The Sequence

of

Immortality

I0649761

The Sequence of Immortality

Laurie Bowler

Published by Laurie Bowler, 2024.

This is a work of fiction. Similarities to real people, places, or events are entirely coincidental.

THE SEQUENCE OF IMMORTALITY

First edition. August 22, 2024.

ISBN: 979-8891701267

Written by Laurie Bowler.

Also by Laurie Bowler

Anima
Angels Blood
The War at Sea
The Shadow of Light
The Hidden Experiment
The Supernatural Agency
The Fire Sorceress
Mystery Magic
The Guild of Shadows
The Sequence of Immortality

Watch for more at https://lauriebowler.com/.

Table of Contents

Chapter One

As I stared at the mocking cursor on my screen, a relentless wave of frustration crashed into my heart, unwelcome and overpowering. The burden of responsibility pressed down on me, a heavy weight I couldn't shake off, as I battled with the creativity block that had seized control of.

In this world, where witches teetered on the edge of existence, shackled by the unyielding laws enforced by the ruling powers, every word I wrote held immense, almost tangible, power. Yet, amidst the pervasive darkness and uncertainty, a glimmer of hope persisted – the enigmatic figure visiting me in my dreams with such unwavering regularity.

Every night, he would materialise in my dreams, a shadowy figure whose identity remained a compelling mystery. His presence wrapped around me like a fog, filling my mind with a thick haze of uncertainty and confusion. A deep, insatiable hunger for answers consumed me as if the truth was a mirage, always out of reach. The more I probed into the enigma of our connection, the more my thoughts twisted and tangled, each attempt to unravel the mystery only deepening my bewilderment. The more recurrent my dreams were, the more I realised the enigmatic figure was an immortal, a vampire, to be exact.

The forbidden nature of our bond—a witch entwined with a vampire—wove an intoxicating tapestry of complexity that thrilled me as much as it terrified me. The wind howled ferociously outside, rattling the windows and sending shivers down my spine, prickling my skin with a keen sense of unease. It felt as if the walls around me harboured ancient secrets whispered by unseen forces to those bold enough to tread the perilous path of the supernatural. This forbidden knowledge seeped into my bones, a heady blend of fear and fascination that I found utterly irresistible.

My assignment was to unearth the truth behind the supernatural beings entwined in the murder of our revered High Witch, Matace—a task that seemed straightforward but was twisted into a labyrinth of complexity by the strict codes these otherworldly creatures followed to remain concealed.

Matace's brutal death haunted me, a shadow that clung to my soul, the wound of his loss festering with every passing day. The deeper I delved into his murder, the more I felt myself spiralling into a pit of despair, each unanswered question tightening a noose around my heart. I found myself gasping for air as the suffocating weight of doom pressed down on me, threatening to crush the last remnants of hope.

In a surge of overwhelming rage and frustration, I slammed my fist onto the table with such force that a jagged crack split its surface, snaking down the centre like a wound. Pain shot through my knuckles, sharp and immediate, but the firestorm of anger roaring inside me eclipsed all else. It was as if an inferno blazed within, consuming every ounce of restraint I had left.

Every path I pursued seemed to dissolve into disappointment, each promising lead vanishing like a wisp of smoke just beyond my reach. The endless maze of dead ends tightened around me, escalating my frustration until I teetered on the edge of desperation, yearning for a way out of the darkness that threatened to swallow me whole.

How could Matace's killer evade justice so effortlessly? The question burned in my mind, a relentless reminder of my failure and the injustice that had been done. I was consumed by a fierce determination to bring the perpetrator to justice, no matter the cost. But even as I steeled myself for the fight ahead, a nagging doubt lingered in my mind. What if I couldn't succeed? What if I was destined to fail? The fear of failure was almost as unbearable as the pain in my hand, but I knew I had no choice but to press on, no matter how difficult the road ahead might be.

From my office nestled deep within the mystical complex, a surge of awe and wonder engulfed me, much like it always did when I looked out the window at the large structure before me. The towering structure held the portals to realms of magic and limitless potential. I was spellbound by the intricately crafted windows and majestic architecture, hinting at the mysterious secrets veiled within its walls. Perhaps the key to the captivating dream figure lay within those walls. The agency is protected by a powerful shield preventing mortals from seeing anything related to the supernatural world.

The figure stood in stark contrast to the darkened room, bathed in the soft, ethereal glow of the moonlight streaming through the window. His sharp and angular silhouette danced against the wall, a captivating and enigmatic presence that commanded attention. I couldn't help but be drawn to his broad, towering stature. Although he was a mere shadow in the night, I could feel the raw, undeniable aura of power and mystery. Despite the distance, I felt an inexplicable pull urging me to uncover the truth shrouding him.

What secrets did this enigmatic stranger hold?

The questions swirled in my mind, a relentless storm fueling my desire to uncover the truth about this enigmatic stranger. As I watched him from afar, his silhouette etched against the window, I couldn't shake the unsettling feeling that he was connected to something far beyond my limited comprehension. He seemed to hold an otherworldly power over me, a power that frightened and intrigued me, like a siren's call I could not resist, drawing me towards the unknown.

But as I sat, my eyes fixed on that intriguing silhouette, one question remained unanswered, a puzzle that taunted me endlessly: What was his name? And would I ever have the courage to find out?

The sharp rap on my office door jolted me from the intense scrutiny of the enigmatic stranger. "Enter," I commanded, my voice tinged with exasperation.

My father entered, his distinguished look and warm smile naturally putting me at ease. Despite his small stature, he exuded a commanding presence, his flawless features and sharp jawline lending him an air of authority. His meticulously combed dark hair gleamed in the warm glow of my office, every strand in place. His black suit and navy blue tie, perfectly knotted, only added to his professional, refined appearance. Shoulders squared and posture erect, he carried himself with an air of unwavering pride and dignity.

"Father!" I cried out, my voice tinged with surprise and alarm. "What on Earth are you doing here?" I gasped in surprise.

"I've come to see how my daughter's new life is faring, Seira Dufey," he said, his voice brimming with warmth and affection. "And to convey a message from your mother." His soft, gentle tone and the sincere kindness in his eyes instantly put anyone at ease. But we had an extraordinary bond with each other.

"Is she alright?" I blurted out, my heart racing with concern as I searched my father's face, looking for any signs of distress. The words tumbled out of my mouth, laced with a sense of dread that gripped me tightly. I hated bad news.

My mind raced as I tried to decipher the reason for his unexpected arrival. Had I forgotten a family event, like the wedding anniversary party I missed a few years ago? The mere thought of it sent a shiver down my spine. Mother had never forgiven me for that. Since then, she had dispatched my father the day before every family gathering as if I were still a child - which, in her eyes, I suppose I would always be. The use of my full name had not escaped my notice; it was a telltale sign that lousy news lay ahead or that I was in deep trouble. My heart pounded as I braced myself for whatever my father had been sent to do or say.

"Is everything alright? Do I need to come home?"

"Seira, she's doing just fine," he chuckled in reply, a mischievous glint in his eye. "She's invited you over for dinner," he explained, his gaze sweeping across the confines of my cramped office. "And I must say, this place is a far cry from your old digs. Tidy, too – not like how you kept things back home?" he teased, a playful jab at my newfound sense of order.

Since I had embraced my witch heritage, my parents had made it clear I was going against their wishes. They were, and still are, in complete and utter denial of the existence of any beings or realms beyond the finite boundaries of Earth, stubbornly clinging to their myopic worldview despite the overwhelming evidence to the contrary.

I had broken my father's heart, the pieces too fragmented to be mended, when I revealed my decision to leave. He couldn't comprehend why I would delve into what he disdainfully dismissed as 'hocus pocus nonsense.' In his eyes, it seemed like a trivial and insignificant path. I had known for years, compliments of my siblings, that I was adopted. My adoption had been a meticulously orchestrated affair, shrouded in secrecy and mystery, leaving me in the dark about my biological heritage.

I discovered my magic abilities by accident; nobody in my mortal life had ever encouraged or helped me develop them. Matace, however, saw beyond my uncertainties and clumsy attempts at mastering my powers. With open arms, he welcomed me into the witching world and shielded me from the dangers I hadn't known were lurking in the shadows. He was more than a mentor; he was a guardian, keeping me by his side and offering unwavering guidance and protection as I navigated the tumultuous waters of my newfound identity. His support and belief in me were not just a lifeline but the essence of my transformation as I grappled with the weight of my magical legacy and the consequences of my choice to pursue it.

"I'm afraid I won't be able to join you for dinner, Dad. I've got a mountain of work piled up, and I can't afford to step away from it right now." I paused, a twinge of guilt creeping into my voice. "Besides, you and Mom have more than enough on your plate dealing with the grandkids. The last thing you need is me there, with my phone constantly buzzing and Josh constantly arguing with me." I tried to lighten the mood with a self-deprecating chuckle, but the weight of my words hung heavy in the air.

"If you're set on explaining to your mother how you're letting her down once more," he said, his voice dripping with resignation and frustration, "I get it. I know this means a lot to you, even though I can't fathom what keeps you occupied all day," he said sadly. "Josh has even asked if you're coming. I know you think he dislikes you, but that's not true. He is your brother. "

I sighed deeply. He would never understand or see that Josh despises me, and he has done so since our parents first took me home. "Dad, I understand if you're disappointed and frustrated with me. I know having family dinners means a lot to you and Mom. But please understand my work is important to me, and I'm not just avoiding this dinner for no reason. I'm sorry if I'm letting you and Mom down once again." I purposely left out any mention of Josh. I didn't want to upset him more than I was by declining the invitation.

Despite my father's constant attempts and pleas to get me to change my mind, I stood firm in my decision. I couldn't join them, not while consumed by Matace's murder. As my father departed, oblivious to the gravity lingering over me, I knew I couldn't let another uncover the killer's identity first. Justice would be served by the laws governing all races' coexistence.

The workday had finally ended, but the relief it should have brought was non-existent. Agitated by an earlier demanding call, I could not wait a moment longer before exiting. Determined to shake off the lingering tension, I vigorously shook my arms, desperately seeking a minor release from the stress, even just for a moment. The entirety of the elder's phone call had replayed in my head for hours.

"Seira," the elder's voice rang out, sharp and commanding, cutting through the silence of my dimly lit office. The weight of his words hung heavily in the air as if they were tangible objects pressing down on my shoulders. "I need you to work faster with the new procedures for the Fae to enter the mortal realm," he barked. "And where's that report I asked for?" His tone left no room for argument, and I felt a sudden pang of anxiety grip my chest.

"The report is on its way," I replied, gripping my pen so tightly it snapped. "You will have it before midnight."

A low, pained groan escaped my lips once he hung up. The idea of working with that specific elder set me on edge and infuriated me. He had not earned the title in any way; it had been passed to him by his father. He is just another spoiled rich kid on a power trip, and he didn't hesitate to make sure I knew how far down the hierarchy I was.

I collected the box of files from my desk and switched off the lights. The weight of the box stacking to the rim with files proved daunting as I strained to balance their weight without dropping anything and closed my office door. With a determined effort, I finally balanced the weight. I closed the door before briskly turning and walking towards the elevator, my footsteps echoing in the empty hallway.

As I approached the elevator, I wearily pressed the button with my forefinger, the weight of the large box of files straining my arm. The numerous files inside the box constantly remind me of my working evening waiting for me tonight. The soft whirring of the ascending elevator car echoed in the hallway, a precursor of the challenges ahead.

As the elevator doors parted, a flurry of hands eagerly snatched the box from my grasp, sending my heart racing. I couldn't physically see over the box and felt vulnerable, not knowing the identity of the box snatcher. As my view cleared, staring back at me was a familiar face and eyes similar to the ones that haunted my dreams. It was Luke, one of the many immortals living in the mortal realm.

Despite knowing each other for a while during working hours, Luke remained tight-lipped about anything that had to do with his job role among mortals. It baffled me that he could perhaps be the source of my nightly dreams, leaving me tossing and turning in bed, or maybe my subconscious was trying to fill the void of a face I couldn't ever see clearly in my dreams. I only ever saw quick flashes of the stranger's eyes. Despite everything, Luke is a typical immortal playboy; he always bragged about his 'hot dates.'

"You?" I scoffed, my voice dripping with a mixture of sarcasm and disbelief. Quickly, I caught myself, and with a forced smile, I added, "I mean, thank you." The words felt foreign on my tongue, a feeble attempt to mask my annoyance.

As he moved to stand next to me, a mischievous grin crept across his face, like a predator eyeing prey. I frantically rubbed at my arms, futilely attempting to hide how uneasy I felt.

Forcing a smile, I faced him. "How's it going?" I asked, stepping into the elevator just a fraction ahead of him. My curiosity was piqued, and I couldn't resist asking, "So, how's the big office move been treating you so far?"

"It's going great, thanks for asking. I couldn't be happier," he replied enthusiastically. "And how about you? I'm eager to hear about the progress on your end, especially considering you're the only one in that part of the building."

I grinned, smoothly redirecting the conversation to myself while discreetly trying to gather details about Luke Granger's elusive office location. Despite scouring official records, he always surprised me with his unexplained sudden appearances. Luke was an enigma - unflappable and privy to all manner of information.

"Nice try, Luke," I quipped, a hint of amusement in my voice. "So, I heard the gossip in the café. You have a hot date lined up for tonight. Care to share the details?"

A vivid memory suddenly resurfaced, transporting me back to our last conversation. Luke had asked for advice on hosting a house party and how to entertain his mortal guests. He had said he'd never invited mortals before and just wanted to be sure they'd be comfortable and enjoy themselves. Attacking mortals is strictly forbidden; the agency provides all the sustenance that every supernatural in the mortal world needs.

"Yep, I've got a date lined up," he grinned boyishly. "And get this; she's actually human. Can you believe it?" His eyes gleamed with a hint of excitement as if he had stumbled upon a hidden treasure.

I stood in the elevator, my gaze fixed intently on him, my mind a whirlwind of unanswered questions. Logically, I knew I shouldn't let him accost a human for his selfish desires; whether his motives were good or bad, they violated the rules. Yet, the intensity weighed heavily, leaving me uncertain about how to proceed.

My heart was pounding in my chest, and waves of panic washed over me as the realisation hit me like a ton of bricks. This can't be happening! I thought in disbelief as I stared at the situation before me. My mind raced frantically, trying to devise a solution; it was my duty to report this. But he's my friend! I didn't want to betray the only friend I had.

Finally, I shrugged helplessly, resorting to a well-worn saying, 'Hear no evil, see no evil,' to console myself and escape the weight of this no-win predicament.

"Luke," I said, my voice trembling slightly, "you're well aware of the rules when it comes to dating a human, and you're a goddamn vampire, for fuck's sake!"

"I love it when you swear," he grinned impishly, not acknowledging my words. "Regardless," he continued, a casual shrug of his shoulders, "humans make better company than the dead, don't you think."

I laughed at his theatrical nose-scrunching, protruding fangs. "I guess so. But your party is still on?"

"Yes. You coming or working late?"

"I'm afraid I can't," I said, a tinge of regret in my voice. He was referring to his party. "I have an overdue report. I'll be out of the agency if the new High Witch Lilly finds out I haven't started."

I could feel the weight of the situation bearing down on me. The consequences of not finishing this report were dire, and the threat of upsetting Lilly didn't appeal to me. My heart raced as I contemplated the possibility of being sacked and never being able to develop my powers. But my loyalty to the agency, my commitment to my work, was unwavering. I knew I had to prioritise this task, no matter the personal cost. The agency was my lifeblood, and I couldn't afford to jeopardise my position.

"That sucks," he said, missing his poor word choice. "They'd be out of their minds to kick you out. You're too damn valuable for them to let go." His eyes narrowed, a hint of menace underlying his tone.

"That woman is capable of anything, and I wouldn't put it past her," I said, my voice laced with disdain. "Nobody in the agency can understand why I was chosen for this role in the first place," I sighed at the memory of my demotion. "They have no idea what she's capable of."

"How so?"

"They look down on me because I don't come from a magical family like they do," I said, my voice tinged with resentment. "My parents adopted me, and I was raised as a human with no idea about my real parents or if they had powers."

"Unbelievable!" he exclaimed, his eyes widening with disbelief. "Well, they'd be fools to cut you out. Hell, you could always find a job with the vampires, you know? Those bloodsuckers would be lucky to have you on their team. Oh wait, I am one!"

I smiled and shook my head at his incorrigible optimism. It was as if he sensed my inner turmoil, appearing with wit and playfulness to lift my spirits. The pinging sound of the elevator stopping and opening the doors brought my attention back to the mission of getting home.

"Well, I've got the files here," I said, firmly grasping the documents. "I'll be in touch soon. In the meantime, have a great time at your party."

"Take it easy," he said, smiling. As the doors started to close, he stopped them and called out. "Hey, if you change your mind, just call."

"Oh, and I suppose you'll hear me over the music with your super hearing, right?" I grinned. "You're going to be too busy flirting with everything in a skirt," I leaned closer, my voice dropping to a low, teasing tone. "When I want you, you'll hear me clearly, whether you like it or not."

He flashed a boyish grin, remarkably younger-looking than other vampires I'd encountered in true form - rugged yet aristocratic, as if assessing me as potential prey. Their haughty air marked them distinct from the human world, as if their immortality gave them a higher status than any other supernatural being.

As I stood before this disarmingly charming vampire, I couldn't shake the uneasy awareness that I was being meticulously appraised, my every breath and movement analysed for any sign of weakness or vulnerability. The predatory edge lurking behind his captivating smile made my skin crawl, a primal instinct warning me of the danger beneath the surface of his alluring façade. With my final grin and wave, Luke allowed the elevator doors to close and was gone. Breathing a deep sigh, I stood alone in the hallway with the large glass doors of the entry and exit to the building in front of me.

A strong sense of unease gripped me as I carefully balanced the delicate files in my trembling arms. The weight of the confidential documents, brimming with sensitive information, pressured me as I hurriedly left the building and started walking towards the sanctuary of my cosy apartment.

It was strictly forbidden to remove any files from the protection of the building, shielded by a powerful enchantment that safeguarded the wealth of esoteric knowledge stored within its hallowed walls. Yet, on this occasion, I summoned the full extent of my latent magical abilities, deftly circumventing the restrictive spell and slipping away unnoticed, driven by a singular purpose – to deliver the critical report to Lilly, Matace's replacement, without a single mistake.

The unshakable feeling that Lilly was deliberately excluding me from the investigation, a suspicion fueled by her longstanding disdain for me that she had never bothered to hide since I first joined the team at Matace's behest, continued to weigh heavily on my mind. She tasked me with uncovering any communication from his final days, hoping to shed light on the shady dealings consuming him before his untimely demise. Despite our professional distance, I was determined to unravel the mystery surrounding Matace's murder and prove my worth to Lilly, showing I wasn't to be underestimated.

After navigating the congested streets and chaotic traffic, I finally reached the store and grabbed the groceries I needed. I jumped back into my car and drove the last few blocks. As I pulled into the familiar driveway, I smiled as my loyal and loving cat, Herbert, sat patiently in front of the door. The minute I exited my car, he ran over; his soft, melodic purrs and affectionate rubs against my leg instantly lifting the heaviness from my heart.

Although it is coincidental, not to mention comical, for a witch to have a cat, Herbert had been part of my family since childhood. This faithful friend has been the one constant in my life, a trustworthy source of comfort and companionship that filled my world with a warmth that defied the darkness that came with the territory of my job.

With a laboured grunt, I hefted the heavy files, the strain rippling through my muscles as I staggered into the room. The stack of documents landed on the cluttered table with a resounding thud, scattering papers and startling Herbert. His low, guttural growl disapproved of being startled and overlooked for his usual welcoming fuss.

I bent down and gently ran my fingers through his soft, lush fur.

"Hello, my boy," I cooed, a warm smile spreading across my face. The loyal canine immediately responded, flopping onto his back, his paws gently patting my hands, silently pleading for his favourite tummy rub. "That's it, my good boy," I chuckled, obliging his unspoken request. Gazing into his adoring eyes, I could almost see the hunger building within him. "Ah, I know what you're after, right?" I teased. "How about we treat you to some salmon for dinner tonight, hm?" The mere mention of his favourite meal had his ears perking up, and I couldn't help but laugh at his unbridled enthusiasm. With a loving pat, I rose to my feet, anticipating the sound of his meows when I presented his meal.

The soft sniffles and delicate mewing sounds reached my ears. I took them as a sign of the cat's appreciation and acceptance of the salmon I put into his bowl. With a gentle touch, I lovingly set the food down. As I watched him eagerly dig in, I couldn't help but imagine the disapproving look on my mother's face if she saw me now, with my single-serving microwave dinner I was putting in the microwave over a home-cooked family dinner. But the demands from one of our highest witches' sudden murder made it unavoidable.

With utmost discretion, Lilly shared a file via our inter-office Mail Portal or MP. This file was a repository of sensitive information, containing detailed images of his physique, and a meticulously compiled list of those present at the crime scene. Using our secure communication channel underscored the secrecy and urgency of our situation.

The microwave beep and rumbling hunger jolted me from gazing at the dimly lit garden outside my eerily silent apartment block. An unsettling hush had settled over the block of flats, starkly contrasting the chaos brewing inside my mind. This eerie atmosphere was unusual for any evening except tonight. I knew there were a lot of new shows, famous magicians, and actors in town, so I wasn't surprised to find the block deadly quiet. It only intensifies the solitude needed to intricately analyse these files.

"Right, Herbert." I focused back on the task at hand, the weight of our mission, like a heavy cloak, pressing upon me. "Got to do some digging for the witch." My jaw tightened with determination as I prepared to delve into the darkness, whatever it may hold.

As I observed him indulge in his meal with a sense of contentment, I retreated to my study. The plush, deep red carpet felt like a luxurious oasis, soothing my weary feet as I gratefully kicked off my uncomfortable high heels. I couldn't help but ponder the perplexing question – why do women, myself included, subject ourselves to such discomfort in the name of fashion?

Plopping down behind my elegant desk, I set aside the food tray, my fingers tingling with anticipation as I waited for my laptop to spring to life. The urge to dive into the files, meticulously cross-referencing every detail for any discrepancies, was overwhelming. Ignoring Lilly's disapproval, I was determined, unwavering in my resolve to uncover the truth behind the death of the one person who had initially believed in me.

I felt a chill run down my spine as the photographs of Matace slipped from my trembling hands, scattering across the floor. The images were a harrowing sight, depicting a man whose body bore the cruel markings of torture. Lash marks crisscrossed his back, while deep nail scars had been etched onto his torso as a mysterious symbol. It was as though some ancient, otherworldly force had inflicted this violence upon him, leaving behind a chilling calling card.

My fork froze mid-air. I stared in shocked silence, and my appetite was suddenly lost. I scanned the testimonies of potential witnesses and perpetrators, searching for any clues to shed light on this horrific act. Yet, the truth of Matace's death remained elusive, shrouded in a veil of mystery and darkness. What dark forces had converged to bring about such a fate? The questions swirled in my mind, leaving me unsettled and unsure of what to make of this chilling discovery.

A pack of savage wolves, feared by all who crossed their path, had brazenly claimed responsibility for their latest grisly killings. The mangled bodies of their victims bore the unmistakable hallmarks of the pack's ferocious assault - deep gashes across exposed flesh and savage bite marks around the neck and head, evidence of the ruthless efficiency of their deadly hunt.

As I meticulously studied the markings, the subtle, varied indents on Matace perplexed me more. The indentations lacked the rough, jagged edges typically associated with the wolf clan. Instead, slight variations and nuances within the patterns left me utterly baffled. Scouring the depths of my extensive knowledge, I found no records of any new or undiscovered breeds within the immediate area.

Scanning the seemingly mundane scene where the lifeless body had been found, nothing immediately caught my attention. Yet, since joining the agency, the haunting possibility of the banished creatures' return refused to leave my mind. Could they have somehow breached the mortal realm?

Delving into my expertise and understanding of their behaviour, I deduced they would likely resort to a comparable disposal site for their victims, as no such locations had ever been documented, explaining the enigmatic markings on Matace's remains. Each supernatural entity possessed distinct methods of killing and disposing of prey, a meticulously catalogued wealth of knowledge within the agency's extensive files.

My heart raced as I stared at Matace's face in the photograph, his once powerful presence now reduced to a mere image. "Nothing?" I spat out the word, my voice laced with a fury I could barely contain. I gripped the edges of the frame, knuckles turning white, as I leaned in closer, searching for answers in those unmoving eyes. "What happened to you?" I demanded, my words barely above a whisper, laced with sorrow and disbelief. "You were so strong, so untouchable. How did this even happen?"

The silence that followed was deafening, taunting me with its lack of response. I felt helpless, powerless to undo the cruel twist of fate that had befallen my once formidable friend. With a shaky breath, I placed the photograph back down, the weight of this mystery pressing heavily upon my soul.

As I scrutinised the captivating photographs meticulously captured by our ministry's elite clean-up specialists, I couldn't help but be awestruck by their unparalleled attention to detail. Every inch of the scene was documented precisely, from the faintest whispers of paranormal phenomena to the unsettling shadows that clung to the walls.

These seasoned professionals moved with unwavering determination, resolute in their mission to erase any evidence of the supernatural before the unsuspecting masses could discover it. Their unwavering commitment to their craft was obvious in their care to leave no trace behind, ensuring the unknown remained a mystery to mortals.

The dimly lit alleyway, with its foreboding dead-end, was infamous for being a hotspot where mortals engaged in illicit drug transactions – a dark, seedy underbelly that lurked in the shadows of the city. In this notorious location, a tragic incident unfolded, one that would shatter the lives of all those involved. The victim was a young mortal named Tom Simmons, only sixteen years old. His death had been brutal and gruesome; his body left abandoned in the alley.

Law enforcement investigators worked tirelessly, painstakingly identifying the victim by comparing his dental records to those in their database – a cold, clinical process that belied the sheer horror of the crime. I instantly dismissed any suspicion of Matace's vengeful involvement in this heinous crime against a mortal - an absurd, unfathomable idea. However, no convictions were made in either world.

The sudden, jarring beep of my computer's notification shattered the serene silence, sending a jolt through me. My pulse quickened as I read Lilly's message in bold, urgent letters. Her words were laced with frustration and emotion as she fervently demanded the report, questioning the brief disruption in the protective spell. A wave of confusion washed over me, and I scrambled to formulate a credible explanation for tampering with her information protection spell, acutely aware of the intensity of her anger bearing down on me.

"I've got the documents you need - I'm bringing them back to file your report, and you'll have it first thing tomorrow morning. I'm going through the photographs right now, and I'll be sure to gather any additional information that could be useful. This is a high-priority situation, and I'm on it." I quickly typed a reply.

I felt drawn to exploring the final locations Matace had visited to unravel the mystery surrounding his last moments on Earth. My journey would take me past shadowy corners and vast fields where Matace had once conducted his awe-inspiring séances, communicating with entities from otherworldly realms. By delving into these enigmatic realms, I hoped to gain insight into the immortal beings associated with our clandestine organisation, 'The Agency,' that Matace had been teaching me about.

I felt a rising sense of unease as I carefully processed the disturbing information. The revelation that he had been spotted strolling down the bustling high street, its rowdy bars luring in the night owls, was deeply unsettling.

The fact that he was last seen in the alley where his life had met its tragic end hinted at a sinister, orchestrated cover-up. Consumed by a burning determination to unravel the truth, I embarked on a perilous journey, visiting various locations and meticulously searching for clues that might expose any information.

Every day at the agency, I felt the oppressive weight of constant surveillance, my every action scrutinised. The reason for this relentless monitoring remained a mystery. Still, I had learned not to question it, fearful of the repercussions. Matace had warned me that venturing alone was dangerous, a caution I had initially brushed aside. Yet, the looming threat of displeasing Lilly and incurring her anger made me seriously reconsider my decision to leave the relative safety of my quarters.

She possessed an uncanny ability to uncover even the slightest indiscretion, especially if someone happened to catch a glimpse of me slipping out under the cover of night and mentioned it to her in passing. The consequences of being caught were not something I dared to experience, for the price would be far too high. Still, the compulsion to retrace Matace's last known steps weighed heavily on my mind, urging me to take the risk.

My mind returned to the time I had first met Matace. As I stood before Matace, his weathered face reflected the wisdom and kindness that had shaped his life. The subtle crinkles around his eyes deepened as he observed my abilities to command the forces of nature, open portals, and manipulate the very fabric of time itself. His warm smile conveyed a profound pride and reverence as if he were witnessing the unfolding of a remarkable destiny. I was both exhilarated and terrified by the sheer power that flowed through me, powers that no other witch had ever possessed. Every spell I attempted, I executed with a potency that surpassed anything anyone had ever seen. It was as if the elements themselves had become extensions of my will, bending to my command with a ferocity that both thrilled and unsettled me.

Matace's gaze held a knowing, almost paternal, quality as he observed the extent of my abilities. I felt a deep connection to the ancient wisdom he embodied at that moment. This connection transcended the boundaries of our physical forms and spoke to the very essence of my being. It was as if he could see into the heart of my soul, understanding the weight of the power I wielded and the responsibility that came with it.

As a hormonal teenager, I first discovered my extraordinary powers during a moment of sheer rage and anguish at the state of the world. Consumed by a rebellious fury, I unintentionally unleashed a powerful hurricane, a force of nature that tore through our neighbourhood, leaving a trail of devastation in its wake. The roaring winds and torrential rains razed everything in their path, much to the horror and dismay of my mother. It was as if my raging hormones had completely overpowered any semblance of rational thought, unleashing a primal, untamed energy that was beyond my control.

The revelation struck me like lightning, jolting me to the core. My mother ushered me back inside our modest home with a sombre expression. She divulged the shocking truth of my origins. To my astonishment, I learned that I did not belong to this world - my existence defied the boundaries of human comprehension.

Despite my extraordinary abilities, I had been categorised as human, a label that never quite fit. In the eyes of an unforgiving society, I was branded a "freak," an aberration to be shunned and feared due to my unique nature. Yet, in the realm of magic and immortals, I was recognised for what I indeed was - a powerful witch, a conduit for forces beyond the mortal plane.

Matace, a wise and perceptive mentor, was the first to perceive the raw potential within me as a fledgling witch. With a warm embrace and open heart, he welcomed me into the agency, becoming my guiding beacon in the realm of magic. Under his tutelage, I blossomed and grew, absorbing his teachings with fervent dedication, my thirst for knowledge unquenchable.

Patiently, Matace nurtured my skills, meticulously moulding and shaping them until I became a formidable force to be reckoned with in sorcery. He waited with unwavering patience, ensuring that I had cultivated inner and outer strength so that I could not only wield my powers but also be responsible enough to wield them for the greater good.

With a gentle yet unyielding hand, Matace introduced me to spells and arcane powers, instilling the crucial lesson of utilising them to help and heal rather than causing harm. His guidance honed my abilities to a razor's edge. It touched the depths of my soul, blossoming into a conscious decision to be a force for good in witchcraft.

Thanks to Matace's unwavering belief in me and his tireless efforts, I now stand tall and confident in my abilities, a living embodiment of the powerful witch he envisioned and nurtured with utmost care. His legacy lives on through me as I strive to emulate his wisdom and compassion, using my powers to better the world around me.

I exhaled a heavy, world-weary sigh as I gingerly slid my worn, familiar shoes onto my feet. With deft fingers, I wrestled my unruly mane into a haphazard ponytail, steeling myself for the night ahead. The world outside had been swallowed in a cloak of darkness, enveloping me in a cocoon of solitude and anonymity.

As I readied myself for whatever the shadows might hold, I took comfort in knowing I was unlikely to cross paths with anyone I knew. The only exception would be if I stumbled upon some otherworldly being, and even then, the prospect held no sway over me. Brushing aside any concerns about potentially incurring Lilly's wrath, I was unfazed by the thought of being recognised.

My thick, insulated coat shielded me from the biting, relentless chill that had crept in since I had unleashed my icy summons. The once vibrant world had been transformed into a frozen wasteland, a reflection of the emptiness that had consumed me since this started. The frigid temperatures, a product of my powers, had caught everyone off guard, leaving the mortals to wander the streets in confusion, their breath hanging in the air as they tried to make sense of the sudden winter storm.

Even the scientists, usually so confident in their knowledge, were left bewildered, unable to fathom how they had missed the signs of the impending freeze. The world had become a frozen, desolate landscape, a harsh mirror to the icy void within my heart.

As I exited my apartment, I took a deep, steadying breath. The hallway's bright lights cast a soothing glow, easing my departure while shielding me from unwanted scrutiny. However, the deafening silence that permeated the building was deeply unsettling, heightening my awareness and leaving me on edge, apprehensive of what might lurk in the shadows.

I hastily crossed the street, clutching my scribbled notes of the unexplored destinations ahead. The soft clicks of my low-heeled shoes against the concrete sidewalk were the only sounds punctuating the eerie silence. Suddenly, a peculiar sensation washed over me, and I couldn't shake the feeling of being watched. My nerves instantly jumped to high alert, every instinct screaming at me to flee.

Yet, as the unnerving feeling of being watched intensified, a strange sense of inner calm washed over me, almost as if I had resigned myself to the situation. The contrast between my rising panic and this unexpected tranquillity left me profoundly unsettled, unsure of what lay in wait around the next corner. I quickened my pace, desperate to reach the safety of my next destination, my heart pounding with each step. The strangeness of my changing feelings reminded me of one person; Blossom.

Shrouded in an air of suspicion, I had the misfortune of encountering a mischievous individual with the unique ability to manipulate emotions. This enigmatic figure had been banished, not for crimes she had committed, but for ones she had been falsely accused of. Blossom, a mischievous soul, had been repeatedly warned by Matace about her reckless behaviour. Yet, she had chosen to disregard his solid advice, leading to dire consequences within the immortal community, who now accused her of sowing chaos in their midst.

Matace and I knew Blossom was not inherently malicious; her mischievous nature bordered on the uncontrollable. The brutal killings of the shape-shifting black bear hunters could not have been orchestrated by Blossom herself, as it was clear from the outset that this was a meticulously planned setup. However, the true motives behind the scheme remained a mystery.

I hurried down the bustling street, but I had to tread carefully to avoid the cracks in the pavement. At the corner, my eyes landed on the first bar on my map, a stone's throw from my home. Yet, the sight that greeted me filled me with unease. The rowdy crowd spilt onto the sidewalk, creating a cacophony of noise and a hazy veil of cigarette smoke that made me wrinkle my nose in disgust.

As I pushed through the crowd of bodies, the overwhelming stench of sweat enveloped me, turning my stomach. It was like stumbling into a fairy tale gone awry, following a trail of breadcrumbs that led not to a magical encounter but to a dingy bar filled with more unpleasant patrons than I could count. I made a mental note always to carry body spray; there was no way I would smell that bad.

The dimly lit room was thick with the hazy stench of smoke and the sounds of shuffling cards as men gathered around small tables, engrossed in their games, their eyes fixed on the game at hand. A few of them glanced up, their looks filled with an unsettling sense of appreciation that made my stomach churn.

Cigarettes dangled from their lips, and pitchers of half-drained beer sat forgotten on the tables.

Amidst the sordid scene, scantily clad women moved through the room, their bodies barely concealed by flimsy, sheer fabrics. Breasts spilt out of low-cut tops, nipples visible through the transparent material. The sight made me long for the biting chill of the outside air, desperate to drag it into this oppressive, suffocating space and force these women to reconsider their revealing attire. The entire atmosphere felt charged with an undercurrent of something sinister, like a tightly coiled spring waiting to snap.

Silently, I approached the dimly lit bar, my gaze locking with the barkeeps. I strived to melt seamlessly into the hazy, smoke-filled atmosphere. Still, the barman's startled reaction betrayed that my presence had not gone undetected.

The bartender flashed a grin, revealing the few remaining teeth in his mouth. "What can I get you?" he asked, his voice laced with a hint of gravel.

I fidgeted uncomfortably as the man next to me leered in my direction, his eyes fixated on my heaving chest. "Orange juice, please," I muttered, shifting uneasily.

"Is that all you want?" he sneered, his brow furrowing in confusion and disdain. " You know what sort of bar this is, don't you, girl?"

"What kind of bar would that be exactly?" I retorted, my gaze narrowing as I fixed them with a stern, no-nonsense stare. The edge in my voice left no room for ambiguity - I was not in the mood for games or evasiveness.

"A mortal's bar," he whispered, leaning across the wood that separated us. "I think you know as well as I do what I'm talking about. What is it you're really after?"

My heart raced, and my mind whirled as I grappled with the stool behind me, desperate for stability. Stunned and speechless,

I planted myself on the wobbly seat, my eyes fixed on the figure before me. How could this excuse of a person possibly know what I was and where I'd come from? The realisation sent a chill down my spine, and I braced myself for the confrontation.

"Excuse me?" I played dumb.

"Don't you dare come at me with that attitude, girl," he growled, his voice laced with a stern warning. He thrust the drink towards me, his eyes narrowing with irritation and barely contained anger.

The loud chatter in the room pounded against my eardrums as if amplifying the tension I felt from the lecherous man beside me. Finally, he succumbed to the drowsy embrace of alcohol, his laboured breath carrying the pungent aroma that hung heavy in the air.

"Alright, let's hear it," the barman growled, aggressively wiping the bar with tattered, grime-stained rags. "What's got your folks crawling back here this time?" His eyes narrowed as he leaned in, his voice dripping with a challenging undertone.

"Back here?" I echoed, my voice laced with suspicion and a hint of defiance. His questions felt like a weighted net, trapping me. I refused to offer any answers until he revealed how he had obtained my identity. I narrowed my eyes, the gears in my mind whirring as I regarded him with caution and curiosity. "The ball is in your court, my friend. I won't play this game unless you show your hand first."

"Clever, aren't you?" he mused, a tinge of admiration in his voice. "They were in here just the other night, you know. Two of them, if my memory serves me right. They grilled me with questions like they were trying to uncover some grand conspiracy." He leaned in closer, his eyes narrowing. "But I saw how they looked around, scoping the place out. They're up to something. I can feel it."

"And what are you?"

"You've got a keen eye, haven't you?" he remarked, a hint of weariness in his voice. "I'm a night owl. I was tasked with watching over particular areas of the Earth, protecting them from the creatures. And what do I get? This dumpster of a place." He paused, a sardonic chuckle escaping his lips. "Forgotten for nearly a decade, I had to find a way to survive. And here I am," he gestured towards me, his expression a mix of amusement and resignation, "yeah, some grand start, mate."

I leaned forward, eyes locked onto him as I slowly sipped my drink. "So, you're a watcher, huh?" The words slipped out, laced with a hint of challenge, daring him to deny it.

"Yes," he said, his voice laced with urgency and importance. "I was tasked with keeping an eye on you, but then Matace had someone else take over that duty and sent me elsewhere. Did you know that?" His eyes narrowed, his expression a mixture of concern and unease as if the thought of this revelation weighed heavily upon him.

"I didn't know that," I said, my brow furrowing in confusion as I shook my head. "You said two people from the agency were in here the other night?" I questioned.

"Yeah, they could have been the Agency, I suppose," he said, his gaze fixed and unwavering. "The blonde-haired woman and some stern-looking bloke accompanying her." He divulged, nodding in between constantly wiping the bar.

"Are you *fucking sure*?" I exclaimed, my eyes widening in disbelief as I stared at him in stunned silence.

The girl with owing blonde hair could only be none other than Lilly. It had to be the head witch guard beside her, tasked with ensuring her safety at all times despite being the High Witch and supposed to be more powerful than anyone or anything. It was clear that Lilly was investigating something. Despite her best efforts to keep a calm facade, it was clear that her hopes of escaping detection were nothing more than wishful thinking.

"She demanded information on Matace," he confided, leaning on the bar. "It was terrible news to hear about his death; I was a little concerned. Wasn't there a binding rule between all species?" he asked. "The one that's supposed to prevent any species or person from coming to harm?"

"Oh, it's there, alright," I affirmed, a grim edge to my voice. "But it's clearly malfunctioned, or Matace wouldn't be dead."

"He sat right where you are only a week or so ago," he said, a mischievous grin spreading across his face. "He was supposed to meet someone here, but they never showed up. I wonder what happened..." His eyes narrowed as he scanned the empty room.

"What did he do?"

"Had a drink, sat down, and we chatted. He promised to re-assign me to watch duties and apologised for ignoring my requests."

"What requests?" I pressed further, my suspicion intensifying with every word. His previous statements had sown seeds of doubt in my mind, transforming him from a mere witness to a potential suspect. He had spoken of his dissatisfaction with his current circumstances, his resentment at being neglected and abandoned on Earth to fend for himself, and his decision to start a makeshift enterprise.

Could the simmering frustration and discontent have pushed him over the edge, driving him to commit a heinous, violent act? The mere thought sent a chilling shiver down the spine as the possibility of such a devastating outcome loomed large, casting an ominous shadow over the situation.

"Returning to my home or being re-assigned was all I could think about," he replied, his voice tinged with hope and apprehension.

"I understand," I affirmed adamantly, a resolute nod punctuating my conviction. "But tell me, how long did he stay there?"

"He waited about an hour," he said, thinking. "He said he was meeting someone to collect information on some new breed he'd heard was being created on the other side of town. He seemed pretty worried about it."

Matace's unexpected decision to dive into this delicate situation left me puzzled. Usually, he would have used his network of spies to gather information while staying aloof. But now, he takes a more daring approach by handling things independently. This change from his usual cautious and analytical style has me worried and intrigued.

Matace is known for his careful and systematic way of dealing with sensitive issues, preferring to observe from a distance rather than getting directly involved. His sudden willingness to take risks and step into unknown territory suggests a significant shift in his thinking. I can't help but wonder if this new approach indicates a bold new strategy that could have a considerable impact.

"Did he, by any chance, say who he was meeting?" I pierced him with a scrutinising gaze, peering over the rim of my glass, desperate for any scrap of information that could prove significant.

"No, he only said he was meeting someone who had vital information on the whereabouts of the location of the new breed so they could be destroyed."

I let out a weary sigh and rubbed my tired eyes. "Alright, I understand," I said, my voice tinged with a hint of reluctance. A momentary pause hung in the air as I gathered my thoughts. "Thank you," I finally managed.

I attempted to escape, but his hand shot out in a swift, calculated movement, clamping around my wrist in a vice-like grip. I was held captive at the bar, and my attempt to escape was prevented. "You need to listen, and listen closely," he said, his grip tightening on my arm as I held his piercing gaze. I figured you would come looking for information; it's common knowledge, the bond between you and Matace." I nodded slowly, my heart heavy, and turned to leave, feeling the intensity of his gaze on my back.

I could practically feel the sheer intensity of his piercing gaze burning into the back of my skull, sending tremors cascading down my spine.

Chapter Two

The refreshing night's ice-cold breeze enveloped me, invigorating my senses and grounding me in reality. Breathing in the crisp, clean air was a welcome change from the stale stench of the bar that lingered on my clothes. As I made my way down the familiar path towards the alley where Matace's body had been found, I couldn't shake the feeling that someone close to him had betrayed him. Rumours circulated about a warning sent to Matace from a witch psychic.

This message had somehow been intercepted before he could receive it. The mystery of the intercepted message and why remained unsolved. It reeked of betrayal and deceit, casting a shadow of suspicion over those closest to him. Despite the murky circumstances surrounding Matace's death, one thing was clear: this was my territory and neighbourhood, and I wouldn't stand for such treachery on my watch.

Witnesses and the psychic's report provided intricate details of Matace's final walk. Starting down the street, he passed through a small field bordered by lush hedges marking the edge of mortal gardens. Moving towards the alley, he slipped through a gap in the fence where the field ended.

"Come on," I groaned as the street stretched miles ahead. "What were you looking for, Matace? And who were you supposed to have met?"

As I walked a few more steps, the familiarity of the location hit me like a ton of bricks. The street, divided by a small field, was a picturesque scene with charming houses on either side. Each home had a neat garden enclosed by carefully manicured hedges. The quaintness of the scene tugged at my heartstrings, invoking memories of my childhood growing up with my adoptive parents. It was a reminder of the simple beauty of everyday mortal life.

I stood in the middle of the field, feeling the soft squelch of the grass beneath my feet. The ground was wet and slippery, my sensible shoes providing much-needed grip. I couldn't see anything unusual around me, but there was an air of anticipation. Something had definitely transpired here, or maybe even further down the alley where Matace had been found. The mystery of what had occurred hung heavy in the air.

The shocking revelation came just hours after his brutal murder, discovered by a young watcher assigned to unconventional duties not found in any official records. Yoko Treiman, a name that stood out in its strangeness, was well-versed in dark magic, summoning evil spirits and malevolent entities capable of wreaking havoc on their targets. Despite his sinister abilities, he had proven to be one of the most talented recruits to have sought membership in the agency. Only a select few could pass through the agency's stringent selection process each year; they had to possess an exceptional power or mastery of spells that set them apart.

I let out a heavy sigh, reluctantly stepping back onto the path, aware that my next stop was the ominous, dimly lit alley ahead. As I walked, the cold air began to creep into my shoes, chilling my bones and sending shivers up my spine, a growing sense of unease trailing me like a spectre. Craving a moment of relief, I veered into a narrow passageway that wound its way towards a cluster of weathered houses. As I cautiously peered around the corner, my breath hitched—there, a shadow flitted swiftly across the road, then disappeared into the consuming darkness.

My heart raced, a wild mix of fear and curiosity surging through me as I grappled with what I had just witnessed. As I pressed on, a creeping realisation dawned—my surroundings seemed subtly warped, as if reality itself had been twisted. The familiar signs and cues that usually guided me were now distorted, altered in such a way that even Lilly, with her sharp tracking skills, would struggle to follow my trail. It was clear—someone was deliberately trying to unnerve me, manipulating my perception and shifting the streets to confuse and disorient me, driving me away from the truth.

I focused on slowing my breathing, using deep, deliberate inhales and exhales to calm my pounding heart as I pressed forward. As I walked, the tension coiled in my shoulders began to loosen, relieving me. With a shaky hand, I reached into my bag and pulled out my worn notebook, its pages filled with scribbles.

My fingers traced over the words until they landed on the notes I had taken at the scene of Matace's murder. The details jumped out at me, stark and vivid – the exact spot where the body had been found, the meticulous layout of the crime scene, every tiny observation painstakingly recorded. I had transcribed each one, determined not to miss a single clue in my quest to solve this chilling mystery.

The alley loomed to my left, beckoning me with its foreboding darkness that seemed to stretch endlessly into the distance. It cast an eerie atmosphere, intensified by the knowledge that a recent murder had taken place there, adding a sense of mystery to the scene. Despite the ominous aura, I knew I had to venture down the alley. The notes indicated that the victim had been discovered halfway down.

If I was fortunate, the faint remnants of the white lines drawn around his body would still be visible, guiding me towards the tragic site.

Entering the alley and flicking my torch on, shaking and searching either side of me, my breath erupted in short spurts. I felt afraid, but I wasn't sure what was affecting me so badly. I was usually very controlled, but today, I felt totally out of my depth; this had to be done to find the truth.

A scuttling sound on my right made me jump, and I stopped to swing the torch in that direction, only to find a rat peering at me with dark, mysterious eyes. The rubbish on either side contained his tiny morsels of food for the night; squeaking with fright, I dropped my torch and found myself in darkness. Bending down and feeling around in the evening for my torch and hoping I wouldn't touch a rat or anything equally disgusting, the scuffling of shoes and the rustle of clothes caught my attention.

As I crept back against the cold, rough surface of the wall, my heart pounded in my chest, the anticipation of the intruder's arrival overwhelming me. The faint sound of shuffling footsteps grew louder, drawing closer with each passing second. I could sense the cautious approach, a silent and menacing presence lingering just out of sight.

I could feel the solid wall pressing against my back, offering me a false sense of security in the darkness. I tensed, preparing myself for whatever was about to emerge from the shadows. The hands that eventually reached out to grab me were not human; they possessed a supernatural strength, cold and inhuman. At that moment, I knew I was not facing a human but something more sinister and powerful.

"Put me down!" I said through clenched teeth as my hair was yanked backwards. "Let me go!" As my elbow jabbed, it collided with something solid, causing a sharp gasp to escape from him and me as pain erupted down my arm. The sudden intake of breath indicated that I had struck a sensitive nerve.

"You've come here to snoop," he growled in the unknown voice. "Now, you'll die. This area is protected from the likes of you from the agency, always poking your nose, missy."

"I don't know who you are," I whispered under my breath, feeling my legs dangle in the air as I was hoisted up from the ground. "Let me..."

He had yanked me up forcefully by my hair, sending sharp pain coursing through my scalp as if my roots were being torn from my head. As I dangled helplessly in his grip, the threat of either death or baldness loomed ominously. The stranger's face hovered just inches from mine, his features a chilling mystery as I frantically searched my memory for any trace of him.

"Who are you?" I stammered, trying to fight his firm grasp on my hair.

"Your worst nightmare," he grinned. "How do you want to die? A bite to the neck," he hissed, tracing his finger down the side of my neck, causing me to shiver. "Or would you prefer it if I shot you and then drank your blood?"

The unexpected growl echoing from the alley's entrance sent a shiver down my spine, followed by the jolt of an unseen assailant barreling into us with a terrifying display of inhuman strength. I was unceremoniously thrown to the ground as the mysterious figure pivoted to confront their rival with a fierce intensity in their eyes.

"I told you she's mine, Tye!" Luke's voice hissed his warning. "Leave her be!"

The sudden, unexpected laughter from Tye pierced through the chaos, mixing with the ferocious hissing and snarling that filled the air. Trash bins were hurled across the room, and bodies collided in a brutal one-on-one battle as clenched fists and angry shouts filled the room. Each violent exchange only fueled the fury of both of them, their rage escalating with every blow and strike.

"Your girlfriend," Tye teased. "Very pretty; she'd make a delicious meal."

"I don't think so," Luke snarled and appeared again, holding a gun in the dim light spread from the moonlight. "Leave, or I'll shoot," he warned, pointing the gun at Tye.

Tye's thunderous roar of incredulous rage reverberated through the air, sending shivers down my spine. With a sudden and forceful stomp, he brought his foot down upon my head. The impact felt like it was crushing my skull into the unforgiving ground. As I lay there, the world around me began to blur and spin, the edges of my vision growing hazy as the ominous embrace of unconsciousness crept closer. In the background, a cacophony of loud bangs echoed, assaulting my ears as I futilely struggled to rise from my defeated position.

"You're safe," Luke's voice said above me. "Stay with me," he urged.

"You lied," I gently whispered, my hand trembling as I reached out to touch him. I needed to feel the coldness of his skin against mine to confirm that he was standing before me and not just a figment of my imagination. "You lied."

"Plenty of time to discuss that later," he muttered, his eyes creasing with concern. "Once you've been to the hospital."

Luke gently lifted me from the cold, hard floor, his strong arms enveloping me in a comforting embrace. As my fingers instinctively gripped his shirt, I felt the warmth of his body against mine, anchoring me in the swirling haze of consciousness. Uncertainty fluttered within me with each fleeting moment of clarity, but as I gazed into his eyes, a sense of calm washed over me.

"You're safe," he said again. "Don't slip away now."

"You lied," I said again, my voice fainter than before. "Why did you lie?"

"I had to keep you alive," he answered, looking straight ahead. "We can talk more later."

I was abruptly jolted by the car's movements, feeling every bump and turn as Lilly's frantic voice filled the air. She was using telepathy to speak to both Luke and me. With a sense of urgency, she quickly called for her most skilled doctors to aid me as we raced towards the hospital.

Luke carefully lifted me from the car, cradling me against his chest with a tenderness that belied his usual rough exterior. I clung to his shirt desperately, my grip only tightening as he held me closer. My eyes struggled to focus on his face, blinking rapidly to clear my vision. A dull ache throbbed in my head, the rhythmic drumming only intensifying with each passing second. I could feel the warm trickle of blood running down my cheek. And yet, Luke remained unfazed, his concern for me outweighing any bloodlust at the sight of my injury.

Upon our arrival, I couldn't help but notice the tension radiating from Lilly as she deftly guided us through the intricate procedures to receive medical assistance from the agency. Her sense of urgency was practically tangible, as she went above and beyond to ensure I received prompt attention despite various obstacles. Evidently, she had been anxiously awaiting our arrival at the hospital. She wasted no time springing into action to facilitate my care.

As I lay in the hospital bed, my head throbbing with pain, I noticed Luke standing off to the side. His presence was both calming and unsettling at the same time. I turned to him, my body aching, longing for answers. The room was silent except for the beeping of machines and the distant sound of footsteps in the hallway. I needed to know what was happening, and Luke was the only one who could provide me with the answers I desperately sought.

"How?" I demanded. "How? Why did you lie to me about who you are?"

I could barely whisper, but I wanted to know why he was following me. His icy gaze bore down on me, but a small smile played on his lips as dimples appeared on his cheeks. As recognition dawned on me, I realised where I had seen that same image. It had haunted my dreams for weeks, with Luke's face appearing as my lover in heated moments that felt all too real. The realisation escaped me until now because my attention was consumed by other things.

"You!" I spoke, just above a whisper, before everything blurred and spun uncontrollably.

My eyes began to close as Luke's lips parted, ready to speak. Slowly, the darkness crept in, embracing me in its icy grip as I drifted into unconsciousness. I felt myself being lifted and placed onto a soft surface, the voices around me sounding muffled and distant. The concerned tones of those speaking to me were barely audible, like whispers in a far-off dream. Despite my best efforts, my eyes refused to open, leaving me to wonder if this was the end. Maybe they were right; the hearing was the last sense to fade as death approached. Was this my final moment?

"How and why was she allowed anywhere near that alley?" Lilly demanded. "Luke, you were assigned to keep her safe, and so far, you've failed; today is a prime example of why vampires cannot help witches with watchers or otherwise."

"I doubt anything I could have done would have kept her safe," Luke remained calm. "She has a mind of her own and does whatever she wants. I followed her, but I was slightly too late. Tye had already gotten hold of her."

"Tye?" Lilly queried. "One of yours?"

"Hardly," Luke defended. "He was banished years ago during the insurgents' rising, so he should be at the top of the list to be found and questioned for the murder. I have no idea why he was there; I was too preoccupied that he had held off Seira and wanted to kill her..."

Once again, the suffocating grip of darkness enveloped me, pulling me deeper into its cold embrace. Yet, amidst the shadows, a deep sense of tranquillity and peace washed over me like a healing balm. It would not have seemed out of place if every witch had been called upon to lend their powers to aid my recovery. I could feel myself being transferred to a secure location, where a magical barrier was erected around me, shielding me from harm and keeping watch over me. The witches' voices murmured softly in the background, their protective spells weaving a cocoon of safety around me. And then, all I could hear was the sound of silence, a comforting stillness that embraced me like a warm blanket.

Time seemed to slip away as I lay there, unaware of the passing of minutes or hours. But then, like a hazy fog lifting, I began to regain consciousness. Gradually, the world around me started to come back into focus. And as I blinked my eyes open, I was met with the sound of someone settling down next to me.

"Luke..."

"I'm here," he whispered beside me. "How do you feel?"

"Rough," I smiled slightly, and my eyes blinked open to find the familiar eyes looking back at me. "Why?"

"I knew you would ask that the minute you opened your eyes," he threw his hands up in mock defeat. "I had to keep you safe. It was something Lilly employed me to do. Someone is targeting the entire agency, but only the witches, including crossbreeds."

"How do you know?" I asked, struggling to sit up.

Luke tenderly nestled the soft pillow under my head. However, there was a noticeable distance between us. The playful and carefree vampire I had once known seemed to have vanished, leaving behind a stranger in his place.

"I can't tell you," he said, looking away briefly. "Lilly will be here in a few minutes. She wants answers, you know that, don't you?"

I remained silent, giving a slight nod in response. I was determined to keep the information I had gleaned to myself for now. I needed to be absolutely sure of the murderer's identity before sharing anything with her.

The gentle caress of the breeze fluttered through the room, causing the blinds to rattle against the windows. At the same time, the sweet fragrance of flowers wafted through the air, announcing Lilly's presence. She glided into the room through the hidden portal reserved for the elite witches, her distinctive scent serving as the only warning of her impending arrival.

"Lilly," I breathed into the silence of the room.

Luke stood by my side, his gaze fixed and unmoving towards the corner of the room. As Lilly's form gradually materialised before us, her presence filled the space until she stood before us. Using the transportation spell had its perks. Lilly was unaware that Matace had passed down the knowledge of that spell to me, and I had fully grasped and mastered it within a day. Such spells reflected one's deep magical heritage and strength, requiring immense power and skill to successfully invoke.

"Seira," she smiled. "You're awake. I'm glad. How do you feel?"

The way she spoke quickly and anxiously scanned the room sent a shiver down my spine as I lay on the bed, feeling the tight bandage wrapped around my head and the cold tube protruding from my wrist, leading to a large bag of saline hanging nearby. At that moment, I only wanted to escape from where I was and be anywhere else but here.

"I'm fine," I answered bravely. "What happened?"

"You don't remember?" she asked, perplexed by my question. "It was Tye, a rather vicious vampire who had been exiled by Matace many years ago. Somehow, he had had help to enter and live on Earth against the agency's knowledge. What were you doing out there on your own? Who knows what might have happened if Luke hadn't followed you?"

"I was trying to locate some details," I defended. "It was nothing much, and I didn't actually unearth anything other than everything that has already been recorded in the files."

"You took the files home, too," she said, "against the agency's rules and beyond the protective spell surrounding all documents, such as those. Whatever has possessed you to do such things?"

"I wanted to trace details," I said. "There's something wrong about the whole thing. It seems like the murderer has had a lot of help from someone privy to inside information."

My voice echoed off the room's walls as Lilly lapsed into a heavy, weighted silence. She lowered her head, allowing her hair to cascade down and create a curtain, shielding her expression from my sight.

Luke carefully disentangled himself from the situation and quietly exited the room. The purposeful sound of his footsteps and his firm gaze in my direction before he closed the door warned me to tread carefully when engaging with the powerful High Witch, lest we risk stirring up unnecessary trouble.

"I see," she said gently. "I can't let you start wandering alone; it's too dangerous, especially now."

"What do you mean 'especially now'?"

"There's been another murder," she answered. "I didn't want to tell you so soon, not until I was sure what we were facing. It seems those close to Matace are being targeted. And so now," she went quiet and struggled to compose herself. "You will have to be under protection at all times."

"Who's been murdered?" I whispered in a barely audible voice, my demand for an answer dripping with insistence.

"Clarette," she answered. "As you know, she was Matace's second in command during his reign over the realm."

"I know," I slumped back against the pillows in shock. "I can't believe it."

The news hit me like a ton of bricks, leaving me utterly devastated. It felt as though a dark cloud of violence and chaos was hovering all around us, creeping ever closer with each passing moment. As the one closest to Matace, I couldn't help but fear that the impending danger would soon reach me. Despite my proximity to him, I knew painfully little about his dealings and the intricate affairs within the realm. The sense of impending doom only intensified my unease and left me feeling unnerved and vulnerable.

"I'll speak to Luke and have him stay with you," she said.

"What do you mean?" I gasped. "Luke can't stay with me all the time," I strongly emphasised the idea of spending the night inside my tiny apartment or wherever he was staying. I prayed it wouldn't be the stereotypical dark and gloomy crypt but something more elegant and sophisticated. I am utterly unfamiliar with the daily lives of vampires as I have never engaged with them on a personal level. In fact, my only interactions with vampires have been strictly business-related, within the confines of my role at the agency.

"I mean all the time, Seira," she said gently but with a firmness evident in her tone. "It's unsafe, and I feel you'll be next or the one after. There are only two of you remaining who were close to Matace. Pepsi is under protection as well."

"Anyone else but Luke," I let out a frustrated groan, burying my face into my pillow once she had departed. Muffled voices reached my ears as Luke and Lilly engaged in a terse exchange outside my closed bedroom door.

"Stay with her and make sure she doesn't do anything dangerous that might get herself killed, and this time," Lilly stopped briefly, "do it properly."

"Properly," he repeated menacingly softly. "Do you know what it's been like to keep up with her? Once she wants to do something, there's no stopping her."

"I'm aware of how stubborn she is," Lilly reprimanded. "Remember, you're under my control now, not Matace's. Until his murderer and the one responsible for the murder of Clarette have been caught and brought to justice, there is no other option but to ensure everyone is kept safe."

"Right," he muttered quietly. "And how does Seira feel about me protecting her? I assume you've told her I've been her watcher for some time now?"

Luke, my watcher, had been observing me without my knowledge for who knows how long. I couldn't believe Matace hadn't mentioned it to me. He was straightforward and wouldn't have kept such an important secret from me.

"Listen," Lilly sighed, "you've been watching her for a while. I've checked, and you've done well to keep her safe. I'm asking on behalf of Seira's guardian, Matace, magic rest his soul, can you please keep her safe for a little while longer?"

"No problem," he responded sharply, with a hint of irritation. "It's like watching a runaway squirrel, though."

The conversation ended, and Luke quietly entered my room, his expression guarded, his emotions hidden beneath a careful facade.

"I'm not asking you to watch me at all," I spoke softly, with a hint of trepidation, as he slowly approached me on the bed. "Actually," I said. "I'll ask you to be re-assigned and get someone else."

"Now, why would you do that?" he grinned suddenly. "Who else will give me tips on handling human women?"

"Well," I huffed. "I think you can forget anything like that. You lied to me; I want to know why?"

"Seira, Seira, Seira," He pronounced my name with a soft, rhythmic cadence as if each syllable was delicately rolling off his tongue. "I had to. If I had told you I was your watcher, you would have told me to get lost," he shrugged. "So, I lied instead, my way of keeping close to you without telling you who I was or my capacity with the agency."

"Where's your office?" I inquired, my hands shaking with excitement as a new realisation dawned on me. Could his office be strategically positioned directly across from mine? The same office where the enigmatic figure seemed to possess the uncanny ability to read my thoughts with eerie accuracy. There was only one explanation for such a formidable power – the presence of a vampire. Their supernatural abilities were unmatched, and the enigmatic figure in the neighbouring office could be Luke himself. Few vampires can read minds, but those who can are said to be from a very ancient vampire bloodline.

"Opposite yours," he said, "I heard you just then," he answered guiltily.

"You still lied," I crossed my arms tightly over my chest in a petulant gesture, my mood sour as I glared out of the window, "and you made me believe in some erotic game you played all the time. Was that to amuse yourself?"

"I'm sorry," he said, appearing harmless and the young mess-around person I'd become used to. "How do you know it was all to amuse myself? Maybe I am serious about that part."

"You're what?" I asked, startled. My voice raised quite a few octaves in the small room. "Don't ever say anything like that again. You know as well I do what will happen if anything like that happens between someone like me and someone like you," my voice plummeted to a hushed urgency as I felt the weight of potential eavesdroppers lurking in the shadows, ready to catch every word of our conversation.

"And why not Seira?" he whispered quietly, stepping closer until his face was a few inches from mine. "Don't you think shaking things up a little inside the agency might be fun? Don't you think we would be good together?"

"No," I carefully inched my way towards the edge of the bed, my fingertips clutching desperately at the edge of the covers to keep myself from falling off the other side. "Get away from me. I don't want to shake things up, and I don't want to be with someone that lies."

"I told you why I did that," he slowly retreated, realising that he was losing the current battle and only managing to further provoke my anger. "I had to so I could keep you as safe as possible. Matace gave me strict instructions to ensure nothing happened to you; you have no idea how special you were to him, Seira," he sighed. "He contacted me every day to ask how you were and what you'd been up to. He wanted to make sure you were happy more than anything else."

"So Matace told you to watch me?"

"Yes," his voice softened as he settled beside me. Leaning in, he rested his elbows on his thighs, his intent gaze fixed on me.

"I don't get it," I said, "I don't understand why my safety would mean so much to Matace. Don't you think that's weird?"

"A little," he admitted. "But it's not something we have to think about, right?"

"Depends on how you look at it, I suppose," I said. "There must be something in his house, some missing evidence that might link something together."

Luke reclined in his chair, a smirk playing on his lips as he observed me intently. His eyes sparkled with amusement while a hint of something else lingered in their depths, unknown and mysterious to me. My thoughts raced chaotically through my mind. I almost felt Luke deciphering them effortlessly, every word and emotion bare before him.

"Don't even consider it," he said quietly. "You're not doing it, and neither am I."

Chapter Three

A faint grin tugged at the corners of my lips as I lay in bed despite the dull, pulsing ache that had taken up residence in my head. It was hardly surprising, given that someone had essentially stomped all over my skull.

"I beg to differ," I responded, my voice level and measured. "I'm afraid I have no idea what you're implying." My expression remained neutral, betraying none of the confusion I felt stirring within. I needed to tread carefully here to avoid revealing any potential vulnerability.

"Oh, I'm well aware," he grinned mischievously from beside me, his eyes twinkling with amusement. "You can't hide a single thought from me, you know. I can hear everything that's going on in your captivating mind." He leisurely stretched his legs in front of him, a hint of curiosity in his voice as he continued, "Most of the time, it's a true delight to listen in on your thoughts. But today, I can't help but sense a touch of unease behind that clever facade of yours."

"And when I was unconscious?" I asked, my voice laced with a hint of curiosity and apprehension.

"Ah, the sweet embrace of peace and quiet," he chuckled, his eyes crinkling with amusement as he gazed at me. The corners of his lips curled into a mischievous grin, hinting at the playful jest behind his words.

With a frustrated huff, I hurled my pillow at him, but he swiftly evaded the soft projectile. Silence fell between us as we sat in the charged stillness, neither willing to break the awkward tension that had settled over the room.

A sharp, throbbing pain pierced through my skull, and I let out a weary sigh. With great effort, I eased myself back against the mattress, my voice barely above a whisper. "I need the nurse," I murmured, hoping for some relief from this relentless headache.

"I'm not surprised," he remarked, "Tye pretty much put everything he had into stomping on your head. If it hadn't been for the witches that came here, you wouldn't have survived."

"The memory of him still sends a shiver down my spine," I recounted, the vivid recollection etching itself in my mind. "Why was he there, though?"

He shrugged casually, his ankles crossed. "Beats me," he said, a hint of nonchalance in his voice. "How he managed to escape his exile, I have no idea. It might have caused a bit of a stir in the dark world, but nothing that's out of the ordinary, really."

"Hmm, interesting," I murmured, my mind racing as I processed the implications. "Do you think there might be a connection between him and the murders?" I asked, leaning forward with a keen expression, eager to unravel the emerging threads of this perplexing case.

"He had clear motives for the murder of Matace but not Clarette," he said, his brow furrowed in contemplation. "What I can't seem to wrap my head around is the reason behind her death. She was the second-in-command, nothing more – so why would someone go to such lengths to eliminate her?"

The mystery hung in the air, the unanswered questions weighing heavily on his mind. There had to be a deeper, more sinister purpose behind Clarette's untimely demise. Still, the clues remained elusive, leaving him grasping for answers amid the confusion.

"Her poor parents must be devastated," I stated solemnly, the weight of their tragedy hanging heavy in the air. The mere thought of their devastation was almost too much to bear. Their world had been shattered, leaving them grappling with a pain no parent should ever have to endure.

The nurse hurried into the room, her footsteps brisk and purposeful. In her hands, she carried a tray laden with painkillers and a glass of water. As she entered, her gaze fell upon Luke, who sat upright, his eyes intently focused on her every move. A faint blush crept across the nurse's cheeks, betraying her momentary self-consciousness under his watchful observation.

Gratitude flooded my voice as I replied, "Thank you."

"And would your boyfriend like anything?" she asked politely, causing me to choke on my drink.

"No, I don't," Luke cut in smoothly, using his smile to disarm whatever she would say next.

As she departed, I swivelled to face him, my gaze locking onto his intently. There was a glint of knowing in his eyes - he had clearly picked up on her unspoken thoughts and knew precisely what she was about to request.

"Did you know what she was going to say?"

"Ah, but the question is, does it truly matter?" he said, teasing me.

"You could have corrected her," I said, yawning and stretching back against the pillow he had replaced behind me.

My eyes drifted closed, and the most pleasant dreams stole around me, taking me to places I hadn't seen before. I found myself amidst sprawling, serene gardens, where the sun's golden rays caressed the lush foliage, unblemished by any clouds that might tarnish the idyllic scene. I sighed at the beautiful experience, not understanding or caring where it came from - only that, for once, I wasn't dreaming of any romantic involvement with Luke.

My dream ended far too soon, dragging me back to consciousness. Blinking open my eyes, I found myself gazing upon Luke's slumped form, his chin resting against his chest as he sat in the chair beside my bed. I studied him, taking in his striking features – a vampire-like allure I had never witnessed in him before. Yet, the feelings that stirred within me were unlike anything I had experienced in our purely professional relationship. I couldn't help but wonder if these emotions had been conjured by the dreams he had implanted in my mind or if they were genuine and authentic.

Regardless, I knew that such feelings could never be acted upon. The boundaries of our working relationship were not to be crossed, no matter the temptation. Still, there was an undeniable shift in the air – a tension that hinted at the possibility of something more, something that both thrilled and terrified me. The agency strictly prohibited any union between a witch and a vampire. Such a forbidden combination would unleash chaos within the agency's walls and beyond. The consequences of defying this rule were too grave a risk for me to consider. The upheaval it would cause for those working inside and outside the agency was not worth the gamble.

"Stop staring," his deep voice broke my trance. "It's rude."

"I wasn't staring at you," I retorted, my voice laced with a hint of annoyance. "What makes you think you're so special that I would even bother with such a thing?" I scoffed, my gaze fixed elsewhere, making it clear that the idea was absurd.

"Because you thought I'm attractive, and you'd like to try something with me - but you're not sure what."

I heaved a weary sigh as I sank back against the plush pillow. I'm going to find out a way I can permanently block his access to my mind.

"For goodness sake, can you just stop?" he snapped, his brow furrowed with irritation as my thoughts disrupted his focus. "It's incredibly distracting."

"When was the last time you ate?"

"Pardon?" he said, his brow furrowing slightly as he turned to face me, his eyes conveying a hint of confusion.

"You heard me, didn't you?" I said impatiently. "So, when was it?"

"Hmm, let me think," he murmured, his fingers nervously running through his messy hair. "I suppose it was the day before yesterday."

"In that case, I'd strongly recommend you make your way to the canteen and fill your stomach before you start longing for a taste of my blood," I said, my voice laced with a hint of playful warning.

"I highly doubt that," he said in a silky-smooth tone, scepticism flickering in his eyes. "It's too salty for my liking."

After saying that, he turned and left, leaving me time to think without worrying about his hearing. I pressed the bell to call the nurse—if there was a time to gain some distance between us, it was now.

Her eyes narrowed as she cautiously peeked around the door. "Yes?" she asked, her tone laced with a hint of concern. "Is everything alright?"

"I'd like to go home now. I feel much better," I said, the relief evident in my voice. "This place has been draining me, but I finally feel like myself again. Can you please bring me the discharge papers and anything I have to sign?"

My tone was firm, and there was a hint of urgency underlying my words. The thought of leaving this place behind filled me with a renewed sense of energy and purpose. I'd had enough of this endless waiting, this stifling environment—I needed to reclaim my freedom, and I needed it now.

"Absolutely not," she declared sternly, her voice laced with concern. "You've been through a terrible experience, barely clinging to life when they carried you in here. You must stay and let us ensure you're fully recovered before even considering leaving." Her piercing gaze bore into me as if she was trying to convey the gravity of the situation. "I won't let you jeopardise your well-being by rushing out of here. You've been through too much already. Please, stay and let us take care of you."

"I'm afraid that's impossible," I responded, my lips curling into a polite yet unyielding smile.

She nodded briefly and bustled back relatively quickly - with Luke trailing behind her, a cup in hand, which I assumed carried his meal. It was an agency rule that all canteens provide food for every creature inside, protecting humans from becoming meals.

Irritation surged through me as I saw him, his cup in hand, undoubtedly carrying his meal. The idea of him shadowing my every move irked me to no end.

"I've been told you're leaving so soon," he muttered, his eyes burning over the rim of his cup. "I hope you weren't expecting to leave without me."

"Surely, you don't think I'd do something like that to you," I said, feigning a look of pure innocence. My gaze met his, a playful challenge glimmering in my eyes. "After all, you're my watcher, aren't you? That means we're bound to be together, always." A coy smile tugged at the corners of my lips. "So I hope you like sleeping outside because there's only room for one at my place."

"Now, you listen up," he said, his voice low and authoritative, as he manoeuvred around the nurse and swiftly removed the IV from my arm. He paused, his piercing gaze locking onto mine. "I've been mulling this over, and I reckon it's far better for you to come stay at my place." His words carried a sense of finality, leaving no room for argument.

What, willingly stay in a crypt? The thought sent a shiver down my spine. The prospect of sleeping a few feet away from a bloodthirsty immortal is enough to make my heart race with dread. However, some people may find confronting danger exciting despite feeling slightly scared. The thought of facing a vampire directly, pushing the limits of our humanity, can be tempting to those who seek adventure. But it is important to remember that willingly putting oneself in the vampire's world is extremely risky and not a risk I personally wanted to take.

I stared at Luke, mouth agape. To my utter astonishment, he erupted into uncontrollable laughter, his entire body shaking. The intensity of his reaction caught me completely off guard, and I found myself utterly speechless, unable to form another sentence. The sheer force of his laughter was infectious, and I couldn't help but be drawn into the moment, my own amusement rising to the surface despite my initial state of bewilderment.

"I guess the arrangement would work," I ventured, "providing you have human food, and it's civilised because humans have certain needs for hunger, thirst and basic human comfort."

"Of course it is," he said hoarsely, his voice thick with emotion. "I may be many things, but a complete monster is not one of them. When you're well enough to go shopping with me, we can stock up on human food tomorrow. But for now, we can grab snacks from the vending machines in the corridor. How does that sound?"

I tilted my head, my brows furrowing slightly. "Well, I suppose it'll be fine," I said, a hint of hesitation in my voice. "But you'll have to handle the shopping – there's no way I'm setting foot in any stores for a while, not after what happened." As I recalled the recent incident, a shiver ran down my spine, the memory still fresh and unsettling.

He considered my response, his eyes flickering with a flare of understanding as he waited quietly for the nurse to finish her duties around the room. I swung my legs over the edge of the bed, my toes barely grazing the cool tile floor beneath. Grabbing the nearest pile of clothes, stained and tattered beyond recognition, I hurried towards the bathroom, eager to change without a vampire's watchful gaze. The thought of him witnessing my vulnerability was not something I was willing to entertain, watcher or not.

Frustrated, I ran my fingers through my tangled, unkempt hair, feeling the knots accumulated without a proper brush. Glancing down at my messy clothes, I sighed heavily, resigning myself to the reality that I had no choice but to go as I was – a dishevelled, disorderly mess. After all, I was about to leave the hospital with a vampire, the forbidden fruit of the realm's most dangerous yet trusted protectors. Did it truly matter how I looked in the grand scheme of things?

His knuckles rapped sharply against the door, echoing through the silence. "Ready?" he called out.

I cautiously pushed the door open, my heart pounding in my chest. Dread gripped me as I prepared to reveal how dirty I looked with my torn, bloodied clothes on. He stood there, hands buried in his pockets, an unsettling cheerfulness about him. Likely a result of the fresh blood he had just consumed, rejuvenating him.

My heart raced as I gripped the car keys, adrenaline coursing through my veins. 'I'm ready,' I declared, the determination in my voice unwavering as I placed the keys in his outstretched hand.

His brow furrowed, and he looked confused. "What on Earth are those?" he asked, his voice laced with a hint of suspicion. "And why in the world would I need them?"

"They are my house keys," I replied, gesturing to my clothes. "We have to swing by there so I can grab some clothes and other essentials. Unless, of course, you don't want me crashing at your place or your creepy-as-hell crypt?" I raised an eyebrow, challenging him to disagree with the shortstop.

"Enough with this crypt nonsense!" he exclaimed, frustration evident in his voice. "I don't live in some dank, dreary crypt," he said. "My place is a proper house, tidy and well-kept, on the other side of town," he explained. "In fact, your belongings have already been moved there." He leaned in, his gaze unwavering. "I assure you, you'll fall in love with my house. Now, we better get a move on if you want out of here. Are you ready?" he asked. "So much for snacks from the vending machine," he muttered.

I spun around, looking at him again, feeling really confused. How could he take my stuff without asking? Was this all planned out before I even realised what was happening?

"How the hell did that happen?" I demanded, struggling to keep up with the sheer magnitude of the situation. My mind raced, entirely out of its element of having my belongings touched by people in the agency I didn't know. It felt like an invasion.

"I asked Lilly to arrange it earlier while you were asleep," he said, holding the door open and gesturing for me to pass through. A subtle smirk played on his lips as he leaned in, his gaze unwavering. "Tell me, did you enjoy your dreams? Were they as peaceful as the ones from a few weeks ago?"

The intensity in his voice sent a shiver down my spine, and I couldn't help but wonder what exactly he had arranged. The air was thick with anticipation, and I knew whatever was to come would be extraordinary.

"My what?" I was amazed again. "How did you know about them?"

"I'm the one who summoned them for you," he said, a hint of arrogance in his voice, unfazed by the fact that he had interrupted my rest time for the hundredth time this month. "And since you didn't like the other ones, I thought I'd provide you with something different today," he said. "I wanted you to sleep peacefully without monsters causing you nightmares."

My nightmares had started a few years ago and plagued me every night. No matter what I did, they always seemed to appear.

"Look, we need to have a long, serious talk about this," I said, my voice laden with frustration and concern. "You need to stop invading my dreams and my thoughts. This has gone on for far too long, and it's just not right and disrespectful. You need to respect my privacy and stop immediately," I said. "If you carry on, I will have no choice but to take drastic measures to protect myself. Do you understand?" The intensity in my tone left no room for argument as I stared him down, my eyes narrowed with a steely determination.

"Listening to your thoughts isn't my choice," Luke pointed out. "It's an inescapable part of my vampire nature, just as giving humans positive dreams is my gift to counteract it. I don't summon distressing visions intentionally. But I'll refrain from both if you promise not to pursue this murder investigation further. You're not equipped to face dangers of this magnitude alone."

"I'm well aware of that," I huffed, frustration lacing my words. "I was only trying to offer my assistance because Matace has been like a father figure to me ever since I joined the agency." My voice trembled with exasperation and yearning, the weight of our relationship pressing heavily on my chest.

We stopped abruptly in the middle of the corridor. Surrounding us were a flurry of beings – some mortal, other creatures of various bizarre descriptions, all scurrying about with their own pressing destinations. The hospital had been engineered to withstand attacks from unknown threats, with its circle of dedicated defenders in the vicinity and protective spells that could hold out until reinforcements arrived. Fortunately, according to the records, nothing of that nature had occurred in nearly a century. Before that, however, the hospital had been viciously assaulted by an army of hounds from a distant, alien world. Their savage snarls and ferocity had inflicted the most profound devastation upon everyone there that fateful night. They had left behind. Only remnants of creatures and people remained, which were used to identify the victims, with a final death toll of three hundred. I was tasked with overseeing everything, ensuring that history would not be granted the opportunity to repeat its most horrific chapters.

"I know," he said softly." And I also know you're not the type to simply give up without a fight. You're the kind of person who will stand their ground, no matter how hard the challenge is."

"Do you blame me?" I asked, my voice barely above a whisper.

"I'm afraid I wouldn't do anything differently," he responded, calm yet resolute. His words had a subtle edge, a hint of a deeper conviction that lay beneath the surface.

I gripped his arm, desperately clinging to it as the world around me spun out of control. My body was betraying me, unable to keep up with the sheer determination coursing through my veins. Yet, I remained steadfast, stubbornly refusing to let this setback keep me from my mission. The hospital walls felt like a cage, trapping me when I needed to be out there, searching for the murderer or, at the very least, contributing to the investigation. Sitting idly by while the perpetrator remained at large was unbearable. I had to get out, no matter the cost to my well-being.

Concern etched across his features, he leaned in, eyes fixed on me. "Are you alright?" He asked worriedly. "You look really pale - is everything okay?"

I laughed wickedly, "What, as pale as you?" The taunt would have ruffled the feathers of any other vampire, but not Luke. His gaze remained unflinching, unperturbed by my jibe. "Sorry," I quickly added, the apology as an afterthought.

"No, don't you dare apologise," he replied, his voice laced with a stern, unyielding edge. "There's absolutely nothing for you to be sorry about."

"No, there most certainly is," I said. "I definitely made a mistake and have been really rude to you. I feel bad about it and wish I could take it back. I know I messed up, and I understand if you can't forgive me, but I want you to know how sorry I am."

Luke didn't hesitate for a moment. He lifted me into his strong arms in one swift motion, insisting on carrying me the rest of the way to the car. I clutched his shirt, my fingers digging into the fabric. His small, low-profile vehicle gleamed under the parking lot lamp, its pristine surface reflecting the light. When I caught sight of the car, I let out a small, involuntary gasp of awe, which only seemed to deepen the satisfaction on Luke's face. But my focus quickly shifted from his triumphant expression to the burning desire to get inside the vehicle and examine it more closely, to run my hands along the sleek exterior and immerse myself in its captivating presence.

"Luke!" I exclaimed, my voice laced with disbelief as I saw the sleek, gleaming vehicle before me. "Is this... is this your car?" The words tumbled from my lips, my heart racing with excitement and sheer disbelief. I couldn't believe my eyes – the sheer presence of this car, which seemed to demand attention, was a far cry from the battered old sedan I had expected Luke to be driving.

"Of course it is," he chuckled, a mischievous glint in his eyes. "Whose else could it possibly be?" He leaned forward, his voice dripping with a smug confidence that bordered on arrogance.

"I have no idea," I responded, my shoulders tensing as I avoided eye contact. "For all I know, you might have taken it without permission."

"Listen up," he declared, his body trembling with laughter. "I'll admit, I may have deceived you before," he reminded me, a mischievous glint in his eyes. "But that doesn't mean I'm about to start lying to you again, and I'm not a thief," his voice dropped to a low, earnest tone, underscoring the weight of his words. "I've never stolen anything in my long ancient life."

"I know," I murmured. "But that doesn't erase the fact that you lied to me time and time again. I foolishly trusted you, only to discover that you were nothing more than a watcher sent to keep an eye on me." My eyes narrowed, the betrayal burning in my chest like a smouldering ember.

"Ah, I could sense it, you know? The way your eyes would linger, the subtle shift in your posture whenever I was around," he teased, lifting the mood. "Deep down, you were captivated by the mystery surrounding me, weren't you? Don't try to deny it. In due time, you'll understand why, but for now, let's acknowledge the undeniable pull you felt towards my enigmatic nature."

He laughed; his smile warmed me, and I couldn't help but secretly agree with him, although I tried my hardest not to show it. Despite my best efforts to hide my feelings, his charm had a way of seeping through my carefully constructed defences, leaving me inwardly captivated by his wit and playful demeanour. The more I tried to resist, the more alluring his presence became, drawing me in like a moth to a flame. He was becoming the same Luke I had known, and I didn't want him to change.

He gripped my body firmly and gently laced me inside his car. Locking his eyes onto mine. "Get in," he laughed.

I slid into the car, sinking into the decadent leather seats that caressed my skin. The interior was a symphony of cool, sleek elegance that captivated me. As I ran my fingers along the impeccable surfaces, I couldn't help but marvel at the sheer luxury of it all. Who possessed the means to have something so exquisitely refined and luxurious? The staggering wealth required to own such a magnificent vehicle left me dumbfounded.

I sank into the seat with a contented sigh, savouring the crisp, refreshing scent that filled the car's interior. My gaze followed Luke as he strode across the parking lot with theatrical flair, his every step a performance. The ordinary mortals milled around us, clustered around their own vehicles, oblivious to the subtle intensity that crackled between us.

I watched a mother's desperate attempts to get her child into the car, only to be met with unwavering resistance. She shouted angrily, scolding and reprimanding the defiant little boy, her voice laced with frustration. But just as quickly, her demeanour shifted, a remarkable transformation occurred. Her expression softened, suffused with a solid and unconditional tenderness. I had only ever witnessed this all-encompassing maternal love in films. This bond went above the physical and emotional realms. My own adoptive mother had loved me dearly and still did, but it lacked the primal, instinctive connection that came from carrying a child for nine months. I always felt a certain level of disconnection with her, and she never treated me the same way as my siblings, her biological children. This mother's gaze held a depth of emotion I could scarcely comprehend, a wellspring of love that seemed to defy logic and reason.

Luke climbed into the passenger seat beside me, a mischievous grin spreading. "So, are you ready to see where I live?" he asked, his voice dripping with anticipation.

I couldn't help but feel a tinge of apprehension, recalling my earlier assumptions about him living in a crypt. My pained expression must have been evident because he laughed, seemingly amused by my continued scepticism.

"Don't worry," he reassured me, his eyes sparkling with a hint of mischief. "I promise it's not as... creepy as you might think." He leaned in closer, his breath tickling my ear, and added in a conspiratorial whisper, "In fact, I think you're going to be pleasantly surprised." He threw his hands up in exasperation, his voice laced with a hint of desperation. "I promise you, it is not some kind of crypt," he insisted. His gaze met mine, "so, tell me, do you have any objections to joining me on this little adventure and perhaps discovering more about each other along the way?" The weight of his words hung in the air, daring me to refuse.

I avoided answering his prying question, letting it hang awkwardly in the heavy air between us. When I cautiously looked at him, his smug smile confirmed that he knew the impact his question had on me. It sparked a battle between my emotions and logic, leaving me in inner turmoil.

Caught between two worlds, he broke down the walls that held me back and unlocked my deepest, secret ambitions. Without even realising it, he sparked a fire within me - the pain of abandonment, the longing for a place to call home. This drove me to take a chance, prove myself in a prestigious organisation, earn a place among the stars, and show that I had something unique.

In the middle of the chilling silence stood Luke - a man who was believed to be dead but was now very much alive and in front of me. He had become my captor, and his actions and words aimed to gain my trust and obedience. I could feel the weight of his control over me as he tried to make me feel at ease in his unfamiliar surroundings. I knew it was for my safety, and everything was happening for a reason. All I wanted was to escape and return to the safety of my own home, away from this unsettling situation. The tension in the car was almost tangible, a feeling of fear lingering in the air. I was trapped, uncertain of his true intentions and powerless in his presence. Luke remained a mysterious and enigmatic figure, keeping his motives hidden from me as he held the cards in terms of being my watcher and, for all intents and purposes, my bodyguard.

"Are you alright?" He looked at me with furrowed brows, his concern evident. His voice carried an unmistakable worry, hinting at the fear of something being amiss. His gaze felt heavy, silently urging me to confide in him. Time seemed to stand still as I felt the urgency to reassure him that everything would be okay.

"Yes," I croaked, my voice hoarse as I sank deeper into the chair, a sharp pain in my chest with every word. "Why on Earth wouldn't I be?" I challenged, my eyes narrowing as I straightened my posture, mustering what little energy I had left to strengthen myself.

"Your thoughts seem a bit scattered," he observed, a hint of concern in his voice. "Are you doing okay? I didn't mean to upset you so much by sending those dreams. I thought I was helping you, giving you something to focus on, but I may have misjudged the situation." He paused, searching my face for any indication of my feelings. "Tell me, what's wrong? I'm here to listen if you're ready to share."

I let out an exasperated sigh; he was utterly oblivious to the profound effect he had on me. Every vivid dream had turned my heart into a quivering mess, making me savour the most extraordinary, intimate details of a love I could never hope to possess. It was mortifyingly embarrassing to think that I had made passionate love to this person in the realms of my dreams without even realising it was him. This felt like an invasion of my innermost feelings and emotions, and I wasn't sure I could ever bring myself to forgive him for subjecting me to this intensely personal, overwhelming experience.

"Stay out of my business and my thoughts, or you'll regret it," I snapped, my words laced with a sharp edge. "I don't think it's fair you did that to me, but I need to try and forget it all," I said, dismissing the matter with a flick of my hand. "Do you promise to stick to your word it won't happen again?"

"Yes," he answered. "I promise you I won't interfere inside your head. I'm sorry," he affirmed. "Oh, look, we're almost there, just up ahead – see that sharp turn?" he said, gesturing with a swift hand motion. When he noticed my nod of understanding, he pressed on with renewed vigour, "It's right beyond that bend, just a stone's throw away."

As we approached the deceptively ordinary-looking house, a shiver of anticipation ran down my spine. After all the tales I had heard about the mysterious vampire residing within, I envisioned a dark, foreboding structure – perhaps a towering castle or a crumbling Gothic manor. Yet, to my utter astonishment, the dwelling before me appeared no different from any other suburban home on the street. The stark contrast between the legends and reality left me bewildered. How could this mundane, nondescript abode be the lair of a creature of the night? Surely, there must be some hidden secrets, some unseen horrors lurking behind those seemingly innocuous walls. All the houses on the street looked the same as Luke drove slowly. My heart raced as I wondered what unspeakable wonders or terrors lay in wait, just out of sight.

As I sat there, transfixed by the differences between expectation and reality, a sense of unease crept up my spine. I knew I was about to enter a world far from the ordinary, where the natural and supernatural boundaries blurred. With a deep breath, I steeled my nerves, eager to unlock the mysteries that lay within.

"You see, I'm not a creature of the night dwelling in some dreary crypt," he said with a playful smirk, helping me out of the car. "Most of us prefer to live a relatively normal life, but there are a few," he paused, his eyes glinting with a hint of mischief, "exceptions to the rule."

The intensity in his voice and the subtle shift in his demeanour as he spoke of the "exceptions" sent a shiver down my spine. An underlying current of mystery and intrigue piqued my curiosity, making me wonder what sort of world he inhabited – a world that seemed to exist just beyond the veil of the ordinary.

"Such as?"

"Tye, for instance," he spat, his face twisting with disdain at the mention of the name. "He fancies himself above the rest of us, and this isn't the first time he's been involved in some dubious scheme. The last time he was caught and exiled, he was attempting to rally his vile coven together. That time, he had trained a small army of savage vampires and newly turned fledglings, attempting to send them to the unsuspecting mortals." His expression darkened, his eyes narrowing with disgust and resentment. "Tye thinks he's untouchable, that the rules don't apply to him. But mark my words, his arrogance and thirst for power will be his downfall. You can only evade justice before it catches up to them."

"Oh no, his past sounds horrible," I gasped, my hand flying to my mouth. "What happened? Did he manage to send any of the new vampires to the public?"

He paused momentarily, clearing his throat as if the words were laced with a bitter aftertaste. "He was apprehended, his treachery exposed, and swiftly exiled from the vampire order of immortality and Earth. The others he had corrupted and turned were completely destroyed. It was too dangerous to keep them alive." His eyes narrowed, a hint of solemn determination lingering in his gaze. "According to the information I've been privy to, Matace himself orchestrated his downfall, issuing the directives that sealed his fate."

"Impossible!" I gasped. "How could it not be documented anywhere?" I muttered, my brow furrowed with confusion. "That information is crucial, yet it's as if it's been erased from every record. There has to be an explanation, something we're missing, as to why someone would need to keep that mission a secret. Do you have any ideas why?"

He shrugged, his brow furrowing with uncertainty. "I'm not entirely sure," he admitted, shrugging. "This was supposed to be a top-secret affair, you know? Strictly confidential, given the sheer scale of the situation and the devastating loss of life." He paused, his gaze darkening. "Do you think that could be why they're keeping everything so tightly under wraps?"

"Absolutely not," I said, my voice firm and unwavering as I shook my head. "Every detail, even the most tragic deaths of mortals, is meticulously recorded. It's all part of a grand plan to track the exiled ones in case they try to return outside of the elder's lifetime, just like Tye has." My eyes narrowed, the weight of the responsibility evident in my expression. "We can't afford to overlook even the slightest of clues."

"Alright, enough of this," he said abruptly, shifting the conversation. His tone held a sense of urgency, as if there wasn't enough time and he was becoming impatient. "Are we going to sit in this car all night, or will we go inside and get you settled?"

The car had barely come to a stop when he sprang into action, leaping out before I could even respond. In the blink of an eye, he had rounded the vehicle and was at my door, hand outstretched in a silent, urgent demand that I join him. There was an electric energy about his movements, a sense of purpose and intensity that demanded I match his pace. Without hesitation, I placed my hand in his, allowing him to guide me swiftly from the car and into the unknown that awaited me.

"Do you ever act human when you're at home?" I asked nervously, glancing around to make sure nobody was looking.

His voice carried a sense of authority as he proclaimed, "Not here. This entire block belongs to me." Sweeping his arm across the empty expanse, he continued, "As you can see, we're the only ones for miles around." The intensity in his gaze left no room for doubt – this was his domain, and he was adamant about it.

I was utterly stunned when I realised he was right. His choice of home was meticulously selected. It was situated down the bottom of the road, far from prying eyes, allowing him the privacy to behave however he pleased within the confines of his own domain. And what a sight to behold—his movements were so lightning-fast that they defied the natural perception of ordinary mortals.

The shiny glass windows of Luke's house looked like they were asking me to come inside. The breeze was swirling around the car, making everything feel magical. Luke was whistling softly, adding to the mysterious atmosphere. As I looked at the house, I noticed all the windows that seemed to hold secrets. The massive front door was the main attraction, towering over everything else. The stone steps leading up to it were grand and elegant. I imagined a 'welcome' mat at the top, waiting for me. I could feel my excitement building as I wondered what adventures awaited me.

"Welcome to my place," he said, a devilish grin spreading across his face as he snatched my small bag from the back seat with a firm grip. The sudden movement sent a jolt of unease through me. Still, I mustered a polite smile to conceal my growing discomfort.

As I followed closely behind him, we approached the front door. He whistled softly, creating a peaceful melody that filled the air around us. The outside of the building was incredibly impressive, but somehow, it still seemed surprisingly ordinary. It was hard to believe that he owned the entire complex. I couldn't help but feel a sense of wonder as I realised that at least forty rooms must be hidden within this massive structure's walls. Why would one person need so much space? The question lingered in my mind, adding a touch of mystery to the whole situation as we approached the entrance.

His eyes gleamed with a mischievous grin as he leaned in. "Oh, I do love a bit of space, don't you?" he purred, his voice low and lilting. I felt the heat rise to my cheeks, and he must have noticed, for his expression softened ever so slightly. "I'm sorry," he said, his tone apologetic. "I'll try not to listen when you're thinking. I guess it's a bad habit, and not having a mortal with me made it a little too easy to hear you." He gave me a rueful smile, a hint of something almost like vulnerability flickering in his gaze.

"But," I interjected, my voice laced with a hint of confusion and challenge, "I was under the impression that you preferred mortal girlfriends."

He let out a loud laugh. "That's exactly what I wanted you to think – a way to throw you off the trail," he said, a sly grin spreading across his face. "Another lie I concocted about myself. I wasn't sure if you had bought into it or not. The idea of me having a human girlfriend seemed to throw you for a loop, didn't it?"

"I'll be honest, I was a bit taken aback," I confessed, my brow furrowing slightly. "I mean, when you asked me for tips on how to date a human, I just couldn't help but wonder - what on Earth made you think I'd be the expert on that?" I let out a small, nervous chuckle. "It's been ages since I've been in the dating game. I'm always too busy, so I'm hardly an expert."

"Wait, what?" he exclaimed, his eyes widening in disbelief. "You're telling me you haven't been on a date in forever? Unbelievable!" he said. "What the hell is wrong with the human guys around here? Don't they realise how incredible you are? How could they possibly let someone like you slip through their fingers?" he said, shaking his head in astonishment.

I couldn't help but laugh at his crazy behaviour. He was so wild and unpredictable, always doing things that shocked and amazed me. He didn't care about following the rules, which was frustrating and exciting. I couldn't resist getting caught up in his dynamic energy. His bold spirit made me want to let go and join in the fun he was having.

"Clearly, they're oblivious to what's so obvious to you," I said, rolling my eyes. "Now, are you going to show me your place or not? It's freezing out here, and I'm shivering in my jacket." I moaned, wrapping my arms around myself to try and retain some warmth.

"Absolutely," he replied, his voice laced with concern. "Forgive me, I should have realised you might be feeling the chill." His eyes narrowed as he studied me, and he swiftly shrugged off his jacket, draping it over my shoulders with a gentle yet decisive motion.

Jangling his keys, he swung the front door wide and motioned for me to go inside first. The huge entrance was surrounded by a stunning collection of glass windows, shining colours into the space. The peaceful white walls paired nicely with the shiny, warm wood floors. As I walked in, the light in front of me sparkled and reflected off the glass like a bunch of little mirrors. Right in the middle of the room was a beautiful silver staircase, spiralling up smoothly and captivatingly. I was so curious that I peered around the first step, and my breath got stuck in my chest as I saw the stairs twisting their way up, offering a mysterious climb to higher floors.

What I saw was so amazing and unbelievable that it was beyond anything I could have imagined. Everything around me looked like it had been twisted and changed crazily, like a kaleidoscope. The world had been torn apart, leaving something unpredictable and strange behind. In this peculiar place, one thing was clear: Luke did not live in a crypt or tomb but in a world of pure fantasy.

"Absolutely remarkable," I breathed, my eyes wide with awe. "I'm utterly impressed. How on Earth did you pull this off?" I couldn't help but marvel at the beautiful details before me, and I felt excited to learn more about the person who created them. My words came out with a sense of amazement.

"I've accumulated a substantial amount of savings over the years," he remarked casually, his gaze fixed upon me. "When you've been around as long as I have, you tend to develop a different perspective on spending compared to the average human." He paused, a faint trace of pride visible in his expression. "So I saved, I invested, and it all culminated in purchasing this place. At first,

I tried smaller accommodations, but they never seemed to provide enough space. As time passed, I constantly uprooted, moving to newer, larger dwellings to accommodate my evolving needs."

His eyes narrowed slightly, a glint of determination flickering within. "It was a necessary but tiresome process that required foresight and discipline most cannot comprehend. But the end result?" He swept his hand, gesturing to the grand surroundings. "Well, you see the fruits of my labour."

"Well, what's the plan now?" I pressed, my voice tinged with a hint of impatience. "Do you still need to keep on the move, or can you finally stay in one place?"

"No," he shook his head. "The agency takes care of the complex's real estate records to show that it has been sold and bought many times, including changing my name numerous times to keep humans from becoming nosy. When I go out, I'm always careful who I see; the only people I can call friends are those from the agency. Vampires can never make human friends, except you," he added quickly.

"Of course," I smiled. "But then I'm with the agency, so I suppose I don't count as much as other humans do."

"Are you a witch, then?" he asked curiously. "You don't act dramatic and mysterious like Lilly, but then you don't seem entirely human either. So, I guess I was just wondering."

I smiled. "Lilly is the High Witch, and with that title comes a great deal of responsibility. While she likes to use her magic to handle every aspect of her life, I prefer to embrace my humanity. I enjoy the simple things, like doing my own laundry and cooking my own meals, rather than relying on magical shortcuts."

"You're completely different than any witch I've met before," he said, his gaze burning with fascination and admiration. "I used to think your kind were a bunch of snobbish, lifeless creatures, but then I was tasked with observing you, and let me tell you,

I was utterly blindsided." He leaned in, his voice lowering to a conspiratorial whisper. "You, my dear, have shattered every preconception I ever had about witches. You're a revelation, a breath of fresh air in a world I thought I had all figured out."

I chuckled nervously and slowly sat down on the bottom step. My legs were shaking a bit, and I had started to feel weak.

"Shall I show you to your room?" he asked gently.

"Absolutely, I'm ready," I replied with a firm nod.

Rather than walk, he swooped me off my feet and held me in his arms as he carried me up the stairs.

"Luke!" I gasped, my voice trembling with suppressed laughter. "For goodness sake, put me down!" I demanded, laughing, struggling against his firm grip as I regained my composure.

"No," he said as he walked up the stairs. "You're too weak. I should have realised earlier. I could smell it, you know."

"Smell what?" I asked, confused.

"I should have realised from the smell you were growing weaker," he replied, a hint of regret lacing his words. "How could I have been so blind? In the future, I'll make sure to keep a closer eye on you, to remember that you're only human and that you need your rest – especially after someone had the gall to stomp on your head." With a softer tone, he continued, "I promise I won't overlook your needs again. You have my word that I'll be more attentive and vigilant in safeguarding your health and well-being. After all you've been through, you deserve nothing less."

My heart raced as a twinge of panic gripped me. For a fleeting moment, I thought he was implying that I stunk – the mere suggestion sent my mind into a frenzy. Discreetly, I began subtly sniffing myself, analysing every inch of my body and clothing, desperately searching for any unpleasant odour. Despite not having bathed since the night before, I couldn't fathom the idea that I could possibly be emitting any foul stench. The mere thought mortified me, sending a shiver down my spine. I wracked my brain, trying to recall any recent activities that could have left me in such a stinking state. The anxiety was unbearable, and I could feel my palms start to sweat as I anxiously awaited his following words, dreading the possibility that I might indeed be the bearer of an undesirable aroma.

He let out a soft chuckle, his body trembling slightly. "No, no, it's not your body I could smell," he murmured, leaning in closer and inhaling deeply. "It's you, my sweet girl. You smell absolutely divine." He buried his nose in my hair, a satisfied smile spreading. "I know I shouldn't say this, being the vampire I am, but I can't help it. You smell absolutely perfect, like nothing I've ever encountered before." His eyes gleamed with hunger and fascination as he gazed at me, his fingers twitching with the urge to reach out and touch.

"Oh gee, thanks," I said sarcastically, wriggling in his arms. "But what was it you could smell?"

"Your body is screaming for rest, and you're fading with each passing second. But don't worry, I'll have a good home-cooked meal ready for you in about an hour if you feel up to it."

My belly unleashed a boisterous, bellowing roar of dismay. In a feeble attempt to silence the embarrassing grumble, I hastily cupped my hand over my abdomen. A muffled snicker suddenly erupted from Luke, seated before me, and in a playful retort, I swiftly swatted his arm.

"Uh, yeah, that should cover it," I replied, mustering a faint smile as I looked up at him. My legs felt like jelly, but I was determined to power through. "So, how much farther to my room? I can walk."

"Not a chance," he said, a playful grin spreading across his face as he looked down at me. "I'll carry you; we're nearly there anyway. You know I might get an elevator, especially for you."

Luke carrying me was honestly wreaking havoc with my insides. His idiotic play at showing me how powerful he seemed to be was a macho display of his strength, which I was already aware of considering his "dead" status in the realm, which said a lot about him in itself. Again, I longed for my dreams to come true, but I knew they never would. He always looked perfect, from his perfectly styled short black hair to his clothing. He had the most amazing blue eyes I have ever seen. I couldn't maintain eye contact for long without feeling myself falling under some strange euphoric spell.

"Oh, for goodness sake," I groaned. "I'm not staying that long, so you don't need to waste your money."

"I have too much money," he said smoothly. "And I don't have anything or anyone to spend it on. I just figured that if I could make it easier for you while you're feeling bad, I will," he said. "And, if I'm going to continue to be your watcher for the rest of your term with the agency, then you might find we have to spend a lot of time together, whether here or at your place. I don't mind."

"I will be better in a few days," I protested. "As for you being my watcher on a full-time basis, let's wait and see how we get on with this temporary deal first."

"Alright, we've arrived," he said, his voice firm and steady, as he gently lowered me to the ground and opened the door with his free hand. "I hope you don't mind, but I have already put some of your things away for you."

"My clothes?" I exclaimed, a sense of panic rising in my chest. My eyes frantically scanned the room, searching for any sign of the missing garments. "Where are they?" I asked. "I really want to shower and change out of these."

"Over on that cupboard," he stated, his finger sharply gesturing towards it. "Is this room okay for you?"

Chapter Four

L uke suddenly looked slightly uncomfortable as he watched me closely in the doorway. I looked around the room and saw how he'd furnished it in soft brown tones with a large four-poster bed in the centre. Adjacent was the ensuite bathroom, and as I peeked inside, I could already see he'd taken the time to add some feminine products for me.

I smiled, realising how hard he worked to ensure my comfort in his house. A gentle feeling of happiness, something I couldn't define, spread through me as I turned to face him.

"This room is beautiful," I said, offering him a reassuring smile. "I'll shower quickly, change, and then go downstairs."

My voice was calm and steady, my words infused with a sense of confidence that put him at ease. I could see the tension leaving his shoulders as he nodded, satisfied with my response.

""Please take your time."

As he approached the door, a sudden shift in his demeanour caught my eye. He turned and glanced around the room before speaking to me.

"And if you're thinking about going after the murderer, I'd appreciate it if you'd let me know so I can do my job."

He knew it was exactly what I was going to do. "Now, what makes you think I would go and do that?" I asked.

He sighed and ran his fingers through his hair. "Because it's exactly what I would do."

Without saying anything else, he suddenly disappeared with a speed only a vampire could possess. I fell onto the edge of the bed, my body feeling heavy and sore. The pain in my head didn't stop; a painful memory of what I went through at the hospital. With a tired sigh, I took off my shoes and lay down on the bed, crossing my arms over my chest as I sank into the softness of the mattress, finding peace in the quiet stillness.

The bedroom was so fancy and nice. I suddenly got jealous, maybe because I didn't want anyone else in this beautiful room or because I wasn't the first to enjoy it. I felt a mix of envy and desire that I couldn't shake off, and with a deep sigh, I sat up.

My dreams were like ghosts that wouldn't leave me alone, playing repeatedly in my head. I couldn't forget those nights when I couldn't sleep, feeling uneasy because of the mysterious person who always felt just out of reach. And now, he was right before me but still just beyond my grasp. There was a clear rule that vampires and witches couldn't be more than colleagues and allies - we couldn't cross that line. Even though my heart wanted to break the rule, I knew I couldn't. The danger was too great, and the punishment too severe to think about.

Even though I tried, I couldn't resist the irresistible force pulling me toward him. I could always feel his intense gaze on me and the electricity between us, tempting me to give in. But I knew I had to stay strong and keep my distance to avoid danger. It was a constant struggle against my desires and longing for something out of reach. I felt trapped between the familiar world and the one I wanted, unsure how to move forward. All I could do was stay strong and focused, hoping the intense desire would eventually fade.

"Ugh, not this again," I sighed in frustration, whispering and shaking my head. It was another one of life's enigmas I had to unravel and make sense of. How could I have been so stupid to believe the dreams were just made up? And to make matters worse, it just had to be a vampire.

A faint chuckle echoed through the silence, sending a chill down my spine. Had I imagined it? With determination, I slowly crept across the room, my heart pounding in my ears. Cautiously, I approached the closet, bracing myself for what I might find. To my utter astonishment, the closet was filled with my own neatly stacked clothes and shoes. The sheer volume of clothing suggested this was no temporary stay – it was considerable enough to justify a stay of weeks, if not months. My mind raced with unanswered questions.

I suddenly realised that I had no control over what was happening. Someone had carefully planned everything for my stay, making me feel scared and uneasy. I heard a creepy laugh again, making me aware that someone else was with me and that I wasn't in charge anymore. I prepared myself for anything that could happen next, staying alert and on edge.

"Ugh, another day, another mystery to unravel," I muttered, releasing a deep, exasperated sigh. I'd love to escape this chaotic mess and return to the comfort of my everyday life. I suppose I have no choice but to dig deeper and get to the bottom of the murder. I clenched my fists, determination flaring in my chest. The sooner I accomplish my plan to continue investigating, the better.

Refreshed from a warm shower, I slipped into a fresh pair of jeans and a clean top, my long brown hair neatly combed into a ponytail. Although the persistent headache continued to throb, I felt a sense of normalcy returning. Rummaging through my bag, I located the medication prescribed by the hospital and quickly swallowed a couple of tablets. As I gazed into the mirror, I was struck by the pallor of my complexion and the haunting, wide-eyed expression that stared back at me. My green eyes look dull, and I look as pale as Luke – despite any attempts to look refreshed, I had failed.

"Perfect," I muttered sarcastically to myself. "Let's hope I don't add more appeal and attraction for Luke."

I wanted to figure out my feelings for Luke, but I feared getting hurt because my life had been tough. Being adopted was hard - it was a secret, and my parents didn't understand what I'd been through. They loved me a lot but didn't get how being a witch was a big part of who I was. Matace, on the other hand, was a fantastic teacher who gave me knowledge that would help me in the future. He saw potential in me and taught me things to help me deal with the challenges ahead with strength and determination.

"Hey, dinner's ready! You all set to join me?" Luke shouted through my closed bedroom door.

He gently knocked on the door while calling. The aroma of the freshly prepared meal wafted through the air, mingling with the anticipation of sharing a meal.

"Absolutely, I'm on my way!" I responded enthusiastically, eagerly making my way towards the source of the call.

I was met with Luke's intense gaze as I grabbed the doorknob and opened the door. His eyes were focused on mine, and he seemed tense as I approached him. The moment felt heavy with anticipation, and I could feel the tension in the air. Luke's presence demanded all my attention, and I found myself drowning the more I stared into his eyes.

Luke reached out and held me at arm's length, smiling. "Steady," he said, preventing me from colliding with him. "Is everything okay?" he asked gently. Unable to speak, I could only nod my head. He abruptly released me and turned away. "Follow me, and I will show you the way to the kitchen," he muttered.

Utterly bewildered and caught off guard, he abruptly shifted his demeanour, treating me like a social outcast.

"Luke," I breathed barely above a whisper, a tinge of apprehension colouring my words. A sense of unease crept up my spine as I gazed at him as he walked away. "Is there something wrong?" I asked, my brow furrowed with concern.

"Nothing!" he replied, turning to face me briefly. "Let's go."

His short and curt response and the way he pressed his lips into a thin line left me in no doubt he was upset over something. It felt like a sharp blade slicing through the atmosphere between us.

I shrugged, perplexed by the subtle shift in the atmosphere and followed Luke while keeping a discrete distance so I didn't piss him off anymore.

With a purposeful stride, he guided me to the dining room, where a solitary place setting awaited. A small, neatly arranged mat marked the spot for my plate, and a glass of water stood ready, its surface glistening invitingly. The scene exuded an air of deliberate preparation, as if he had purposely gone out of his way to set the table just for me.

"Are you not joining me?" I questioned, my brow furrowing with curiosity.

"Seira, I'm a vampire," he said sternly, his words laced with a hint of impatience. "I don't eat human food." His piercing gaze bore into me, leaving no room for misunderstanding. "Sit down," he ordered.

He turned away briskly, gathering the food tray. As he busied himself, setting up sandwiches and steaming hot tea before me, he spoke, "I've been thinking." A pensive look crossed his face. "I don't think it's wise for us to go after the murderer." His words were laced with caution, his brow furrowed with concern.

I paused, my hand frozen midway to my lips. "Luke," I sighed, a hint of exasperation creeping into my voice. "What's the matter?" I turned to face him, my brow furrowed with concern. His expression troubled me, and I couldn't help but feel the unease wash over me. "Talk to me," I urged, my tone gentle yet insistent, desperate to understand what was weighing on his mind.

"Nothing?" he scoffed, his voice dripping with sarcasm. His eyes narrowed, and he leaned forward, his body language radiating a subtle yet discernable defiance as if daring me to question his curt reply further.

"I'm sorry, but I need you to tell me what's going on," I said, my voice filled with concern. "I truly don't understand what I've done to upset you. Please, help me understand so I can make it right." I leaned forward, my brow furrowed, desperately seeking an explanation. "I never meant to say anything to hurt you, but if I have, I want to know so I can apologise and make amends. I care about you and don't want any distance between us. So, please, won't you help me figure this out?"

"You didn't say a word," he retorted, his brow furrowing with frustration and confusion. "Let's just leave it be, shall we?" His tone was curt, but there was an underlying unease, as if he was desperate to avoid delving deeper.

Bristling with frustration, I stayed silent in the face of his abrupt, hostile reaction. His once-amicable demeanour had transformed into that of an adversary, the change so rapid and jarring that it left me reeling.

Annoyed and fed up, I slammed my palm against the tabletop, making it tremble as the sandwich tumbled from my grasp and crashed to the floor at his feet. "Tell me!" I demanded, my voice laced with a desperate edge as I leaned forward, eyes burning fiercely.

My firm and angry reaction seemed to calm him down, making him stop and stare at me in surprise and confusion. I don't think he expected me to react so strongly or for his mood to suddenly change.

"Do you realise how intoxicating you are to me?" he asked gently. "Do you know what I want to do to you? It seems your shower has amplified how your scent makes me feel."

I shook my head, eyes locked on him, waiting to see what he'd do next. I knew he was stronger than me and could easily beat me in a fight. He moved around me, getting closer. His movements were smooth and dangerous, but his eyes never left me. I felt scared and anxious, with my heart beating fast and sweat running down my back. I stood firm, determined not to run and let him chase me. I wouldn't let him catch me without a fight.

He stepped closer, his piercing gaze fixed on me. "Do you know what would happen to us if your dreams came true?" The intensity in his voice sent a shiver down my spine.

Finally, it made more sense. He was struggling with his needs as a vampire and the urge to protect me.

He inhaled deeply, savouring my scent. "Your smell, it's intoxicating. I'm damn close to losing control around you." His body tensed, years of hard-won discipline now teetering on the edge. "All those years I spent keeping myself in check, and you waltzed into my life and shattered it all." He moved even closer, his eyes burning with an unspoken hunger. "Small amounts of time with you were torturous, but now you're here, in my home. I can smell you everywhere, and it's driving me mad."

"Luke," I uttered his name, my voice trembling with a hint of trepidation. "I-I don't... I don't mean to smell so," I paused, searching for the right words, "captivating." My words came out faintly, almost a whisper, betraying my growing tension.

He walked around me one last time, his intense, predatory energy hanging in the air. Suddenly, he appeared right before me, his face close to mine. He grabbed my arms tightly, like a vice, and his lips moved slightly as he took a deep breath, almost like he was enjoying my fear. His eyes stared intensely at me, making my heart beat fast, and my breath stop in my throat.

"Too late," he sneered, his eyes glinting maliciously. Panic gripped me as I realised the gravity of the situation. "Seira, you'd better run to your room and lock the door," he warned, his voice dripping with a chilling sense of urgency.

"W-w-why?" I stammered, my voice quivering with fear and trepidation. The weight of his command hung heavy in the air, like a dark cloud looming over me, filling my mind with dread and uncertainty about the horrors he might inflict.

"Because I'm losing control around you, having you here with me, smelling you so close and knowing I can take you if I wanted to."

I bolted from the table, the chair scraping harshly across the floor as it toppled over. My legs felt like lead, anchored to the spot by a primal fear that clawed its way up my throat. His dark, stormy eyes locked onto mine, a cruel sneer twisting his lips. The air crackled with tension, thick and suffocating, as if the room held its breath in anticipation.

"Please, don't do this," I breathed, trembling in the thick silence. "Luke, you have to control it. Fight it." Each word was a desperate plea, a lifeline thrown across the chasm of his burgeoning darkness.

"I can't," he snarled the word, a guttural growl that sent shivers down my spine.

With his face contorted in a fierce snarl, Luke flung himself in the opposite direction, his voice a desperate rasp as he urged me to flee. "Run!" he commanded, the word a guttural eruption from his parched throat. The urgency in his voice and the fear in his eyes made me react quickly. Adrenaline rushed through me as I ran as fast as I could, matching the panicked beat of my heart with each step.

My heart raced, and I ran to my room, taking the stairs quickly
and loudly. I shut the door behind me, scared of what might be
outside. I whispered words of protection and felt a comforting
energy around me. I lie on my bed, breathing heavily, feeling safe
from potential dangers. My heart beat fast, and I could feel the
terror of Luke approaching. His movements were threateningly
silent, and I clung to my protective barrier. I didn't understand why
Luke acted this way or why his hunger was suddenly out of control,
and I felt desperate and afraid. I tried to remember what I knew
about vampires, wondering if this one was different or dangerous.

I stood and made my way to my bedroom door. I listened
intently at the door and waited for his footsteps to charge up the
stairs and for him to try and break the door in. The door wouldn't
hold him for long. It was a flimsy barrier between me and the
nightmare waiting on the other side. But I had one advantage: the
protective bubble I had woven around myself. It wouldn't stop him
entirely, but it would buy me time and weaken him. Long enough
to find an escape. My fingers tightened around the doorknob as
his form materialised through the door's frosted glass. He reached
out, his hand a blur of inhuman speed, and slammed against the
wood. The door shuddered, splintering at the edges and cracking
loudly. The hinges dislodged from the frame, and the door hung by
its lock.

"Luke?" I breathed, my heart pounding as I turned and ran
back to the bed. My fingers gripped the bedsheets, knuckles
turning white with tension. "You have to control it." I strained to
make out any familiar silhouette in the shadows, my mind racing
with a million possibilities, each more unsettling than the last.

Seconds ticked by, each one an eternity as I waited silently for
a response that never came. The house now felt eerily still, like a
tomb. Perched on the edge of the bed, my legs tucked beneath
me, I leaned to the side, chin resting on my arms, eyes fixed on

the door, anticipating it to be flung open at any moment. Fatigue crept up, weighing my eyelids down, and a throbbing ache pulsed through my head, making me feel nauseous. The hospital stay had left me drained, and I hadn't so much as touched a morsel of food since then, my appetite long forgotten in the face of the unfolding anxiety.

Exhaustion tugged at my eyelids, but I fought to keep them open. With a crazed, thirsty vampire on the loose, I couldn't afford to succumb to the siren call of sleep. Still, my body betrayed me, and gradually, my eyes fluttered closed.

"Just a short doze," I murmured, making a desperate bargain with myself. "Nothing more." The world around me faded, and I drifted into a realm of unconsciousness, knowing that I was powerless to resist its pull. Every moment I spent asleep was a moment of vulnerability, a chance for Luke to close in and strike. Yet, the exhaustion gnawing at me for hours refused to be ignored. I just hoped my protective barrier would remain in place while I slept.

As I sank deeper into sleep's embrace, a tiny part of my mind remained alert, a flickering flame of awareness in the darkness. I clung to it, straining to stay conscious and maintain my vigilance. But the harder I tried, the more the darkness threatened to envelop me, and I knew that I was losing the battle against sleep's pull.

Finally, the unmistakable sound of a car engine roared to life outside, the tyres screeching as Luke angrily manoeuvred the vehicle, waking me up. I knew he had left the building and would likely return once he had calmed down and sated his hunger. The abrupt departure and the intensity with which Luke operated his car demonstrated his agitated mind. I could almost picture his tense grip on the steering wheel, his knuckles turning white as he navigated the streets, eager to put distance between himself and the situation. Yet, I also knew that his departure was only temporary, that he would return once he had regained his composure and tended to his basic needs. The image of him coming back, perhaps more level-headed and ready to face the circumstances that had driven him away, lingered in my mind.

A deep sigh escaped my lips as I closed my eyes, and there they were – the familiar images of Luke dancing beneath my eyelids. The same haunting dreams that plagued me now enveloped me again, pulling me under their irresistible spell. For a fleeting moment, I yearned for something different, something more from this relationship with Luke – a desperate desire to break free from the relentless cycle of these recurring visions. Finally, the dreams ended, and I had successfully forced them out.

Overcome by a deep, dreamless slumber, I remained blissfully unaware of how much time passed until the morning light pierced through the half-drawn blinds, jolting me awake. As I slowly regained consciousness, I noticed my coverlet had been carefully tucked around me and my shoes neatly arranged at the foot of the bed. The realisation dawned on me that Luke must have silently slipped into the room at some point during the night, likely to ensure my well-being. The thoughtful gesture filled me with warmth as I imagined him moving with quiet concern, ensuring my comfort while I lay oblivious to the world, lost in a peaceful, restorative sleep.

The intensity of the sunlight filtering in, combined with the evidence of Luke's attentive care, made me acutely aware of my surroundings and the events. I felt a surge of appreciation for his unwavering presence and the comfort he had provided, even in the stillness of the night.

"Seira," he murmured, his voice barely above a whisper, as he leaned forward in the chair at the far end of the room, his eyes filled with concern. "Are you alright?"

A deep, weary yawn escaped my lips, and I couldn't help but question the authenticity of my current state. Was I awake, or was this another dream? The uncertainty gnawed at me, leaving me in limbo, unsure of the true nature of my consciousness.

"I'm fine," I mumbled, my words slightly slurred as I fought to shrug off the sleepiness. "This feels like such a pleasant dream." I managed a small smile in his direction.

"You're not dreaming, Seira," he said, his voice low and sincere. "This is real. I'm sorry about last night." The words hung in the air, laden with a weight I couldn't quite decipher. Still, the intensity of his gaze left me breathless, as if he was willing me to understand the depth of his remorse.

I felt my heart beating fast as I sat up suddenly in bed, brushing my hair out of my face to see him better. His eyes were full of regret, and his smile was peaceful – a significant change from the Luke I knew from our agency days. The carefree, fun guy who always made me laugh seemed like a distant memory now. Looking at him, I thought about the rules that kept vampires and humans from getting too close. The unspoken laws of our relationship weighed heavily on me, reminding me that our connection, while tempting, was risky and unpredictable.

"Wait, this isn't some kind of dream, is it?" I blurted out, my voice dripping with disbelief. My eyes widened as I stared at the figure sitting at the foot of my bed, unable to comprehend the reality of the situation. "You're actually here, right in front of me?"

My voice showed that I was astonished, confused, and slightly nervous. I couldn't believe what I saw - I did not expect to see this so soon. My heart raced as I tried to understand what was happening before me.

"Yes," he replied, his voice tinged with regret. "I'm afraid I can't come any closer because of the protective bubble surrounding you. I had to carefully drape the coverlet over you and wait until your feet emerged from beneath the barrier just so I could remove your shoes," he paused, a concerned expression crossing his features. "Did I startle you in the process? I hope not. I didn't mean to scare you again."

"Sort of," I answered uncertainly. "But I didn't understand; one minute, you were fine, and then you wanted to have me for dinner. What happened?"

I leaned in closer, trying to read his expression for any hints that could explain what was going on. My eyes showed how much I cared and how eager I was to figure out what had happened. The suspense of waiting for an answer made my heart beat faster, and I was sure Luke could feel the tension in the room.

He sighed deeply, his brow furrowed with frustration and longing. "I honestly don't know what it is," he admitted, his gaze locked on me. "There's just something about how you smell that draws me in, like a magnetic pull I can't resist." He paused, running a hand through his hair as he struggled to find the right words. "Most of the time, I can keep it under control, push those feelings down. But now that you're here and knowing you'll be around for a while, I..." He shook his head, a look of vulnerability flashing across his features. "I let my guard slip, just for a second. And before I knew it, I wanted you so badly it was almost physically painful."

"Lovely," I retorted, my voice dripping with thick sarcasm. "So, let me get this straight - you're telling me that me being here with you is why you couldn't bear to be in the same room as me?" I fixed my gaze upon them, my eyes narrowed with a challenging intensity, demanding a response to help me understand.

"That's right," he said, shifting uncomfortably in his seat. His gaze was fixed on the ground, unable to meet my eyes. "I don't want you to be afraid of me, but I understand if you are. I promise it won't happen again." His voice was laced with a hint of desperation, as if he were pleading for my understanding and forgiveness.

How can I know for sure? This question has been on my mind, making me want a clear answer. I must find a way to eliminate this doubt and figure out the truth. I'm determined to find a foolproof way to know the truth without any doubts. I'm willing to look closely at the evidence and search thoroughly for the answer I need. I won't rest until I confidently say I know the truth.

"Anyway," he said, a hint of mischief in his voice. "You've always got your trusty shield to protect you in case I get hungry again," he leaned in, smiling, trying to lighten the mood.

"I understand your concern, but I'm not sure using my shield all the time around you is the best solution," I replied, my voice tinged with unease. ""Luke, I don't think it's a good idea for me to be here if you can't handle being around me. I don't know why my smell causes you so much pull."

I spoke kindly but firmly, wanting to talk more and figure out why he was uncomfortable. I tried to handle the situation delicately and make sure we both understood each other before deciding what to do next.

"Grief?" he stammered, his voice laden with emotion. "No, no, not at all," he quickly clarified. "It's quite the opposite, in fact. I feel drawn to you. The urge to taste you is almost overwhelming," his eyes darkened with longing, yet a strange sorrow lingered there. "But I won't – I can't – take that from you. Your life is precious, and it would be a tragedy to see it wasted. If the time ever comes when you're ready to embrace immortality, know that I'll be here, waiting to offer you that gift. Until then, I'll cherish our time, even if I can never truly make you mine."

"Am I supposed to feel reassured by that?" His words sent a shiver down my spine, leaving me in turmoil. Part of me yearned for the sweet release to be with him in any way I wanted, while another tried to distance myself from him entirely. Yet, I was torn between the pull of my desires and the unwavering loyalty I owed to the agency's rules.

The atmosphere was tense, emotions simmering beneath the surface. I struggled with conflicting thoughts and feelings, feeling stuck and unsure of what to do. His words strongly impacted me, stirring up a whirlwind of emotions. I knew I had to choose, but the pressure was suffocating. The agency's rules felt like chains holding me from following my true desires. The fear of what could happen if I broke those rules weighed heavily on me, making each step forward feel uncertain.

"I know you don't expect that from me," he chuckled, his eyes sparkling with amusement. "But hey, that's what makes our friendship so great, doesn't it? We can be ourselves, no judgments, just good old-fashioned fun." His smile was warm and genuine. "We're still friends, right? I wouldn't have it any other way."

A warm smile spread as I replied, "I guess." I replied. "Can I get up now?"

"Yes," he said. "Seira, I know you're still afraid of me," he said, his voice laced with frustration and concern. "But you have to understand, I would never hurt you. Even if I lost control, I would have found a way to stop myself. This shield around you – it breaks my heart to see you feel the need to hide from me like that."

I surveyed the information, puzzled by how he behaved with me today. It was as if last night's events had been a mere figment of my imagination, a dream that never truly occurred.

Gathering my courage, I looked into his eyes and asked, "Luke, did you control my dreams last night?" My voice wavered slightly as I removed my shield, exposing my vulnerability to him.

"No," he replied firmly, his voice laced with a hint of resolve. "I had no intention of pushing those boundaries or crossing any more lines. I had already promised not to and was determined to keep my word."

"Oh?" I whispered softly, taking a moment to stop thinking and look at him. My forehead creased slightly with a mix of interest and slight distraction.

What on Earth had I been dreaming about? I was much happier knowing it was Luke summoning and placing them in my head without worrying that I was fantasising about him.

With a heavy sigh, I grabbed my brush and ran it through my tangled hair. As I sat back, I noticed Luke watching me intently. His eyes narrowed in a quizzical gaze, and his expression widened, conveying a sense of curiosity and intrigue as he observed me.

"Did you really dream about me last night?" he asked, his voice thick with emotion and a hint of disbelief.

"I thought I made it clear that I don't want you reading my mind," I retorted sharply, frustrated by the intrusion. "And you told me you wouldn't, didn't you?" I fixed my gaze on them, my eyes narrowing as I waited for a response.

He sighed deeply, his fingers anxiously raking through his messy hair. "I know," he said. "But you did, didn't you?" He asked as he searched my face for any sign of denial or remorse.

"Yes, Luke," I exhaled, a hint of resignation. "I did," I admitted, meeting his gaze with a solemn nod.

"Damn it," he cursed, slapping his leg in frustration. "We can't let this get in the way, and we both need to act like mature, responsible adults. This has to end; I never should have planted those ideas in your mind, and if I hadn't, we wouldn't be in this predicament. Seira," he said, "I need you to forget everything I've put inside your head; it's only a dream, and you know it can't become a reality. Neither of us can let it happen, not unless you're dying, and then I'll offer you the immortality you deserve. Letting you die would be a tremendous waste, both for the world and for the agency."

My mouth felt dry, and I couldn't think straight. I licked my lips nervously, trying to find the right words, but I was too shocked to respond. His words had left me speechless and frozen, and I didn't know how to react.

He chuckled nervously, and his unease was evident as he waited for my response. "Well, what do you say?" he said again.

"You're absolutely right," I replied, my voice firm and resolute. "I've already decided that we can only ever be colleagues, nothing more." I paused, carefully considering my next words. "And Luke," I continued, my gaze locked with his. "I'm determined to investigate these murders, no matter what it takes."

"I had a feeling you might," he said, a faint smile on his lips. "I'm more than happy for you to examine the records and go through that stuff, but I need you to understand something very clearly - I don't want you to do anything else beyond that. That means no snooping around, leaving the house to search for anything on your own, and no asking anyone questions. Do I make myself absolutely clear?" He spoke in a strong and severe tone, looking directly at me without any doubt. His voice showed his instructions' seriousness and importance, making it clear that I had to follow them. Obviously, he wouldn't allow me to disobey the rules he had set.

"Right," I said, smiling. "Got it!"

Luke hurried out of the room, gently shutting the door. Under his breath, he muttered something about needing to make urgent phone calls and attend to a pressing business matter.

I was happy to be by myself, enjoying the peaceful quiet that let me think deeply. The headache I had before was gone; it was just a faint memory. But now my stomach was growling, reminding me that I hadn't eaten in a while.

I felt sore and tense as I quickly washed up and wore clean clothes. Dark bruises covered my skin, especially around my neck, showing the violence of Tye's assault. The bruises were a painful reminder of what had happened to me. Thankfully, someone had packed a scarf for me, which I wrapped tightly around my neck to hide the worst injuries.

I stood at the top of the stairs and watched Luke in the dark hallway, whispering into the phone. The deep voice on the other end seemed like a man. Luke looked serious and focused, his brow creased with concentration and his shoulders tense. I couldn't hear what they said, but I could tell it was important. I decided to sit on the top step and wait, unsure whether to go down or not.

"I've made it crystal clear that I simply can't take on this task," he asserted firmly, his voice laced with a steely resolve as his voice got louder. "Absolutely not. There's no way I'm doing this, and that's my final word on the matter."

He listened carefully to the person on the phone, looking focused. I was sitting on the stairs, unsure what to do next. The atmosphere was tense as I thought about my choices, feeling excited and scared simultaneously.

"Listen up," he said, his voice firm. "You can do whatever you want, but she's not coming with us. And trust me, you won't change my mind on this. You know as well as I do how dangerous it is to bring a human, especially a witch, along." His eyes narrowed, and he leaned in, his expression deadly serious. "The risks are just too high. We can't afford to have her jeopardise the entire mission. So, that's the end of it. No more discussion."

I could tell they were talking about me, but I couldn't figure out exactly what they said. I tried hard to piece together their conversation, but it only made me more anxious. I didn't know what part I played in their mysterious discussion, which made me even more unsettled. The uncertainty bothered me, and I wanted to understand what they were trying to say.

The receiver's sharp click echoed in the silence, followed by his voice. "Seira, you can come down now. I'm sorry about that. I was on the phone."

"No worries," I responded with a warm, reassuring smile. I was excited as I walked down the stairs; the excitement of seeing a lot more of this beautiful house was evident in the way I hurried to reach the hallway at the bottom. It was so big that I

couldn't believe it! I was amazed by the grand and impressive details I saw as I kept walking.

The rooms connected to the main entrance were all uniquely decorated. Some looked bright and open, with big windows letting in lots of natural light from outside. On the other hand, the rest of the rooms were deliberately designed to block out the outside world, making you feel like they held a hidden secret. You could feel a mysterious atmosphere as you explored these interestingly decorated spaces. It seemed like each room had a story to tell, but it was being kept hidden by the fancy decorations. This made you curious and urged you to uncover the hidden truths underneath the carefully arranged design.

The kitchen felt organised and ready for cooking. The tall stools were inviting, encouraging people to sit and enjoy the cooking process. The pots and pans were neatly placed, showing that someone took great care in arranging them. The appliances were neatly lined up against the wall, waiting to be used. A giant table stood in the centre of the room, a veritable command centre for the morning meal, providing easy access to all the necessary accoutrements. The kitchen emanated a sense of anticipation as if it were eagerly awaiting the arrival of its next guest.

This kitchen was more than just a place to cook. It was like a fancy room where amazing meals were made. The tall chairs, the organised pots and pans, the food machines, and the big table all worked together perfectly and invitingly. It looked unused, as everything seemed so shiny and new, like it had only been stripped of its manufacturer's plastic layer.

A feminine voice suddenly cut through the silence, startling me as someone spoke directly behind me. "You must be Seira," the woman declared in her authoritative and curious tone.

I jumped in surprise, my heart racing, as the quiet suddenly broke. I hadn't heard anyone approaching, so the sudden interruption caught me off guard.

"Hello," I managed to say, my voice raspy and unsure, fully aware of how plain and unremarkable I appeared next to this woman whose beauty was the kind I had always secretly envied. "I'm Seira," I introduced myself, my heart pounding with nerves and self-consciousness as I took in her captivating presence.

"Hello, Seira," she greeted warmly, a friendly smile spreading across her face. "It's a pleasure to meet you. I'm Darcy, and I'm so glad we've finally had the chance to meet in person." Her tone was inviting, exuding a genuine enthusiasm to get to know the other person better, but something felt off about her.

I blinked in confusion, my gaze meeting her piercing stare. "Darcy?" I echoed, the name rolling off my tongue with a tinge of uncertainty. "I'm sorry, but do I know you?" The words tumbled out, flustered, my heart racing as I tried to place the familiar-sounding name and the face that accompanied it.

"No," she chuckled. "But you might have stumbled upon my photographs scattered around the place. I've known Luke for quite a while now; we've more or less grown and changed together, side by side."

"Changed?" I questioned, my brow furrowing in confusion. I struggled to keep up with the sudden shift in the conversation. "I'm afraid I don't quite understand what you're getting at," I admitted, my tone laced with uncertainty as I searched her face for clues to decipher her meaning.

"You know, turned into vampires," she rolled her eyes.

"Oh, so you're a..."

"Yes," she replied, a coy smile spreading across her face. "I'm dead too, but it's not all bad, you know. There are quite a few perks to this whole 'being dead' thing." She leaned in conspiratorially, her eyes sparkling with mischief. "For one, I can beat a grown man at arm wrestling. How many living, breathing girls do you know who can pull that off, huh?" She chuckled, clearly amused by the idea. Leaning back, she gestured towards a nearby table. "Anyway, enough about my supernatural arm strength. You look like you could use some breakfast. What do you say - care to join me?"

She spoke really fast, and I couldn't understand what she was saying. Somehow, I caught something about breakfast, and she quickly left to go to the other side of the tidy kitchen. As she talked about herself, I got lost in my thoughts. I went to the windows, still thinking and looking outside but not seeing.

I opened the glass door to the side of the window and felt a gentle breeze on my face. It made my hair move, and I took a big breath. The flowers in the garden smelled exquisite and made me happy. I looked at the swing in the yard, and it was moving nicely as if the wind was playing with it. The sun was shining on the grass, making it look pretty and warm. I felt connected to nature, and the urge to touch the ground and connect properly was overwhelming. My connection was my special place to relax and enjoy the world's beauty.

One unique aspect of my many abilities is my command over the elements. I can make it happen if I want it to be hot, like summer. And if I want it to snow, I can make that happen, too. People around me don't realise some other force is controlling the weather. I usually try not to use that specific power because I worry about its effect on global warming. Humans think that any sudden weather changes are because of global warming, and they go about their lives like busy ants, not knowing the true power at work. Another witch had a similar power, but she had a significant difference. Blossom's power was different - she couldn't control her emotions linked to the elements. Her emotions wreaked havoc with the weather whenever she entered the mortal realm.

"Do you like the garden?"

I turned around and saw Luke standing a short distance away. He wore loose pants and a light shirt, looking peaceful and calm. It was a significant change from before when things were tense between us. Now, he looked welcoming and relaxed, with no sign of his previous thirst.

I gazed out at the sprawling garden, captivated by its beauty. "What a stunning day," I remarked, my eyes drinking in the serene landscape. "Do you spend much time in your garden?"

"No, not really," he said softly, "I only go out there when I need to talk to the gardener. And yeah, just like Darcy, he's a vampire, too."

"A vampire gardener?" I grinned. "How intriguing."

"I don't usually have any time for hobbies," he said, a hint of amusement in his voice. "But Darcy, she loves to cook."

"And talk," I interrupted. "She likes to talk."

"Yeah, that's the thing," he said, a hint of annoyance in his voice. "I should have been here to introduce you. She's been a fixture in my life for years and won't leave me be. As soon as she found out I had a mortal staying with me, she insisted on making you breakfast this morning." His eyes narrowed, and he let out a frustrated sigh. "I'm sorry about that. She can be a bit...overbearing, to say the least. But I appreciate you putting up with her. Hopefully, she'll get the hint and give us some space soon."

I sipped the refreshing orange juice and said, "Ahh, this is perfect." Then, gazing around at the picturesque setting, I continued, "This would be the ideal spot for an amazing picnic."

"Do you enjoy picnics, Seira?" He asked curiously.

He spoke softly and leaned against the doorframe, his gaze drawing me in with charm.

"I'm not that into them anymore," I said quietly. "I used to love them when I was young, but people change as they grow up, don't they? As you get older, it's just not the same." My words carried a hint of wistfulness as I remembered a few family picnics.

He stepped closer, standing beside me, close enough that our arms almost brushed. The room felt charged with energy, and I could sense his body heat nearby, making me want to close the space between us. I could feel the excitement building as my heart raced, resisting the temptation to touch him and experience the warmth of our skin together.

His intense gaze felt like it was studying me intensely. I tried not to look back at him because I knew it could lead to trouble. He was mysterious and difficult to understand, and I didn't want him around. I had to stick to the rules, no matter what.

"Your breakfast is ready," he said, his voice warm and gentle. "I need to get going now. There's plenty to do today, you know." He paused, a hint of concern in his eyes. "Will you be okay until later? We can do something together then if you'd like."

I spoke with confidence, even though my voice was shaky. I looked directly into his eyes, intensely wanting to reach and touch him. I shook my head and stated firmly, "I will be perfectly fine on my own," I reassured. "Guess I'll dive into those reports all day." I paused, then added, "I can access the agency files from here, right?"

He chuckled softly, "You'll find everything you need in the second-floor study. But don't forget our deal." I raised my brows at him in question; I intended to stick to our deal to a certain extent, anyway. Luke sighed and smiled. "The one where you said you wouldn't try and find the murderer, and we'll wait it out here."

"No, Luke," I said sadly. "That was your deal, not mine!"

I turned and walked away when I heard Darcy scrapping breakfast onto the plate. "Drumroll, please!" she exclaimed, beaming with pride as I stepped through the doorway. "Your breakfast masterpiece has arrived!"

Vampires, known for their extraordinary powers, were terrible at cooking. The idea that they could successfully cook was just not accurate. I wondered where Luke kept his meals and if he'd eaten this morning.

"Well," Darcy leaned in, eyes fixed on me as I settled into my seat and took the first bite. "How is it?"

Her fingers fidgeted with the cloth, a nervous habit she couldn't shake. Dressed in a light blue apron, her fair hair framing her face, she looked the part of a dutiful maid. But by the way, she twisted the bottom of her apron in her hands, she was clearly nervous as she anxiously awaited my response.

"Mmm, it's amazing!" I gushed, smiling as I struggled to swallow the food.

The food was awful. It was super salty, probably because Darcy had forgotten how human food tasted. Even though it was way too salty, I still smiled and tried to be friendly, not wanting to hurt her feelings.

"Fantastic work!" I exclaimed, neatly folding my napkin. "That was truly wonderful."

I was confused that she couldn't hear what I was thinking. My thoughts were deafening and could have been heard from far away. Then, I heard Luke's voice reminding Darcy he was cooking tonight coming from the study, which proved that my thoughts were super loud, and he'd heard them. When Darcy opened the fridge, I immediately spotted the blood-filled cartons inside - the answer to my earlier question about Luke's dietary habits. I bolted out of the kitchen, relieved to be free. Gleefully, I deceived Darcy as she busied herself tidying up.

Last night was bizarre, and I felt so confused. The way things were between us felt off and made me feel uncomfortable. I couldn't understand what was happening, which greatly bothered me.

It took me a while to find the mysterious study Luke had mentioned. The first room I saw was full of toys, which was strange because Luke lived alone and didn't have kids. The second room looked like someone else's bedroom, making me curious about who else lived there.

Luke's voice came from behind me. "You found the study, I see." A hint of satisfaction tinged his words.

I whirled around, startled by the sound of his voice. Heat rushed to my cheeks as the thoughts racing through my mind came flooding back.

"Luke," I said, my voice trembling slightly. "What's with the kid's playroom? I don't understand."

He casually shrugged his shoulders, a slight smile playing on his lips. His nonchalant gesture showed a mix of not caring and a hint of amusement, suggesting there was more going on in his mind than met the eye.

"Darcy has a wide network of human connections, but she's adamant about not being affiliated with any agency, refusing to join one. The humans in her life trust her to occasionally care for their children, and I make it a bit more convenient for her to bring them here and let them play. So, don't you like children?"

"No, it's not that at all," I quickly responded, instantly regretting my question. "I think kids are great. I'm sorry. It was so rude of me to ask. I just wondered why you had a room full of toys, that's all," I said quickly. "Luke, how do you feel about me staying here? I mean, honestly."

"No, it's quite alright," he said softly. "I like having you here with me. It's been far too long since I've had some company." He paused, his eyes filled with sincerity. "And please, don't worry about last night. I feel terrible about it, truly. It won't happen again, I promise."

"No worries," I said, dismissing the issue casually. "It's really not a big deal."

"Will we ever be like we used to be?" he asked, his voice tinted with a glimmer of hope and a hint of apprehension.

"Huh? What are you talking about?" I blurted out, utterly perplexed. "I'm exactly the same as always. I haven't done a single thing differently!" My brow furrowed as I tried to make sense of their puzzling statement.

"No, you're not," he said. "You're holding me at arm's length. You were different to when you didn't know who I was or my job."

"So were you, Luke," I answered. "So were you."

I quickly turned around and walked into the study. I felt thrilled seeing the big desk and comfy chair ready for me. It was much nicer than my tiny home office with its uncomfortable desk and my cat always sitting next to me.

"Luke!" I cried out, instantly racked with guilt for abandoning him.

He emerged from behind the door, maintaining his distance, his eyes fixed on the room, alert and cautious. "Yes?"

"What about my cat?" I blurted out, my voice laced with concern.

"A cat?" he asked, his lips curling into a deliberate, unhurried smile. "I wasn't aware you had one."

"Well, you do now," I answered. "Can he come here?"

"I'll send someone over to collect him right away."

I watched him leave, then sighed heavily as I sat at the desk. The computer made a loud beep. The new computer was fast, a nice change from the old one that was slow and outdated.

Chapter Five

I sat forward, my eyes locked on the screen, fingers furiously jotting down notes as I sifted through Lilly's secret files. A sense of unease grew within me as I read, my heart sinking at the sight of my name mentioned in connection to an assault that had never occurred. It was clear that the location had likely been fabricated, a protective measure to shield me from those causing unrest in the realm and to safeguard Matace and his inner circle.

The eyewitness statements lined up with the events detailed in the paper files Lilly had sent my way, adding a chilling layer of authenticity to the fabricated narrative. It was all part of a carefully crafted web, one that left me powerless. Lilly had made it abundantly clear—I was not to help investigate, nor was I permitted to offer any input. She had effectively barred me from snooping around or contributing any ideas, leaving me trapped in the dark.

My home network was tethered to the agency, every keystroke and search was monitored, and a detailed report was sent directly to Lilly. She scrutinised my every move, questioning my actions with relentless precision. The suffocating surveillance left me no room to breathe, let alone operate freely.

But Luke's network was a different story. It wasn't connected to the agency, a loophole I knew how to exploit. I had learned how to slip past the agency's firewall, a ghost in the system, undetected whenever I wasn't on my home network. It was my only way to dig deeper, to uncover the truth hidden within the layers of deception that Lilly had woven.

The investigation had ground to a frustrating halt. Every lead we pursued led to dead ends, and the silence from potential witnesses was deafening. It seemed like no one wanted to talk—or perhaps they were too terrified to speak up. Fear hung over the realm like a thick, suffocating fog.

The only person who seemed to have any real knowledge was the bar owner. But could we truly trust him? His recent firing by the agency cast a shadow of doubt over everything he said. Had he been silenced because he knew too much, or was he somehow involved in Matace's death? The possibilities churned in my mind, each one more unsettling than the last.

And then there was Tye. His sudden, vicious attack on me had thrown everything into chaos. What role did he play in this tangled web? His involvement was shrouded in mystery, adding another layer of confusion to an already baffling situation. None of it made sense, and the more I tried to piece it together, the more the truth seemed to slip through my fingers like sand.

Matace's grand estate stood like a sentinel on a steep hill overlooking the city, a towering white mansion that had captured the imagination of locals for years. Its imposing presence was the subject of countless stories, whispered among the children who dared to brave the treacherous journey up the mountain. They hoped to catch a glimpse of the rumoured ghosts said to haunt the grounds or to dare each other to approach the ominous black door at the mansion's entrance.

Matace, the enigmatic owner, seemed to relish the eerie legends surrounding his home, adding to the estate's already energetic air of mystery. The mansion had been long abandoned, its windows dark and empty, until the agency assigned Lilly to live there. With her arrival, the estate took on a new life, though its secrets remained locked away behind those tall, silent walls.

As an agent, I had been granted permission to explore the mansion, to delve into its hidden corners and uncover whatever secrets it held. The thought thrilled me—wandering through the shadowed halls, uncovering the mysteries that had intrigued so many for so long. But beneath the excitement, a sense of unease gnawed at me. What could be lurking within Matace's home? What had the estate witnessed in its long, silent vigil above the city?

The anticipation was electric, but it was cut short when Lilly was handed the keys. My welcome was abruptly terminated, leaving me with a lingering curiosity and anxiety that only deepened as I thought about the unexplored mysteries behind Matace's grand facade.

I decided to wait until Luke was preoccupied before beginning my secret adventure. By my bedroom window, a trellis covered in thick vines offered a perfect escape route. The drop to the ground wasn't too far, and I could easily reach it without arousing suspicion.

From there, I planned to walk to my destination, choosing to forgo magic entirely. I knew that if I cast even the smallest spell, Lilly would sense it instantly. Matace had drilled this into me during our training—sometimes, it was better to rely on wit and physical skill rather than magic. Now was the perfect time to put that lesson into practice.

The thought of sneaking around without the aid of magic made my heart race, but it also filled me with a quiet determination. I just needed to act like a human, blending in and doing everything by hand. It was time to see if all those lessons had truly prepared me for this moment.

As a desk clerk, I didn't understand why I had to learn so many spells. My main job was to keep records, update reports, and search for news about supernatural beings. It felt like a lot of extra work that didn't make sense with my regular office tasks. Learning many spells was confusing and frustrating. Why did someone like me need to know all this weird stuff?

I often felt a deep sense of overwhelm, caught between the mundane routine of my everyday job and the gravity of the tasks I was truly responsible for. The contrast was jarring—filing reports and managing paperwork while simultaneously handling matters of critical importance. Even though the broader picture often eluded me, I understood on some level that my work carried immense weight.

Each day, I collected information with a heightened sense of urgency, knowing that the accuracy of my reports and my vigilance in monitoring the news could have far-reaching consequences. The stakes were always high, even if they weren't immediately visible to me.

There were times when doubt crept in, making me question my abilities and whether I was truly up to the task. But the weight of responsibility was a powerful motivator. It drove me to work harder, to push through uncertainty, and to strive for excellence in everything I did, knowing that the world could hinge on the details I managed.

A sudden urge to catch up on the news struck me, compelling me to hurry downstairs in search of the newspaper. The familiar rustle of pages and the scent of ink always grounded me in a way that online updates never could. But as I began my search, I quickly realised it was more challenging to locate than I had anticipated.

I could have easily checked the latest headlines online, but I craved the focus and clarity that only a physical paper could offer—no distractions, just the news in its purest form. My eyes scanned the room, searching for where it might be tucked away.

After a few moments of looking around, I finally spotted a stack of newspapers tucked neatly in the cabinet by the front door. They were organised in careful layers, with issues from the past week and month resting atop one another. The sight reassured me, a comforting reminder of the importance of staying informed.

Even in a world where technology reigns supreme and supernatural beings move unseen among us, the simple act of holding a newspaper reminded me of the necessity to remain vigilant. Staying up to date wasn't just a habit; it was a crucial part of navigating the ever-changing world around me.

I carefully looked through the papers, focusing on the reports of deaths and gruesome murders. They were especially disturbing and pushed the limits of what was creepy. I needed to find any connections to Matace's sudden death, especially after hearing about a new, dangerous breed that might be spreading.

It was a scary thought that anyone could do such a terrible thing. The last time something like this happened was almost twenty years ago, with appalling consequences. Wild animals were set free in revenge, causing much destruction. The person behind this cruel plan was a crazy, angry lover who thought his family was trying to hurt him.

Instead of talking to them about it, he planned this vicious attack. It turned into a violent fight between the families, with the wild animals making it even more chaotic. Sadly, innocent people who were just going about their day got caught up in the violence, too.

The agents had to be very sneaky and convincing to keep the public unaware of the supernatural creatures living on Earth.

"There you are," Luke exclaimed, walking through the door, "I have someone here keen to meet you."

Grinning, he held my cat towards me, who immediately recognised me and pounced from the safe confounds of Luke's coat. He leapt into my lap, purring happily and rubbing his fur all over me.

"Hello, boy," I whispered. "The bad man forgot all about you, didn't he?"

Without waiting for a reply, Luke walked over and expertly picked up my cat, looked him in the eye, and received a loud hiss of dislike.

"I don't think he likes me," he complained. "You want to see how I convinced the wretched animal to come out from under the bed?"

"Really," I asked, genuinely shocked. "That's funny; he's never like that."

"Don't worry," Luke laughed, placing the cat on the floor and warily watching him. "Animals can sense who we are and don't tend to offer a nice cuddle." I laughed at his expression, which was painful, to say the least. "What are you doing with the papers?"

"I'm just searching for anything that might link to Matace," I muttered, cringing as the atmosphere shifted. He seemed to become cold and withdrawn. "But it's only so I can send a report to Lilly. Don't worry; I'm not going anywhere," I added quickly.

"You'd better not," he warned. "You won't get far anyway. I run fast, you know I do, and I'll catch you and lock you in your room if I have to. It's my job to keep you safe, and I plan on doing that."

"You and your job," I said crossly. "Luke, where's this article gone?"

The paper had been torn, the article missing with a hole in its place that peered through the next page.

"I don't know," he stalked away, leaving me to gape at his departing back.

I frowned, confusion knitting my brow. He knew exactly where it was and had deliberately taken it away. It became clear that Luke was trying to protect me, keeping me from finding it or even leaving his house. The atmosphere grew tense, thick with unspoken words and hidden motives.

It felt as though he was intentionally keeping me in the dark, restricting my freedom in ways I couldn't fully understand. The weight of his actions pressed down on me, filling the air with a sense of foreboding. What was he hiding? What was he so desperate to prevent me from discovering?

The situation grew more intense with each passing moment, the uncertainty gnawing at me. I felt torn, caught between a burning desire to uncover the truth and the unsettling sensation of being trapped, unable to fully grasp his reasons. The more I thought about it, the more the mystery deepened, leaving me restless and uneasy.

"Well," I whispered inside the bubble of silence I'd conjured so Luke wouldn't hear me speaking out loud. "If he thinks I won't find them for one minute, he has underestimated me. What do you think, boy?" I chuckled as he scampered back onto my lap, nestling in for a much-needed cuddle. Absently, I ran my fingers through his soft fur, pondering where Luke would hide things.

How long can one vampire tolerate the company of a mortal who, according to him, smells as irresistible as I do? The thought lingered, a mix of curiosity and unease creeping in. But it was too late to dwell on it. He had already followed through on his earlier threat, blocking my internet access entirely. There would be no way for me to view the latest death reports or any other news.

Determined to find another way, I decided to bide my time. I'd wait until he was distracted or had left the house before making my move.

Restless, I wandered back downstairs and sought out Luke. His room was more like a den, a private retreat with a masculine charm. The space was dominated by a fully stocked bar, its polished surface gleaming under the low lights. Bottles of spirits lined the shelves, each one more exotic than the last. A snooker table took up the centre of the room; its green felt inviting and well-used. A large sports TV hung on the wall, flickering with highlights from a recent game. A jukebox stood in the corner, its vibrant lights casting a warm glow across the room.

The space felt lived-in, a sanctuary where Luke could escape the burdens of his otherworldly existence. But as I stood there, surrounded by the trappings of his carefully curated life, the questions gnawed at me. What was he hiding? And how much longer could I pretend that everything was fine?

"Oh, hi," he turned to smile from the snooker table. "Everything ok?"

"Yes, fine," I said. "Mind if I play?"

He stared at me and quickly recovered; instead, he turned and quickly threw a towel over his glass.

"You don't have to do that because of me," I laughed. "I don't mind you drinking, and I know what you drink."

"I was trying to preserve your feelings," he grins. "But hey, since you gave me advice on girls, I guess I don't have to preserve anything. I never thanked you for that, did I?"

"No," I replied. "But none of it was true, so there's no need to."

"Not everything I told you was a lie," he answered thoughtfully. "I need you to know that. You'll discover which parts were true and which I had to make up to get you on my side. Do you remember what you first said to me?"

I thought back, my mind spiralling over the many conversations I'd had with him, the times he'd made me laugh, and then it hit me.

"Oh yeah," I laughed. "You asked me if I knew anything about a love spell. I told you in no uncertain terms that a vampire, someone already dead, shouldn't be trying to steal someone's warm heart because theirs is stone cold."

"Exactly," he laughed, "I can't believe you said that to me, but it got you talking to me, and I think you ended up giving me a short counselling session."

"I did," I smiled.

"What do you want to drink?"

"I'll take a cola," I said, standing facing the table and picking up his abandoned cue.

My sense of stupidity was about to become a reality. In all honesty, I'd never played snooker, but I had played some pool with my dad when I was a kid, and if all that was required of me was to poke the ball with the stick, then that's what I could do.

"Do you know how to play?"

"Of course," I lied. "I used to play all the time with my father."

"I see," he said. "Well, take your shot then."

Time ticked by, the clock making as much noise as my heavy breathing. I felt pretty silly standing here pretending I knew how to play this game just so I could spread my scent around him and get him to run off in the opposite direction, leaving me to snoop inside his study without being observed.

"You're taking a long time," he commented, standing beside me. "Would you like me to help you?"

"No," I answered stubbornly. "I can play this game. I err...concentrating,"

"Is that what you call it," he said, hiding his amusement. "Well, I'll stand here and wait then."

You do that, mister, I thought, much to his delight because he heard me and choked on his drink.

I struck the cue, hoping the ball didn't rebound and bounce off the table. To my delight, by fluke or a sheer miracle and without any spells being used, the ball struck, and I managed to pocket one of the balls.

"Well done," he said, standing next to me. "Good shot," he praised, watching me.

I darted swiftly, leaving my scent in the air, enticing him. He caught the fragrance and abruptly turned away, unable to resist its allure. The smell had cast a spell, enveloping him completely.

"Can you not move that fast again," he asked gently without raising his voice. "That was too strong for me to take."

"I thought you were alright with your drink, and it wouldn't have much of an effect, you know, with my scent around you."

"Damn," he punched the side of the table, and I watched as the leg collapsed, and the table ended up crooked on the floor. "It doesn't matter whether I've fed or not around you; for some reason, I can't control my need to taste you. Your smell is just drawing me to the edge of my self-control, and I don't know if I can live under the same roof as you for the next few months."

I felt a sharp, painful stab of guilt in my heart, but it was all necessary to find the information I needed. I had to get rid of him or get him to keep his distance so I could sneak out tonight without being seen or heard.

"I'm sorry," I gasped, "I didn't realise."

"I think you did," he rounded on me, his face unhappy and his self-control slipping. "It's almost like you have just done that on purpose," he said, staring at me.

"I wouldn't do that," I defended heavily, "Luke, you have to believe I wouldn't endanger my own life now, would I?"

He studied me intently, his gaze piercing through me. Without a word, he turned on his heel and strode out of the room, his steps quick and purposeful. As he reached the doorway, he muttered something about purchasing another snooker table.

I heard some noises at the back door before he left. It seemed like he was trying to get away from me and get control of his strong desire. After leaving the game room, I quickly went to his study and saw a pile of files on his desk. I couldn't resist looking through them and found some information Lilly had sent.

"The sneaky liar," I said vehemently. "How could he?"

He had been secretly investigating the murders, despite warning me not to search the news for anything unusual. His curiosity got the better of him, and he sought out information to piece together the mystery. Frustration simmered within me as I sifted through the files he had gathered. There was nothing new—just scraps of evidence, none of it substantial enough to point a finger at anyone. It was a tedious exercise, and my impatience grew. Bored, I decided to abandon the files altogether and head to Matace's house instead.

As I prepared to leave, the distant roar of a motorcycle engine reached my ears. The sound grew louder, then faded into the distance, confirming that Luke had gone out. A wave of relief washed over me, and I savoured the thought of finally being alone. The house felt lighter, and less oppressive, and I allowed myself a moment to breathe.

Earlier, Darcy had proudly declared her breakfast a 'masterpiece' before leaving. Her enthusiasm was endearing, but I silently wished she hadn't insisted on making breakfast tomorrow. A simple bowl of cereal or a slice of toast would have suited me just fine. Yet, as I stood there in the quiet, I couldn't help but appreciate the solitude. The absence of Luke and Darcy gave me the space I needed to think, to plan my next move without their watchful eyes.

As I gently closed the file, a few paper clippings slipped out and fluttered down, landing on the desk with a soft rustle. My fingers hesitated before I picked them up, a sense of unease settling in my chest. The words on the fragile pages sent a chill down my spine.

According to the mortal world, several recent attacks had been carried out with a level of brutality that hinted at a deranged serial killer. The reports described how a group of young people, out for a night of dancing in a local field, had been savagely attacked. The perpetrators, according to eyewitness accounts, were creatures with enlarged bodies and more than one head. The exact number of heads remained unclear, adding an element of terrifying uncertainty.

This bizarre-sounding beast was unlike anything documented in the supernatural archives. My pulse quickened as I realised the implications—something new and deadly was lurking in the shadows, evading identification even among those familiar with the supernatural world. The paper clippings felt heavy in my hand, the weight of the unknown pressing down on me as I stared at the words, trying to make sense of the horror they described.

The attack was devastating, leaving only one survivor—though his life was forever changed. Disfigured and scarred beyond recognition, the poor man would likely never step out in public again. His face had been so severely damaged that plastic surgeons had to painstakingly reconstruct it, each procedure a desperate attempt to restore a fragment of his former self.

I knew the agency had quietly summoned those skilled specialists. The guilt over what had happened weighed heavily on everyone within our ranks. The responsibility for the tragedy clung to us like a shadow, a burden that would haunt each of us for the rest of our lives.

Tye's name was scrawled across the top of the articles, the ink haphazardly smeared as if written in a hurry. Lilly's familiar handwriting led the charge, with what seemed to be Luke's following closely behind. A timeline of dates and brief accounts detailed his movements, meticulously recorded as if they had been laying out a trail, tracking his every step.

My eyes widened as I read on. Tye had been meeting with Matace in secret, and the frequency of their encounters was more than suspicious. My breath caught in my throat as the pieces began to fit together. The evidence was undeniable, staring back at me like a sinister puzzle finally falling into place.

My heart pounded as I absorbed the chilling reality—Tye was deeply entangled in this, just as I had feared. His involvement ran far deeper than I had imagined, and now, the truth was glaringly clear. The weight of the revelation pressed down on me, filling me with a sense of urgency and dread.

I was certain now—Tye was the one Matace had met on the night of his murder, and it was Tye who had killed him. The realisation sent a chill racing down my spine, making me shudder involuntarily. The weight of the truth settled heavily on my shoulders, cold and unforgiving.

I carefully returned the files to their original place, ensuring everything appeared undisturbed. But before I did, I quickly scribbled down the key details Luke and Lilly had recorded, using a crumpled scrap of paper I found in the trash. The makeshift backup plan gave me a small sense of security. If the files ever disappeared or Luke realised I had been snooping, at least I wouldn't be left empty-handed.

The tension in the air was palpable as I tucked the paper away, my mind racing with the implications of what I had uncovered. Each step I took away from the files felt heavier, weighed down by the dark knowledge I now carried.

I hurried up the stairs, taking them two at a time. Reaching my room just in time, I quietly closed the door behind me and sprawled on the bed, pretending to read a book. Moments later, Luke poked his head around the door, his face twisted in a scowl.

"Again," he said, grimacing. "Sorry."

"Hey," I waved. "No problem."

I mulled over the information, my thoughts churning as I carefully placed the book on my pillow. Moving quietly, I crossed the room and silently locked the bedroom door, ensuring the latch didn't make a sound. Luke had vanished as suddenly as he had appeared, slipping away into the night like a shadow.

Knowing his ways, I suspected he was brooding somewhere, trying to keep a safe distance. It was his method of protecting himself from succumbing to his vampiric urges—a battle he fought daily. For a vampire, Luke displayed a remarkable level of restraint over his emotions, but it was a constant struggle, one I could sense simmering beneath his composed exterior.

The air in the room felt heavy, thick with tension as I contemplated his sudden departure. His strange, abrupt actions only deepened my curiosity and heightened my anxiety. I could almost feel the intense emotions bubbling beneath his calm surface, like a storm barely contained, a wild side he fought to keep in check. The thought of it all sent a shiver down my spine, leaving me with an unsettling mix of concern and intrigue.

Even though he seemed calm, I couldn't shake the feeling that he could suddenly change and become dangerous. The thought made me nervous, but I was still fascinated by this mysterious and risky person, like a moth drawn to a flame. I couldn't resist the temptation of the unknown, even though I knew danger could be ahead.

I struggled to open the window, its weight pressing against me as if resisting my efforts. The frame was stubborn, stuck in place, and with each attempt, my frustration grew. The metal clasps, meant to be secure, emitted a loud, grating squeak that echoed through the room.

Determined to fix the problem, I rummaged through the bathroom and found a bottle of oil-based lotion. I quickly squirted the contents onto the window hinges, the thick liquid seeping into the joints. After a few moments, the irritating noise vanished, replaced by the smooth, silent glide of the window finally giving way. A small victory, but it felt good to have resolved the issue quietly.

Climbing out of the window proved easier than I had anticipated. But descending the trellis was an entirely different story. The vines, thick and thorny, wrapped around the wood with sharp tendrils that clawed at my skin. Each movement was a battle, the jagged bits of wood scratching me as I tried to maintain my grip.

By the time I reached the ground, my hands and arms were stinging. I glanced down and saw thin lines of blood where the thorns had cut into my skin, a stark reminder of the dangers I had just faced. The sight made me pause, the adrenaline fading as the reality of my situation set in. Perhaps I needed to rethink this risky plan—next time, the consequences could be far worse.

I was getting close to solving the mystery of Matace's murder. His house was the last place I needed to search for answers. I was convinced that I would find something important there that would help me figure out who killed him. The idea of confronting the killer or killers made me anxious, but I was determined to find out the truth no matter what.

Defeating someone as powerful as Matace would require either a formidable group or an individual of unimaginable strength. The brutality with which he was brought down still haunts me, the terrifying events playing over and over in my mind, refusing to fade.

Yet, as gruesome as Matace's death was, the murder of Clarette was even more horrific, a nightmarish scene that left a deep scar on those who witnessed it. A human had stumbled upon her mutilated body, the gruesome sight sending chills down their spine. Her abdomen had been viciously torn open, her intestines spilling out onto the ground in a sickening display.

But that wasn't the worst of it. Her other vital organs appeared to have been either crushed or completely removed, as though they had been taken—or perhaps even consumed. The sheer savagery of it all was almost too much to comprehend, a macabre tableau that lingered in the shadows of my thoughts, a constant reminder of the darkness lurking just beneath the surface of our world.

I froze in my tracks, mid-step, as Luke's voice rang out, shouting my name. The trellis beneath me creaked ominously, straining under my weight. I wasn't heavy, but this structure wasn't designed to bear the burden of a person and looked really old.

"Seira," he called somewhere in the house. "Are you still in your room?"

His heavy footsteps thundered down the corridor and echoed through the empty halls. I hurried, darting down the remaining distance, desperate to escape. Suddenly, I felt the ground rush to meet me when my foot missed the gap, and I landed with a jarring thud. Searing pain shot through my ankle, and I winced, the swelling already visible. The agony was intense, making me wince with every movement.

"Shit!" I exclaimed quietly.

I raced toward Matace's house, my ankle throbbing with each agonising step. The pain was intense, a sharp reminder of my injury, but I hadn't realised until now just how closely Luke could hear my every word and thought. His presence loomed in my mind, but I couldn't let it slow me down. The urgency of the situation overpowered everything else.

With each stride, the excruciating pain threatened to pull me under, but I pressed on, determined to reach my destination no matter the cost. The pounding of my feet against the ground echoed in my ears, blending with the rapid, frantic beating of my heart.

I knew time was against me. The weight of the moment bore down on me as I half ran, half limped across Luke's front yard. My only focus was getting to Matace's house, and nothing—not the pain, not the distance—could stop me.

"Seira!" Luke's voice bellowed out the bedroom window.

I heard the front door creak open, followed by a loud, forceful slam that reverberated through the walls, causing the wood to tremble under the sheer impact. His temper had clearly flared, consuming him entirely. The anger in that slam was unmistakable, a sharp reminder of the tension hanging in the air.

Without wasting a moment, I hurried toward the edge of the garden, my heart pounding in my chest. I pushed through the narrow gap in the hedge, the branches scratching and clinging to my skin as I forced my way through. Each scrape felt like a fresh sting, adding to the pain already radiating from the thorns that had torn into me while descending the trellis earlier.

My body ached with every movement, the combined injuries weighing me down, but there was no time to dwell on the pain. I needed to get away, to put distance between myself and the growing storm of his rage. The thorns and branches left their marks, but I pushed forward, driven by the need to escape, knowing that the discomfort I felt now was nothing compared to what could come if I didn't.

"Great," I muttered, running and limping along the street. My first time taking a chance and escaping, and I had enough injuries and blood that I may as well wear a neon flashing light to call all predators for dinner.

I crept along the pavement in front of Luke's house, simultaneously watching the main road. Despite my best efforts, I couldn't locate Luke anywhere. He was nowhere to be seen, and

I couldn't even detect the slightest sound of his approach. I knew vampires were masters of their craft – possessing unparalleled speed, strength, and the uncanny ability to appear before their unsuspecting victims without warning. They moved with a silent, predatory grace that sent a chill down my spine.

"Will you stop," the voice hissed in my ear. I whirled around, but no one was there. Shrugging it off as the wind, I continued running, dragging my injured foot.

Shaking off the uneasy feeling gnawing at my gut, I quickened my pace down the road, wincing as a sharp pain shot through my ankle with every step. But I pushed through the discomfort, the thrill of narrowly escaping a vampire still coursing through my veins. The excitement fueled me, making me feel alive despite the throbbing pain.

I was determined to reach Matace's house, the only place left to search. Luke had warned me against it, his words echoing in my mind, but I couldn't be swayed. The mystery surrounding the murders gnawed at me, and I was committed to uncovering the truth, no matter the cost.

A strong, unyielding desire to find answers drove me forward, a force too powerful to ignore. Nothing would stop me from fulfilling my mission. My determination was a relentless fire, burning within me, each painful step bringing me closer to the truth I so desperately sought.

"For God's sake, Seira," I thought I heard him say. "Just stop, would you."

"No chance," I muttered, grinning and pretending he was there.

The darkness of the evening enveloped me, its comforting embrace like a warm hug, making me feel secure and concealed. My dark clothes melded seamlessly with the shadows, keeping me hidden from prying eyes. Yet, I knew that to immortals, my scent was as distinct as any other human's—a beacon that could easily betray me.

I pressed myself against the rough bark of a tall tree, leaning into its sturdy trunk for support. My ankle throbbed painfully, and I quickly massaged the swollen, tender area, wincing as I felt the inflammation beneath my fingers. The pain was a sharp reminder of my vulnerability.

This was the moment to act. I needed to create a shield, an invisible barrier that would protect me from anyone who might seek to claim what was mine—my blood, my life. The shadows cloaked me, but it was the shield that would keep me truly safe, warding off any immortals who might be drawn to the scent of my humanity.

My heart pounded as I focused, drawing on my inner strength to form the protective barrier around me, knowing it was the only thing standing between me and the dangers lurking in the night.

The protective bubble enveloped me like a misty cloud, soothing my nerves and providing a much-needed sense of safety. Despite the calm it offered, I could still feel the presence of vampires nearby, their dark energy sending shivers down my spine. Fear surged through me, fueling my determination as I sprinted through the night, dodging obstacles with desperate agility.

My heightened senses sharpened with every step, allowing me to detect the dangers lurking in the shadows. Every sound, every flicker of movement, was a potential threat, but I navigated my way toward safety, my heart pounding in my chest. As I neared Matace's house, the path ahead gradually became clearer, the imposing structure emerging from the darkness.

I wished desperately that I could teleport there, to simply vanish from where I stood and reappear at Matace's doorstep. Walking felt too slow and too vulnerable, but using the portal tunnels came with its own risks. If I used them, Lilly would immediately know I was alone, unprotected by Luke. The thought was unsettling—no vampire had ever dared to use the portals, and their effectiveness was uncertain. The unknown loomed large, yet I pressed on, driven by the urgent need to reach Matace's house and the safety it promised.

I felt increasingly excited as I got closer to Matace's house; my goal was so close. I was curious and a little nervous about what I would find there. I was tempted to take a shortcut through a mysterious portal. Still, I was worried about what might happen if Lilly was alerted to my magic use. I took slow steps towards the house, staying focused and alert, ready to see what awaited me.

I stopped walking when a sharp pain in my side made me feel like I couldn't continue. I leaned against the driveway stoned wall, feeling their rough texture. The house was completely dark at night, making me feel as if the darkness was surrounding me and getting closer as if it would engulf me completely.

"I've been waiting for you," Luke stepped out of the shadows, angrily watching me. "I knew you were headed here. Why didn't you stop when I called you?"

"Luke," I gasped, "How did you get here without me seeing you?"

"I know you sensed me," he said, looking at the bubble around me. "Hence, you covered yourself," he shook his head. "Good idea, but I'd rather you didn't climb down the trellis and leave the safety of my house."

"I felt like a prisoner," I complained. "And besides, unless you're thinking of tying me up, I'll do anything I damn well please."

"I'm strongly considering what you've just said," he remarked, laughing at me. "But until then, you'll have to put up with me following you."

I shrugged and hobbled towards the house, my wretched ankle throbbing and hurting; I almost wished I hadn't climbed down the trellis. I released the protective shield.

"You're injured," he commented. "Let me help you." He walked alongside me and placed his arm around my waist, allowing me to put all my body weight on him.

"Do you think it's a good idea?"

"I know what you did earlier, Seira," he reprimanded. "That wasn't nice. I should have known you'd use anything to get rid of me for your little plan. However," he said. "I'm not totally useless, and I can control my thirst for your blood a little longer, and I promise not to bite you."

I watched him carefully, not sure if I could rely on him. He belonged to our group, but that didn't guarantee his loyalty. Would he attack me suddenly, biting me and killing me? The idea made me shudder. Even if he did betray me, he would face punishment from the others, but that didn't make me feel any better.

"Are you serious?"

"Yes," he laughed. "Don't look so shocked; I told you earlier that, for some reason, having you in such close proximity has wreaked havoc with my self-control. I cannot explain it, and I won't even try, but there's something about you that I can't shake off."

"I know what you mean," I smiled shyly. "I've dreamt about you without wanting to, and I know you didn't put the dreams inside my head. They appeared; whatever this is has to end. We can't get involved with each other romantically and can only ever be colleagues."

"I agree," he said softly. "Now, how about a lift up to the house?"

Before I could react, he scooped me up and ran at full speed, making me slightly nauseous from the whizzing scenery.

"Luke," I chuckled, "this is the first time any vampire has done this."

"I should hope so," he whispered. "Now, what if I agree to help you unravel this mystery of the murders, as long as you promise to tell me everything you know and find out?"

"And will you tell me when Lilly tells you stuff?"

"I will," he agreed meekly. "But we must work together, and you can't wander about alone. You could be next on the list, and I want to protect you, not because it's my job but because I want to."

I understood precisely what he meant. If people close to Matace were being targeted and killed, I knew I was probably next. It wouldn't be a good situation, that's for sure. I'm sure the person behind it had their own messed up reasons. But I knew it wasn't up to me to decide what should happen to them.

The high court would have to handle it, and I had a feeling they wouldn't be lenient. In the sacred chambers of the High Court, Lilly and the respected elders of the immortal institutes gathered to discuss the fate of the accused. Their eyes showed their seriousness, and they spoke quietly but firmly. This was their routine every time they met in court.

"Listen," Luke whispered, silencing my voice with his hand over my mouth. "Can you hear that?"

I looked at the house and heard a sad, spooky sound from the garden. It sounded like a mix of an animal and something magical. The creepy sound made me feel scared but also curious. I wanted to find out where it was coming from.

"What is it?" I asked softly, keeping my voice as low as he had been.

"I don't know," he shook his head. "But I think we're going to find out."

The words had barely left his lips when I saw a movement out of the corner of my eye. Emerging from the shadows, a dark figure materialised around the eastern corner. Squinting into the darkness, I couldn't distinguish what it was – was it a single animal or more? The creature shuffled along, its black coat blending seamlessly with the night.

A soft, mournful moan drifted on the breeze, and its tail swung with a strange, newfound emotion. As it drew closer, the shadows cast against the house wall revealed the unmistakable outline of multiple heads. My heart raced, my pulse pounding in my ears. Where were the other creatures hiding? I strained my eyes, desperately trying to pierce the veil of blackness, but the unknown lurking in the darkness filled me with a growing sense of unease.

"What are they?"

"I'm not sure," Luke whispered, holding me tightly against him. His hands were placed against my waist, and his body remained dangerously close to me. "I haven't seen anything like this in a long time."

The animal's ears perked up, and it froze mid-step, one leg raised as it began to sniff the air and let out a low, menacing growl. The other two heads soon followed suit, sensing the impending danger. Panic gripped me as I tried to summon a protective bubble around myself, desperately hoping to shield Luke. Still, the witches' magic seemed unwilling to cooperate. According to Matace, these creatures did not belong in this world – they were outsiders, unwelcome intruders and therefore, any protection spell cast by a witch wouldn't extend to anything from hell.

I held my breath, every muscle tensed, as the animals circled closer, their eyes gleaming with predatory intent. The air was tense, and I knew I had to act quickly to survive this encounter.

"I don't think it saw us," Luke whispered softly. "I think it smells and senses our presence more than anything."

"Let's get inside the house," I nodded and gestured towards the trap door beside us. "This way."

I trusted him completely as he opened the door, standing watchful while I stepped inside the room. His eyes remained vigilant, scanning our surroundings, even as I paused on the stairs, uncertain of what he might do next. I had to stay close to him—he was my guardian, after all. I had already hurt my ankle trying to deceive him before, and I couldn't afford to break his trust again.

As we began to descend the dark, narrow staircase, a wave of nervousness washed over me. My heart pounded in my chest, each step making me more aware of the dangers we faced. His presence was reassuring, but it also heightened my awareness of the gravity of the situation. I had to stay strong, knowing he was the only thing standing between me and the perils lurking in the shadows.

The atmosphere was tense and thick with silence as we walked through the dimly lit hallway. The faint light cast eerie shadows on the walls, and the sound of our footsteps echoed ominously, making the task ahead feel even more daunting. I knew I couldn't afford to make any mistakes. One misstep could put me in grave danger and shatter any hope of uncovering the secrets I sought.

Guilt gnawed at me for not simply asking Luke to bring me here. The thought of him possibly trying to drink my blood lingered at the back of my mind, a mix of fear and forbidden curiosity. I had secretly wondered how it would feel, but I knew such thoughts were dangerous, especially with Luke's probing nature.

As we moved deeper into the hall, I purposely allowed some of my thoughts to surface, knowing Luke was likely reading them. It felt as though a fog clouded my mind, a telltale sign that he was sifting through my thoughts, searching for something. The sensation was both unsettling and strangely intimate, reminding me of the delicate balance between trust and the unspoken dangers that surrounded us.

"Please stop thinking so loud," he moaned. "It's affecting my thoughts, and I need to keep my wits. Just for the record, though," he stopped beside me as I looked up into the eyes that always

seemed to be catapulting themselves into my head. "I'm not angry
with you for deceiving me; I will not eat you, and I will protect you.
Please stop thinking about anything other than that; it would help."

"No, just don't intrude inside my head again." I grinned at him,
savouring the satisfaction of getting under his skin.

He had been appearing in my dreams and thoughts, so I
decided to do the same to him. Luke led the way as we quietly went
down the stairs. He kept a lookout, making sure I was safe. The
atmosphere was tense, and I felt excited.

Revenge felt empowering, and turning the tables on him was
satisfying. As we moved stealthily through the shadows, I felt a
growing excitement at the prospect of catching him off guard.

"It's clear," he whispered, beckoning me forward. "Come on."

"It looks like we're in the cellar," I whispered, trying not to
stumble and fall against him. His back was facing me, and I knew
he could feel the pain I was in. That much was evident by how his
hand swept towards me and held onto my elbow; he attempted to
hold me up while I perched my injured ankle against one of the
many sacks lining the wall. "I hope there are no rats down here," I
said.

I shivered at the thoughts and heard Luke's faint rumble of
laughter.

"I feel you're safe for now," he muttered. "I can't hear any of
them anyway. They must be resting."

"Are you kidding me?"

"Nope," he said and pointed to the floor where I could make
out the soft droppings that had been recently left behind. "Just
don't scream if any of them come out."

"I won't," I whispered, shivering violently. "Where's the door to
the upstairs then?"

"Over there, I think," he said. "Are you walking alright, or do
you want me to carry you?"

"I think I'm alright," I said, hoping he wouldn't decide to carry me against my will. It was wrong with us holding hands, and I hoped it didn't give him the wrong signal.

"Good." He turned to smile at me and squeezed my fingers reassuringly as he stepped towards the door. He turned the handle gently and muttered a curse when it didn't give.

"It's locked," he said.

"You think," I said sarcastically. "Open it then."

He sighed. "Anyone behind this door will hear us if I do that."

"So," I shrugged. "I have my shield and a vampire to protect me."

He smiled and let go of my hand. A pang of loss and a desperate yearning to cling to him swept through me, catching me off guard and stumbling on the small, shallow step I'd stood on to be closer to Luke.

The handle yanked back violently in Luke's hand, splintering the wood. Shards flew towards me, grazing my cheeks with their razor-sharp edges. The sudden impact stung, and I winced at the sharp pain.

"Great," I said, my voice muffled by my sleeve as I tried to stop them from catching me. "Another injury to add to my human body."

"Are you ok?"

Luke's eyes widened with concern when he noticed the tiny, crimson droplets on my cheek. Instantly, I whirled away, blocking his view. I couldn't bear the thought of him losing control and being unable to withstand the sight or scent of my blood. The idea made my heart race.

"Get away from me," I slapped his hand away angrily. "You can't see it, and I want you to hold your nose."

"Why?" he laughed softly. "I'm finding the smell of your blood oddly comforting, having you so near to me. Since earlier, Seira, I'm in complete control and gradually getting used to how you smell," he explained. "Let me see."

"Don't touch me, Luke," I warned through clenched teeth. "I'm telling you. Don't you dare touch me!"

The floor trembled beneath my feet, the unsteady vibrations causing me to lose my balance. I crashed into the door frame clumsily as I tried to stop myself from falling but failed and instead slithered to the floor with a heavy thud. The sudden impact sent a jolt through my body, leaving me momentarily disoriented on the ground.

"Ouch," I rubbed my bruised back. "What was that?"

"You don't know?" he asked with genuine surprise, crossing his face. "You honestly have no idea what just happened?"

I shook my head, feeling dazed and confused and bruised with the new injuries to add to my old ones.

"Seira," he clucked his tongue, smiling gently down at me and holding his hand for me to take. "You're an entirely new experience. I have only seen it a handful of times. The power inside you is like a magnetic force drawing nature's energy."

"What are you talking about?" I snapped, pulling my hands free from his.

His touch ignited a fire deep within me, a dangerous spark that should have been left alone. He was a vampire, and I was a witch—an impossible match that went against all rules. Being together would be like reliving the story of Adam and Eve, constantly giving in to the forbidden fruit's lure and testing our world's limits. The results would be catastrophic. Darkness would emerge from every vampire, whether exiled or wandering the Earth. Additionally, anger and disgust from other realms would target me, creating an overwhelming storm of consequences.

"I'll explain later," he answered. "We'd better get inside. We've already made enough noise for anyone to come and investigate, and we don't want to face any questions."

Chapter Six

Luke stepped into the house first, guiding me inside. The first room we entered was a large kitchen that flowed into the dining room. The house was enormous but well-organised, and the spotless cleanliness immediately caught my attention.

The strong, sharp smell in the air made me cover my nose to stop myself from coughing or gagging. For some reason, being in Matace's home made me feel uneasy. I had never been here before, not even when he was alive, and the unfamiliar setting made me feel out of place.

"This way," Luke nodded toward the study door. He could see it was wide open, and the windows faced outside into the garden.

Startled, I jumped back and hid behind Luke when I saw two menacing eyes staring at us through the glass. Luke held me steady, using his body to shield me and pushing me gently against the wall. I waited behind Luke. He gently took my hand and led me forward when the danger was gone. We entered the study, and he quickly closed the curtains to make sure we were safe.

"Won't they see you've just done that?" I asked, "Closing the curtains, I mean."

"Probably," he said, "what choice do I have? Either that or they'll see us in here and come in."

"True," I whispered.

"Where do you want to start?"

"I guess I'll start with the desk, and you start over there." I gestured towards the shelves, laden with thick ring binders stuffed with documents. I had no idea what they contained, but I was almost sure we'd find something to help us in this room – before they came after me for whatever reason.

I sat at the large desk covered with a stack of papers. I went through them, hoping to find something interesting, but they were mostly boring. The only sound in the room was the quiet rustling of paper as I flipped through the documents. Luke stayed silent, watching as I lost interest in the files. He turned away and started selecting ring binders to go through.

The room was covered in rich, warm wooden panels on every wall. Above, the ceiling featured a beautiful mural of fairies dancing gracefully. The artist's delicate brush strokes made their angelic wings look enchanting. The fairies' faces were detailed and extravagant, with silver and gold ribbons woven into the painting. Subtle, ancient symbols were hidden throughout the mural, hinting at the timeless secrets and mysteries that gave this space an exclusive and enduring aura.

"I feel like this is absolutely useless," Luke commented as he shuffled through another file. "We'll need more than just today to look through all this."

"Stop moaning and get on with it, would you?"

"I'm not moaning," he smiled. "I'm saying it's a futile attempt to find something that might not even be here in the first place."

"It's here," I said, "I don't know how I know, but I do."

I powered on Matace's computer, hoping it might shed some light on the ongoing murder investigation. The cursor flashed, demanding a password. Before I could stop myself, my fingers danced across the keyboard as if guided by an unseen force. It was a peculiar sensation, like someone had taken control of my movements, desperate to show me what to do, to grant me access to the information I so desperately needed.

"Hey Luke," I squeaked excitedly, "Come here, look at this."

The answer lay hidden in the first password-protected documents, like a whisper amidst the chaos. Though not entirely clear or comprehensive, it was enough to unveil the truth about the creatures being developed. This truth fascinated and unsettled me.

"It looks like phrases taken from websites during a Google search," Luke said as he leaned over the chair behind me. "Look," he pointed at the screen. "Doesn't that part relate to the mythological creature, you know, the three-headed animal?"

"Sure is," I agreed. "That species hasn't been around in many centuries, and most people started to believe they were pure myths, but I guess someone found a way to develop them and bring them back into this age. We can't let this animal get out and loose amongst anyone, whether they're human or not. They are a danger to all species."

"I know," he sighed, distractedly running his fingers through his hair. "It's dangerous. The people involved are trying to cover their tracks as best they can. If they find out you've had a look at these documents, then you're next on the list—that's providing they don't already think you're involved and helped Matace before his death."

"Well," I slapped my hands together, "I'm involved now, aren't I?"

"And so am I as your protector," he answered dryly.

The howling wind battered the windows, causing the crystal chandelier to tremble and chime. As Luke plunged the room into darkness, the computer screen flickered, illuminating the documents. Seized by a sense of urgency, I quickly whipped out my phone. I snapped a picture of the three-headed beast on the web page, determined to capture this startling discovery.

As Luke lunged towards me, his hand firmly grasped mine, yanking me out of the seat. The papers scattered, cascading to the floor. A single document caught my eye, promising something intriguing. I snatched it up without hesitation and tucked it securely into my bra, determined not to lose this newfound treasure.

A thick mist crept up behind us, and the eerie whispers of someone using the vortex tunnels echoed through the house, unsettling the animals outside. Their anguished howls pierced the air, interrupting the surrounding nature as I heard the loud screeching of birds and howls of dogs living nearby, amongst a few.

Luke scooped me up and dashed through the house, his steps swift and silent. We rushed to the cellar where we had entered, and he hurried out the door, his pace unwavering as he carried me to safety.

My heart raced with exhilaration and fear as the animals gathered around the front door, their wagging tails casting eerie shadows on the walls. As I watched the shadows, a shocking realisation dawned on me.

The shadows revealed three heads joined at the neck - dark, dangerous, and unmistakably the Cerberus, the mythical creature Matace had fought so hard to keep from being revived. Their presence meant that their efforts to silence the Cerberus had ultimately failed.

"Put me down," I whispered when we'd run clear enough from the house. Being as close as this to Luke was disconcerting, and my pulse raced impossibly fast. "Please."

He froze, scanning our surroundings before carefully setting me down, his gaze probing mine. His eyes smouldered, perfectly reading my fiery blush of embarrassment. A smirk tugged at his lips as his fingers brushed my cheek, erasing any chill as I felt heat spreading through my body, mesmerised by his eyes. My mind screamed, 'No,' but my traitorous body ached for more.

"Stop," I shoved him away, taking control of my inner feelings and allowing the rules to seep back inside me, "You know nothing like that can happen. And besides, you might get over excited and eat me."

Playfully teasing him was far more effective than anything I could have said. It worked as he grinned back at me, his eyes locked onto mine with a captivating gaze.

"You're right," he grinned, "And I'd better not eat you either. The world is far more interesting with you, and I wouldn't want to be here without you, would I?"

I smiled, a wave of relief washing over me. The danger had retreated, fleeing far from the house. Should I tell him what I had witnessed? Or wait until we were safely back at his place?

The rolling hills passed by as we walked in silence. Neither of us knew what to say after our intensely close encounter. My heart raced, adrenaline still coursing through my veins. I couldn't shake the moment's intensity—how his eyes had locked onto mine, the electricity that crackled between us.

I longed to break the deafening silence. To reach out and touch him. To seek comfort in his embrace. But uncertainty hung thick in the air. I held my tongue, waiting to reveal what I had seen.

The clouds rolled by in the sky, and the moonlight cast our silhouettes as we pressed on. The trees swayed softly in the strengthening breeze. Luke, ever the gentleman, removed his jacket and draped it around my shoulders. His fingers lingered, perhaps a moment too long, on my collarbone. But his gaze remained fixated on the task at hand, never meeting my eyes.

His house gradually came into sight, or what I still preferred to call a crypt. The darkness enveloped us as Luke took my hand and guided me over the small, gently flowing creek. The lamp lights danced in the water, creating a mesmerising reflection of the stunning beauty that surrounded his home.

As we approached the house, a sense of anticipation and excitement grew within me. The grandeur of the estate and the warmth of Luke's presence made my heart race. The darkness amplified the place's allure, casting an almost ethereal glow over the grounds.

With each step, the details of the house became more pronounced, its architectural elegance and ornate features captivating my senses. The gentle murmur of the creek and the flickering of the lamps added to the enchanting atmosphere, making me feel as if I had been transported to a magical, secluded world.

"Luke," I started, "I need to check some stuff on the internet."

"I gathered you might say that," he said softly. "I've reconnected it anyway. I didn't think you would back away from the idea of finding Matace's murderer without a fight, but next time," he turned to me, "can you use the front door and not climb down the trellis? It wasn't built to withstand the weight of any kind, and I have a feeling you've damaged it."

"Sorry," I grumbled. "But if you weren't such a taskmaster and a jailer, then I wouldn't have had to do it, would I?"

"A jailer," he chuckled, "Hardly. But next time, I might consider it."

"There won't be a next time," I said. "Can we go inside?"

His touch sent shivers down my spine, a mix of cold air and growing excitement impossible to ignore. I tried desperately to push these feelings aside, knowing it was for the best. But his hands lingered, teasing and tormenting, their warmth seeping through the innocence of the contact.

His presence was overwhelming, filling the space between us with tension. With each passing moment, the electricity building between us became harder to resist. It crackled in the air, making my resolve waver as I struggled to maintain control.

He reached for my hand, but I quickly pulled it away, refusing his touch. Behind me, I heard a faint, mocking chuckle, spurring me forward. My ankle throbbed with pain, causing me to sway slightly, but the discomfort only fueled my determination. I marched towards the front door, driven by an urgent need to find the answers I desperately sought.

"Does it hurt?" he inquired beside me.

"It's a little painful," I admitted shrugging. "But I'll handle it and plant a healing spell around the area when I'm alone inside my room."

"I thought you might say that," he said,."Do you ever resort to normal stuff, you know, like mortal medicine?"

"Sometimes," I answered honestly. "But it depends entirely on the situation. One like this needs me to be in top form, which doesn't include resting my ankle and waiting until the swelling goes down, which is the advice from any mortal practising doctor."

Luke's house was eerily quiet, the dimly lit rooms amplifying the hollow echo reverberating through the sparsely furnished spaces. Though he would never admit it, he found a strange comfort in displacing the minimal furnishings he had scattered around the house. Yet, nothing seemed to subdue the lingering sense of emptiness that permeated the air. This heaviness weighed upon the soul.

His self-proclaimed "crypt"—as I still liked to call it—stood empty. The haunting silence was almost suffocating, and the shadows cast a shroud of melancholy over the entire dwelling.

"I'll leave you to it," he said, his harsh voice disturbing my thoughts. "I need to go and do some things."

"Another words," I coughed discreetly, "you need to eat?"

"Hm..." he said and marched away from me toward his private suit, which consisted of the entire top three floors of his home.

I watched him vanish up the stairs, his back hunched as he dashed at an inhuman speed. His vampirism was a dark and mysterious force.

Rushing into the study, I hastily retrieved the crumpled paper in my bra. The distinct handwriting confirmed that Matace had written it.

Matace had carefully created a timeline complete with names. To my shock, I saw my name, "Seira," written on it. Underneath, the words sent a chill through me: "Luke must protect her from the evil that prevails and will undoubtedly surround her and destroy her soul." I felt a shiver down my spine as I tried to understand this.

Clearly, Luke knew something I didn't, and Matace had tasked him with keeping me safe from a coming darkness. The seriousness of the situation weighed heavily on me, and I knew I had to find out the truth, no matter what it took.

The timeline was straightforward, with a detailed map leading to a small section of the forbidden woods in the dreaded vortex – the very same place that every witch was strictly forbidden to enter due to the horrific atrocities within. I suddenly remembered the barman.

He had more questions that needed answering. These pages recorded his name and specific details about the investigation that Matace had been secretly orchestrating. It was clear now that he had not been honest with me earlier and had deliberately tried to mislead me.

"What's that?" Luke asked, appearing behind me like a silent predator.

The paper slipped from my grasp, fluttering to the floor. But before it could land, Luke darted forward, snatching it up. His eyes widened as he scanned the contents, brows raised in surprise.

Slowly, he lifted his gaze to meet mine, a silent question hanging between us. I sat behind the desk, steeling myself, ready to face him and uncover the truth.

"You tell me," I said bravely.

"I don't know what you're asking me to tell you," he replied, evading my question.

"Don't be like that, Luke," I snapped. "Matace wrote that note, and it has something about me there. So before you start lying to me again," anger began to flare, and my voice hitched up a notch, "tell me the truth, or do all vampires lie?"

"My race," he pounded on the desk in front of me, "are exactly like humans; we lie and cheat the same as humans do; there is nothing about us that could be assumed to be demoralising wrong, aside from the fact that we drink blood to live."

"So if that's the case, then you won't have a problem answering my questions, will you?"

"Go on," he said, carefully measuring his words and composing himself.

"What is it Matace asked you to do to protect me, and what exactly are you protecting me from?"

Luke sighed. "He approached me when I was working in my office; he asked for complete discretion and needed you protected."

"From what?"

"He said it was an unknown force, a new race built being resurrected that no one expected to rise again and that your life was the key to survival."

"Why my life?" I asked, stunned at the new revelations.

"Because of your heritage," he sighed and slumped into the seat opposite me, his resignation to my questions clearly evident in his composed self. "Do you know who you are? Do you know anything about your birth?"

"I don't understand," I said. "I'm adopted, and my adoptive parents are mortals. My witch skills surprised my parents and me when I was younger, something I dabbled into accidentally during my hormonal years. Then, I found a book in the library and really got into it."

He smiled, the slow, soft smile I was becoming accustomed to, the one that told me I was being naive and didn't have a clue.

"You know," he said. "That's one thing I've always liked the most about you."

"What?" I asked, surprised.

"The fact that you have no idea who you are or where you've come from," he replied. "You're going to be shocked and scared, and I want you to remember that I'm here to protect you."

"I'm waiting," I breathed slowly, "tell me everything you know."

Luke leaned back, his face obscured by the soft, enveloping shadows that danced across the dimly lit room. The clock's steady ticks echoed in the silence as I held my breath, my gaze fixed on him. The tension mounted with each passing second, the air thick with unspoken thoughts.

I could feel the weight of his presence, the gravity of his pause, as if the world had paused to hold its breath alongside me, anticipating his following words.

"You were born in the highest of secrecy for the purposes of the realm, to become the last remaining High Witch that could ever be made. Your bloodline stems from frozen cells of the first witches that stepped on Earth amongst other beings."

"Do you mean Cerberus?"

"Yes," he said distractedly. "That's exactly who I mean. Your blood was crossed with Matace's because you had to be made with the strongest bloodline possible to be created as a perfected person like they wanted."

"But I don't understand," I said, shaking my head. "Why would they want that for me?"

"To stop the one thing everyone was most afraid of," he answered kindly, "your birth was surrounded by mystery, and you were born on a different realm millions of miles from here for your own safety and then quickly handed over to your adoptive parents who were sworn to secrecy."

"So they knew all along?" I asked, suddenly feeling sick as I dreaded his reply.

"Yes," he nodded. I slumped in my seat, and it felt like everything had started to spin around me. "Are you okay?" His voice was soft, and concern shone in his eyes.

"Not really," I said sadly. "But you know, it's not every day you find out one of your natural parents is the same person who's just been murdered, and I'm some kind of weird crossbreed freak nurtured in a lab and made to perfection. Only," I paused, "I'm not perfect, am I?" I stood and walked to look out of the window.

He swivelled around in his chair, the moonlight casting a soft glow over his partially obscured face. I felt my breath catch in my throat, overwhelmed by the sheer magnificence unfolding before me. His eyes, captivating beyond my wildest dreams, and his hair, delicately groomed around his features, enraptured my senses. The entire scene felt like a vision of pure, unadulterated beauty. Luke's allure was getting harder to resist.

As the clouds obscured the moonlight, the room fell into a deep, enveloping darkness. Suddenly, I was plunged back into the shadows, a sensation that almost felt like a dream—not one of reservations but of raw, unfiltered truth, no matter how terrifying and dramatic it may have seemed. The darkness was all-consuming, pressing in on me from every side, and the moment's intensity was paralysing, leaving me with a sense of both dread and unwavering clarity.

I stood transfixed and moved closer to stare out of the grand window. The trees swayed gently as the birds bid their final farewells, their melodies carried on the wind. In the distance, an owl's haunting hoot echoed, and the creek babbled noisily, its waters glimmering through the lush foliage that paved a path across the grass.

The dew-kissed leaves that had grown tall enough to be seen through the window and grew just below twinkled back at me as the night stretched, casting a shroud of mystery and wonder over the world beyond the window. My mind raced, grappling with the events that had unfolded and the profound truths about my heritage and birthright. My link to nature enabled me to see many things others couldn't.

The intensity of this revelation gripped me, filling my heart with a dizzying mixture of emotions—awe, uncertainty, and a deep sense of connection to a past shrouded in secrecy. I stood, transfixed, as the weight of this discovery sank in, transforming the familiar landscape into a canvas of transformative potential.

"Luke," I said softly. "Does that mean that Matace is my father?"

He appeared behind me, his chest lightly brushed against my back as his soft, inhumane breathing whispered softly against the skin on my neck. I shivered with the delightful feeling he aroused inside of me.

"I'm afraid," he admitted. "He is one of many of your fathers. But most likely, it is one of the strongest ones inside your DNA. None of this was supposed to be revealed to you, and I was sworn to secrecy."

"Then why tell me?" I asked softly, enjoying the feeling of having him so close behind me that I could feel his strength and draw comfort from it.

"Because," he swallowed. "You're hell-bent on finding out who killed Matace, and I can't allow the discovery to come to light another way but from me. I care about what happens to you and that people, including me, have hidden many secrets from you for the sake of the realm."

I turned and met his gaze, and the realisation of everything unfolding between us finally set me free. As he looked down at me, the longing in his eyes was powerful, igniting a fire that made my heart race uncontrollably.

Gently, he leaned in, and our bodies naturally gravitated towards each other. As our lips met, the world around us faded away. It was as if the outside world had suddenly frozen in time. All thoughts vanished, and there was only the intensity of our kiss.

Our lips met in a passionate embrace, our mouths exploring each other with a desperate hunger. But just as quickly, I pulled away, my heart racing with the knowledge of the perilous consequences if anyone discovered any romance between a witch and a vampire. The risks were too significant, and I wouldn't take the chance because it would endanger Luke's life. It's now clear that I have fallen hopelessly in love with him.

"Luke, we shouldn't do this," I said, my voice trembling as I gripped his shirt tightly. "It's dangerous for both of us. We need to be careful."

"No one has to know," he whispered, caressing my cheek with a feather-light touch.

"If anyone finds out, it'll ruin everything," I said, my voice tense with worry. "We'll be banished, forced apart, and I can't bear being separated from you. We must be careful, or we will never have a future together."

"I will find you," he answered gently. "Allow this, us, just for this one night, Seira. Let me show you what love feels like; let me guide you through the forbidden path and let the walls drop,"

"I can't," I whispered shakily. "I can't."

I forced myself to step back, feeling the icy glass of the window press against my skin through the thin material of my blouse. Luke stood before me, his determination only adding to my momentary confusion. So much was happening at once, and I didn't want Luke to get hurt. Neither did I want him banished. Just the thought of losing him felt like a vice had clamped around my heart and crushed it.

"One day," he said gently, "you'll realise we are meant to be. Whether we are supposed to be destined to live in exile, I don't know, but you will figure out you're supposed to be with me, and I hope it's sooner rather than later."

Instead of confronting him, I hurried to the safety of my room, his words echoing in my mind, deepening the turmoil within me. Once inside, I collapsed face-first onto the bed, my tears of anguish soaking into the sheets. The weight of Luke's revelations about my past crushed me, and the memory of the passionate kiss we had shared only intensified my confusion.

I had fallen for him, unprepared and unaware, and now that realisation overwhelmed me. He was the one person who had been truthful with me, and that truth was both a comfort and a curse.

I stayed in my room, wrapped in the turmoil of my emotions. Sometime later, Luke came to find me.

The gentle knocking on the door caught my attention. I turned to see Luke enter the room, carrying a tray filled with various foods for me.

"I've brought you some food," he said, placing the tray beside me. "I thought you might be hungry."

I nodded and licked my lips, using the back of my hand to dry my wet cheeks.

"Have you been crying?" he asked gently, concern showing on his face.

"It's nothing," I muttered thickly through another onslaught of unshed tears. "Thank you for the food."

"Don't cry," he said, sitting beside me on the bed and taking me in his arms. "It'll all be okay."

"I doubt it," I managed a shaky smile when I pulled away from him. "There's some stuff I haven't told you yet."

"Oh," he said, placing a small napkin before me. "Tell me."

I hesitated. This moment felt like one I wanted to freeze in time. I knew this memory would forever be etched in my mind. Still, nothing could compare to the intensity of his lips on mine just moments ago—a sensation that would now haunt my dreams. It would be a moment in my life I wouldn't forget.

"Those guards," I began. "You know the ones from Matace's house."

"Yes, the dogs," he interrupted, handing me a small sandwich, "Eat, please."

I took a small bite of the sandwich, savouring the creamy flavour as it melted in my mouth. Cautiously, I met his watchful gaze, knowing I had to pay tribute to the offering he had placed before me. The intensity of his stare made my heart race, but I continued chewing, determined to honour his gesture.

"They weren't dogs." I shook my head. "They were Cerberus."

The room fell silent as Luke settled beside me, his eyes blinking rapidly in an attempt to process the new information about the peculiar guard dogs outside. His once neatly pressed clothes were now crumpled, a testament to his effort in carrying me. Still, he seemed oblivious to his appearance, his focus entirely consumed by the task.

I watched his profile, mesmerised by his captivating features. Like a flawless sculpture, his face seemed carved from stone, with his hair delicately framing the tip of his ears. The perfect, blood-red lips that had locked with mine in a passionate embrace now beckoned me to taste them again. With great self-control, I resisted the temptation.

"Do you mean the same three-headed creatures from the myths and the same ones on the document you found?"

I nodded, swallowing down another mouthful of the delicious sandwiches. "Yes," I said hastily. "They're back. Matace must have discovered they'd been resurrected. Only someone with tremendous power can resurrect those creatures; even then, it's impossible without losing your power. They will only be commanded by that person. I know only one, other than Matace, who is powerful enough to resurrect them."

"Lilly," we both said in unison.

"So if she's brought them back, then she must be trying to take over the entire realm; obviously, being the High Witch isn't good enough for her," he added dryly. "We can't tell Lilly anything we know."

"Right again," I answered between mouthfuls of food. "It wouldn't be wise to tell her anything right now. We must find out why she's resurrected them and find Matace's murderer. I feel she wants bigger things other than bringing them back to life. Whatever she's doing inside his house must be dangerous. Hence, she's brought them back to guard her and the house and keep the secrets locked inside."

"That's another thing I like about you," he commented slowly. "The way you're so wise, and you never give up. I've watched you many times and seen your determination to keep going even when things weren't going according to plan. You've done a lot of good inside the agency, you know?"

I smiled back at Luke, sat, ate the sandwiches, and drank hot tea while Luke looked out the window. It was a comfortable silence; each of us focused on our thoughts. I want to know why Lilly needed the Cerberus and what she hoped to gain.

"Thank you for not stopping me from looking into all this much more," I said.

"You would have done it anyway," he laughed.

"Luke," I replied as a sudden thought came to me. "I need to visit that bar again."

"Why?" he sighed. "Do you want to go tonight? Or won't your ankle be up to the challenge?"

"I'll put a spell on it to heal it faster," I replied. "We need to go and just listen to anything in the bar. Lilly has already been there, and hopefully, we can gather some intel about her."

"Are you sure you put a spell on your ankle? I thought you could only use the elements of the Earth," he mimicked me so directly and correctly, his teasing changing the atmosphere between us.

I playfully slapped his arm, but instead of a soft, fleshy impact, my hand collided with something unyielding, like stone. His skin felt rigid and unmoving beneath my palm, and I couldn't help but wonder if he was carved from marble. The force of my slap barely registered on his expression, and he let out a deep, rumbling laugh that seemed to reverberate through his entire body.

"Come on," he sighed. "We'd better get ready if you want to go and find some answers. But I warn you, some of the answers you're not going to like, and they will cause more harm than good; nothing is going to come out of this, and I'm worried about your safety."

"In what way?"

"I want you to go disguised tonight," he answered, "I've got something you can wear," he rummaged in the wardrobe and produced clothes worn by the demonic immortals that were granted passage through the Earth to reach other realms nearby. "You'll have to wear this," he said. "If anyone catches a sniff you're investigating, you'll have so many people after you trying to destroy you. Matace placed you in adoptive care for your own safety, and then you turned up all by yourself without any help asking to join the realm," he explained. "Poor Matace nearly had a heart attack when he read a report about an unknown magic user outside the agency. He knew it was you."

"I traced my own witchcraft heritage, and somehow I knew I had to be here," I defended myself, feeling criticised for returning. "My parents weren't happy, and I suppose that, with how I was made, they were right to be angry with me."

"Well, I can't blame them, but then you're always determined and stubborn," he pointed out. "You wouldn't have listened anyway."

"You're right," I smiled.

"Now, change into that costume. Matace cooked up it, and nobody can see it's spell-ridden. Lilly will detect any magic you use, so you can't use it to disguise yourself. Still, this costume was created by Matace, so she shouldn't be able to detect it as quickly, if she can at all. And besides, you're going to look damn demonic and hot!" He grinned mischievously and tossed the costume in my direction. I quickly stepped forward and snatched it out of the air, watching as he hastily left the room, eager to be done with this task for the evening.

Wincing in pain, I eased myself back down on the edge of the bed, cradling my throbbing ankle between my fingers. My mind drifted to a forgotten chapter of my past – the spell book I had rescued as a child, a secret treasure I had hidden away from prying eyes. I remembered the day I had found it, discarded in the gutter on my way home. Overjoyed at discovering this new, mysterious book, I hastily stashed it away in my private den, deep within the garden. Only when I was absolutely sure that no one was watching would I dare to peek inside, my heart racing with curiosity and trepidation.

The pages of the ancient book were worn, and the spells had been written over, rendering many of them ineffective. Yet, the mesmerising handwriting drew me back to the book repeatedly. I had reached a point where I had started dreaming of wielding the power of a mighty witch. The words "The Realm" were etched onto the back cover, and through a chance discovery, I learned of the hidden creatures that roamed the Earth. A sense of wonder and trepidation gripped me as I delved deeper into the secrets concealed within the weathered pages, eager to uncover the true nature of this mysterious realm.

As a young aspiring witch, I spent countless hours in the pages of spell books borrowed from the local library. In the solitude of our garden, I'd practice my magical craft, sometimes with explosive results, leaving a trail of miserable weather in my wake. However, my mother's disapproval was ever-present, especially when my father caught me mid-spell, desperately trying to transform the school bully into a croaking frog while forcing him to hop like a kangaroo. It was a foolish thing to do, yet I found it equally entertaining and exhilarating, particularly after all the years he'd spent tormenting me.

My parents had vehemently opposed my use of witchcraft. Still, I couldn't resist the allure of the realm beyond my doorstep – the one where Matace had welcomed me with open arms. I felt woefully inadequate compared to the others who had auditioned alongside me that day. Yet, I knew I had one exceptional skill - mastering the elements. Calling upon this power, I conjured raging storms, dazzling sunshine, and Earth-shaking tremors. A whirlwind of sheer terror materialised at my command. Still, I swiftly dissipated it, my control over the forces of nature absolute.

"Well done," Matace clapped happily, laughing, his eyes twinkling. "I loved that little show. Now tell me," he searched the eyes of the others in the room and found I was the only one brave enough to stand and openly gawp at him. Where did you learn to do that?"

"Well, sir," I replied, "I learnt it at the bottom of my parent's garden."

"Really," he asked, amused by my response. "Well, little one, would you like to join us? I am sincerely overjoyed with your show and your determination."

The moment he smiled and offered me the position, I couldn't contain my excitement. I let out a triumphant whoop and practically flew out the door. It was almost too much to believe – in my wildest dreams, I had never imagined I'd be granted entry into this prestigious realm, let alone be asked to join him as one of his advisors. It was an honour beyond my wildest expectations, and I was brimming with joy and disbelief. The magnitude of this opportunity was almost overwhelming, but I knew I had to seize it with both hands.

After Matace's sudden passing, Lilly swiftly demoted me, declaring that I lacked the qualifications to be one of her trusted advisors. She had already handpicked her successor; I was not in that selection. Faced with this unexpected dismissal, I retreated without protest. I was driven by respect and the dread of losing even the slightest foothold in the agency realm that held such profound significance.

"Are you ready?" Luke asked from the doorway, peeking around the door. "I see you aren't."

"Sorry," I mumbled, hastily grabbing the costume and throwing it quickly over my clothes, "There," I stood in front of him with my arms outstretched. "How do I look?"

"You still look a little mortal," he groaned. "Try putting a spell on your eyes to turn them red or something."

"Right," I said, and I developed my own spell to make it work just for me. I felt my body moving with the whirl of magic I could feel wrapping itself around me, the whispering of my words and the sudden scorching pain in my eyeballs. "How's that?" I asked, gasping from the pain.

"Better," he said, concern showing in his eyes. "Did that hurt?"

"Like hell," I replied. "But all done now, and I've managed to heal my ankle simultaneously, so no worries now," I said quickly. "All transformation spells hurt. We are using magic to manipulate and change our bodies," I explained.

"Hm..." he muttered, "Let's go."

Stepping out into the eerie silence of the night, this was the hour when the supernatural beings emerged from the shadows. The demons and immortals roamed freely, their true nature hidden from the unsuspecting mortals who slept soundly safe in their homes around them. The darkness provided the perfect cover for these entities to move about undetected, their presence a closely guarded secret.

"I think Lilly is at the bottom of everything," I said. "Her name has been tangled more than once."

"How so?" He asked gently, helping me step over the fallen branches on the floor as we crossed his garden.

"Matace's note, and I remember the barman said to me before that she'd turned up there with someone, but I assumed she'd been trying to gather information," I explained. "And she's the only one I know who would use the vortex tunnels to travel around without risking being seen or discovered, only for some reason, I can't sense when the tunnels are being opened."

"Will you stop," he groaned. "Do you ever listen?"

The howling wind surged around us, creating a powerful illusion of a raging storm. It felt like someone had conjured a vicious gale, whipping and swirling angrily, trying to push us back. But Luke's firm grip on my waist kept me steady, preventing me from being swept away by the fierce gusts that threatened to overwhelm us.

"Your Matace's child in a way," he repeated from earlier. "You're made with particular handpicked DNA, which makes you the highest in the realm. As weird as it may be to you," he stopped and pulled me closer as my fingers gripped his coat. "You're made to be the one who can do almost everything. And with that comes incredible power which cannot be overthrown by some stupid female thinking she can get the better of you, and by that, I mean Lilly."

Frozen in place, I gawked at him, the gusting wind yanking the hood off my disguise, unleashing my hair to dance wildly in the air. Luke's eyes softened, and he pulled me close, wrapping me tightly to his side as he strode purposefully through his garden.

"Seira," he breathed in my ear. "Can you please do something about this damn wind?"

I grinned and distanced myself from him, clambering atop a fallen, massive tree limb nearby. The wind grew stronger and louder, its power impossible to ignore. Someone with great strength was clearly controlling it, trying to create obstacles for anyone outside and stopping anyone from travelling.

I hummed the familiar words, feeling a magical connection to the Earth and the elements around me. The lights shone brightly, crackling with energy, and I drew that power into myself. The fight against my unseen enemy was brutal, leaving me weak and tired. But as I battled, an intense energy and determination surged, driving me to overcome the challenge.

When the first tornado suddenly appeared, I couldn't help but laugh at the raging storm. Through the howling winds and flying debris, I saw Luke's panicked face repeatedly. I could barely hear his desperate shouts, telling me to be careful as he clung to a nearby tree for dear life. The moment's intensity filled me with excitement, even though the tornado was tearing everything apart.

The storm's threatening centre came closer, daring me to face it. The wild storm communicated with me, roaring and crashing uncontrollably toward the fragile houses below. The once peaceful area was now filled with the raw and fierce power of the elements.

"No!" I yelled, my voice laced with venom. I flung my hands out, desperate to escape the situation I had unwittingly found myself in. Deep within the raging storm, I could faintly hear Lilly's wicked laughter, her cruel cackle echoing in my ears as ghostly glimpses of her appeared now and again through the storm.

"Lilly!" I snapped, my voice laced with urgency. "What in the world are you thinking?"

No response. She had disappeared from my line of sight. Gradually, I regained control over the raging storm. I calmed the eye of the storm and banished it back into the skies, shifting the clouds to reveal the night moonlit sky.

"Luke," I whispered into the dark, my voice tinged with desperation. "Where are you?"

"Right here," he said, his voice steady beside me.

My body had weakened from the intense battle with another powerful being, and I collapsed to the ground. Luke was quick to help me up, his hands constantly checking my skin, his eyes filled with concern. I took a deep, shaky breath, trying to regain my strength.

"Hey, what's with the sniffing? Are you eyeing me like a piece of meat or something?"

"Seira," he said, a mischievous glint in his eyes, "I can smell if you're bleeding." He leaned in, his voice lowering to a conspiratorial whisper. "If you are, we might have to postpone our little outing and try again another night." The corners of his mouth curled up in a devious smile as he studied my reaction, his gaze burning with a predatory intensity.

"Well, I'm not bleeding," I smiled, "Why is it so dark?"

"You used the power from the lamp lights around here and blew them out," he answered, "I didn't know until then how you could draw power like that. You were amazing."

"What did I look like?"

"The lightning was a bit unsettling," he said lightly. "It was like a scene straight out of a horror movie happening before me," he explained. "Seira, you're truly powerful, and you've got to have faith in yourself."

I wavered a bit as he guided me forward; the storm had quieted, leaving an eerie calm and a faint reminder of its previous power. Luke, ever vigilant and on guard for any danger, continued forward, and I kept up with him. My breaths were short and strained as I tried to stay composed despite the lingering unease.

"We're almost there," he said gruffly as we approached the road leading directly to the bar on the other side. "Pull your hood up, and don't say a word. If there's any useful information, I'll pass it along to you. But the last thing we need is for anyone to know you're here. Your attempts to dig into those details have already caused enough suspicion."

His voice had a sense of urgency, stressing the need to be careful. The situation was clearly delicate, and I could feel the tension in his behaviour. I nodded and pulled up my hood, preparing myself for what was ahead. We had to be discreet to find the answers we sought without attracting unwanted attention.

I prepared myself, still shaken by the failed attempt but eager to find new leads. I knew the barman wouldn't give up his information easily—we'd have to force it out of him. That's where my vampire protector came in. We walked into the bar casually. It wasn't unusual to see a demon with a vampire; both were feared and respected in and out of the underworld and the agency.

"Stay by my side," Luke breathed, his voice urgent and laced with concern. His lips hardly moved, yet his words echoed in my mind as if he had whispered them directly into my ear. The intensity of his gaze held me captive, sending shivers down my spine as the weight of his unspoken message settled upon me. "Can you see the end of the bar?" he asked.

Hiding under my heavy hood, I peeked out carefully. My eyes struggled to see through the thin fabric as I looked around the room. Feeling uneasy, I quickly found a stool and sat down, my heart pounding.

Lilly was deeply conversing with the bartender in the dimly lit bar, whose details were scribbled on the scrap of paper I had taken from Matace's place. Their voices were hard to hear over the noise of the patrons drinking and smoking. The acrid smoke stung my nose, and I tried to block it with my sleeve.

"Stop it," Luke said firmly, his brow furrowing. "No demon would ever cover their nose like that."

"No witch worth their salt should have to skulk in some grimy, smoke-choked dive, masquerading as some ugly demon. That's not how we do things."

"You're breathtaking, even in disguise," he murmured, a mischievous glint in his eyes. Turning back to the bar, he waved over the approaching bartender. "One pint of O-neg, and..." He paused, locking eyes with me. "What's your poison tonight?"

I firmly shook my head, making it clear that I had no intention of drinking blood or engaging in anything remotely demonic in this place. The thought of it made my stomach churn with disgust.

"My friend doesn't seem to want anything, so just the pint of blood would be fantastic," he said.

As the bartender turned away, I felt the hairs on the back of my neck stand on end, and a chill of fear trickled down my spine. The tension was thick, and I couldn't shake the feeling that something terrible was about to happen. The idea of getting caught made me shiver. The stakes were high, and the consequences of being discovered could be severe. I couldn't afford any mistakes. My heart pounded as I gathered my courage, determined to follow the plan despite the risk.

"Don't look up," he warned beside me. "Tye's arrived with some others."

"What if he sees you?"

He put a finger to his lips. "Shhh... I'm just here enjoying a nice cold one. If he comes over to me, head for the door, and I'll be right behind you."

I accepted that I had to leave. Casting a protective spell was out of the question because Lilly would sense it and know another witch was nearby. Even though I was nervous, I had no choice but to go.

"Move!" Luke commanded, his voice sharp and uncompromising.

Chapter Seven

A s casually as I could, I stood and made my way towards the door, conscious of the curious gazes of the creatures around me. They lounged at the tables, some sipping crimson blood. In contrast, others indulged in mortal alcoholic drinks deemed safe for their kind, ensuring they wouldn't become overly intoxicated and pose a threat to humans.

"Well, well, well," I heard Tye say softly, "If it isn't the ever-heroic Luke," he quipped. "And where, dare I ask, is the luscious Seira?"

"I don't have to and won't answer that, Tye," Luke said sternly. "Why are you here? Out to murder someone?"

Tye laughed. "Out for a drink," he answered, ignoring the dig about murder. "Want to join me?"

"Not really," Luke replied. "I was passing through and couldn't win against the forever call or the smell of the blood, so I dropped by for a quick taste."

"The good old-fashioned thirst, hey," Tye chuckled. "Well, I'll join you for at least one."

"Who's your friend?"

"What friend?"

"The one who just left the bar," Tye said.

"I have no idea who that is," Luke replied. "Like I said, I was only passing by. Whoever the demon is, they aren't interested in friendly chat."

They stood in plain sight, their voices cutting through the bar's chatter. Tye leaned in close to Luke, his eyes locked onto him, unblinking and intense. Their conversation flowed casually, but the weight of Tye's words held Luke captive, his gaze unwavering and cold-hearted.

"You should tell her to stop investigating," he warned. "It's becoming noticed, and she's headed up on the list as the next to die. I'm only telling you as an old comrade to another," he said. "Do you remember the old days, Luke?"

"I'm not one of your comrades anymore, Tye," Luke snapped. "I've moved on since the old days, and I'm not happy about the things I've done in the past or the terror I've caused," he replied and then leaned closer to him. "If one hair on Seira's head is touched by you, mark my words that I'll be coming after you."

Lilly's melodic voice abruptly interrupted the hushed conversation as she approached. Her flowing garments swirled around her, making her appear almost ethereal, like a divine being. However, her lack of confidence was evident in the presence of the single male guard who accompanied her.

"Tye," she chimed gently. "Oh, and I'm honoured to meet you again so soon, Luke."

Luke leaned in, his eyes locked with hers in an intense, unspoken challenge. Slowly, deliberately, he bent down and pressed his lips to her outstretched hand, his touch featherlight but charged with unwavering intention. The air crackled with the electricity of their silent confrontation as they engaged in a battle of wills, neither willing to back down.

"Lilly," he breathed, charm seeping into his voice, making my skin crawl from outside. "How lovely to make your acquaintance so soon. But I'm afraid I have to leave. This was only a drop-by drink before my duties resumed."

"Yes," she breathed. "You must keep our darling young witch Seira safe, right?"

"Indeed I do," he said, downing the remainder of his drink.

The cloaked figure loomed behind me, its heavy footsteps echoing on the pavement as it crossed the street. I saw its dark silhouette in the corner of my eye. The figure's presence sent a chill down my spine. Its voice was rough and forced, an apparent attempt to conceal its true identity. My heart raced, and I knew I had to act quickly before this mysterious stranger got closer.

"Come with me," it said. "I have something significant to show you."

"I'm not coming with you," I replied gently. "Who are you?"

"Neither friend or enemy," it said. "Bring your friend and meet me in the alleyway where Matace breathed his last breath."

I peered out under my hooded cloak. My eyes fixated on the dark, cloaked figure as it descended the dimly lit road, heading straight towards the ominous alleyway. My heart raced, pounding frantically in my chest, the anticipation and unease building with every step the mysterious figure took.

The air was thick with tension, and I couldn't help but wonder what this shadowy figure was. A sense of dread crept up my spine. I held my breath, watching intently as the figure vanished into the alley. The unease left me desperate to uncover the truth behind this eerie encounter.

"What happened?" Luke demanded when he reached my side and pulled me away from the bar by the elbow. "I can hear your heart thumping, and it's deafening."

"There was someone out here just now," I replied. "A cloaked figure. They want to meet us in the alleyway where Matace died."

"Do you think that's wise?"

"What choice do we have?" I shrugged. "They might have something we need to know, and besides, we can defend ourselves if it's a trap or something."

I felt a profound realisation growing inside me, driven by the intense controversy around me. The seriousness of the situation was evident, and I wrestled with a deep understanding of its complexities. The debate sparked something within me, making me want to explore the details with more focus and awareness. In my mind, I was questioning why Luke was so tense and stressed. It's not like we couldn't defend ourselves if we had to.

"I'm not stressed," he muttered through clenched teeth, "I'm worried. This may well be a trap."

"I didn't say anything," I answered. "And you shouldn't be inside my head," I snapped. "It could be a trap, but if it isn't, we would miss out on much-needed information," I pointed out.

"I know."

The alleyway loomed ahead, a dark and ominous tunnel that seemed to pull us forward. This was the place where Tye had brutally stomped on my head and where Matace had met his end. The shadows stretched out, daring us to enter the unknown, filling us with dread and anticipation.

Luke's firm grip on my arm held me pinned firmly to his side but pushed me against the wall as he navigated the cluttered alley, moving through scattered boxes and debris. My fingers clung to his jacket, panic rising as sweat trickled down my forehead. The distant sound of shuffling feet made us freeze, and my heart pounded in the tense silence.

"Who's there?" Luke demanded. "Show yourself."

"It is I," came the faked gruff voice. "Are you both here?"

"We are," Luke answered sternly. "Show yourself."

A diminutive cloaked figure emerged among the scattered debris, swiftly followed by three others donning the same hooded cloak. They were all tethered together by a rope, their movements synchronising as they approached. Slowly, they removed their hoods, revealing mischievous grins and eyes that gleamed with an unnerving intensity as they fixed their gaze upon me.

"We are a part of the Cronomiun race," she retched slightly when she sniffed me. "I see you're completely human."

"Well, yes," I replied bravely, reaching out to clutch Luke's hand tightly. "What the hell is a Cronomiun?"

For the first time in my extensive study of the diverse races inhabiting Earth and other dimensions, this is my first encounter with this race. Their fiery, glowing eyes and deathly pale faces, with the skin around their eyes appearing scorched, their unnaturally high cheekbones and tightly stretched skin, all warned me to approach them with caution and vigilance.

"My dear young child," she answered. "You contain part of our DNA. You were made to be a part of us, and the day of reckoning is near."

"I don't have your DNA," I muttered. "Don't be so absurd. What powers do you have?"

She let out a chilling cackle, her mouth burning with intense flames dancing and flicking inside. The fiery heat radiated from her lips, adding a powerful sense of menace to her presence.

"Steady," Luke whispered when he saw her approach closely.

Her gaze locked onto mine, intense and unwavering. Slowly, she raised her hand and caressed my cheek, her touch feather-soft and electrifying. My skin tingled under her delicate fingertips, and I shivered involuntarily. Without thinking, I reached out and placed my hand on top of hers as if drawn to her by an unseen force.

A surprising, exciting feeling flowed through us, making the alleyway look like it was moving and changing, revealing a beautiful new world. The lush, green forest wrapped around me, filling my senses with its bright colours. There were people on the ground, bowing their heads in respect. The lines between different worlds had blended, taking me to a place full of magic and secrets.

The pull of the discovery of the unknown. I faced the unusual woman, and a smile crept across my lips. She reciprocated the gesture, beckoning me to move forward. Luke stood by my side as if in a trance. Together, we navigated through the crowd, who continued to pay their respects to me.

The energy faded, and suddenly, we were surrounded by people, their smiles illuminated by the dull light. We followed the path back to the alleyway, which had now come back into focus. The moment felt charged with longing, as if the vibrant atmosphere had disappeared, leaving us yearning for its return.

Shadows crept across the alley, cloaking us in a suffocating darkness. The blackness enveloped us, seeping into every corner and leaving us disoriented and uneasy.

"What was that?" I gasped.

"That was our world, where you partly belong," she explained. "The people have been waiting for your return for some time," she answered, "We're honoured to make your acquaintance."

"Err...Luke," I began. "Any ideas?"

"You know what," he replied softly. "I've heard strange things have happened before, so just go with it for now. What's your name?"

"We do not keep names," she replied. "They are a symbol of self-possession, and we prefer to fight as one—one person, one army united to fight and fall..."

"Don't tell me," I choked between laughter, "as one."

"You mock me," she accused. "A sign of your human genes, no doubt," she said. "I have come to warn you against the onslaught Lilly has prepared for you."

"What do you mean?"

"You have tempted her anger, and in that, she will attempt to destroy you to keep her secret safe; this is the falling of our race and yours combined unless you find a way to counteract the half-breeds and all dangerous mythological creatures she is intent on bringing back to life."

"We already know about the Cerberus," I interrupted. "We can destroy them."

She scrutinised me intently, her eyes burning with an intense fire that partially illuminated the dimly lit alleyway. Her companions stood in a row with their heads lowered. Another one approached me, arms outstretched, and firmly grasped me, pulling me into a different dimensional realm, but this time without Luke.

"Where are we?" I asked, clasping what I thought was Luke's hand, but it was the Cronomium's hand instead.

"Sh," he murmured lightly. "Watch."

I stood high above a mysterious, uncharted world. Peering down, I saw the darkness lurking beneath my feet. Suddenly, a distant roar echoed, sending a shiver down my spine. Yet, driven by curiosity, I pressed on toward the source of the unsettling sound.

"Tell me where we are, please," I begged.

"We are on Earth," he replied. "This is what it shall become in a few months from today. I have the power to bridge time and the future and see all things before they happen, whether they are good or not. Unless you stop Lilly before she discovers how to kill you and discovers the spell that will release the vortex to create and bring back to life the deadliest of monsters the Earth shall ever see."

"Are you serious?" I asked, amazed that he could see all of this. "Your leader woman says I'm a part of your race, so what power do I have?"

"You will have to learn that one for yourself," he answered. "Look down there."

As I followed the line of his outstretched finger, a dawning sense of realisation slowly crept over me, like a chill running down my spine. Suddenly, the shadows seemed to come alive, erupting into a deafening roar, like a chorus of primal fury.

The humans scattered in a frantic, panicked attempt to escape the ferocious, lumbering beasts, their terrified cries echoing through the darkness. But Lilly remained rooted to the spot, steadfast in the face of the impending danger, her eyes fixed on the approaching creatures, and she looked calm.

Her dress swirled around her like a living tornado, its movements hypnotic and entrancing as she stood, frozen in place, completely consumed by the dark magic enveloping her. The air crackled with malevolent energy, the very essence of her power radiating outward in ominous waves.

Monsters under her control obeyed her every command with eerie precision. They seized innocent bystanders, their claws wrapping around them like iron shackles, and hurled them toward her as if they were mere playthings—sacrifices to feed her insatiable hunger for power. Each victim was drawn into her orbit, their terror unmistakable as they were offered up to the dark forces swirling around her.

The intensity of her spells was beyond anything I had ever witnessed. The sheer, terrifying force of her magic left me trembling, caught between fear and awe. I could only watch in horror as she reached the apex of her power, the dark energy coursing through her, growing stronger with each passing second.

Deep down, I knew there was no stopping her now. Her power had reached a crescendo, a force of destruction that was beyond any mortal's ability to contain. I was helpless, a mere spectator to the chaos she unleashed, powerless to intervene as she prepared to unleash her ultimate fury upon the world.

"I can't stop her," I gasped, "it's impossible. I'm not a strong witch."

"You're stronger than you think," he answered; his eyes widened a fraction. "We have to go back. She is calling for us. Can you feel it?"

To my utter bewilderment, I felt an irresistible tug, as if an invisible rope had been fastened to me, forcefully dragging me back toward the gloom of the alleyway. There, Luke stood, gripping my body tightly in his arms, cradling me as I crumpled from the overwhelming force of the power. The alluring pull was impossible to resist, like a magnetic force tugging at every fibre of my being, compelling me to return to the darkness. My limbs felt heavy, my senses clouded as if an unseen force was controlling me.

Helpless, I allowed myself to be drawn back into Luke's arms. Luke held me close as if trying to shield me from the intensity of the power surging inside me. The sensation was terrifying and intoxicating, a dizzying mix of fear and an inexplicable desire to surrender to the darkness.

"Seira," I heard Luke whisper, stroking my hair. "Can you hear me?"

I mumbled a vague response, and then my eyes snapped open. I stared at him, then shifted my gaze to the end of the alleyway. We were utterly alone now. The creatures had vanished, but their chilling message still hung in the air, leaving me trembling with dread. The sheer force I had to confront and somehow overcome weighed heavily on my mind, filling me with a sense of impending doom.

"What happened?" I dared to ask, licking my dry lips.

"I'm not sure," he responded.

"I remember going into the future with one of them but nothing else."

"You went into the future?" he asked gently. "Whoa, steady., he said as I swayed.

"Come on, let's get back. I have a lot to tell you," I urged. "We can..."

Luke swept me off my feet, and I let out a small yelp of surprise, cradling me in his sturdy arms as he carried me the rest of the way to his house. The sight that awaited us was a wondrous haven, a safe refuge from the harrowing ordeal that had left me weakened and helpless, a state I had never experienced before meeting Luke.

As we approached, Darcy stood in the garden, talking with another man. Their presence at this dark, late hour could only mean one thing - trouble was brewing. I felt a chill run down my spine, knowing that whatever was unfolding was bound to be ominous.

Luke's touch provided a sense of security, but I couldn't shake the unease that gripped me. Something was amiss, and the impending danger lurking in the shadows only heightened my apprehension. I clung to Luke, seeking his strength and protection, my heart pounding with fear and uncertainty as we neared the confrontation that awaited us.

As we drew near, they both swivelled to face us. Luke handled me with tenderness, gently lowering me back to the ground. His arm remained firmly wrapped around my waist as if he was reluctant to let me go. I could feel the warmth of his touch, the strength in his grasp, and the underlying current of protectiveness in his every movement.

"Darcy," he greeted softly, "Benjamin."

"We need to talk," Darcy responded, using an entirely different tone than I'd heard her use before. "Without her."

"She stays," he commanded, his voice firm as he extended his hand, stopping her speaking attempt. His eyes locked onto hers, an unwavering determination etched across his features. "What is it?" he demanded.

"Luke, the situation has taken a dire turn. The things Seira has found out have created a threat. Your arrival at the bar tonight has caused complete chaos among the demons guarding Lilly," Darcy said, her voice laced with urgency and frustration as she fixed me with a stern gaze.

Benjamin spoke for the first time. His voice sounded gruff, yet there was something softly compelling about him. "I see Seira is staying here with you. Is it wise to have a mortal inside the house with you, Luke?"

"That's nothing to do with you," Luke snapped. "Now tell me, what threat are you talking about?"

"Those same cursed creatures she dressed herself as tonight, that's who," Darcy spat, her voice laced with venom. "You've brought so much trouble, especially by dressing her up as one of their kind. They are furious at the disrespect and are on their way here, plus they are great supporters of Lilly."

"I know how you feel about them because of the past," Luke said gently.

"Their entire race are vicious killers, Luke," Darcy snapped. "And we could do without that kind of heat of them."

Darcy's words oozed with anger, her calm facade demolished by a raging fury. Just hearing about those demons ignited a deep hatred in her, as if they represented all the hardships and suffering she had ever faced.

"I get it, Darcy," Luke replied, his brow furrowing as he leaned forward, his gaze fixed on the two people before him. "But there's nothing we can do about it now except make sure we are prepared to fight if we need to when they arrive," he said. "That doesn't explain your attitude towards Sierra or why it takes both of you to tell me."

They looked at each other desperately, but no solution was in sight. The silence in the air was suffocating, and I clung to Luke, feeling vulnerable and protected. Luke said nothing else; he just turned and returned to the house. The cold air made me shiver as exhaustion crept in. I dragged myself up the stairs, yawning each step, feeling increasingly drained.

"Tired?" he inquired, "Let's get you settled in bed, and we'll talk in the morning."

"What about what Darcy said?" I asked, yawning.

"The demons won't be here for a few days. They aren't known for their speed, so don't worry. If anything, it's more important that you get some rest so we can adequately prepare for their arrival."

"But..."

Luke pressed his finger across my lips to stop me from speaking and guided me up the stairs, his hand on the small of my back, leading me to my room. Gently, he eased me down onto the bed, the mattress cradling me as he tenderly covered me with the soft, warm blankets. The unexpected touch of his lips on mine sent a shiver through my body. I found myself lost in the intensity of his gaze, my eyes fluttering closed as I surrendered to his affection.

I let out a deep sigh as I gave in to the darkness of sleep. My nightmare began, and it felt like a giant hand gripped me tightly, drowning me in fear. The nightmare scenes in my mind were terrifying, making me feel like I was stuck in a living hell that I couldn't escape from. My nightmare swiftly transformed, and in its stead, I found myself captivated by the piercing gaze of the one person I had come to depend on, unknowingly and unexpectedly. Luke's presence sent my heart racing, and my mind became consumed by nothing but him.

His intense gaze pierced me, stirring up a rush of emotions that almost engulfed me. I felt a strong pull towards him, like he had put me under a spell, rendering me helpless in his enchanting aura. Every part of me ached for his touch, hug, and undivided focus.

As I drifted into my dream, the world around me faded into a distant blur, leaving only one thing in sharp focus—my connection with Luke. He consumed my thoughts, captivating my every sense and leaving me yearning for more. His presence in my life was like a storm, chaotic and unpredictable, yet impossible to resist.

Luke's playful nature always brought a smile to my face, his jokes a light in the darkness. But there was also a depth to him, a seriousness that commanded attention when needed. His intense gaze could silence a room, drawing all eyes to him. Being with him was a whirlwind of emotions, stirring feelings inside me that I had never experienced before.

In my dream, we were together beneath a vast, beautiful sky, the air filled with music that seemed to soothe us both. The moment was intimate and tender—a perfect escape from the harshness of reality. In his arms, I felt safe and cherished, wrapped in a love that made everything else fade away. It was as if time stood still, allowing us to savour each second together.

Even as I began to wake, the memory of his touch and the scent of him lingered, a precious moment I clung to with all my heart. The dream left me with a mix of emotions—a sadness at having to leave that perfect world behind, a warmth from the connection we shared, and a deep desire to hold onto that feeling forever.

Jerking awake, I scanned the room in a frenzied panic and anger, desperate to find him. But the bed and room were empty, solidifying it was only a torturous dream.

"Luke!" I shouted, jumping from the bed. "Luke!" Seething with rage, I marched to the windows and violently yanked the curtains open. The sheer force of my action caused the curtains to tear away from the curtain rod, cascading down in a dishevelled heap.

"Yes," he appeared inside the doorway. "What's wrong?"

"What the hell are you playing at?" I demanded, my blood boiling in a fury.

He was incredibly bold in entering my dreams and showing images of us together, especially since he knew I had feelings for him. It felt like he was deliberately tormenting me as the visions continued to replay in my head and make me feel uncomfortable and upset. I felt unease and sadness, making it hard to think clearly. I stared at him angrily, wondering why he would invade my thoughts like that.

"Uh, hey there," he mumbled, his brow furrowed in bewilderment as he ran a hand through his dishevelled hair. "You look a little... off today. Rough night or something?" he asked, his tone laced with concern.

"Nothing I'm sure you didn't aim to fix," I replied sweetly. "Why did you enter my dreams again? How dare you? I thought we'd had this conversation once before and agreed," I pointed out. "We agreed you would stay the hell out of my head and keep to your side of the bargain."

He looked mischievous and amused, as though he was enjoying my anger. I felt really frustrated and grabbed a pillow to throw at him. He dodged it easily with a quick dive and seemed even more amused.

"I think someone needs to control their temper," he remarked. "And as for entering your dreams," he replied silkily, "I think you'll find you dreamt of me all by yourself. I can't say I blame you," he continued, "I mean, who wouldn't dream of someone as irresistible as me?"

Filled with anger, I quickly moved toward him, trying to attack. However, he quickly caught me and held me close. Looking at me, his playful look had turned serious and intense.

"Seira," he murmured, his voice low and urgent, "when will you finally accept that this thing between us is here to stay?"

The gentleness in his voice caught me off guard, but the underlying happiness simmering beneath the surface was real. His eyes held a soft, almost tender gaze. The situation felt strange, with so many unspoken feelings between us that I'm sure he could sense everything as acutely as I could.

He suddenly let go of me, steadying me on my feet. Then, with a mischievous wink, he turned and swiftly exited the room. When he encountered Darcy in the corridor, his voice erupted in a loud, vehement hiss, dripping with intensity and disdain.

"I see your girlfriend needs to be controlled," she said. "Or do you need a cage for the witch?"

"Leave it out, Darcy," he warned through gritted teeth. "Leave her alone. I thought you liked her."

"I did," she admitted. "Probably still do, but now she's brought danger directly here to you, Luke, and that's something I cannot condone, no matter who they are."

"That's my decision to make," he snapped. "She won't be for much longer. As soon as she finds the answers and the key to whatever Lilly wants, it's over."

"What, and you're letting her walk away, just like that?" she asked, snapping her fingers to emphasise the point.

"No vampire can have a witch in their lives for long," he answered. "It's an impossibility."

I heard his heavy footsteps thundering down the corridor, each quickened step sending a wave of dread through me. As I lay there, knocked down and utterly bewildered, a sense of relief washed over me—this ordeal would soon be over. I could finally regain my self-respect and put an end to these foolish romantic fantasies about being involved with a vampire.

For heaven's sake, he was dead—what was wrong with me? Was I ill? Or was it the intoxicating allure of being wanted, of feeling needed by someone, that was driving me to the brink of madness? These questions circled my mind, but no matter the answers, one thing was certain—I had to suppress the emotions and feelings he stirred within me.

I needed to remain intact, aloof from his magnetic pull, and resist the profound effect he seemed to have on my heart. Whatever strange spell he had cast over me, I was determined to break free before it consumed me entirely.

"Knock, knock," Darcy called as she popped around the doorway. "Alright, to come in?"

I cautiously nodded, keeping a wary eye on her. Her frosty words from last night still echoed in my mind. The warmth and hospitality she had shown me when she made that rather unappetising breakfast were now replaced by a chilly demeanour. I couldn't help but wonder what had changed and whether her initial welcome had been genuine or merely a facade.

"Can I ask you something?" she said, her tone shifting to a playful, whimsical cadence. I felt a flutter in my chest as I looked at her, the most captivating vampire I had ever encountered.

"Sure," I replied, my fingers frantically running through my dishevelled hair, desperate to appear more presentable. Of all the times I had to look less than perfect, it had to be now when faced with this ethereal beauty.

"How much do you like him?" she asked, her gaze piercing me and her curiosity clearly visible.

"Pardon," I hesitated, my hands frozen in the air. "What did you say?"

"You know," she laughed, her voice almost sounding like wind chimes outside. "Luke, how much do you like him?"

I couldn't stand to see her face anymore. I clenched my teeth and tried to find the courage to confront her. A small part of me hoped I could somehow trick her with a magical spell to hide how much I cared about him. But deep down, I knew I couldn't lie, even if it meant avoiding the hurt of talking to her. My feelings were too strong to express, and I couldn't bring myself to share them with her, no matter how much she asked.

"I deeply cherish him as a trusted friend, a wise advisor, and my protector," I responded, trying to sound convincing. "Nothing more, nothing less. He holds a unique and irreplaceable role in my life." I paused, allowing the weight of my words to settle. "Our bond is built on loyalty, trust and mutual respect – a connection that goes further than the boundaries of just friendship."

"Wait a second," she blurted, her eyes narrowing as she studied my face. "I could've sworn I just heard your thoughts saying something completely different before you shut them down. Is there a particular reason I might have picked up on that?" Her tone was laced with a hint of accusation, as if she was onto something I was trying to hide.

"I have no clue what you're on about," I replied, shrugging my shoulders dismissively. "Is there something specific you need, Darcy? I must get ready and talk to Luke." My voice held a slight edge, betraying my impatience. I shifted my weight, eager to finish this conversation.

Her creepy laugh made me feel scared. Even though she looked nice, her smile had a scary feeling as she looked at me with evil eyes. It was clear that there was something bad about her that I couldn't ignore.

"Listen to my warning, my dear," she hissed, her voice dripping with venom. "Never get involved with a vampire, especially not Luke. He's been off-limits for years, and I've been trying to claim him for myself." She paused, her movements suddenly blurring as she surged forward, standing mere inches from me. Holding her thumb and forefinger together, she whispered, "I was this close to getting him to like me, to develop feelings for me." Her eyes bore into mine, the intensity of her gaze almost overwhelming. "So, don't you dare rain on my parade, young one," she snarled, "or I'll be the one coming after you, not Lilly."

She quickly turned around and violently closed the door, loudly echoing. I fell to the floor, feeling small and defeated, with a heavy heart, realising that she was struggling with her feelings for him just like I was with my own emotions.

"Don't worry," I muttered softly. "I won't be raining on anyone's parade. He's all yours."

I abruptly stood up, physically shaking myself as a deafening clap of thunder echoed through the sky. Dark clouds rolled in, rapidly blotting out the once-sunny day and plunging the room and the outside world into a gloomy, ominous atmosphere. The sudden shift in the weather was uncanny, almost as if a powerful, supernatural force had summoned it.

A shiver of unease slid down my spine, the chilling realisation dawning on me that the extraordinary display before me could only be the work of a powerful witch. As I pieced together the pieces, dread settled in my gut as I came to the horrifying conclusion that only Lilly could be responsible again.

Her blatant show of power sent a wave of fear coursing through me, causing the shadows to deepen and the air to grow thick with tension. The atmosphere crackled with an intensity that made me feel like reality was being pushed to its limits. I dread what the mortals thought about all these sudden weather changes.

"Oh well, Lilly," I muttered. "You can bring the storm, but you will not bring a war to this world."

I started to run a hot bath, the steam rising like a veil between me and the world outside. As I stepped into the water, a newfound sense of determination coursed through my veins. I attacked my skin with a rag, scrubbing with such force that it left angry marks and raw patches in its wake. Each stroke felt like a battle, as if I were waging war against the lingering memories of Luke's tender touch.

But I gritted my teeth and soldiered on, knowing that this painful ritual was necessary. The sacrifice of physical closeness was a price I had to pay for our survival. As I finished cleansing myself, a deep sigh escaped my lips, carrying the bittersweet taste of longing and regret.

No longer would I feel the warmth of Luke's lips on mine or the gentle entwining of our fingers in moments of intimacy. The thought pierced my heart like a dagger, the ache almost unbearable. But I knew it was a sacrifice I had to make to protect us both. The distance between us had to remain, a necessary barrier against the dangers that lurked in the shadows.

With a heavy heart, I resigned myself to a life without the joy of being swept off my feet by the man I loved. The bathwater cooled around me, reflecting the chill that settled in my soul as I accepted the lonely path I had chosen.

"Seira!" Luke's voice thundered through the house, rising above the deafening crack of lightning that split the sky.

The sudden burst of light flooded the room, revealing every corner with a haunting glow before slipping away into the blackness. The electric energy in the air intensified, crackling with an almost tangible tension as the storm outside raged on, leaving my heart racing with anticipation of the unknown.

"Coming," I shouted back.

With a surge of adrenaline, I made a hasty retreat from the room, my heart pounding in my chest. Fear gripped me as I snuck a final glance behind me, the once familiar surroundings looming with menacing shadows in the darkness. The bed, which had always been a source of comfort, now seemed almost threatening in the eerie gloom.

Feet pounding, I raced down the stairs, my frantic steps echoing loudly on the cold tiles. The curved stairwell loomed ahead. I shuddered at the realisation that my clumsy movements would make me a poor fit for the stealthy ways of the vampire. The thought of becoming one of the vampires sent a chill down my spine, a fate that I would only consider as a last resort when faced with certain death.

Eager to find Luke, I swiftly approached the direction his voice had come from, soon spotting Benjamin and Darcy in the dining room. As I entered, all three sets of eyes turned to greet me, their gazes locking with mine. The enticing aroma of freshly brewed coffee wafted through the air, causing my mouth to water and my impatient stomach to rumble in anticipation of the impending breakfast.

Darcy swiftly exited the room and reappeared moments later, carrying a plate of freshly baked pancakes. Her smile was soft, almost like the one I had seen the other day. It was puzzling to witness how she could seamlessly transition between two vastly different personas, a trait that seemed to be another intriguing aspect of vampire nature - one that I was still exploring and attempting to understand fully.

"You're here," Luke clapped from his seat at the head of the table, his hands tightly holding a mug. "Good. I'm glad. I'd like you to meet Benjamin officially."

I stood at the entrance, consumed by a mixture of anxiety and excitement. The rapid thumping of my heart echoed in my ears while a swarm of butterflies danced wildly in my stomach. I couldn't ignore the sudden surge of realisation that I was on the brink of coming face-to-face with another vampire.

As I braced myself for yet another encounter, I couldn't help but wonder how many more of these nerve-wracking meetings I would have to endure before I could break free from Luke's control and escape this suffocating place. It was the only way to keep my feelings towards him in check and maintain a distance.

"Hi," I croaked. "Nice to meet you."

I remained perfectly still, resisting the urge to extend my hand or make any physical contact. On the other hand, Luke leaned back in his chair, casually wiping the faint traces of redness from his lips. I suspected he had just finished his morning 'meal,' I wished Luke didn't need to hide it from me; it's not like he had to.

But then, I guess the less I saw of their vampiric rituals, the easier it would be for me to leave him and return to my own comparatively mundane existence. The only way I could save Luke from being harmed by Lilly or any of her minions is to leave his world. To do that, I knew I had to distance myself completely.

"Nice to meet you properly," he drawled from across the table. "Come closer. I would like to see this girl who has the immortal world in such uproar."

With few choices left, I walked closer to him, using the table as a shield. I stood my ground, confident that Luke would protect me. I was determined to keep a safe distance, no matter what. The atmosphere was tense, but I wasn't going to give in. My heart was pounding, but I was determined. I looked him in the eye, unafraid and prepared for whatever he might do.

"I see you're young," he commented. "And you have an incredible power surrounding you."

"Benjamin," Darcy laughed. "Don't start with all that again," she rolled her eyes and turned to me. "Benjamin likes to think he can sense auras of people, but in reality, he's just a blood-sucking vampire like the rest of us."

Her smile seemed to dim slightly as if she couldn't hold it in place, briefly showing the false facade of her friendliness.

"Come and sit down," Luke patted the seat beside him. "We have some information we need to share with you."

Luke looked happy and calm, unaffected by what had happened. This confused me because it was odd. I sat in the chair across from him, ignoring the one he offered. He seemed angry initially, but then he just shrugged and sat back down. Darcy and Benjamin sat beside each other, their own gloomy auras evident. My magic had unlocked the feelings and emotions of those around me, a skill I had been trying to perfect for a while but couldn't quite master. For unknown reasons, it had chosen today to activate.

The room hummed with an almost tangible tension so dense it felt like it could be physically sliced through. Despite the heavy weight of unease that seemed to envelop everyone else, Luke appeared completely unaffected, his bright and cheerful persona standing starkly against the sombre backdrop. As I watched him, a memory suddenly flickered to life in my mind of the first time Matace had demonstrated the aura spell to me.

"I'm going to teach you something today," he'd said after we walked around the agency grounds. "My young one," he began, "I want to teach you as much as possible while my life is still on Earth. Once I cross the boundaries into the other realm belonging to souls, I cannot contact you at all. But I will be watching over you."

"Please don't talk like that," I whispered to him, "You're not dying, are you?"

"Oh, no," he chuckled. "Of course not, but you don't know what's going to happen tomorrow, and you should never take a day for granted."

"I know," I'd replied.

Our leisurely stroll occurred on a bright Sunday afternoon, with the sun rising above us. The birds chirped melodious tunes in the background as we wandered around the grounds. Basking in the warm, unusual sunshine (which I had conjured to impress Matace), he acted fatherly, taking me under his wing.

He advised me who I could trust and who the creatures destined to be evil and failures were. I absorbed his words like a sponge, listening attentively, knowing this knowledge was crucial for my rise and becoming the best I could be.

The stroll felt invigorating and meaningful. Matace's guidance was invaluable, and I hung on to his every word, eager to learn and grow. The lush, verdant surroundings and the cheerful birdsong created a serene, almost enchanting atmosphere, making the experience all the more impactful.

I felt a deep sense of purpose and determination to listen to Matace's wisdom and use it to propel myself forward in the realm. His fatherly demeanour and the trust he placed in me fueled my resolve, and I was determined not to let him down.

Once we had stepped inside the house, Matace unveiled the well-worn spellbook he had relied on for years. The pocket-sized volume bore the marks of its extensive use, its binding hastily repaired with tape and its pages brittle from countless incantations. The book demanded the utmost care and reverence, a tangible testament to the magic it contained.

A sense of anticipation filled the air as Matace flipped through the weathered pages. This unassuming book, battered by time, held the key to unlocking powers beyond our comprehension. Its tattered appearance belied the incredible knowledge it possessed, waiting to be tapped by those skilled enough to harness its arcane secrets.

The book's presence radiated an aura of mystery and power, hinting at the extraordinary feats it had facilitated over the years.

With each turn of the page, we felt the weight of history and the promise of the unknown, for this spellbook was no ordinary tome – it was a gateway to a world of magic that lay just beyond our reach.

"This," he coughed slightly, "is my most prized book. This is where all my homemade spells are documented; when I do die, Seira," he'd turned serious eyes to mine and placed the book into my hands. "This will be yours to keep and treasure as much as I have. Be warned, some spells are homemade concoctions to prevent war and slaughters. In contrast, others are for the power of goodness and nothing more."

Utterly captivated by his mesmerising speech, I could only manage a silent nod of understanding. The sheer weight of being in the company of one of the realm's most legendary and revered witches left me in awe, a humbling privilege I scarcely dared to believe. And that same person tutoring me and guiding me was a pure honour.

"We need to discuss what we need to do about these demons coming after you, Seira," Luke cut through my thoughts, his voice clear and deep. "Are you listening?" he asked with restrained impatience.

"What...?" I asked, visibly shaking my head. "Yes, sorry, I was thinking about something."

"Care to share?" he asked smoothly, watching as I smothered my pancakes in syrup.

"Not really," I said abruptly, covering the uncomfortable moment. "What's this about demons?"

"They're coming here to speak to you," Darcy answered. "They have a lot of issues with you and the information you have gathered so far. I don't think you can hold them off either," she added. "Especially not with magic." Her final sentence was a mere whisper inside the room. Her eyes glazed over with unconcealed anger as she watched Luke instantly become protective of me.

"That's enough, Darcy," he said. "Don't speak to her like that," he reprimanded. "What do you think we should do, Seira?" He spun around, locking his gaze with mine. His broad shoulders blocked the other two, who sat motionless, their unblinking eyes fixed and their faces set in a hardened, unreadable expression.

"Do you think you two can at least try and pretend to act a little human around me, please?" I complained. "It's a little off-putting eating breakfast with walking talking statues."

"Now, who's being rude," Darcy replied.

With a sudden burst of energy, she rose from her seat, her fingers gripping the table's edge as she leaned across, her eyes fixed on me with an intense gaze. In one swift motion, she reached out and seized a fistful of my shirt, yanking me forcefully towards her. I barely had time to react before she pulled me out of my chair, the force of her movements catching me by surprise.

Her eyes blazed with unbridled fury, a deep, angry crease forming between her brows as her expression twisted into a scowl. I could see the rage simmering within her, her face tightening with the intensity of her emotions as if her very features were on the verge of shattering.

"I should warn you," she spat. "Don't..."

Luke abruptly rose from his chair, the force shattering it into fragments scattered across the floor. His eyes burned with a furious intensity as he lunged across the narrow space, tackling Darcy and slamming her to the ground. The two grappled fiercely, their limbs entangled in a desperate struggle. Darcy tried to break free, but Luke's grip was relentless, his muscles straining with raw, unbridled aggression.

Her piercing screams of outrage and disbelief echoed through the room, causing me to instinctively clamp my hands over my ears in a desperate, childlike attempt to shield myself from the overwhelming sound. Erecting a mental barrier around myself, I slowly backed away towards the furthest wall, my eyes fixed on the chaotic scene unfolding before me as Luke and Darcy grappled in a fierce, unrelenting struggle.

He leaned in close, his breath hot against her ear as he whispered fervently, his voice so low it was almost lost in the stillness. I strained to catch even a fragment of their hushed exchange, but the words remained just out of reach, like shadows in the dark.

Then, without warning, their demeanours shifted. The air between them thickened with tension, crackling with the sudden surge of hostility. In an instant, they lunged toward each other, hands outstretched in a clash of wills.

Luke moved with a predatory speed, reaching her first. His fingers clamped down on her with a rough, unyielding grip, and with a surge of aggression, he shoved her hard. She careened into the wall with a sickening thud, the force of the impact sending her crumpling to the ground in a graceless heap. Her limbs tangled awkwardly as she landed, a dishevelled pile of shock and pain on the cold floor.

"I told you never to hurt her, Darcy," Luke seethed. "You made your promise to leave her be. What made you do that?" he hissed.

The room was filled with a foreboding hiss and deep growl, their menacing tones bouncing off the walls and permeating the atmosphere with unease. The sound was so powerful that it caused the fragile light fixtures to shake and the silverware to clatter noisily. Suddenly, without warning, the plates on the table crashed to the ground and broke into pieces, scattering in all directions.

As I stood with my back against the cold wall, a sudden rush of energy filled the room, swirling around me like elusive tendrils of smoke. In response, I instinctively raised my protective shield.

Taking a cue from the spell Matace had meticulously taught me, I delved into the realm of auras and emotions, allowing my senses to navigate the unseen currents surrounding us.

The scene before me unfolded like a vivid tapestry of raw emotions, each thread weaving a complex and tangled web of feelings. Luke, usually composed and calm, now simmered like a storm on the brink of eruption. His aura pulsed with fiery rage and confusion, a swirling mass of intense emotions barely contained beneath the surface.

In stark contrast, Darcy radiated a powerful energy that blazed with anger and jealousy. Her feelings toward Luke—and perhaps even toward me—poured out in waves, their heat rapidly accumulating in the room. The air between us crackled with tension, thick with the unspoken turmoil that hung heavy like a storm cloud.

The room had become a battleground of emotions, each one vying for dominance in an invisible dance of auras. The clash of conflicting energies created an atmosphere so dense it was almost suffocating, the weight of it pressing down on me as I stood at the centre of their silent war.

Caught in this web of simmering tension, I struggled to ignore the powerful feelings surging between them, trying vainly to push them back and restore a sense of calm. But the more I tried, the more the situation seemed to unravel. Amidst the chaos, Benjamin stood apart, his aura exuding a sense of amusement and tranquillity. Refusing to get drawn into the argument, he simply observed the unfolding drama with a detached, almost entertained expression.

The air crackled with the weight of unspoken words and unresolved issues, leaving me to navigate this intricate emotional landscape with great care and uncertainty.

"Stop!" Benjamin shouted above the din. "Come on now. We are all old friends with a new friend. What's this about?"

Luke's eyes widened in surprise as my protective shield flared, a shimmering barrier of raw energy glowing with undeniable power. He took a step back, his movements slow and cautious as he evaluated the strength of my defences. Frustration creased his features, his jaw tightening with barely contained anger.

Without speaking, Luke retreated to another seat, muttering under his breath about how Darcy would be responsible for the damage. His words were almost drowned out by the crackling energy surrounding me, but the tension in the air was unmistakable. It pressed down on us, thick and suffocating, a silent battle of wills brewing between us.

Luke's gaze remained sharp and calculating, his eyes locked on me as if searching for the slightest sign of weakness. He was waiting, watching for the moment I might relax and let the shield down. But I held firm, knowing there was no way I could lower my defences while Darcy's anger still radiated like a dark storm cloud in the room.

Darcy's features twisted in a mask of pure fury, her cheeks flushed and her eyes ablaze with anger as she rose to her feet. She stomped fiercely with each step across the room, echoing like a thunderclap. As she turned her gaze towards me, her eyes bore into my soul with a fiery intensity that threatened to consume me whole. Her jaw clenched so tightly I could see the muscles straining against her skin, a physical manifestation of the rage boiling within her.

In contrast, Luke stood nearby, and his expression was now calm and composed as he silently communicated with Darcy. His eyes conveyed a silent plea for her to back down and let go of our heavy hostility. His subtle gestures spoke volumes, urging her to leave me be and to defuse the tension that threatened to erupt into something far more volatile. It was a delicate dance of emotions, a silent struggle for control in the face of overwhelming anger.

I stood resolute, unwavering in the face of the vampire before me. The mere presence of the creature did not instil fear within me; instead, it fueled my determination. I knew the weaknesses and vulnerabilities of vampires, and I was confident in my ability to exploit them. The anticipation of the impending battle electrified the air around me, but I remained composed and centred. I was fully prepared to take on the undead creature, armed with knowledge and strategy, ready to confront her if she wanted this to happen.

"Seira," Luke said softly, disturbing my reverie. "Please sit down and finish what's left of your breakfast. Darcy, go outside and sort yourself out. This is no place for you to fight, and neither is it the right time with demons heading this way."

I settled into my seat, my eyes warily fixed on Darcy. Luke remained calm, his composure unwavering even as Darcy stormed out of the house, slamming the back door behind her. Benjamin, sensing the tension, quietly excused himself from the table.

His eyes met mine, gentle and kind, but the mischievous grin on his lips was unmistakable, hidden from Luke's view. I managed a few more breakfast bites before giving up entirely, suddenly losing my appetite. Luke remained silent, and I couldn't stand the silence any longer.

"When will they arrive?" I asked, breaking the silence. "I mean, how long do we have?"

Luke's intense gaze bore holes into my soul as he scrutinised every flicker of my expressions. It felt like he was peeling back layers of my mind, searching for clues to uncover the truth behind my emotions.

"I believe they're arriving sometime after six," he replied quietly. "I doubt you'll be here, though, will you?"

"Will you stop me if I decide to leave?"

"Depends," he relaxed backwards in his chair, tipping it so the front legs no longer touched the floor but remained balanced. "On whether you'll take me to whatever you're thinking about doing this time."

"I'm not thinking of anything," I answered, which was true enough; my mind had remained deliberately clear, no words had entered, and I tried desperately hard not to think about him. "Anyway," I sighed. "You don't want to be around me as much as I don't want to be around you. Clearly, we have feelings for each other that complicate the entire situation. We need space between us, and Darcy needs you."

His eyebrows rose, and his hands clasped the back of his head. "I seriously doubt even you don't believe we should be apart, nor do you have any idea about my feelings or thoughts on this situation," he said. "Not even your magical powers stretch that far, do they?"

He was the most infuriating individual I had ever encountered. I hated it when he answered my questions with another question or when he questioned my powers.

"Alright," I said, springing to my feet. "I'm going to follow Lilly. Now that she knows what we're up to, we must be careful. Something is missing in all of this, Luke," I said. "Don't you get that feeling as well?"

"Get what?" he asked, a small, tight smile playing around his mouth. "I don't understand what you're saying."

I stomped my foot in frustration and gritted my teeth. The case with Matace and Lilly was more complicated than it seemed. The Cerberus creatures were alive again, but they could be defeated easily. However, there was more to this mystery we hadn't figured out yet. The more I thought about it, the more I was sure there was a hidden layer to this mystery we hadn't uncovered.

The puzzle was a mystery to me, and I couldn't understand it. Only by following Lilly could I figure out what she really wanted.

We knew she wanted to take over the world and destroy everything we cared about. But I couldn't quite piece it all together, no matter how hard I tried. Her plans were big and scary. Each step she took made things more risky and uncertain. She was playing a dangerous game, leading us towards disaster.

I knew I had to act to uncover the truth before it was too late. But the puzzle pieces continued to elude me, taunting me with their complexity and the ever-shifting nature of Lilly's plans. The world hung in the balance, and I was running out of time to put the pieces together and stop her.

"There's something off; I can feel it," I said, my words laced with growing frustration, much to Luke's apparent amusement. "The pieces don't add up, not how we thought they did. She's hiding something, I'm sure of it." I took a deep breath, trying to control the rising tension in my voice. "This whole thing feels too neat, too perfect. There's more to the story, and I intend to find out what it is."

Chapter Eight

"What do you think she could be hiding?" he asked thoughtfully, "I mean," he shrugged, "what else is there that she can possibly want to hide?"

"I'm not sure," I answered. "But we have to follow her to find out."

I didn't wait for his response and hastily exited the room, the scraping of his chair echoing behind me as he got up from the table. To my relief, no footsteps followed, and I was thankful to avoid another confrontation with him.

The tension in the air had become suffocating, and I needed to escape before it threatened to consume me entirely. As I hurried down the hallway, my heart pounded in my chest, the adrenaline coursing through my veins. I couldn't bear arguing with him again, not when the wounds from our last argument still felt raw and unhealed.

"Seira," he called from the bottom of the stairs. "Don't go alone; wait for me, and I'll come with you. If only to make sure you are safe."

I didn't bother to turn around and face him. His words were laced with a soft yet ominous tone, a clear warning that I shouldn't leave without him.

Quickening, I hurried up the remaining stairs back to my room. I needed to change into my sneakers—for comfort and to be able to run if necessary. I couldn't shake the feeling of being watched, trapped in a web of his unwavering gaze. My heart raced as I contemplated my next move, knowing that defying him could have dire consequences.

A sudden thought flickered, and I almost immediately heard Luke's loud laughter.

"Oh, you can keep on listening, mister," I muttered, my voice laced with a subtle warning. The words slipped out, clear and deliberate, leaving no room for misunderstanding. "Trust me, it will only get worse from here."

His chuckle sent a wave of irritation through me. Undeterred, he whistled another cheerful tune, clearly revelling in my discomfort. It was as if he derived some twisted pleasure from antagonising me, determined to provoke the worst in me, even as my feelings for him continued to grow without my consent.

Gritting my teeth, I felt a surge of resolve to end his infuriating habit of effortlessly reading my thoughts. His nonchalant disregard for my emotions only fueled my determination to confront him and reclaim a sense of control over the situation.

"I'm ready," I shouted. "Hope that hurt your ears."

"On the contrary," he suddenly announced from behind me, causing me to jump with a startled yelp and hastily back away. "Sorry, I didn't mean to startle you," he said, extending his hands as if to steady me.

I expertly manoeuvred around them, dodging his grasp. A grin slowly spread across his face, reminiscent of the old, teasing Luke I remembered.

"I was going to say," he continued, the grin widening, "your shouting has no effect on me whatsoever. However, if you were to scream, let's say, in the throes of passion, I'm sure it would be absolutely deafening."

His words were filled with a strong suggestion, making me feel a shiver of fear. How he looked at me with intensity and a predatory gleam in his eyes made me feel uncomfortable. His bold and taunting comments made me feel trapped and cornered. I wanted to run away from the tense atmosphere that had built up between us.

"Pathetic," I scoffed, my eyes narrowing as I turned away, focusing on retying my shoelaces. "Your so-called passionate encounters hold no appeal for me." I paused, glaring at him over my shoulder. "And need I remind you, vampire and witch are not meant to mingle, let alone become romantically involved." My voice dripped with disdain. "We've already broken enough of the rules, and I have no intention of making any more mistakes, Luke. Not when the consequences could be dire."

"I won't tell if you won't tell," he replied, gently swinging me around so I stood face to face, looking directly into his eyes. "And besides, who will tell?"

I thought about his question for a while and suddenly realised the answer. I moved away from him gently, his hands slowly letting go of my waist. He looked amused, as if he had enjoyed seeing me move away from him and fight my feelings.

"I can assure you," I replied, my voice dripping with sarcasm. "It will be Darcy who tells if anything more than work happens between us. She's in love with you."

My words made him laugh. He tried hard to control himself but failed and eventually managed to stop laughing. Although he looked like he was holding back his laughter, his face twisted with amusement and a struggle to keep a straight face.

"I don't think so," he shook his head. "She has her own string of lovers. She doesn't date vampires; she's strictly a mortal's only kind of girl," he replied, wriggling his eyebrows at me dramatically.

I couldn't help but burst out laughing at his funny face. Luke always knew how to make any situation happier, no matter how sad. He was quick and charming and could easily change the mood of a conversation. His jokes and funny gestures always surprised me. Just when I was feeling down, he would say something funny or do something silly that made me feel better. It was like he had a unique power to vanish any bad mood and bring happiness instead.

I marvelled at his uncanny talent for reading the room and knowing exactly what to do or say to make me forget my worries and focus on the brighter side. All my troubles melted away then, replaced by the warm laughter Luke had so effortlessly evoked.

"You know," I smiled, "she does love you. She threatened me to keep away from you, telling me she has been after you for years and has gotten this close," I quickly mimicked her voice and snapped my fingers. "Only to have someone like me tear it all away."

Luke's expression changed again, showing a different side of himself. He had many different personalities, each unique and intriguing. The serious look on his face showed that he was not amused, but I could see anger simmering in his eyes.

His gaze intensified, his features becoming harder as the emotion inside him grew. It felt like a storm was brewing in him, hiding behind a calm exterior. The air around him felt dangerous, as if he dared anyone to challenge the darkness inside him. I could have kicked myself for mentioning what Darcy had said.

"She won't get away with threatening you under my roof," he answered darkly. "There's no way I will let her do that again."

"Hey," I shrugged quickly and collected my jacket. "It's not your fault. And like you said," I began to try to lighten the situation. "She likes mortals, not vampires, which counts you out, right? And anyway," I carried on in a rush. "You prefer mortals too, don't you?"

My big mouth spluttered the remainder of the sentence in a heated moment and backfired straight back at me when I realised what I had said.

"Oh no, Seira," he replied, his tone softened, "only one mortal who also happens to be a witch, in particular..."

Suddenly, Benjamin yelled for Luke to come downstairs right away. Luke ran out of the room at lightning speed while I struggled to keep up with his fast pace. My normal human steps couldn't keep up with his superhuman speed. Benjamin's tone of voice had made Luke move quickly as if he had a sudden surge of adrenaline, his steps seeming almost effortless as he ran up the stairs. In contrast, I struggled to keep up, moving slowly with heavy footsteps.

Benjamin shouted again, which echoed loudly, making Luke hurry with worry. I felt tense and anxious as I followed closely, my heart beating fast.

"What the hell is going on?" Luke shouted, his voice echoing through the halls. "Benjamin, you had better tell me quickly!" he demanded, his brow furrowed with impatience and a hint of concern.

The order scared me a lot, like a strict drill sergeant yelling at me. The tone was so powerful that it made me shake with fear. It wasn't a simple request – it was a strong demand for instant obedience. The words felt heavy and made me feel anxious. I felt like I had no control, like a new recruit facing a demanding boss.

"They're nearly here!" Benjamin yelled, his voice laced with urgency. "They'll arrive in about an hour," he added, his eyes fixed on the horizon.

Luke's expression turned blank as he hurried to join Benjamin by the window overlooking the hill behind his house. "Then we don't have any more time," he said, his jaw set with determination. "Go get Darcy, quickly!"

Benjamin nodded sharply and ran past Luke and me. Luke stood his ground, his gaze unwavering as he scanned the distance for any sign of the unwelcome visitors.

"We'll have to confront them together, but I really hope they'll come to their senses and not want to engage in battle here. There's no way I will let my home be destroyed without a fight."

As I looked out the window, I saw the mist getting thicker in the distance, which meant that the portals were used a lot. The air smelled bad, like rotten cheese, meaning demons were nearby. I was thankful that I didn't have that smell. The smell identified a demon and let witches know there were demons nearby.

"What do we do?" I asked.

"Quickly, raise your shield!" he commanded, his voice urgent and authoritative. "And Benjamin, don't just stand there staring – go fetch Darcy immediately. Where is she, for goodness sake?"

I hadn't heard him approach and jumped when I realised he was standing right behind me.

"She's been brooding ever since you handed her that humiliating defeat," he chuckled, the memory still fresh in his mind. "I'll go back and drag her out of her hiding spot right now."

Luke, looking serious, stood next to me. His eyes were fixed on the swirling mist, scanning it carefully. The portals were getting busy, and we needed Lilly to arrive soon. Tension filled the air, and I could sense the seriousness of the situation. Luke's jaw was tight, and his forehead was wrinkled, showing he knew our danger. The mist kept appearing and disappearing, reminding us of our unstable situation.

I shifted my weight, my muscles tense, ready to react at a moment's notice. The fate of everything hung in the balance, and I couldn't help but feel a sense of unease creeping up my spine. If Lilly showed up with those portals, it would be an all-out war, and I wasn't sure we were ready for it.

I took a step back, focusing intently. "Alright, I'm setting up my shield now," I said with determination.

"Excellent," he responded with a nod of approval. "But make sure you stay behind me when they arrive. I'm not sure if they intend to harm you or join us."

I didn't hesitate, my voice firm. "No, I'm standing on the front line. There's no way I'm hiding behind you."

A calm buzzing sound filled the air, and a shiny shield appeared around me. The bubble grew slowly, wrapping me in protection. There didn't seem to be any danger, so the shield stayed put, ensuring not to harm my friend Luke. Matace created these shields to keep witches safe. They could also learn and improve each time they were used. Unlike the spells we cast, these shields were meant to be a friend in times of danger, defending against any enemies that came near.

When the shield formed, it glowed softly, making me feel safe and calm. The humming got louder as the shield got stronger. It was a powerful and flexible defence, better than any spell I could have used.

A mischievous smile played on his lips as he teased, "Very nice." Darcy's heels clicking on the floor below caught his attention, and he turned away, saying, "I'll be right back."

His gaze lingered momentarily, his eyes sparkling with a hint of playfulness. The air was charged with a subtle tension as he made his way downstairs, his footsteps echoing in the silence. Darcy's presence had ignited a spark within him, and he seemed eager to speak to her before she joined us.

I sat firmly on the ledge by the window, my gaze fixed upon the once-vibrant sky. But now, it had been warped by a sinister force, transforming the once azure expanse into a bleak, dreary canvas. The sheer sight of it sent a chill down my spine, leaving me to wonder if the gloomy atmosphere was merely a figment of my imagination or a tangible manifestation of the dark magic that had descended upon the world.

The once-radiant sun had disappeared from the sky as if it, too, sensed the impending peril. The world outside had gone dark, shrouded in an ominous veil of uncertainty. Within the confines of this humble abode, we stood resolute. Our hearts steeled for the inevitable confrontation.

The air crackled with tension, and the shadows seemed to close in, taunting us with the unseen threat that lurked beyond the walls. Yet, we were undaunted, our determination unwavering. We were prepared to face whatever danger lay in wait, ready to defend our sanctuary with every fibre of our being.

The silence was deafening, broken only by the faint sounds of our own breathing as we waited with bated breath for the storm to arrive. We knew that the battle ahead would be fierce. Still, we were united, a band of steadfast companions, ready to stand our ground and fight for survival.

"Cut the crap, Darcy!" Luke's voice boomed with fury. "Why the hell did you threaten her? I've made it crystal clear a million times that there's no chance anything will ever happen between us!" he spat angrily.

"Luke," she said, her voice trembling with emotion. "I never intended to upset her. I was only trying to shield you because the last thing you need right now is to be entangled with a mortal witch. Why can't you just be with me? Why can't you see me as more than a friend?" Her words were laced with a desperate plea. The intensity of her feelings was evident, the longing in her voice undeniable. She wanted him to see her, choose her, love her in the way she loved him.

The question hung in the air, thick and unresolved. Suddenly, a loud thud echoed through the room, followed by the sharp crash of something colliding with the wall. Luke's voice rang out, laced with curses that shattered the tense silence.

"I don't need your protection, Darcy!" he shouted, his voice laced with frustration. "There is nothing between Seira and me. I'm her protector, and that's it. When will you learn to mind your own business? You're a guest in my house, just like she is, but she treats this place with respect while you take advantage of it every chance you get, ever since the day we met. Your life," he continued, his tone dangerously low and filled with anger, "has been nothing short of a mistake, both in your mortal existence and now in your immortal one. You refuse to study and make something of yourself, even though there are countless opportunities at the immortal schools designed to cater to the needs of all immortals, including vampires like you."

"But L-l-Luke," she cried out, her voice trembling with emotion. "I tried so hard; you know I did. Why won't you believe me?" Her words were laced with a desperate need for understanding, the hurt and disappointment on her face.

"Hah!" he spat out, his voice dripping with contempt. "One measly visit? That's hardly enough, don't you think?" His eyes narrowed as he continued, "And let's not forget how you spent that time - busy locking lips with the mortal teacher in the corner. Mind you, the one who was just there on work experience and was about to become a student witch." He leaned in, his expression darkening. "You really went and ruined his chances, didn't you? Alongside your own, I might add."

Years ago, I realised I had been adopted, and now Darcy was experiencing the same earth-shattering revelation. I couldn't help but feel a deep empathy for her—the struggle to find one's rightful place in the mortal or immortal world is a universal experience.

We all yearn for that perfect little niche, that snug and secure corner where we can comfortably belong. Darcy deserved my unwavering support and compassion as she embarked on this journey of self-discovery, determined to uncover her true identity and carve out her own unique space in the grand tapestry of existence.

"Luke!" I called out, echoing down the eerie, dimly lit corridor. "You need to come here. Now!"

I heard his irritated growl, followed by the thunderous pounding of his steps as he approached me. The onslaging mist outside had completely obscured the view from the window, leaving only the closest treetops visible. I knew even those would vanish from sight soon enough, swallowed by the relentless, blistering haze.

The demons surged forward, their ferocity and determination evident. Their hunger for domination had nearly been sated centuries ago. Still, mortals had intervened, forging their own paths and uncovering the secrets of magic to guide them. The past remained a hazy veil of truth, obscured by the demons' wrath and their recollections of slander, treachery, and guilt.

"What is it?" he asked as he reached my side, his gaze fixed out the window, unflinching, as if he had anticipated their approach.

"I have an idea," I hesitated, uncertain if he would be receptive. The plan was risky, the darkest journey I had ever considered.

With a deep breath, I steeled myself. I prepared to unveil my idea, knowing it could make the difference between triumph and utter devastation.

He cocked his head impatiently, his piercing gaze locking onto mine, demanding an answer. "Well?" His voice was sharp, his words tinged with impatience. "Are you going to tell me? We don't have all day."

I cleared my throat nervously and tried again, "Look, we should get out of here before they show up. I don't think they're coming for a friendly chat. The way they are marching towards us, they're clearly here for a fight." I didn't give him a chance to respond as I continued, "If we leave now and follow Lilly, it might buy us some time before she manages to catch up and kill us." My heart was racing, and I could feel the urgency in my voice. The situation was growing more dire by the second, and we needed to act fast to survive.

I waited with bated breath, but he remained silent, his gaze fixed beyond me towards the encroaching mist that had shrouded the small corridor and the window in the darkness. Despite the lights being on, the approaching demons cast a pall of darkness, their wrath fueled by a relentless vengeance against anyone who dared to reside within or work alongside their realm.

Sadly, that included Luke and me. The air grew heavy with a sense of dread, the atmosphere charged with the ominous presence of these malevolent entities. Their fury seemed to crackle and hiss like a raging storm about to break. I could feel the hairs on the back of my neck stand on end, and a shiver ran down my spine as the shadows seemed to close in, threatening to swallow us whole.

Rubbing his chin, he furrowed his brow and responded pensively, "Ah, I understand now. Let me think this through carefully..."

The thunderous pounding of feet shattered his sentence. The stairs trembled under the weight of the advancing horde. A mist enveloped Benjamin and a group of other vampires.

Benjamin emerged from the mist, leading a group of forty others. They moved close together, their eyes darting warily, taking in their surroundings. "Luke," Benjamin called out, his voice cutting through the eerie silence. The group followed closely behind him, their footsteps echoing in the thick, damp air. They seemed on edge, unsure of what lay ahead. Their senses heightened as they navigated the shroud of mist.

"What's going on here? Who are these people?" Luke acknowledged a few of them with a nod, which they returned. Gritting his teeth, he demanded, "Speak up, Benjamin. I'm waiting."

"They're here," he said, his voice laced with urgency. "The demons have come to fight, not just because Sierra pretended to be one of them, as you were told. They lied to us." His eyes narrowed, a determined glint in them. "I've brought my friends to help us fend them off, but their numbers are greater than anticipated," he explained. "Luke, you, me, and Darcy, we can't hold them all back alone. I have a witch friend who kindly used a spell to obscure us so we could use vampire speed to get here."

"Hmm, I understand. Thank you," Luke uttered, his gaze locking with mine. I dropped my shield just as he firmly grasped my upper arms. "We'll go with your plan and track her down, but you'd better be right about this." Turning to face Benjamin and the others, he continued. "You all stay here and hold them off until we return. We are going to track Lilly and find out what hold she has over those demons so we can stop them," he explained. "Good luck, my friends."

Luke sounded urgent and serious, making it clear the situation was serious. He held onto my arms tightly, showing that he believed in me. I could feel the seriousness of the task and sensed the tension building as Benjamin and the others got ready to confront the enemy. The action quickly intensified, with a sudden explosion causing me to fall into Luke's arms. He caught me and helped me regain my balance before letting go.

Darcy burst into the room, her eyes wide with alarm. "Luke!" she exclaimed, her voice tense and urgent. "Did you hear that? What was that noise?"

"That was their final ultimatum – surrender or face the consequences. You'll remain here with Benjamin and the others to fend them off. We're going to pursue Lilly and end this madness once and for all," he declared, his voice carrying a sense of urgency.

She turned towards the window, her brow furrowed with concern. "How exactly do you expect us to hold them off?" she muttered, her eyes scanning the horizon for any sign of the approaching threat.

A thick, swirling mist enveloped us, and the mysterious figures I had encountered before materialised once more. Their faces were shrouded in shadows, and their eyes burned with an otherworldly intensity. I knew that the Cronomiun had arrived.

"We're here, Seira," the female leader whispered beside me. "Tell us where you need us to be, and we'll be there."

I could feel the tense energy in the air as the Cronomiun's presence filled the room. I knew I had to make crucial decisions that could impact everything. There was no time to waste - I had to act fast.

"Stay right here," I said, turning to face her with a reassuring smile. "Help the others while we're gone. We'll be back as soon as possible," I added, my voice urgent and determined.

"How do you plan to venture forth?" she inquired, her voice laced with concern. "The portal passages are overrun with demons, their sinister presence lurking, ready to pounce on any who dare to cross their path," she warned, her gaze fixed upon me with a mixture of trepidation and urgency.

"Luke," I said, my gaze fixed on her captivating form. Her beauty was mesmerising even though her features, illuminated by the blazing fire, would be considered horrific in the mortal realm. To me, she was the most breathtaking creature I had ever laid eyes on, and her companions were no less enchanting.

He tapped his foot impatiently on the ground. "Well..." The smoke from the fire to the east drifted our way, filling the once-clean air and stealing the oxygen I needed to survive, replacing it with an intoxicating haze that invaded my lungs.

I coughed and continued, "I was going to say we'll have to use my tunnel. Matace helped me create a hidden passage; now, we must rely on it. I'm unsure if it will work for you since vampires have never tried it."

"There's only one way to find out," he said, his voice tinged with a hint of bravery. "But we need to hurry; they're almost here. A few more minutes, and we won't be able to escape without being caught."

I nodded, my heart pounding. Stepping away from the group, I focused my energy, swirling my hands and chanting the ancient words that would unlock the secret network of tunnels I had created. This was our only chance to slip away undetected.

The swirling dark vortex started to materialise, the captivating blue light pulsing in my palms as I moved my hands in gentle circular motions, steadily building energy until it coalesced into a substantial size. Just as I neared completion, a second warning shot struck the house, shaking me and causing me to stumble. My head collided with the wall, and I felt a trickle of blood run down my cheek.

Undeterred, I rose, determined to open the gateway and complete my journey. The passage now has a more immersive and intense tone, with more descriptive language to convey the visual and sensory details. The wording has been simplified, making the narrative more engaging and accessible. The meaning and overall sequence of events remain the same but with a heightened sense of drama and momentum.

The gaping, blackened mouth loomed before me, growing larger and more menacing with each passing moment. It swirled and churned, a vortex of darkness beckoning me to enter its depths. The witch within me stirred, her cries for freedom echoing in my mind, urging me to join the magical unknown.

The enormity of the shadowy maw filled my vision, its sheer size and the depth of its darkness captivating me. I stood transfixed, torn between trepidation and the overwhelming desire to embrace the unknown, to let the witch break free and revel in the magic that awaited me. The moment felt pregnant with possibility, the air thick with anticipation, as if the fabric of reality hung in the balance, waiting for me to choose.

With shoulders hunched, Luke stepped beside me and grasped my hand tightly. We bid farewell to the others with one final, lingering glance. Their voices raised in a chorus of well-wishes as they braced themselves to hold off the approaching evil. The apparitions had finally descended, smothering the house with their malevolent presence.

Shadows seemed to cling to the walls, and an oppressive chill filled the air as if the very essence of darkness had taken hold of the place. We could feel their malicious intentions seeping into the fabric of the building, an aura of dread and foreboding that made the hairs on the back of our necks stand on end.

Reluctantly, we turned and hurried away, our only hope being that our companions would have the strength and resolve to withstand the onslaught of these ghastly, otherworldly forces. Their struggle weighed heavily on our hearts, but we knew we had to escape, lest we, too, be consumed by the ravenous, spectral horde.

"Hurry up, Seira!" Luke barked, shoving me forcefully from behind. His grip on my arm tightened as he pushed me harder, leaving no room for hesitation. "Get in there, now," he demanded, his voice laced with a threatening edge that sent a shiver down my spine.

I lurched forward, my heart pounding, and reached out, grasping frantically for his hand. Our fingers intertwined as I pulled him inside, my grip tight and desperate, determined not to let him slip away.

Spinning out of control, Luke and I hurtled into the pitch-black abyss of the vortex tunnel before us. I desperately clung to his hand as his face flashed in and out of view, the dizzying journey feeling like it would never end. Our destination was

Matace's house – where we knew we could spy on Lilly and implement our plan.

"Luke!" I cried out, my voice trembling with panic. "We're spiralling out of control, falling into the unknown!" I gripped his arm tightly, my knuckles turning white. "We should have landed by now. I don't know how much longer I can hold on. Can you... can you hang on if I let go?"

My heart pounded as the world spun around us in a dizzying blur. The air rushed past, deafening in its roar. I could feel the terror coursing through my veins, making my hands shake uncontrollably.

"Forget everything else and just do what you need to do right now!" he yelled urgently, his voice laced with desperation. "There's no time to waste, so move it!"

With a deep breath, I withdrew my hand from his and extended my palms outward, focusing intently as I summoned the full force of my powers to my fingertips. The swirling vortex all around us crackled with energy.

Still, I could feel the protective barrier closing in, shielding the tunnel from outside interference. It was a trap to keep witches like myself safe from harm until we reached our intended destination. The magic surrounding us was unyielding, blocking any attempts at breaking through. This comprehensive entrapment would ensure our safe passage.

I steeled my nerves, feeling the raw power coursing through me as I maintained the delicate balance to navigate this treacherous portal. The slightest misstep could have catastrophic consequences, but I refused to falter. With unwavering determination, I pressed forward, guiding us deeper into the swirling vortex, my focus never wavering for an instant.

"This is so frustrating!" I cried out in exasperation, my voice laced with desperation. The task at hand had me completely stumped, and I felt a wave of helplessness wash over me as I stared at the uncooperative device or system in front of me. The words tumbled out of my mouth, dripping with annoyance and disbelief, as I struggled to understand what had gone wrong. The sheer sense of failure and the growing realisation that I couldn't find a solution only fueled my agitation, causing me to let out a frustrated exclamation that echoed through the passage.

Relentlessly, I battled against the overwhelming force, pushing back with every ounce of my inner strength, even as my mortal body grew weaker. My stubborn determination refused to waver, and slowly, the dim light at the end of the chaotic maelstrom grew larger and brighter. The swirling vortex tossed us around mercilessly, like clothes tumbling in a frenzied washing machine, fighting to keep us trapped at the bottom of Matace's yard.

But I refused to give in, driven by an unwavering will to break free and reach that elusive opening we desperately needed. The intensity of the struggle was palpable, every muscle strained, every nerve on edge, as I poured everything I had into this desperate bid for escape. The roar of the vortex filled my ears, and the dizzying swirl of motion threatened to overwhelm me. Still, I pressed on, driven by an unbreakable resolve to emerge from this maelstrom and find the path to safety.

The luminous intensity surged without any prior notice, propelling us out of the vortex at a startling velocity. Alarm gripped me as I somersaulted through the air, careening towards the ground. With a sudden impact, I found myself perched atop a sturdy tree branch, my bottom pointing skyward, the rough bark of the trunk pressed against my back. The unexpected landing left me disoriented, my senses reeling from the rapid transition.

"Ow!" I hissed through gritted teeth, desperately trying to regain my balance and get a proper view of my surroundings. "Luke," I breathed out, my voice barely above a whisper, a sense of urgency and concern lacing my words.

He had vanished completely, and not even a single sound could be heard, which wasn't surprising. The vampire's steps were as silent as the grave, honed over centuries of hunting. This unnerving trait had not diminished over time, leaving me on edge, frantically groping around to find my way down.

There was no other option but to take a leap of faith. Summoning the last of my strength, I felt my body become weightless, as if floating on air. The breeze gently lifted me from the tree, and I rotated slowly, desperate to glimpse Luke. I had to be extra cautious lest the Cerberus spot me.

The thick, impenetrable darkness made it nearly impossible to distinguish any distinct shapes. Yet, the foul, putrid stench of the three-headed beast was unmistakable, closing in on me rapidly. Its fierce, guttural growls, echoing through the shadows, sent a shiver of pure terror down my spine. I feared the worst - that Luke had already fallen victim to the monstrous creature's deadly grasp.

"Luke!" I called out, my voice echoing through the eerie darkness. My heart pounded as I strained to hear any sign of him, any indication that he was still out there, trapped within the swirling vortex. The uncertainty weighed heavily upon me. I couldn't help but worry that his vampiric nature had not been enough to protect him from the vortex's ravenous grip.

Panic began to creep in as the silence stretched on, interrupted only by the faint howling of the wind. I clutched my hands into tight fists, nails digging into my palms. Where was he? Had the vortex consumed him completely, leaving no trace behind? The thought sent a chill down my spine, fueling my determination to find him, no matter the cost.

"Luke, please..." I pleaded, my voice cracking with emotion. "Where are you? Answer me!" I needed to know he was still out there, fighting to return to me. The uncertainty was maddening, and I couldn't bear losing him to the darkness.

I was met with complete silence, as if the world had been muted. Puzzlingly, he had vanished without a trace. Slowly, I lowered myself down, my feet gently caressing the soft blades of grass. Gradually, my entire body descended, and I felt the familiar weight of my form return, replacing the weightless sensation that had enveloped me during the ascent. The transition was seamless, and I found myself grounded once more, my senses heightened and my awareness sharper than before.

"This can't be happening," I said, my heart pounding with fear for Luke's safety. "Where the hell is he? I've got to find him, fast." My eyes frantically searched every corner of the dimly lit room. The deafening silence only heightened my sense of dread. I couldn't shake the feeling that something terrible had happened to him. I had to act quickly before it was too late.

"Must you keep referring to me as 'hell' all the time?" he asked with a mischievous grin, his eyes sparkling with a hint of playfulness as he stood behind me. "I mean, I know vampires are often associated with the underworld and are supposed to be as wicked as the depths of hell itself." He cocked his head slightly, his tone becoming more lighthearted. "But I'd like to think I've proven myself to be quite different from that stereotype, don't you agree?"

I gave him a forceful shove on the shoulder, first for ignoring my questions and then again for nearly giving me a heart attack. The impact sent him stumbling back a few steps, his eyes wide with surprise and alarm. I glared at him, my heart pounding, fuming at his blatant disregard for my concerns and how he had suddenly materialised, startling me.

"It actually worked!" I exclaimed, my voice laced with disbelief and excitement. You're here with me, on the other side of the witch's portal!" I looked around in awe, taking in the unfamiliar surroundings, the air thick with a sense of otherworldly magic. The realisation of our successful passage through the mystical gateway filled me with wonder and trepidation as we now found ourselves in uncharted territory, unsure of what challenges might lie ahead.

"I'm right here, staring you down," he retorted sarcastically, a mischievous glint in his eyes. "Can you believe no one's thought of this before?" he scoffed, a wry smile tugging at the corners of his mouth. His words dripped with amusement. The tension in the room thickened as he relished the moment, waiting to see how they would react to his bold, provocative statement.

Before I could respond, the thundering sound of paws against the ground drew near. Instinctively, we scrambled into the dense thicket of overgrown thistles beside us. The sharp thorns sank into my skin, tearing it away and drawing more blood. My head continued to ooze slowly from the earlier impact, the pain pulsing with each heartbeat. The situation had become increasingly intense. I knew we needed to find a way to escape quickly before the approaching threat caught up.

"You're bleeding," Luke said in a low, tense voice, his gaze fixed on the Cerberus beast prowling ahead of us. "I can smell it. If I can smell it, that thing can too." He nodded towards the creature, which had lifted its three heads, its many eyes narrowing menacingly as it caught our scent.

The Cerberus snarled, the deep, guttural sound sending a shiver down my spine. All three heads were now focused on our location, the beast having detected the scent of fresh blood. Its massive paws thundered against the ground as it started to stalk towards us, its jaws parting to reveal rows of razor-sharp teeth.

"Damn it!" I cursed under my breath, quickly covering the injury on my arm with my free hand. I frantically cast the healing spell, hoping it would take effect quickly. The searing pain was unbearable, but I couldn't afford to waste any time. "This spell better work fast," I growled, my brow furrowed with determination as I waited anxiously for the magic to take hold.

"We don't have a second to spare," Luke whispered urgently, his voice laced with urgency. "We need to keep moving until you're fully healed, and that creature can't pick up our scent anymore." His eyes darted around the dimly lit surroundings, constantly scanning for signs of danger. The air was tense as we quickened our pace, our footsteps echoing in the eerie silence. The need to escape was consuming, driving us forward relentlessly. "Stay close to me," Luke commanded, gripping my arm firmly. "We can't afford to be separated. We have to keep going, no matter what."

His words were laced with a sense of desperation, underscoring the gravity of the situation. The thought of the creature catching our trail sent a chill down my spine, and I knew we had to move with haste if we wanted to survive.

"Screw this, let's just take the fight to that thing," I urged, my voice laced with determination. "We can't keep running forever. We need to end this, once and for all." My hands clenched into fists as the adrenaline coursed through my body, the anticipation of the coming battle evident. "It's time we stopped playing the victim and showed that bastard who's in charge around here."

"Shut it!" he barked, his voice laced with irritation. "For once, just listen to me without your know-it-all attitude. Is that too much to ask?" His brow furrowed, and his eyes narrowed as he glared at me, clearly fed up with my tendency to argue back. The sharpness in his tone made it clear he was in no mood for discussion - he wanted me to listen and comply without question.

Gritting my teeth, I grabbed the man and slapped him hard, my hand still clutching the wound where the blood gushed freely. Thistles had slashed my skin, and the crimson liquid spilt onto the ground, dripping steadily. The Cerberus caught the scent of the blood. It reared up on its hind legs, its eyes glinting with a feral intensity I had never witnessed before nor even believed possible.

It lunged forward with a speed that took my breath away, its jaws snapping viciously.

The ancient records housed at the realm's central archives revealed a startling truth about these enigmatic creatures. Burdened by their immense size and the peculiar addition of a triple-headed physique, they were clearly not built for swift movement. This anatomical compromise significantly impacted their speed, rendering them lumbering, slow-paced entities, easily captured and contained.

As I observed the creature's movements, it was evident that some magical enchantment had been cast upon it. Most likely the work of the powerful sorcerer, Lilly, the creature's actions were unnaturally swift, belying its natural sluggish nature. This sudden burst of speed and agility hinted at the potent magical forces at play, transforming the creature into a formidable yet captivating sight.

I tightened my grip on Luke's arm, my heart pounding urgently. "It's here," I warned in a hushed but frantic tone. "We have to fight this one, no matter what."

The ominous presence loomed closer, and I could feel the weight of the situation bearing down on us. We had to be ready, every muscle tensed, eyes scanning the darkness for any sign of the impending threat. This was no time for hesitation – we had to meet this challenge head-on and give it everything we had.

He let out a deep, weary sigh. "If we fight this one, he'll summon the rest of them, and all hell will break loose right here, right now," he said with a sense of dread and resignation. The thought of facing the entire group filled him with a growing sense of unease, and he knew they had to tread carefully to avoid an all-out confrontation that could spiral out of control.

"Hmm..." I shrugged, my brow furrowing in confusion as I struggled to grasp the meaning behind his words. The uncertainty in his tone left me feeling a little lost. I searched his face for any additional clues that might help me understand what he was trying to convey. With a slight tilt of my head, I waited patiently for him to elaborate, my curiosity piqued, but my comprehension still elusive.

"'So," he said, mocking my voice with a condescending tone, his eyes narrowing. "We can't take on all of them. There's just the two of us against a whole group - about a dozen, I'd say. Doesn't exactly seem like a fair fight, does it?" He laughed harshly, shaking his head as he studied me, his expression mixed with amusement and disdain.

The way he mimicked my voice, his arrogance, and his look down on me made my blood boil. I clenched my fists, every muscle in my body tensing up, as I glared back at him, ready to show him how wrong he was.

Anger boiled at Luke's condescending tone, but I swallowed it and forced a smile. I nodded in reluctant acceptance, knowing he was right. With more than a dozen of them and Lilly's spells and mischief awaiting us inside, our chances were slim to none. Attempting to confront them would only alert Lilly, allowing her to flee and complete her sinister plan uninterrupted. The bitter taste of defeat lingered on my tongue, but I knew we had to bide our time and find a smarter way to stop her.

The massive Cerberus beast collapsed beside me, its three pairs of intense eyes locked onto mine, and its powerful jaws panted heavily. Sensing my presence, the creature suddenly sprang to its feet, towering over me.

It assumed a menacing fighting stance, its massive paws angrily pawing the ground and kicking up a billowing cloud of dust and dirt. Panic surged through me, and I felt Luke's hands firmly pushing me backwards, urging me to retreat as the enraged Cerberus growled and prepared to attack.

The beast's guttural roar sent shivers down his spine, but he refused to back down. With adrenaline, he launched onto the creature's broad back, his hands desperately grasping the thick, pulsing neck. The beast thrashed and bucked, but he held on, his muscles straining against the sheer power of the creature.

Luke's trembling fingers desperately rummaged through the animal's thick, coarse fur, frantically searching for a heartbeat. I lay there, sprawled in a disorganised heap, observing him bravely confront the terrifying creature. The air was tense as he risked his safety to subdue the vicious beast.

"Seira!" he barked, his voice laced with irritation. "I could really use your help here, you know," he demanded, his brow furrowing with frustration as he glared at me, silently urging me to come to his aid.

I charged towards the beast, my eyes narrowed with determination. In one swift motion, I launched myself, soaring through the air and latching onto its hind legs. I yanked the creature down with every ounce of strength, sending it crashing. Its limbs buckled under the force of my weight and its own inability to withstand the assault. The beast let out an anguished whimper as it hit the Earth with a resounding thud, trapping my legs beneath its massive form.

"Get off me!" I grunted, pushing against his heavy frame with all my might. The sharp pain in my side intensified as I struggled to free myself from his crushing grip. My muscles strained, adrenaline coursing through me as I desperately tried to shove him away.

As I observed, one of the creatures' heads swivelled toward me, its jaws gaping and snapping with a relentless determination to strike. It was driven by an unwavering instinct to survive and protect its master, even at the cost of its own life. These deadly animals were rarely documented to have been defeated. Still, Lilly possessed the power to summon their life force back to the Earth, using them as her defenders.

"Seira," Luke gasped, "Come over here and grab anything sharp you can find. Or, if you're able, use your magic to deal with this threat."

"There's no magical solution to end a living being," I cried out, desperately evading the massive, snapping jaws and the guttural growls that were hurled at me with each of its menacing attacks. "That's dark sorcery, and I only wield the power of white magic. I thought you were aware of that," I pleaded.

"Figures," he groaned in exasperation. "What the hell are you doing?" he demanded, his voice dripping with frustration.

Frustration boiled within me as his impatient tone grated on my nerves. I gritted my teeth, glaring at him. "Can't you see I'm filing my nails? What did you think I was doing, just sitting around?" I snapped, the irritation dripping from my words.

He laughed harshly and joylessly as he frantically grappled like a cowboy at a rodeo. His arms flailed about, pulling in all directions, and his bottom was violently tossed around, slamming back down onto its neck with a sickening thud.

I fought against the relentless grip of the weight of the body on top of me, desperately trying to break free. The thick, viscous substance clung to me, its slimy tendrils wrapping around my body, weighing me down. The sticky wetness seeped into my hair, dripping down my neck and shoulders, refusing to let go. The unforgiving goop seemed to merge with my very being, trapping me in its unyielding embrace.

"Coming," I hurried forward, my breath in short gasps. The third head swivelled towards me, its lips peeled back in a menacing snarl, revealing a maw filled with jagged, razor-sharp teeth. I edged closer, the gap between us barely an inch wide. I had to move cautiously or risk becoming this beast's next meal.

I could feel my heart pounding in my chest as I steeled my nerves and pressed on, determined not to let this creature's savage display deter me from my goal.

In desperation, I frantically scanned the area, desperately searching for a sharp object. Without hesitation, I reached out and slapped myself sharply, berating my foolishness. Suddenly, I realised the solution was right at my fingertips. Determined, I summoned the dagger belonging to one of the greatest witches of all time, Mathelda Gravely.

Before her reign, a lineage of influential leaders had left their indelible mark on the realm, each contributing unique spells and unwavering goodness to our hallowed circle. Now, with the legendary dagger in hand, I felt a surge of strength and purpose course through me, ready to face whatever challenges lay ahead.

Determined, I lunged towards the beast's neck, where Luke's hand still gripped. Gritting my teeth, I plunged the dagger into the thick, vulnerable folds of skin, seeking the vital life source within. The blade sliced through the flesh with ease, a wet, sickening sound accompanying its descent. Luke watched intently as the neck twisted and convulsed, the creature's struggle for survival growing weaker with each passing moment.

A final, agonising gasp escaped its lips, and then the head came crashing down, thundering against the ground. Without hesitation, Luke jumped down, shaking the dirt from his trousers and wiping his hands clean on the front of his shirt. The deed was done, and grim satisfaction settled over him.

"Ah, I see you've finally finished the task," he remarked, a hint of satisfaction in his voice. His expression shifted as he saw me, his brows furrowing in concern. What happened to you? You look like you've been swallowed and spat back out again!" he exclaimed, his eyes scanning me from head to toe.

"No way!" I exclaimed, my voice tinged with a hint of exasperation. "I was the one pinned down, trapped beneath its massive limbs as it droned on and on, relentlessly weighing me down." I could still feel the weight of the creature's legs pressing against me, the sensation of being helplessly immobilised as it continued its endless monologue.

A wide grin spread as he uttered, "Nice." His eyes lit up with genuine enthusiasm, and the corners of his mouth turned upward, creating a look of pure delight. The simple yet impactful response conveyed his genuine appreciation and excitement about whatever had just occurred.

The putrid odour of the beast was suffocating, making it difficult to breathe. As we hurried away, I quickly cast a spell to mask the scent, ensuring the other members of the deathly circle would not be alerted to our escape. The fragrance of nothing now pervaded the air, effectively concealing the absence of our lost comrade from their senses.

The creature's looming presence faded with each step, and the oppressive atmosphere lifted. We had narrowly evaded the clutches of another beast, and our only focus now was putting as much distance as possible between us and the incident scene. The intensity of the encounter had left us shaken. Still, the successful application of my spell provided a glimmer of relief in our hasty retreat.

"What's our next move?" Luke's voice echoed with urgency as he grasped my arm, pulling me down into the cover of another dense hedge. How can we be sure she's here?" His words carried a note of desperation, the need for a plan evident in how he searched my eyes for answers.

The environment felt alive, the rustling of leaves and the occasional snap of a twig heightening our senses. We were in a high-stakes game, and the stakes had never been higher.

"Trust me," I said, a confident grin spreading. "She's in there, I can feel it. The power radiating from within is overwhelming - it's no wonder I felt so strange earlier. Matace told me that when a witch expels a massive surge of magical energy all at once, it can cause others in the area to experience a sense of discomfort, even nausea, to a degree.

I could practically taste the raw magic in the air, an electric current that made the hairs on the back of my neck stand on end. The power was palpable and undeniable—a tangible force that seemed to linger and press around us.

Whatever was happening inside those walls, it was clear that an incredible amount of arcane energy was being unleashed. My pulse quickened with trepidation and excitement. We were standing on the precipice of something monumental; I could feel it in my bones. Whatever lay beyond that door, we were about to bear witness to it. Taking a steadying breath, I steeled my nerves and moved to push the portal open, ready to confront the source of this overwhelming magical disturbance.

"Hmm, I see," he murmured, his brow furrowing as he contemplated the situation. "This magic you've just wielded – could it potentially alert her to your presence here?" His voice carried an underlying note of concern, the weight of the implications evident in his words.

I firmly shook my head, refusing the offer. My eyes were laser-focused, scanning the horizon for any sign of a portal opening or the slightest movement from within the ominous house. The air crackled with tension, and I knew I couldn't let my guard down—not even for a second. Every nerve was on edge, my senses sharpened and primed to respond at the slightest hint of danger. The stakes were perilously high, and I remained vigilant, my gaze steady and focused as I scoured my surroundings for any clue that might lead me to my objective.

"No," I answered, "It wasn't enough for anyone to trace the location or the source. The magic I used was relatively small compared to other spells I could have used."

We moved stealthily alongside the house, keeping our bodies parallel to the towering walls. The Cerberus were noisily devouring their meal, their jaws snapping and crunching through the bones with a sickening sound. Shuddering, I felt a deep sense of revulsion at the sight of the grisly remains being consumed by these monstrous creatures. I couldn't even tell if the morsels were the remnants of an animal or something far more sinister – and given my growing distrust of Lilly, I didn't want to know.

"Look," my companion whispered, nudging me and nodding towards the house. In the dim light, I could see Lilly moving quickly but gracefully down the corridor inside, her movements marked by a sense of urgency. "Where is she going?" he asked, his voice laced with suspicion.

"I'm not sure," I responded, considering the layout of the building in my mind. "The library is that way, but I don't see any other obvious destinations."

He let out a snort of derision. "I highly doubt she's there to read anything of substance." He paused, brow furrowing. "Are you absolutely certain there's nowhere else she could be heading?"

"No, I haven't seen anything unusual," I said, my voice laced with uncertainty. "Unless, of course, there's something hidden by magic that we can't see." I peered intently at the object, my brow furrowed as I searched for any sign of the extraordinary.

"Oh, fantastic!" he retorted with heavy sarcasm, his voice dripping with frustration. "Not only do we have a deranged witch on our hands, but now there's also this mysterious hidden area that we know absolutely nothing about. Who knows what sinister plans she's brewing up in there?" he continued, his words laced with dread and apprehension.

"We're so close now, I can practically feel it," I said, pinching my thumb and finger together for emphasis. "Just outside, ready to see what she's up to. We can watch her without her ever knowing we're here." My heart raced with anticipation, the thrill of the hunt coursing me. This was our chance to uncover the truth, to finally get the answers we'd been seeking. I couldn't take my eyes off the building ahead, every muscle tense, poised to spring into action at the first sign of movement.

He watched intently as Lilly glided gracefully down the dimly lit corridor, her dress billowing behind her. Her hair was perfectly coiffed, yet her eyes held a dark, unsettling gaze that belied a sinister nature.

A malevolence surrounded her, darkened by her own consuming hatred and the allure of the dark magic that enveloped her. Unaware of its insidious grip, the magic steadily ensnared her soul, drawing her ever closer to the fiery pits of the underworld. The evil witches and those condemned to death by the kingdom reigned supreme in this realm.

Chapter Nine

"So, do we just sit here and wait?" Luke asked, settling down to watch for a while longer.

"No," I said. "We go inside. We have to see what she's up to, or we won't stand a chance of doing anything even remotely good."

"Are you serious?" he gasped, watching me closely, his eyes screwed up into slits; he was trying to figure out if I was joking or being serious.

"I'm dead serious," I said in a low, unwavering tone as I stealthily crept out from the thick hedge towards the towering, ancient wall.

My heart pounded with adrenaline as I cautiously scanned the area, alert for any signs of movement or potential threats. Every step was calculated, and my body tensed and was ready to react at the slightest provocation. The weight of the situation hung heavy in the air, underscoring the gravity of what lay ahead.

The Cerberus, the fearsome three-headed hounds, were engaged in a ravenous frenzy over their meal. Their heads snorted and guzzled down the food, each fighting viciously against the others in a desperate attempt to claim dominance over the territory of their shared feast.

Seeing the intensity of their struggle, we pressed ourselves tightly against the wall, flattening our bodies as we cautiously made our way towards the other side of the house. Our hearts raced, wondering if we could find a safe entry point to access the interior without drawing the attention of the savage beasts.

As we cautiously made our way to the back of the house, I was struck with anticipation. To my surprise, there stood a small, unassuming door - an entrance that promised access to the unknown. Whether it would lead us directly to Lilly's whereabouts, I couldn't say for sure.

But this was our chance, our opportunity to uncover the truth finally. With a deep breath, we approached the door, ready to face whatever lay beyond. The possibilities swirled in my mind, fueling my determination to see this through. We had come this far, and the mystery was about to unfold.

"Come on, this way!" I said urgently, grabbing his sleeve and pulling him towards the door. "I bet we can get in through here. Do you think you can pick the lock?" My heart raced with anticipation as I eyed the door, searching for any signs of a vulnerable entry point. The stakes were high, and I knew we needed to move quickly to pull this off.

"There's no way I can pick a lock. It's not something they teach in vampire school," he replied dryly. "I can, however, kick it in."

He looked at it and measured its size. The solidness of the door ignited ideas inside my head about ways we could discreetly get through it. The light above the door held my curiosity for a while longer; it was an alarm mechanism I hadn't encountered before. Matace hadn't told me about any alarms he'd placed around the house, so I supposed it was new.

"Luke," I said, my voice urgent as I pointed at the blinking alarm panel. "That's an alarm system. We'll need to disable it first, or she'll know we're inside." My heart raced, the adrenaline coursing through my veins. Time was of the essence, and I couldn't afford any mistakes. I glanced around, taking in the details of the room, searching for the best way to approach the situation without alerting our target.

"Look, I'm no professional thief or anything," he said, his voice laced with uncertainty. "I have no idea how we're supposed to disable that alarm system. This is completely new territory for me."

The tension in the air was thick as he spoke, the gravity of their situation weighing heavily on his mind. He knew they were walking a fine line, and any misstep could have dire consequences. But he was determined to see this through, even if it meant stepping out of his comfort zone and trying something he'd never done before.

"Get ready!" I exclaimed, my voice brimming with excitement. Swiftly, I gathered the necessary tools, their metallic edges gleaming under the bright light. With a confident grin, I presented them, eager to put them to work and show Luke some of my skills.

As I was growing up with my adoptive parents, one of my friends was a shady character. He had a troubling past and often spoke to me about the ways he would locate the homes of the wealthy so he could steal their valuables and sell them to support his younger siblings.

Listening to his stories, I felt a deep sense of pity for my friend. I could feel his desperation and helplessness, knowing he had to resort to risky and unethical means just to put food on the table for his family.

At the time, I didn't have the powerful magical abilities I possess now. All I could do was listen and offer what little comfort and compassion I could muster. The weight of his struggles bore heavily on my heart, and I wished I could have done more to help him and his family escape their dire circumstances.

Each tale I had been exposed to was meticulously crafted, delving into the intricate details of disabling alarms even before I reached my twelfth birthday. I had a huge advantage if I harboured any ambitions of becoming a burglar. Equipped with the knowledge to effortlessly get into any home and navigate through the shadows the way he'd shown me.

"Do you have experience disabling alarms? I'm guessing they don't exactly teach that at witch school, right?" he chuckled as he helped boost me up to the alarm panel.

His grin was mischievous, and a glint of excitement danced in his eyes, hinting at the thrill of this illicit endeavour. I took a deep breath, feeling the adrenaline going through my veins. This was it – the moment we'd been planning for. With his assistance, I reached up and carefully examined the alarm, searching for the correct wires to disconnect.

I carefully removed the sharp tools between my clenched teeth, trying not to lose focus. Bracing myself against the sturdy wall, I felt Luke's reassuring grip clasped together, forming a secure platform to stand on. His steadfast support gave me the confidence to push forward and reach my goals, no matter how daunting they seemed.

"I didn't get the chance to attend that fancy witch school like the rest of them," I grumbled, my voice dripping with bitterness. "Back home with my so-called parents - or should I say, my adoptive parents," I quickly clarified, "I knew all sorts of shady characters. Probably half of them are rotting in jail by now, but let me tell you, they sure taught me a thing or two about their dirty little tricks." I paused, the corner of my mouth twitching in a sardonic smile. "They even offered me a spot in their criminal gangs, but I politely told them to shove it. I wanted no part in their illegal stuff."

"Oh," He chuckled deeply, his voice rumbling through the room as he swayed me gently. I instinctively reached out, my fingers clinging to the wall to steady myself against his playful movements. The man's laughter had a deeper, more captivating quality to it. The way he moved me, almost like testing my balance, created a playful tension. I had to react quickly, grabbing the wall to keep my footing, heightening the engaging nature of the moment.

"Quit with the laughing and focus on keeping me steady, would you?" I hissed through gritted teeth, my frustration mounting. "This is not an easy task, in case you haven't noticed." My voice dripped with annoyance as I struggled to maintain my balance; every muscle tensed with the effort. The situation was far from amusing, and I wished Luke would take it more seriously.

He froze in place, his grin unwavering, and I glanced down to see him winking up at me. With swift, practised motions, my hands worked rhythmically, reaching for the wires nestled beneath and behind the alarm box. I sliced through them cautiously, severing the connection and plunging the light into darkness, the glass enclosure remaining unbroken.

"Almost there," I said, hurriedly shifting the box and lowering it to Luke. He snatched it up deftly, cradling it in his arms while maintaining a firm grip on my legs. "There, I'm done," I announced, satisfaction evident. "Now we can head inside, but we'll need to be extra careful to keep the noise to a minimum. If we creep, we should be able to slip in undetected."

"Me, make noise?" he replied, "I'll show you how quiet vampires can be."

As we traded lighthearted banter, it provided a much-needed buffer against the looming seriousness of the situation and the uncertainty ahead. It was almost uncanny that I could manually disable the alarm without resorting to supernatural abilities.

After all, I had been raised entirely in the mortal world, where magic was nothing more than a figment of imagination. It was purely by chance that I discovered the truth about my identity and the extraordinary powers that lay dormant within me.

An overwhelming and startling revelation, shattering the already bleak and gloomy state of my life - a secret I had meticulously concealed from my parents for their own peace of mind. If they had known the truth, it would have sent them spiralling into a state of anxiety and distress.

Despite the lessons I had absorbed in school and the countless shady individuals I had encountered along the way, I always felt a strange, unshakable sense of belonging to something far greater. It was as though I were connected to a deeper purpose that continually eluded my understanding. I couldn't quite grasp it, yet the feeling was always there—persistent and insistent, as if whispering from the edges of my consciousness.

This elusive connection seemed to transcend my everyday experiences, hinting at a reality beyond what I could see or touch. The uncertainty only heightened its intensity, making it feel like I was reaching out to grasp the edges of a vast tapestry that refused to reveal its full pattern to me.

It was a constant undercurrent in my life, a nagging sensation that there was more to my existence than what was immediately apparent. This feeling of being tethered to something indefinable yet vitally important fueled my curiosity, driving me to explore the hidden depths of my existence. I was always searching, always striving to uncover the elusive truth that lingered just out of reach, like a distant star on the horizon of my soul.

"Are you ready?" he breathed, his voice barely above a whisper. His eyes gleamed with a mixture of anticipation and concern. "I thought you would use your magic to disable the alarm. What happened?" he asked, his brow furrowing with curiosity.

"I was born and raised in the ordinary, non-magical world," I said as I crouched on the floor, "And I've picked up a few tricks along the way. The spell I'd need to disable that barrier and let us through would be far more powerful than simply summoning some tools to help. She would have sensed it in an instant."

My voice carried a sense of urgency and slight apprehension. The barrier before us was a formidable obstacle that required careful consideration. I knew the risks of bypassing it, but the need to press forward was palpable.

The contrast between my mundane upbringing and the extraordinary nature of our current predicament was stark. I had been thrust into this world of magic, and now I had to rely on my wits and limited knowledge to navigate these uncharted waters. The weight of the situation was heavy, but I was determined to find a way through, no matter the cost.

"So summoning items isn't a powerful spell then?"

"No," I shook my head firmly, "It's a simple spell that witches use frequently when they can't be bothered to wait. We try to blend into the mortal world as best we can without relying on magic, just like vampires do."

He chuckled softly and tucked a stray strand of hair behind my ear, his touch sending a shiver down my spine. "I see," he mused, his eyes gleaming with curiosity. "Are you ready for us to head inside then?"

His words were laced with a subtle, alluring charm, and I found myself drawn to him, captivated by the intensity of his gaze. The air between us crackled with an undeniable tension, and I knew that stepping inside with him would only deepen the connection we were forging. Nevertheless, I steeled myself, determined to maintain my composure and keep our relationship on a professional footing, at least for now.

"Yes," I said hastily, my gaze on the Cerberus. Their thunderous snores echoed through the cavernous space between us, sending shivers down my spine. "Hurry, please," I urged, my voice laced with urgency.

With their three massive heads resting atop their muscular bodies, the Cerberus lay sprawled out before us, their slumber seemingly oblivious to the pressing matter. Their snores, a deep and rumbling symphony, filled the hollow expanse, making my heart race with anticipation.

Satisfied with my remark, he swiftly but resolutely kicked the door. He relentlessly repeated the forceful action until the latch inside gave way under the relentless pounding. Determined to gain entry, his blows grew more intense, the sound of the door rattling against the frame echoing through the space. His face was set in a focused expression, brow furrowed as he continued his assault on the barrier separating him from his goal. Each impact reverberated, the lock steadily weakening with each strike until, finally, the catch gave way, the door swinging open to grant him access.

"Nicely done!" I exclaimed, a hint of pride in my voice. "You managed to open the door without shattering it this time." I couldn't help but recall the previous incident when the door had been left in pieces, and a sense of relief washed over me that we had avoided a repeat of that debacle.

"I have my own unique purpose and value," he retorted sharply, a subtle intensity lacing his words. His gaze bore into me, unwavering, as if challenging me to understand the depth and significance of his role. The conviction in his voice was unmistakable, leaving no room for doubt or dismissal. It was a bold and unapologetic statement, a declaration of his worth and the integral part he played in the grand scheme of things.

He strode into the corridor, his gaze unwavering as he scrutinised the dimly lit passageway ahead. There were no other doors or side paths—this was the sole entrance and exit, the only way in and the only way out. His heart raced, his senses on high alert, as he prepared for whatever lay beyond. The air was thick with tension, and he gripped his weapon tightly, ready to confront any potential danger that might await them.

"I can't hear a single sound coming from within," he whispered nervously, his brow furrowed with concern. "It's as if the place is completely empty, like there's no one there at all." His voice trailed off, the eerie silence unsettling him. He pressed his ear against the door, straining to catch even the faintest hint of movement or activity. Still, the deafening stillness was all-consuming, leaving him with a growing sense of unease.

"She's still inside," I responded, my voice laced with urgency. "I would have felt the telltale vibrations if she tried to escape through any arcane portals." My senses were on high alert, scanning the area for the slightest disturbance. The air seemed to crackle with an unseen energy, and I knew she could make her move at any moment.

"It's pitch-black everywhere!" I can barely see my own hand in front of my face. The oppressive darkness is suffocating, enveloping me like a thick, heavy blanket. I strain my eyes, desperately trying to make out any semblance of light, but it's all just an inky, endless void. The shadows are closing in, making me feel trapped and disoriented. "When is this infernal darkness going to end?"

"When a witch turns wicked," I faltered, "the shadows coil around her, like vines wrapping their tendrils, ready to drag her soul into the abyss of damnation. The scorching flames of her malevolence will inevitably consume her, devouring her essence and life until she ceases to exist."

Luke halted and pivoted towards me, a gentle smile tugging at the corners of his mouth. His piercing gaze locked onto mine, scrutinising me intently as if he could see directly into the depths of my soul. The intensity of his eyes captivated me, drawing me in and making it impossible to look away.

"Exactly how much time did you devote to your studies?" The question was laced with a hint of curiosity and urgency. His eyes narrowed slightly as he leaned in, eager to uncover the details of his academic diligence.

Matace was an exceptional teacher who had me diligently studying every day. I was utterly perplexed as to why. "Why?" I asked, my brow furrowed in confusion.

Luke gently reached out and tenderly stroked my cheek, a small smile on his lips. "Because," he said, his voice soft and captivating, "you just recited a passage from one of the most historically significant books, word for word. That demonstrates an incredible grasp of the details you've absorbed through your studies. I'm truly impressed."

My heart raced with a flutter, pounding fiercely against my chest. I took a deep breath, willing to slow down as I gradually pulled myself out of his enchanting spell. Sensing my resolute determination, he retreated, backing away cautiously. Without another word, he continued his stride down the dimly lit corridor, leaving me to regain my composure.

The door at the opposite end stood unlocked, a silent invitation into the heart of the house. No one was guarding this section, leaving us with a clear path forward. The layout was straightforward, a simple arrangement of corridors that posed little obstacle should Lilly have any protectors waiting within, determined to safeguard her and her life.

The lack of security filled us with unease, and the eeriness of the silent hallways heightened our senses. Yet, this was our chance, the moment we had been waiting for. We had to move quickly, anticipating potential threats emerging from the shadows, ready to confront them head-on if necessary. Lilly's safety depended on our swift and decisive action.

"This way!" I whispered urgently, grabbing Luke's arm as he started to head in the wrong direction. "Trust me, I know the layout of this place."

Without waiting for a response, I took the lead, moving with cat-like stealth around the house. Every step was deliberate, every breath controlled, as I navigated the silent, empty rooms. My senses are on high alert for any sign of danger. I couldn't afford to make a single mistake – our lives depended on it.

Luke remained vigilant, his grip tightening on my upper arm as the slightest sound echoed through the darkness.

My eyes strained to adjust, and my feet cautiously navigated the familiar furniture, knowing Lilly would have been hard-pressed to rearrange any of it without our notice. Luke's heightened senses kept us on high alert. Every creak, every shifting shadow, sent a jolt of adrenaline through my body. I held my breath, my heart pounding in my ears, as Luke's unwavering focus guided us through the unseen dangers.

"Should we go to where she is?" I urged him, my voice laced with a sense of urgency. The situation felt tense, and I couldn't shake the feeling that time was of the essence. I needed his response, and I needed it now.

"Got any other bright ideas?" he growled, his voice dripping with menace as he leaned in closer, his hot breath tickling my ear. "Or were you thinking of taking a closer look at the rooms, see if there's anything worth swiping?" His eyes gleamed with a dangerous spark, daring me to make a move.

"How in the world did you find out about that?" I asked, my eyes narrowing with suspicion. My voice had a sharp, demanding edge, signalling that I would not take any evasive answers. "I thought I had kept that information under the tightest lock and key. So, tell me, what do you know, and how did you uncover it?"

He was recounting my previous encounters with the cunning thieves and the captivating demonstrations of their crafty techniques. The memory of those secretive meetings lingered vividly, igniting a sense of intrigue and fascination within me.

The thieves had skillfully unveiled the inner workings of their trade, leaving me both awed and unsettled by the sheer dexterity they possessed. Their stealthy movements and ingenious methods left an indelible mark, stirring my mind with curiosity and unease.

"I can see right into your thoughts," he said casually, a faint smile on his lips. "I'm relieved you've resisted the temptation to join those dark forces. It means your spirit has remained pure and untainted by the corrupting influence of evil." His piercing gaze held mine, conveying a sense of profound understanding and approval.

"That's absolutely true," I snapped, frustration seeping into my tone. "But how has that knowledge actually helped me in any meaningful way?" I threw my hands up in exasperation, my mind racing with the situation's futility. "It's all good to have the facts, but what good are they if I can't apply them to make a real difference?" I shook my head, my jaw clenched as I searched for a solution that seemed increasingly out of reach.

"More than you know."

With a firm grip, he seized my arm. He yanked me forward, leading me swiftly towards where he had spotted Lilly entering. As we hurried through the larger room, unease crept up my spine. To our utter bewilderment, the room was completely empty, and Lilly was nowhere to be found.

"Where the hell did she go?" he exclaimed, his eyes widening in bewilderment. He scanned the room frantically, his heart racing as he tried to make sense of her sudden disappearance. His brow furrowed, and a sense of urgency gripped him, propelling him to search every corner, desperate to uncover her whereabouts.

"I have an idea."

He watched me intently, his eyes narrowing as he noticed my hands start to move. Sensing the impending magic, he instinctively stepped back, his body tensing in anticipation. I knew I had to be cautious, so I carefully conjured the weakest spell I could recall, my palms beginning to glow softly in the darkness.

I couldn't risk arousing Lilly's suspicions – the magic had to be subtle, barely noticeable, yet powerful enough to achieve my goal. My heart pounded as I focused on the task, the faint illumination casting an ethereal light across the room. I had to be precise, leaving no room for error lest I jeopardise the entire operation.

The swirling vortex tore from my grasp, a whirlwind of energy scouring the room. It sought out any hidden dimensions, concealed chambers cloaked in magical obscurity, determined to uncover their elusive locations.

The parallel vortex ripped free from my hands, a twisting, roiling torrent of power that swept across the room. It quested relentlessly, hunting for any trace of another dimension, any secret chambers shrouded in arcane obfuscation, driven to pierce the veil and expose their hidden whereabouts.

"What is that thing?" he whispered beside me, his eyes fixed on the mysterious object with curiosity and unease. He leaned in closer, his body tense as if ready to spring into action at the slightest provocation. The air around us seemed to crackle with anticipation, and I could feel the hairs on the back of my neck stand on end.

"This is a parallel dimension," I responded, my eyes meticulously scanning the anomaly before me. I carefully guided it, preventing it from careening around in confusion. "It's seeking out anything dimensional or hidden in this world - anything that can be consumed by the unseen magical forces at work here."

The energy of the parallel realm was palpable, a pulsing, otherworldly presence that seemed to hum with ancient power. I could feel the hairs on the back of my neck standing on end as I observed its restless movements, searching, probing for a way to breach our reality.

"Is it a powerful spell?" The words were laced with a sense of wonder and a hint of apprehension. The sheer power radiating from the enchantment was palpable, sending shivers down the observer's spine. The air crackled with an electric energy, hinting at the immense potency of the mystical incantation.

"Nah," I let out a low, amused chuckle, "This is pretty flimsy, so it won't really throw her off," I quickly added, "She's actively looking for anything out of the ordinary. And if that's the case, we're in deep trouble - she'll spot us in a heartbeat. But for now, we're in the clear."

The relentless vortex hunter halted abruptly, its senses on high alert. Hesitant yet determined, it tugged at me, urging me to return to the spot where it detected something unusual. The intensity of its movements conveyed a palpable sense of unease, as if it had stumbled upon a disturbance in the fabric of the parallel world. With growing anticipation, I allowed the vortex hunter to guide me, my curiosity piqued by the prospect of uncovering a hidden mystery.

As I focused, I could feel the intense, otherworldly energy emanating from the room's far end. The spell's protective veil had not been strong enough to shield it from the weakest of my incantations, which took me by surprise and filled me with a sense of unease.

The power radiating from that corner was like a tangible force pressing against my senses. It was as if the air had been charged with primal, untamed magic, crackling with an undercurrent of danger. I found myself captivated by the raw, untamed nature of this energy. Yet, it also filled me with a growing sense of trepidation.

What could be the source of such potent and unrefined magic? And why had my own spell breached the protective barrier with such ease? These questions weighed heavily on my mind, fueling a growing sense of unease and the desire to delve deeper into this mysterious phenomenon.

Lilly's magic had been a constant in her life, a reliable force that guided her every step. But lately, something seemed off. Had she become careless in her craft, or was she orchestrating a clever test, waiting for someone to uncover the truth? The uncertainty hung thick in the air, a challenge that demanded to be met.

I channelled the powerful parallel vortex, its swirling energy enveloping me as I stepped through the spell. The arcane energies crackled and hissed, the very fabric of the enchantment unravelling before my eyes. With a sharp intake of breath, I watched as the spell dissolved into nothingness, dissipating into the air around us. Behind me, I heard Luke's astonished gasp, his eyes wide with wonder at the display of magical prowess.

"Where the hell did it go?" Luke asked, his eyes frantically scanning the room.

"I've sent it ahead to see for us," I said, calm yet tinged with anticipation. "It will return shortly, bringing us news and images of whatever lies hidden behind that cryptic enchantment." I paused, my gaze fixed on the horizon, eagerly awaiting the scout's arrival. The air was thick with a sense of suspense, as if the world held its breath, waiting to unveil its secrets.

"Hmm," he muttered, his brow furrowing with suspicion. "Do you think she's playing us for fools?" The edge in his voice betrayed his growing unease as he considered the possibility that they were being led astray by the woman's deceptive actions.

"To be honest, I have no idea," I responded, a sense of unease creeping into my voice. "It's highly unusual for a witch to open the back doors, exposing the weakest of spells. I'm not taking any risks here - not a single one." My brow furrowed as I spoke, my eyes scanning the area with heightened vigilance. The situation felt off, and I couldn't let my guard down for a second.

The hunter burst back into sight, spinning and twirling with a frenzied energy. Suddenly, they landed right in the palm of my hand. I closed my eyes, feeling a rush of anticipation as I plunged headfirst into the captivating, enchanted realm hidden behind the spell.

A sense of unease washed over me as I stepped into the room. The air was thick with an unsettling stillness, and the disarray around me only heightened the tension. Lilly stood in the centre of it all, her back turned to me, her hands moving with mechanical precision on an item perched on the table.

There was an eerie detachment to her movements, as if she were disconnected from the world around her. The darkness seemed to cling to her, slowly enveloping her, yet she remained oblivious to its insidious presence. A palpable unease had replaced the normalcy that once defined this space. This silent foreboding crept into the fabric of the room.

Gratitude surged through me as I whispered, 'Thank you.' With a decisive gesture, I released the swirling vortex, allowing it to return to its rightful place. The task was complete, and our venture had been secured on the opposite side of the room.

"We need to find a way in and fast! The clock is ticking, and our mission is on the line. Tell me, what's our plan of attack?"

"Quickly, follow me down this path!" I urged, my voice laced with urgency. My eyes narrowed, scanning the area as I gestured decisively towards the narrow, winding trail ahead. "This way, hurry!" I added, my tone leaving no room for hesitation as I began swiftly walking along the route, beckoning him to keep pace.

I grasped his hand firmly and guided him to the secluded corner, where we vanished from sight within the concealed chambers. The unnerving darkness persisted, enveloping us with a palpable sense of unease. The feeling of anxiety rippled through me, consuming my senses.

"Where is she?" Luke whispered, his voice laced with a tone of desperation.

I urgently shushed him, my finger pressed firmly against my lips. We needed to be as quiet as possible lest we alert Lilly to our presence. Whatever she was up to, we had to see it ourselves to ensure we could intervene. The anticipation was palpable, and I could feel my heart pounding as we crept closer, desperate to glimpse Lilly's mysterious activities.

We crouched behind a pile of crates, their musty odour assaulting our senses. The stench was sickening, a nauseating blend of rotting flesh and other indescribable scents that made my stomach churn.

I clamped a hand over my mouth and nose, desperately trying to muffle any sound that might give away our hiding spot. The air was thick and heavy, with an overwhelming stench that threatened to engulf us at any moment. Lilly was consumed by the darkness and hadn't noticed our presence.

Luke gently pulled me closer, his arm draped around my shoulders, and discreetly gestured for me to stay silent. Lilly was so intensely focused, her brow furrowed in concentration, that she remained oblivious to the peculiar blend of witch and vampire scents swirling around her. The unfamiliar, almost palpable aroma would have instantly alerted any attentive witch to the presence of something extraordinary. This supernatural mixture should have set off alarm bells.

"Oh, no," she blurted out, frustration evident in her voice. Slamming her fists against the cold, metal table, she shook her head in disbelief. The object wobbled and clanged against the sides, echoing her growing irritation. Her brow furrowed, and her expression darkened, conveying a sense of utter disappointment in herself.

I couldn't believe my eyes as a human hand, dripping with blood, suddenly fell from the table and swung limply on the floor. The pool of crimson liquid rapidly spread, engulfing the woman's feet. Still, she remained utterly oblivious, her focus entirely consumed by the work she desperately tried to complete.

The sight was horrifying, the severed hand twitching and the blood gushing out in alarming quantities. Yet the woman paid no notice, her features contorted with intense concentration as she remained locked in her task, seemingly immune to the gruesome scene unfolding around her. The contrast between her calm, determined expression and the shocking violence of the situation created an unsettling atmosphere.

She shuffled her feet nervously, moving slightly to her left, giving us a clear view of the table and the ominous object she was working on. I gasped involuntarily, and Lilly turned sharply. Her shrewd eyes darted around the room, a flicker of anger flashing in their depths.

To my horror, I no longer recognised my friend, the once-revered leader of the realm. She had been consumed by a greed that had slowly frozen her heart, transforming her into a shell of her former self, lost to all within the realm. The only way to free her from this evil was through her imminent demise.

The image before me was truly horrific – a half-formed creature, a twisted amalgamation of human and inhuman features. The humanised head was shrouded in a tangled mass of hair, while the hands resembled a human's. Still, the rest of the body was a grotesque mash-up of unrecognisable parts, haphazardly assembled into a singularly disturbing form.

"Oh no," she muttered, her voice barely above a whisper - starkly contrasting her usual confident tone. "I've messed it up again. These stupid instructions are so confusing!" She stared down at the task before her, her brow furrowed in frustration as she tried to decipher the steps again.

Fuming frustrated, she crumpled the paper in her fist and hurled it forcefully across the room. The paper sailed through the air, a testament to the raw emotion bubbling within her. Her temper flared, ignited by her inability to accomplish a task that had eluded her.

We watched in tense silence as she opened a shimmering portal, the gateway to a realm beyond our reach. She stepped through the swirling vortex with a determined stride, vanishing from our sight. At that moment, she had safely harboured her ideas and the plan she had hoped to develop, leaving us to wonder what lay on the other side.

"Hurry!" I exclaimed urgently, grasping Luke's hand and pulling him forward as I hastily opened another portal to match Lilly's. "We have to go through it right away!" My heart raced with urgency and dread.

The situation was dire, and we needed to act fast. I tugged Luke along, my grip tight, as I flung the portal open. The shimmering, unstable gateway beckoned us to step through without delay.

His gaze frantically swept across the room, a growing sense of dread etched on his face. "What is this place?" he muttered, his voice laced with bewilderment and fear.

I froze mid-action, my hands still stretched out, desperately trying to maintain the portal's opening, leading us to Lilly's location. In my brief moments, I surveyed the atrocious scene before me. Lifeless bodies were strewn about the room, their vacant eyes staring back at me, silently pleading for me to uncover the secrets Lilly had been guarding.

The sheer revulsion I felt was nothing compared to Luke's reaction. He recoiled in horror, stumbling backwards and colliding with me with an inhuman force. The impact sent me reeling sideways as I struggled to maintain my balance and the portal's integrity.

"Agh!" I hissed through clenched teeth, wincing as I gently prodded the tender, swollen skin on my throbbing leg. "What happened?" I asked, my voice laced with concern as I examined the angry, reddish-purple bruise blossoming across my limb.

Panic surged as I frantically sat up, desperately grasping the closing portal, determined not to lose the crucial information I had just obtained. Suddenly, he seized me, whipping me around and obstructing my view, preventing me from seeing anything further.

My heart pounded with a mix of fear and adrenaline as I struggled against his unyielding grip; my senses heightened, desperate to catch a glimpse of what lay beyond the portal before it vanished altogether.

"Keep your eyes forward," he commanded, his voice laced with urgency. "We need to catch up to her now!" He quickened his pace, his eyes laser-focused on the retreating figure in the distance. The situation demanded swift action, and he couldn't afford any distractions. Determination was etched across his features as he pushed forward, driven by an overwhelming need to overtake their target before it was too late.

Despite his smile, an unsettling chill ran down my spine. His grin was forced and unnatural, conveying an unspoken message: "You really don't want to see what I've just witnessed." If I had more time, I would have pushed past him to investigate the matter myself. Still, the heavy vibrations of the dissipating portal were weighing heavily on the energy I was pouring into it to keep it alive.

"Come on," I replied, mustering a brave smile in return, though a sense of dread lingered in the air.

Together, we ventured into the unknown, crossing the boundaries of parallel worlds and entering a realm I had always dreaded. It was a land where the evil demons reigned supreme, their malevolent hearts orchestrating a sinister plot that threatened both the realm and the very existence of the human race.

The air was thick with a palpable sense of dread, and the ground seemed to tremble beneath our feet as we navigated this treacherous landscape. The demons, with their twisted forms and piercing cries, seemed to lurk in every shadow, their malicious intentions burning in their soulless eyes.

The fabric of reality seemed to warp and distort, leaving us disoriented and vulnerable. Yet, with a deep breath and a steely resolve, we pressed on, determined to confront the darkness that had taken hold of this realm and restore the cruelly disrupted balance.

"Ugh, I despise this wretched place," I muttered, shuddering as I peered through the eerie, glowing portal. The air felt thick and oppressive, sending a chill down my spine. "I can't believe she had the nerve to come here, of all places." My heart raced with dread and disbelief, the weight of the situation settling heavily on my shoulders. The portal seemed to beckon, a tantalising yet ominous invitation to enter this twisted, foreboding realm.

"Is this what I think it is?"

I solemnly nodded and stepped into the crisp yet hazy atmosphere. "Yes, it is indeed," I replied, a sombre tone in my voice. "The atrocities committed by those sent here are truly abhorrent and vile. This desolate place is their punishment - a life of exile, forever banished from the comforts of the world they once knew, forced to endure the company of their fellow outcasts, with no hope of ever returning to the Earth they once called home."

The words hung heavily in the air, the weight of their meaning palpable. I couldn't help but feel a deep sense of unease, a visceral understanding of the profound suffering endured by those condemned to this isolated, forsaken realm. The misty landscape seemed to mirror the bleakness of their existence, a constant reminder of the high price they had paid for their transgressions.

"It's well chosen," he said, looking around him, "Why is the air so misty?"

When I flipped through the picture books from the realm, I couldn't help but notice how they had portrayed the exiled world in a rather sunshiny and idyllic manner. The realm's depiction didn't match the harsh realities faced by the exiled ones. It was as if they wanted to present the outside world as a refreshing escape rather than the bleak and hopeless place it was.

"I'm not sure, but it looks like some kind of dark magic," I said, my voice laced with uncertainty and a hint of trepidation. The air around us seemed to crackle with an unseen energy, and a chill ran down my spine as I stared at the strange, otherworldly phenomenon before us. "It's like nothing I've ever seen before. We must be cautious – this could be a powerful, dangerous spell."

He jabbed me sharply with his elbow, a smug grin on his face. "Well, what are you waiting for?" he said as I turned to face him, my eyebrows arched in response. His tone was taunting, his expression a challenge. "Go on, take a look," he pressed, his eyes gleaming with a hint of mischief.

I stretched out my hands, searching the air for the familiar thrumming of magic. The force I encountered was immense, far beyond my abilities. It slammed me backwards, slamming my body against a tree and sending me crashing to the ground. The spell had been fortified, locked down against other witches.

There was no way to trace its origins, no way for me to counter the curse that had been unleashed upon the world. The power pulsed through the air, oppressive and unforgiving. I lay there, stunned, feeling the weight of this unknown magic pressing down on me, sapping my strength. Whatever had been set in motion was beyond my control, and I knew I had to act quickly before it consumed everything in its path.

"Seira!" he shouted, his voice laced with urgency as he hurried towards me. His eyes were wide with concern, and he reached out, grasping my arms firmly yet gently. "Are you okay?" he asked, his brow furrowed with worry.

"Absolutely," I breathed, trembling with awe and caution. The current had been jarring, a powerful surge that sent shivers down my spine. "Tracing the spell would be far too risky for both of us. Let's not even bother trying." I paused, searching his face, hoping he would understand the gravity of the situation. "Can you bear with the mist for a little while longer?" I pleaded, my eyes imploring him to agree.

He chuckled, a low, reassuring sound that put me at ease. He gently helped me sit up, his strong arms cradling my body as I leaned against him. The warmth of his presence was a welcome comfort in the hazy, uncertain atmosphere.

"Of course," he chuckled, a mischievous grin spreading across his face as he shook with laughter. "I'll do whatever it takes to get us out of this place as soon as possible. This whole area just gives me the chills - it's unsettling being here." He shuddered visibly, glancing around the eerie, dimly lit surroundings.

"Now," I said, my voice dripping with sarcasm, "Are you really sure it's this world and not that you've finally realised how much of a vampire you truly are that's haunting you?"

He froze, his eyes boring into mine with an expression I couldn't decipher. As much as I tried to untangle my feelings for him, they only seemed to grow more complex the more time we spent together. It was a thrilling yet confusing predicament we both knew was forbidden.

We could never make it work, and that harsh reality hung heavy between us. The tension between us crackled like electricity. I watched him closely, waiting for his response, my heart pounding. This was a delicate dance, one mistake, and everything could come crashing down around us.

My mouth felt like sandpaper as I licked my lips anxiously. "Luke," I said, trembling, "We need to leave. Now."

I sprang to my feet, hastily brushing off the grime and debris clinging to my body. It was a futile effort, as the other filth I had amassed clung stubbornly to my clothes. I looked more akin to a feral creature dwelling in the desolate streets than the witch I was meant to portray.

"Come on," he urged, his voice firm yet laced with concern. Gently, he took hold of my arm, guiding me forward, his touch a steady anchor amidst the turmoil of my wavering steps. I felt the resistance in my body, a silent protest, but without a word, he released me, falling into stride by my side. The air between us grew thick with unspoken questions. "Do you think she's meeting someone?" he asked, his gaze cutting sideways, searching my face for any flicker of insight or emotion.

"I have no idea," I responded bluntly, the uncertainty weighing heavily on my words. "But of one thing, I am certain," I continued, a grave tone seeping into my voice. "Her soul has already been consumed by the shadows, trapping her in a downward spiral that no amount of magic can undo. The darkness has taken hold, consuming her heart and dragging it deep into the fiery pits of damnation. At this point, her fate is all but sealed – she is beyond saving, her path leading ever further into the abyss."

"Hmm, I see," he murmured, his brow furrowing in deep contemplation. His gaze sharpened, piercing through the uncertainties as he leaned forward, his voice tinged with urgency. "Now, tell me, where exactly did she go?"

"This way!" I exclaimed, my voice laced with urgency. I couldn't help but notice the faint shimmer of the portal silently trailing behind her, a ghostly presence that seemed to cling to her every move. "The portal has followed her, most likely on her command.

It's as if tethered to her, unwilling or unable to disappear like ours just did."

Luke's eyes narrowed, and his brow furrowed with curiosity and apprehension. The air seemed to crackle with unspoken tension as if this lingering portal had subtly warped the very fabric of reality. He couldn't shake the feeling that there was more to this than met the eye, that this was just the beginning of a complex and potentially perilous journey.

As he followed me, Luke couldn't help but glance over his shoulder, his senses heightened, ever vigilant for any sudden shifts or changes in the ethereal landscape surrounding them. I felt slightly safer knowing he remained as vigilant as he was so I could use spells and magic with any disruptions.

My trained eyes, honed by Matace's meticulous instruction, meticulously followed her portal's swirling, misty aftermath. The ethereal tendrils danced and trailed in her wake, awaiting their following command.

In contrast, Lilly's approach to magic had become increasingly sloppy, while with each incantation, my own skills grew stronger. It was almost unnerving to realise I was surpassing the abilities of one I had once considered my superior.

"Are we nearly there?" my companion whispered behind me, his gaze darting nervously around the overgrown, unforgiving terrain.

The world had been meticulously crafted, born from the twisted demands of the damned demons banished to this realm of exile. Every nuance, every detail had been painstakingly considered to ensure their suffering would be minimised, their comfort prioritised.

It was a world designed to cater to the very beings who had committed the most heinous acts. This twisted irony defied all notions of justice. Yet, in this domain of the damned, there was an underlying principle that refused to bend – no one, not even the most vile of creatures, would be forced to endure torment. It was a bizarre and unsettling reality, a world where the wicked were treated with compassion that seemed to mock the concept of retribution.

The overgrown area was a menacing labyrinth of thorn-laced bushes and gnarled, twisted trees, the perfect lair for the slithering demons of the underworld. Their bodies seamlessly integrated with the surrounding nature, blending in like a chameleon, allowing them to shapeshift and conceal themselves from potential predators effortlessly.

The thick, tangled vegetation cast eerie shadows, creating a suffocating, sinister atmosphere that instilled a sense of dread and unease. One could almost feel the presence of the malevolent entities lurking within, their piercing eyes watching and their sharp talons poised to strike at the slightest provocation. The area exuded an aura of pure malevolence, a testament to the unholy forces claiming it as their domain.

A deep, rumbling voice suddenly echoed across the space, freezing us in our tracks. "What is someone from the realm doing here?" it demanded, the words booming and reverberating around us, laced with a palpable sense of authority and suspicion.

The voice's origin remained elusive as it reverberated from every direction, surrounding us in a bone-chilling cacophony. Its deep, bellowing timbre filled the void, evoking a sense of unnerving power that belied the apparent gentleness of its tone.

However, this fleeting impression was quickly shattered by the sheer severity of the ominous world we had stumbled into, a realm that exuded a palpable aura of dread and uncertainty.

"Who are you?" I shouted. The air thickened with unspoken tension as if everything around us held its breath, waiting for a response. My heart raced, my palms grew sweaty, and a shiver ran down my spine. I felt exposed and vulnerable at this moment, as if the stranger could see straight through my soul's depths.

Luke tensed his muscles, his body poised and coiled like a predatory feline, ready to spring into action at the slightest provocation. His piercing gaze scanned the shadows, searching for any sign of the unseen threat that had prompted his instinctive, vampire-like defensive stance.

The air felt charged with an electric tension, as if the atmosphere was bracing for the impending clash. Luke's senses were heightened, his reflexes honed to a razor's edge, and he was prepared to react with lightning-fast precision against whatever dark force dared to challenge him.

"Cease your resistance, for I harbour no ill intent towards you," the entity said, its voice resonating with a soothing yet commanding tone. "I pose no threat and seek only to engage in peaceful discourse."

A blinding, otherworldly light suddenly materialised before our eyes, its radiance pulsating and swirling erratically. The luminous apparition then hovered in midair, gradually coalescing into the distinct form of a human figure.

"My name is Ahmed," he said, his voice carrying a subtle confidence that immediately commanded attention. He cocked his head slightly, his piercing gaze studying me intently, a hint of curiosity dancing in his eyes. "And you must be," he paused, the corners of his lips curling into a subtle smile, "Seira."

My heart raced, adrenaline coursing through my veins as I gasped in shock, the realisation striking me like a lightning bolt. This creature, this entity of pure darkness, knew my name – the same Ahmed who had been banished for his demonic intrusions, his malevolent acts tearing apart the very fabric of mortal lives, transforming them into crazed murderers and perpetrators of unimaginable crimes, condemned by the unyielding laws of the mortal realm.

"Ahmed," I said, trembling with fear and trepidation yet laced with a hint of cautious kindness. "How... how is this possible? It's been so long, far too long, since we last crossed paths." I steeled myself, bracing for the inevitable confrontation, for the malicious intent that I knew lurked within this ancient being.

"I know," he exclaimed, a mischievous grin spreading across his face. "I'm doing just peachy!" His eyes sparkled with a hint of intrigue as he leaned in closer. "You see, I'm quite the connoisseur of the latest happenings around these parts. Whenever a new face graces our realm, I get the juiciest tidbits of information." He chuckled, his voice dripping with a playful sense of superiority. "Ah, yes, I remember when you were still finding your footing here. Watching the newcomers navigate this world is always such a delightful source of entertainment for me."

"I remember you, though the memory is a faint echo in the recesses of my mind," I responded, struggling to keep my voice steady and composed. The mere sight of this familiar face had stirred something within me, a flickering flame of recognition that refused to be extinguished. "But tell me, have you noticed anything unusual happening around these parts? Any strange occurrences that have been weighing on your mind?" I leaned in slightly, my gaze sharpening as I sought to discern any hint of unease or concern in their expression.

Tension hung thick as I leaned in, my heart pounding. Luke positioned himself firmly between us, his face a stony mask, but his body language screamed volumes. He stood as an unyielding barrier, a human shield, determined to protect me from the creature's malevolent intent.

His arms were crossed tightly over his chest, muscles coiled with readiness. His narrowed eyes were laser-focused, tracking the beast's subtle twitch and movement before us. I could feel the energy crackling between Luke and the creature, like a coiled spring on the brink of snapping.

The atmosphere was suffocating, the tension so thick it felt tangible, as if I could reach out and grasp it in my hands. Luke's unwavering stance and the creature's predatory stillness created a standoff that seemed to stretch for eternity. The silence between them was deafening, the anticipation hanging in the air heavy and oppressive.

I held my breath, fully aware that any sudden move could shatter the fragile equilibrium, unleashing a storm of untamed fury. The moment teetered on a knife's edge, the outcome uncertain, but the intensity undeniable.

"Listen, you two," I said, my voice laced with urgency. "Now is not the time or place to be airing your differences. Whatever issues you have, you must put them aside and work together." I paused, letting the weight of my words sink in, before continuing with a tone of finality. "This situation is too important for your squabbles to get in the way. I need you both to put your differences aside and focus on the task. The stakes are too high for us to be divided right now. Can I count on you to put your egos aside and do what's necessary?"

"What on Earth makes you think a scumbag like him is worth your time?" Luke spat, his brows furrowing in a mix of disgust and incredulity. His voice dripped with contempt as he leaned in, eyes narrowed, scrutinising the person standing before him. "That lowlife's not fit to lick the dirt off your boots. So tell me, what could you possibly see in a worthless piece of trash like him?"

With a delighted chuckle, Ahmed's form shook slightly. The mortal body he had chosen to inhabit was far from his usual appearance – a volatile and passively disagreeable visage, hideous and unapproachable to behold. His true essence, a being of immense power and otherworldly prowess, was concealed beneath this grotesque facade, adding to the intrigue and unease that radiated from his presence.

"Luke," I said, my voice firm and commanding, "It's time to stand up. This man doesn't mean us any harm, and I've come to trust him." Luke's nostrils flared in a derisive snort, and his scepticism was evident in the tense set of his shoulders as he reluctantly complied with my request. The air was thick with a palpable tension, and I could feel the unease emanating from him, but I knew we had to confront this situation head-on.

"Well, well, look who's amassed their own personal security detail these days," Ahmed remarked, his eyes gleaming with amusement at Luke's reaction. "If you're looking for Lilly, she breezed through a few moments ago. Headed that way, into the cave across the way." He jerked his chin towards the dark, foreboding opening in the rock face. "Although I can't imagine what she wants in there. That place is nothing but death and solitude, my friend."

The cave's gaping maw loomed before them, a yawning void that seemed to suck the very light from the air. Shadows danced along the uneven walls, hinting at the unseen perils within. A chill ran down Luke's spine, and he couldn't help but wonder what could possibly compel Lilly to venture into such a forsaken place.

I nodded firmly, determined to move forward despite Luke's hesitation. I could feel his piercing gaze burning into my back as he lingered behind, his eyes narrowed into tiny, angry slits. Reluctantly, he had no choice but to acquiesce to my wishes, refraining from harming Ahmed or causing a scene.

The tension in the air was palpable, but I refused to be deterred. My resolve was unwavering as I pressed on, leaving Luke to grapple with his resentment and frustration. The situation crackled with an unresolved conflict, but I remained steadfast, unwilling to back down or allow the volatile emotions to erupt into chaos.

"How the hell do you know him?" he demanded, his voice gruff and laced with a tangible undercurrent of suspicion. His brow furrowed, and his eyes narrowed, scrutinising the person before him as if trying to uncover a hidden truth. The unspoken questions hanging between them, waiting to be answered.

"He was exiled for something completely stupid a few years ago. It's his fault, but I never believed it warranted exiling him here. They could have chosen a better location where he could have learnt how to reign in his power and then return and work for the realm. It just felt like a waste," I reluctantly admitted.

I could never fathom how Ahmed's crimes warranted such a severe punishment – exile to this desolate, barren world. The realm's decision to banish him entirely from our realm felt unjust, even for the gravest of offences. Perhaps I simply lacked the entire understanding of his atrocities and the depth of their impact on the mortals involved. But Ahmed's unique magical abilities and shapeshifting prowess could have been a valuable asset to our realm, a revelation we could have harnessed in our past adventures.

Instead, he now languishes in this harsh, unforgiving landscape, his extraordinary gifts forever lost to us. The thought of his wasted potential and the missed opportunities to use his powers for the greater good fills me with a deep, gnawing sense of regret. Suppose only the realm had shown more leniency and willingness to rehabilitate rather than cast him out entirely. In that case, we may have gained a powerful ally rather than losing him to this desolate exile.

"Are you out of your mind?" he exclaimed, his voice laced with disbelief and indignation. "How can you even consider talking like that after everything he's done?" he continued, his words dripping with a palpable sense of outrage and contempt. His eyes narrowed, and his brow furrowed as he struggled to comprehend the sheer audacity of the suggestion. The air around them seemed to crackle with the intensity of his reaction, leaving no doubt about the depth of his conviction.

I stopped in my tracks, pivoting to confront him head-on. Once soft and gentle, my gaze now sharpened with a newfound intensity. I locked eyes with him, my stare unwavering, conveying a resolute determination that demanded his full attention. The air seemed to crackle with the weight of the moment as we stood, poised for what was to come, the tension palpable between us.

"So you know what he did?" I asked.

"Of course," he uttered, his voice laced with defiance and discomfort. "Why wouldn't I know? After all, I am a demon, though a gentler creature than that abhorrent monster."

His brow furrowed, and his eyes narrowed as he spoke, the weight of his demonic nature evident in every word. The air around him seemed to crackle with a palpable energy, a subtle reminder of the powers that lay dormant within him, waiting to be unleashed should the need arise.

Yet, there was also a hint of reluctance in his tone, a trace of discomfort at the very notion of his own demonic heritage. He was not like the monstrous entity that had preceded him, and he took pride in that distinction, even as he acknowledged the darkness that resided within him.

"He's not as bad as you think," I argued softly, trying to diffuse the tension. "Trust me, we've dealt with much worse than him before." The sound of rustling bushes behind us indicated we had company. Luke quickly grabbed me and pulled me into the nearest cover of shrubbery, holding me tightly against his side.

Peering cautiously through the foliage, we watched Lilly emerge from the cave Ahmed had directed us towards. She seemed unharmed, floating effortlessly above the ground, her feet barely grazing the ground as she moved with an almost arrogant grace. Turning her head in our direction, her gaze passed over us without detection, as if unaware of our presence, wholly absorbed in her triumph.

I recoiled in shock, nearly losing my footing as I witnessed the horrifying transformation unfolding before me. Lilly's eyes had darkened, the pupils expanding until they consumed the entire white, leaving nothing but an abyss of blackness. The sight sent a chill down my spine, a stark reminder of a phenomenon long documented in the realm. This grim fate befell a witch who had surrendered her soul to the malevolent spells she once commanded.

The reality of Lilly's descent hit me with full force. She had plunged far deeper into the shadowy abyss than I had ever imagined, a revelation that filled me with genuine dread. Though we were never close, a pang of empathy pierced through me as I recognised the depth of her anguish. This was the most severe case the realm had ever recorded, and the weight of that realisation left me profoundly unsettled.

The sheer gravity of her condition gripped me with an intensity I had never known. It was as if the darkness that consumed Lilly was reaching out, clawing at my sense of security, leaving me with an overwhelming feeling of unease. The atmosphere was thick with the foreboding presence of her transformation, a stark reminder of the dangers lurking within the shadows of our world.

"Did you see her eyes?" he exclaimed beside me, his gaze transfixed and his voice tinged with a hint of awe. His eyes were wide, blinking rapidly as if he, too, couldn't believe the spectacle unfolding before them. The intensity in his voice and the captivated expression on his face suggested that what he had witnessed was nothing short of extraordinary, leaving him in mesmerised disbelief.

"I did," I sighed, the weight of the words heavy on my chest. "It's too late for her now. All we can do is pray we stop whatever twisted scheme she's concocted before another innocent life is claimed by her callous hand." My voice was laced with a sombre resignation, the realisation that we may already be too late to prevent further tragedy. The stakes had never been higher, and the urgency to uncover her sinister plans burned like a flickering flame in the pit of my stomach. We had to act quickly before the darkness she had unleashed consumed us all.

"Well," he said, his voice laced with urgency and determination. "I'm here for one purpose: to keep you from being killed. Your name has been marked as the next on the list, and I'll be damned if I let that happen on my watch." His eyes narrowed, a steely resolve reflected in his gaze as he spoke. "I've been tasked with ensuring your survival, and that's exactly what I intend to do. No matter what it takes, I won't let you slip through my fingers now."

His words hung in the air like a thick fog obscuring the truth. I had no desire to explore their hidden meanings, not right now. More pressing matters demanded my focus, which required my undivided attention. Whatever existed between us, whatever unresolved tension or unspoken emotions, would have to wait. I couldn't afford to dwell on it, not when critical decisions were to be made.

Only when the time was right, when I had the counsel of a trusted confidant by my side, would I dare unpack our relationship's complexities. Their insight and guidance would be invaluable in charting the best course of action and navigating the treacherous waters between us.

Until then, I would keep my feelings locked away, steeling my mind against the temptation to delve into the underlying implications of his words. The stakes were too high, the consequences too severe, to risk getting distracted by personal matters.

We held our breath, anticipation palpable, as she navigated the final bend in the valley. Her once airy, carefree responses to perceived threats had been overtaken and consumed by a now almost demonic, evil state of being. Teetering precariously on the precipice, she balanced, poised to embrace the transformation into an actual demon fully.

The air grew thick with tension as we watched the final stages of her metamorphosis. Her movements became jerky and erratic, as if her very soul was being ripped apart and remoulded into something dark and sinister. The once gentle cadence of her voice had been replaced by a guttural, primal growl that sent chills down our spines.

In that harrowing moment, we knew there was no turning back. She had crossed the threshold, her humanity extinguished, consumed by the relentless darkness that now consumed her very being. The demon within had triumphed, and we could only watch in horrified awe as she embraced her newfound, malevolent existence.

The colossal cave yawned before us, its cavernous maw menacing as we drew near. Ominous shadows danced across the entrance, and the fluttering of unseen wings sent a shiver down my spine. The eerie, guttural moans that emanated from within had my heart pounding in my chest, and I fought to maintain a calm facade beside Luke.

I knew he would be tempted to shield me from the unknown dangers that lurked within, but I steeled my nerves and willed myself to appear as resolute as possible. The darkness beckoned, its siren call both alluring and terrifying, daring us to venture into its depths. With a deep breath, I stepped forward, determined to face whatever lay ahead, even as the unseen denizens of the cave scattered at our approach.

Chapter Ten

Once we stepped through the threshold into the cave, the inhabitants greeted us with a surprising level of acceptance despite my uncertainty about what awaited us. The damp, dimly lit interior felt almost welcoming, as if the walls embraced our presence, inviting us to explore the mysteries ahead.

The inhabitants exhaled thick plumes of smoke from their flaring nostrils, their agitated movements echoing through the confines of the cave dwelling. The presumed males of this particular clan pawed at the ground restlessly, their powerful frames radiating an undercurrent of discontent that reverberated all around us. The air was charged with an underlying tension, the beasts' disconcerting nature palpable in every clenched muscle and furtive glance.

As I had anticipated, Lilly had achieved whatever dark purpose brought her here, leaving the formidable creatures in the cave agitated and on edge. The growls and low rumbles that filled the air were a testament to the unease she had stirred within them. Their animalistic responses heightened the already tangible sense of danger that thickened the atmosphere.

Ferocious snarls echoed through the cavern, each more menacing than the last, causing me to falter momentarily. The largest of the pack, its massive frame towering over me like a living shadow, charged forward with unbridled aggression. The ground trembled beneath its weight as it closed the distance between us, its fiery eyes locked onto mine.

Just as it seemed the beast would crash into me, it halted abruptly, inches from my body. The air between us crackled with tension as the creature whirled around, its powerful hindquarters launching it in the opposite direction. This was no mere show of force; it was a test of my resilience, a challenge to my loyalty to their clan.

The sheer intensity of their savage growls and the raw ferocity of their movements sent a chill down my spine, but I refused to back down. I stood my ground, heart pounding, determined to prove my worth in the face of this formidable challenge. The creatures circled me, their eyes glinting with primal intelligence. I knew that this was the moment that would define my place among them.

It was the first time I had ever seen these monstrous creatures, and the sight of them sent a shiver down my spine. They were a rare and elusive species, known only to exist in the realm's furthest, most untamed reaches. These beasts were utterly alien to our world, incapable of assimilating or conforming to the ways of civilised lands. Their very presence exuded an air of untamed ferocity. This raw and primal energy seemed to defy all attempts at domestication.

Their hulking forms were covered in thick, gnarled hide, each movement imbued with a primal grace that belied their immense size and power. The glint of their predatory eyes and the gnashing of their razor-sharp fangs filled me with awe and dread. These creatures answered to no one, beholden to no laws or customs but their own savage instincts.

The air around them seemed charged with a wild, uncontainable force, a testament to the pure, unbridled power coursing through their veins. I could feel the weight of their presence pressing down on me, a constant reminder that I was in the company of beings far beyond the reach of human control.

Standing face to face with these enigmatic and dangerous beasts, I deeply and profoundly respected the sheer, untamed might they embodied. They were a testament to the enduring power of the wild, a reminder that there were still places in this world where the untamed reigned supreme, beyond the reach of mortal control or influence. It was a humbling and exhilarating experience that left an indelible mark on my soul.

The Meniagier were creatures of myth, confined to the pages of ancient tomes that meticulously chronicled the realm's storied history. Over the centuries, these enigmatic beings had ascended to legendary status, renowned for their relentless attacks and unmatched prowess as guardians of the realm. Their endurance against the harshest weather conditions and resilience in the face of any assault had solidified their reputation as formidable protectors.

Yet, despite their fearsome reputation, this was the first time anyone had succeeded in taming the Meniagier for long. The creatures remained elusive, defying others' attempts to bend them to their will. Historical accounts spoke of their insatiable hunger, a dark force that consumed any living being who dared to challenge their untamed nature.

Their wild spirit and unyielding ferocity continued to captivate the imagination of the realm's denizens. Tales of the Meniagier's raw power and the mystery that shrouded them were passed down through generations, each story deepening the allure of these legendary creatures. In every whispered legend and ancient text, the Meniagier symbolised the wild, untameable forces that lay just beyond the edge of civilisation.

I stood cornered, trapped in the eerie confines of the cave. Luke, mere feet away, gripped my hand tightly, his clammy palm betraying his mounting tension. Despite his icy, inhuman touch, his skin still glistened with sweat, a stark reminder that he, too, was subject to the physical demands of this unsettling situation. The juxtaposition of his otherworldly nature and the all-too-human response of his body sent a shiver down my spine, a testament to the precarious nature of our circumstances.

The menacing, ebony-haired Meniagier beasts converged upon us, their colossal frames intertwined in razor-sharp claws and gnashing teeth. The creatures seemed to move in a frenzied, synchronised dance, each jostling and shoving, desperate to prove their dominance. The air reverberated with their guttural snarls and the thunderous crash of their massive bodies colliding as they engaged in a fierce, primal display of power and supremacy.

Their presence was unsettling, a haunting terror that gnawed at the edges of sanity. Enormous, yellowed teeth jutted from their gaping maws, each fang as large as a fully grown human, gleaming ominously in the dim light. Matted, shaggy black fur cascaded to the ground, obscuring their hulking forms beneath a tangled mass of darkness.

Perched atop their heads were a pair of formidable horns, grotesque and unnervingly fluid in their movements. One horn arched further back while the other jutted just above the tail, capable of swaying and bending in ways that defied the limits of imagination. Their appearance was alien and unnatural, teetering on the brink of the horrific.

The mere sight of these otherworldly creatures sent a chill down my spine. Their very existence seemed to challenge the boundaries of what was natural, leaving a lingering sense of unease and dread in their wake. It was a sight that would be forever etched into my memory, a chilling reminder of the strange and unknown that lurks in the darkest corners of the world.

"They definitely don't look friendly," Luke remarked. "And we are surrounded."

"You think?" I squeaked, the shrill tone of my voice piercing the air and eliciting a chorus of agitated growls from the surrounding beasts.

Laced with sarcasm, my words only further antagonised the already restless creatures. Their hackles raised, and their eyes gleamed with a primal fury that was freakish and frightening. The tension in the air was palpable, and I couldn't help but inwardly curse my own tactless outburst, knowing full well that it had only succeeded in provoking the beasts even more.

The powerful display of brotherly camaraderie against trespassing intruders was captivating to behold. The most enormous beast in the group effortlessly somersaulted through the air, landing firmly on its sturdy hindquarters.

With unbridled momentum, it bounded forward, planting its muscular forelegs onto the ground and unleashing a series of forceful snorts. The impact of its hooves against the solid, cemented surface carved deep, aggressive furrows into the Earth, conveying a palpable sense of dominance and unyielding protection of their territory.

A spark of inspiration ignited within me. I leaned in, barely excited, and whispered, "I've got an idea."

The concept traced its origins back to the journals of a powerful realm witch who, in a bold and ill-fated attempt, had sought to tame the savage beasts. Her efforts ended in tragedy, her life cut short by the very creatures she sought to control. Matace, ever the advocate for expanding one's knowledge, had stumbled upon this journal centuries ago and had since entrusted it to me.

He had impressed upon me the importance of understanding the diverse inhabitants of the realm, emphasising that doing so would not only broaden my knowledge but might also reveal hidden powers within me that had yet to be fully harnessed. The weight of his words settled heavily on my shoulders, filling me with a profound sense of purpose and urgency to explore every detail within the pages of that ancient journal.

Holding the journal, I felt the echoes of the witch's last moments, her ambition, and her ultimate demise. The tattered pages seemed to hum with dark energy, beckoning me to uncover the secrets they held, secrets that could shape my path within the realm. The task before me was daunting, yet it also made me eager to unlock the mysteries hidden in these timeworn pages.

My spell began to manifest itself into a dark, shapeless image, conjured to match the size and speed of the Meniagier beasts; frighteningly, it launched itself across towards them with the aim of attack, striking down anything that moved swiftly into its path, following my directions and instructions.

The dark, sinister entity I had unwittingly manifested and sought to control was a constant threat. This plague-like shadow clung to me relentlessly. This was the Meniagier's greatest weakness, a vulnerability exploited by many witches who had attempted to tame these formidable beasts. One such witch had summoned another dark lord, only to become a mere morsel for the creature. Still, his chilling notes found their way into the hands of the powerful Matace.

"Remarkable, Seira!" Luke exclaimed beside me, his voice brimming with admiration as he witnessed my swift and decisive action, harnessing the full power of my arcane knowledge and abilities. "Absolutely brilliant! Now, how about you do that same mesmerising display, oh, say, about eleven more times?" he teased, his excitement palpable.

I shot him a determined look and shouted, "Not a chance, Luke! Conjuring these dark lords may be impressive, but it's also utterly draining. The sheer effort to manifest and control them is enough to leave me spent." I shook my head, a hint of exasperation creeping into my tone. "I'm afraid I'll have to pass on an encore performance – at least for now."

He pressed himself tightly against the corner, his eyes wide with terror, transfixed by the ferocious display unfolding before him. The beasts' snarling intensified, their hackles raised as they reared up on their hind legs, their movements' sheer size and power filling the air with a palpable menace.

Suddenly, one of the more enormous beasts, emboldened by the pack's numbers, broke free from the group and launched towards me, its jaws gaping wide, a primal roar rumbling from its chest. The creature's muscles rippled beneath its thick fur as it charged, its razor-sharp claws poised to tear and rend.

The beast's massive form loomed closer, its ragged breath and thunderous footsteps reverberating through the dank, shadowy cave. Every step it took sent tremors through the ground, shaking the very foundation of the cavern. I narrowly evaded its grasping claws, my breath caught in my throat as my heart pounded violently in my ears, each beat a desperate reminder of the danger.

Then, in a blinding flash, my dark lord unleashed a devastating counterattack. A surge of searing light erupted from his hands, instantly obliterating the looming threat. The cave was suddenly bathed in an ethereal brilliance, shards of light splintering across the dripping, moss-covered walls.

Droplets of water clinging to the stone were illuminated like crystalline tears. Their delicate weight caused them to trickle down the uneven surfaces as if the cave wept in awe and sorrow at the raw display of power. The air crackled with residual energy, a palpable reminder of the arcane forces at play. The ozone-tinged scent of magic filled my senses, sharp and electric, leaving me breathless in the aftermath of the confrontation.

The beasts were a sight to behold, their true grandeur far surpassing the mere photographs kept within the headquarters.

Thick, coarse fur hung from their massive frames, reminiscent of the shaggy mane of a mighty buffalo. Their horns, gleaming with a sharp and deadly edge, were a testament to their wielding power. The vibrant colours that adorned their forms held a more profound significance. This visual cue distinguished the leaders from the females and other members of their kind.

As I observed these majestic creatures up close, I couldn't help but feel a sense of awe and trepidation. Their presence exuded an aura of raw, untamed strength that permeated the air around them. Their piercing gazes, filled with primal intelligence, seemed to bore into my soul, reminding me of the untamed wilderness they called home. It was a humbling experience, a reminder that these were not mere beasts but living embodiments of nature's untamed power.

The pack parted, and an even more powerful, menacing beast stepped forward, looming over me. I couldn't fathom how anything could surpass the sheer size of the previous creature. Yet, this new monstrosity towered above me, its massive frame casting a daunting shadow. It thrust its face mere inches from mine, its repulsive, stomach-churning breath washing over me in suffocating waves.

I fought the overwhelming urge to gag, the acrid stench burning my nostrils and threatening to elicit a violent retching response. This was nothing like the romanticised depictions in movies, where the beast and the heroine seemed to share a mutual understanding, their breath allegedly fresh and pleasant. No, this beast couldn't be bothered with the basic hygiene of toothpaste or mints - it was a nightmare made flesh, its foul exhalations assaulting my senses and filling me with revulsion.

I dared not breathe, not even allowing a single muscle on my face to twitch. Luke inched toward me, his movements cautious and deliberate. But before he could reach me, a thunderous roar erupted from one of the beast's nearby mates, the sound so powerful it knocked him backwards, forcing him to retreat. He had no choice but to leave me, facing the colossal creature alone.

The beast's imposing presence loomed over me, its sheer proximity making the danger all too real. It could easily rip my head clean off my shoulders and spit me out without a second thought. Towering at a dangerously massive fifteen feet, its enormous bulk and the ferocious gleam of its jagged teeth left no doubt that it could devour me for breakfast without hesitation.

The information I had received about this realm had yet to prepare me for this monstrous entity's terrifying scale and ferocity. Its presence was overwhelming, a nightmare of raw power and primal rage. If I managed to survive this encounter, I vowed to correct the grievous underestimation of such a beast. But as it towered over me, I could only hope that I would live long enough to do so.

Suddenly and sharply, the massive horn began to move, slowly edging in my direction. Luke finally reached me and stood behind me, his hand firmly gripping the fabric of my clothing on my lower back, ready to launch me away from the beast if necessary.

My hands trembled with a mix of anticipation and dread as the sharpness of the tip threatened to slice through my skin. The horn inched closer, its pointed tip drawing dangerously near my face. I held my breath, bracing for the worst, when suddenly, the tip touched me gently, almost searchingly. Sensing my nervousness, the creature backed away slightly, shaking its head. Its tongue lolled to the side of its mouth, almost comically, as if trying to reassure me uniquely. After all, I had entered its domain.

Puffs of cloudy breath escaped its massive nostrils and mouth, leaving small indents on my skin as it explored me. Its eyes flashed with unfamiliar messages, a strange gentleness lurking beneath the depths, rapidly rising to the surface. The creature's sudden familiarity with me seemed to shock it, and its eyes widened in what appeared to be a mix of wonder and apprehension.

The creature's serpentine tongue suddenly darted out, swiping across my cheek in a sloppy, uncalled-for gesture. The wet, slimy appendage left a glistening trail of saliva in its wake, a viscous and unpleasant sensation that lingered on my skin, sending a shudder down my spine. The intrusive, aggressive nature of the action left me feeling violated and deeply unsettled, as if the creature had breached an unspoken boundary. It asserted its dominance over me in a primal, predatory manner.

Out of the corner of my eye, I noticed Luke's face contort into a grimace as he struggled to stifle a burst of laughter. The beast, seemingly unfazed, turned its gaze towards him and began to stomp its feet in a bizarre, tribal-like dance.

Instantly, the others joined in, the thunderous pounding dislodging the loose rocks lining the cave walls and plummeting to the ground, shattering into countless jagged fragments upon impact. The deafening cacophony was both enigmatic and disorienting, an unexpected turn of events I could never have imagined encountering, both for myself and the Meniagier.

"Luke," I hissed through gritted teeth, "Get away from me. Now."

His whisper, as low as the one I had used, was laced with a palpable undercurrent of worry and concern. The words hung in the air, their weight pressing upon me as he asked, "What if they hurt you? Or try to hurt you?"

I felt his words like a physical force, their intensity sending a shiver down my spine. The softness in his tone, the raw emotion that underscored it, tugged at my heart, softening my resolve once more. His gaze bore into mine, searching, pleading, desperate to convey the depth of his fears for my safety.

At that moment, I was acutely aware of the vulnerability in his expression, the mask of composure cracking to reveal the vulnerability beneath. It was a side of him I had rarely glimpsed, and it stirred something deep within me, a longing to reassure him, to wrap him in my arms and shield him from the world's dangers.

"No, I don't believe they will," I responded, my voice barely above a whisper. A subtle smile tugged at the corners of my lips as I gazed intently at the scene unfolding before me. "This is their way of welcoming me, of embracing me into their fold. Isn't it amazing?"

The air seemed to crackle with an underlying current of anticipation, the weight of their acceptance palpable. My heart raced with a mixture of trepidation and exhilaration, the significance of this moment not lost on me. It was as if the very fabric of the world had shifted, realigning to accommodate my presence among them – a testament to the power of their tacit approval.

"Astounding!" he gasped, his voice quivering with awe and trepidation. "Perilous and reckless – those are some of the milder terms I would use to describe it." His eyes widened, and his brow furrowed as he grappled with the sheer magnitude of what he was witnessing. The air seemed to crackle with a sense of unease, and the weight of the situation hung heavy in the atmosphere. "It's a daring, even foolhardy, endeavour – one that could have disastrous consequences if not handled with the utmost care and precision," he continued, his words laced with a palpable mixture of fascination and dread.

I offered a soft, reassuring smile and turned to face him, determined to convey my courage. Standing tall, I felt a sense of quiet defiance, knowing that, in some ways, I was a stronger presence than him, even as a vampire. Sensing my unwavering resolve, he retreated, his movements cautious and uncertain. The eerie silence that had blanketed the cave suddenly intensified, the lack of sound palpable and heavy, accentuating the tension in the air.

Spiritually, I felt an overwhelming connection, a profound bond with those around me. This was no ordinary event; it was a momentous chapter in history, a pivotal occasion for which countless souls had sacrificed everything. The weight of this realisation pressed heavily upon me as I stood amid this extraordinary setting, fully aware of the significance of the moment and the lives that had paved the way for it.

The air buzzed with a tangible energy, a reverence that seemed to seep into every fibre of my being. It was as if the very fabric of reality had shifted, transporting me to a realm where the physical and the ethereal boundaries blurred. In this sacred space, the transformative experience brought forth the yearnings and aspirations that had driven generations before me.

I felt humbled, almost insignificant, to be part of something greater than myself. The reverence of the occasion echoed within me, filling me with a sense of purpose and continuity, a link in the chain of countless souls who had dreamt of this moment long before I ever existed.

I slowly reached out, my fingers trembling with trepidation and awe. Tentatively, I touched the velvety nose of the majestic beast before me, feeling the warm, soft flesh beneath my fingertips. The creature eyed me warily, its eyes flickering with a guarded curiosity as I edged closer, my movements cautious and deliberate.

A shiver ran down my spine as I felt the raw power and untamed energy radiating from the beast. Mustering my courage, I whispered soft words of encouragement, my voice low and soothing, like a gentle lullaby. I felt my way along the thick, muscular length of its neck, marvelling at its hide's intricate patterns and the creature's sheer size.

Suddenly, the beast's horn moved aside, granting me permission to proceed. I inched forward, my fingertips caressing the smooth, curved surface, and then, with a gentle flick, the horn brushed against my hair, causing me to giggle in delighted surprise. At that moment, the barrier between us seemed to melt away. I felt a deep, primal connection with the magnificent animal before me.

"Shh, it's alright; I won't let anyone hurt you," I whispered gently, my voice laced with a soothing intensity. I reached out, my movements calm and deliberate, offering the assurance of safety and protection. My eyes locked with theirs, conveying a steadfast determination to shield them from harm. "You're safe now, I promise," I continued, my tone firm yet compassionate, intent on easing their evident distress.

The beast's coarse fur felt uneven beneath my caressing fingers. It was thick in some areas but surprisingly sparse in others, belying its rugged, formidable appearance. As I gently threaded my fingers through its mane, the softness of the individual strands surprised me, a stark contrast to the creature's overall wild, untamed look.

Remarkably, the animal allowed me to approach it, seemingly letting down its guard and exhibiting a gentleness I had not anticipated. A glint of trust flickered in its eyes, a testament to its hidden, gentle nature beneath its imposing exterior. I eased myself closer, drawn in by the captivating interplay of textures and the unexpected tenderness radiating from this magnificent, powerful being.

I was mere inches from its gaping jaws, close enough to feel the hot, putrid breath on my face. In that heart-pounding moment, I was sure that the massive beast would lunge forward and seize me in its powerful jaws, tearing me from the ground and flinging me onto its towering back. The sickening realisation of the dizzying height beneath me only heightened my terror as I clung desperately to the creature's coarse, tangled mane, my fingers trembling with sheer panic.

The Meniagier, the mighty beast I sat upon, turned slowly, almost as if acutely aware of the dizzying height between me and the ground far below. The sheer drop was genuinely terrifying, and I dared not even glance down, not even to glimpse Luke's reaction.

The ground seemed to beckon from an eternity away, and the slightest misstep could send me plummeting into the abyss. My heart raced, and my grip on the Meniagier's rough hide tightened, every fibre of my being focused on maintaining my precarious perch atop this towering creature.

Grinning with the achievement, I was sure my grin would soon split my cheeks; I twisted around to see Luke, who remained statuesque in the corner, without flinching. His smile was firmly plastered on his face.

I saw him being guarded by another Meniagier, so he was encompassed and unable to move; his aura sent out a message of impatience and boredom, and I reacted by poking my tongue out at him, acting like a child who'd just been given a brand new sparkly toy to play with.

The hulking beast loomed before me, its powerful presence demanding attention. As if presenting me to its pack, I watched in rapt fascination as the other creatures began to bow and lower themselves to the ground, their submissive gestures clearly displaying reverence. I felt a surge of unease, unsure why I was being accorded such unexpected honour. The air crackled with a palpable tension, and I found myself captivated by the sheer intensity of the moment, my heart pounding with apprehension and intrigue.

A sacred and enigmatic ritual, a custom shrouded in mystery, reserved solely for those deemed worthy of the highest esteem and reverence. This rite of passage, a hallowed tradition, welcomed me into their esteemed ranks, embracing me as a cherished member of their tightly-knit pack.

The air crackled with a palpable sense of anticipation as I was ushered into the sacred space, my heart pounding with apprehension and honour. The elders, their faces etched with weathered wisdom, gazed upon me with a profound gaze, silently bestowing their trust and acceptance.

The ritual unfolded with reverence, each gesture and utterance steeped in centuries-old significance. I felt a deep connection to the ancestral lineage that had preserved this sacred tradition. This humbling and transformative experience forever marked my place within this revered group.

A surge of exhilaration swept through me as I realised they accepted me. I couldn't quite fathom it - the pungent aroma that had once overwhelmed my senses no longer bothered me, and the urge to gag or cover my mouth had vanished.

It was as if a profound connection had been forged, and these incredible yet profoundly misunderstood creatures had become a part of me in a peculiar, almost mystical way. The intensity of the experience was overwhelming. I felt a sense of belonging, a strange kinship with these beings that had once seemed alien and intimidating. Once a place of discomfort, the cave had now transformed into a sanctuary. In this realm, I felt truly accepted and understood.

Every fibre of my being vibrated with a sense of wonder and belonging. The initial trepidation had given way to a deep, unwavering trust. I was no longer an outsider but a welcome member of their enigmatic community, bound by an inexplicable, almost spiritual connection that transcended the boundaries of the physical world.

Deliberately, the Meniagier lowered its massive, hulking frame, gradually bending in the middle. With a careful, controlled motion, it gently eased its great, bulbous body onto the ground, allowing me to slip down from its towering height and onto the floor below. Luke watched, his eyes wide and intensely focused, his gaze fixed upon me with a passive yet captivated interest.

"Did you see that?" I exclaimed, my heart pounding with excitement. My eyes were wide, and I couldn't contain the exhilaration. The sight had been so unexpected, so breathtaking, that I couldn't help but gasp with wonder. I turned to my companion, my expression brimming with awe and anticipation, eager to share this incredible moment with them.

"I did," he responded, his voice laced with unease. His eyes darted nervously, searching for a way to escape this situation. "Do you think we can leave now?" he added, his tone almost pleading.

I couldn't help but laugh, the sound reverberating through the crowd surrounding us. The gleeful laughter seemed to cut through the tension, my voice ringing with a sense of confidence and amusement that contrasted sharply with my companion's discomfort.

The scene was charged with profound energy, as if the air was alive with an undercurrent of excitement and anticipation. I could feel the weight of the people's gaze upon us, their curiosity and interest palpable. It was as if they were waiting to see how this encounter would unfold, eager to witness the unfolding drama.

"Without a doubt, they are gentle creatures," I affirmed, my voice brimming with conviction. The words tumbled out, tinged with wonder, as I contemplated the gentle nature of the beings before me. Their graceful and measured movements belied a profound serenity that enveloped the air around us. I was captivated, my initial scepticism giving way to a growing appreciation for their tranquil presence. "Yes, they truly are gentle," I reiterated, my gaze locked on the captivating display unfolding before us, the awe in my tone impossible to conceal.

"Ah, how astute of you," he retorted with a hint of sarcasm, his voice dripping with dry, sardonic amusement. The subtle roll of his eyes and the imperceptible curl of his lips betrayed his utter indifference to the apparent observation as if he were addressing a rather slow-witted child. His response, laced with a subtle, mocking edge, conveyed a clear message: that the statement had been so self-evident that it was barely worth acknowledging.

The Meniagier were sprawled on the ground, their laboured breathing echoing in the eerie stillness. I approached them cautiously, my heart pounding with trepidation and concern. Their large, soulful eyes locked onto mine, pleading for help, their gaze conveying a wistful vulnerability that tugged at my heart.

I knelt beside them, speaking in a low, soothing tone to offer comfort and reassurance. The Meniagier seemed to understand, their bodies relaxing slightly under my gentle touch. But behind me, Luke shifted nervously, his impatience apparent, the tension in the air thick and unforgiving.

After much inner turmoil, I finally resolved to depart from these peculiar creatures, which various individuals had misunderstood and misrepresented over the years. Contrary to the fierce and monstrous depictions in rumours and documented tales, these animals were no more ferocious than vampires—an odd and conflicting revelation. The field journals had failed to capture their profound yearning to be loved and nurtured, a strange but deeply poignant emotional need.

"Did you catch that?" I asked urgently the moment we stepped outside. My heart was pounding, and I couldn't help but replay the interaction in my mind, analysing every subtle shift in their expressions and body language. "The way they reacted to me – it was like I had just sprouted a second head! The tension was detectible, and I could practically feel their eyes boring into me, judging and scrutinising my every move." I searched his face, desperate for some reassurance or insight. "What do you think that was all about?"

"Yes, I did," he confessed, a hint of reluctance in his voice. "Quite commendable, I must say." He paused, his gaze sweeping the environment around them. "But have you taken the time to observe the air since we stepped outside? The way it seems to cling to us, heavy with an unnatural stillness, as if the atmosphere is holding its breath in anticipation?"

I trembled at the sheer acerbity in his voice. His words struck me like a cold, unforgiving gale, chilling me. His demeanour, once placid, now morphed into an icy disposition, cutting through the air with a harsh edge. The man before me had transformed, his countenance hardening as he honed in on the subject. He was determined to seize control of the discussion with an iron grip.

The air had shifted, the once-familiar atmosphere now foreign and unsettling. Lilly's presence had vanished, her scent a faint memory on the breeze. I cursed myself for being distracted by the beasts, allowing her to slip away while I was occupied. Any orbs that might have guided my portal home had dissipated, leaving me adrift and uncertain in this alien landscape.

The change was palpable, a weight pressing down, the world around me transformed in her absence. I strained to catch any trace of her, any lingering hint that she had been here, but the silence was deafening. Time seemed to slow, every moment an eternity, as I grappled with the realisation that she was gone, my only means of return fading with her. The urgency built within me, a rising tide of desperation.

I had to find her and follow the trail before it vanished altogether. The stakes had never been higher, and the need to reconnect with her was overwhelming. This world had become a cold, empty place without her light to guide me, and I knew I had to act quickly before the darkness closed in completely.

"Damn it!" I spat out the words through gritted teeth, my frustration palpable. "She's long gone by now," I growled, the realisation stinging like a slap. My heart raced as I frantically scanned the empty street, hoping to glimpse her retreating figure. Still, she had vanished without a trace, leaving me with a bitter taste of regret and missed opportunities.

"I understand," he replied, his tone soothing yet firm. "We must return to the house immediately. There's a huge fight, and the demons aren't giving up or listening."

His words were weighted with urgency, the situation demanding their swift action. The air crackled with tension, the distant sounds of the ongoing conflict urging them to make haste. His eyes narrowed, a steely determination shining through as he met my gaze, silently conveying the gravity of the situation. Without further delay, he gestured towards the path leading back to the house, his steps quickening as he led the way, his resolve unwavering in the face of the challenges ahead.

His gentle yet insistent reminder of the epic battle raging in the complex he called his home was enough to ignite my determination to set things straight. However, without any clue where the deranged witch Lilly had vanished to, our only viable option was to return and see if anything remained of his house – if the walls had survived the onslaught of the demons' rampage.

Battles involving such malevolent forces often left behind a scene of utter devastation, with bare walls and piles of rubble littering the ground, their toll on human life far exceeding that of any other conflict. The gravity of the situation weighed heavily, and I knew we needed to act quickly before the body count climbed any higher.

"You're absolutely right," I hastily concurred, swiftly conjuring a shimmering portal to transport us into the lush, verdant garden surrounding his home. "Come on!" I urged, my voice laced with a sense of urgency as I noticed him staring at me with a perplexed expression, his brow furrowed and his gaze unwavering.

"You're getting the hang of using your magic, right?"

"I suppose I am," I agreed, "I don't really keep a count of how fast I use my spells; it all comes naturally and lately," I said, "I've found some new strength that I can't understand that's been helping me to get them right without screwing them up."

The journey back to his place was shrouded in a deafening silence, the air thick with unspoken dread. As we finally reached the familiar property, the scene that unfolded before us was nothing short of devastating. Stepping onto the soft, scorched grass, we were greeted by a harrowing sight.

Thick, billowing clouds of smoke engulfed the area, obscuring the once-proud structure that had been his dream home. The air was heavy with the acrid stench of destruction, and the crackle of the ongoing blaze sent chills down our spines.

We could almost feel the anguish of the once-vibrant home in the eerie silence that now surrounded it, reduced to nothing more than a smouldering ruin. The devastation was immense, its scale so overwhelming that it left us both stunned, struggling to grasp the moment's weight. The building shuddered violently under relentless blasts of scorching flames that pummeled its structure, a scene so apocalyptic it seemed ripped from the depths of a nightmare.

Never in my wildest dreams could I have imagined witnessing such a horrific spectacle firsthand. This was no figment of imagination, no fleeting horror from a movie screen—this was reality. The Earth was not meant to be the domain of demons or any other unholy entities that were never supposed to exist. And yet, here they were, unfolding a terrifying display before the eyes of mortals.

The sight was so jarring that it threatened to tear apart the very fabric of our world, a world that had fought desperately to conceal the presence of such horrors. The ferocity of the assault was beyond comprehension, shattering any illusion of safety and plunging us all into a nightmare of unimaginable proportions. The flames roared a monstrous force of destruction, leaving us standing helplessly amid chaos, our minds struggling to process the reality of what we were witnessing.

"Luke," I urgently tugged at his sleeve, my voice laced with desperation, "What can we possibly do? The situation is slipping through our fingers, and we must act quickly before it's too late." I could feel the tension building in my chest as I pleaded with him, my eyes searching his face for any sign of a solution. The moment's weight pressed down on us, demanding an immediate response.

"Alright, let's head inside," he said, his gaze sweeping the area with urgency. "We have to do something to help; we have no other choice." His voice carried a resolute tone, underscoring the gravity of the situation. The tension in the air was almost suffocating as he made the decision, and the weight of responsibility was evident in every word and gesture.

We cautiously made our way through the hazy, smoke-filled terrain, our footsteps muffled to avoid drawing the attention of the demonic entities lurking nearby. In the murky depths, I caught a glimpse of one of the demons, its piercing gaze fixed directly on me.

A shiver of fear coursed through my body, the umpteenth time since we embarked on this perilous investigation. I stopped abruptly, tugging Luke's sleeve and gesturing intently towards the ominous presence in the distance.

I was abruptly torn away from Luke's presence and thrust into a foreign, unsettling realm belonging to the demons. Unease gripped me as I stood in a shallow pit at the foot of an ominous altar, nervously awaiting the arrival of their malevolent leader.

The air crackled with unmistakable strain, the restless rattling of chains echoing all around as the demonic horde heralded the approach of their dark master. I held my breath, every muscle in my body tensing, paralysed with a debilitating fear. The air seemed to grow thick and heavy, suffocating me as I stood rooted to the spot, terrified to make the slightest movement or sound lest I incur the wrath of the impending demonic presence.

He loomed over me, seated imposingly in the chair, a malevolent grin etched across his features. Raising his arms, he commanded silence and obedience from his people, a gesture that demanded reverence. I felt a deep respect for these individuals and a profound desire to ensure their safety – to prevent any of them from suffering the fate that befell a demon's demise, whatever that might entail.

My surroundings were unfamiliar, and a sense of unease crept up my spine. "Where am I?" I uttered, the words escaping my lips with a hint of desperation. A pang of worry overcame me as I frantically searched the room. "Where's Luke?" I demanded, my voice laced with concern and a tinge of panic. The uncertainty of my situation weighed heavily, and I couldn't help but wonder what had happened and where my friend had disappeared.

I scanned the area frantically, my eyes darting in every direction, but he was nowhere to be seen. Yet, I could sense his presence, lingering like a ghostly spectre just out of reach. It was as if my physical form remained anchored to the very spot where I had last been while my spirit had been violently torn from it, transported to this strange, unsettling realm.

"Silence, witch!" he growled, his face mere inches from mine. His eyes were dark and unfathomable, like bottomless pits with no discernible end. "You have no place to speak here, within this hallowed circle," he spat, his voice dripping with contempt and a remarkable sense of power.

I let out a deep, weary sigh. How could I have forgotten that crucial detail? Matace had shown me something about these peculiar beings long ago – a strange congregation of demons that posed no real threat unless provoked and pushed beyond their limits. Once an insider was ushered into their sacred circle, they were bound by an unbreakable silence, forbidden to utter a single word.

Just by posing one seemingly harmless question, I could have been swiftly banished back to the world he once inhabited, where he would have immediately and mercilessly ended my life. The mere thought sent a shiver down my spine, a chill that gripped me with a sense of dread and unease. I should have been more cautious and vigilant in recalling Matace's warnings. Now, I feared the consequences of my careless actions might come back to haunt me in the most horrifying of ways.

"We are here, witch," he growled, his voice dripping with malice and contempt. His piercing gaze locked onto mine, his eyes burning with suspicion and an unwavering determination to pass judgment. "To determine whether we should spare your life or simply snuff it out like a flickering candle. So, do you have any final words you wish to utter before we decide your fate?" he demanded, his tone leaving no room for negotiation.

"I apologise for my bluntness," I responded, my tone laced with a hint of frustration, "but I truly fail to comprehend the reason for my presence here. It strikes me as rather peculiar that you've wielded such considerable influence over me while adorned in one of your archaic robes, effectively disguising yourself." My gaze narrowed as I sought to unravel the underlying purpose behind this unexpected encounter, my curiosity mingling with a subtle sense of unease.

A sudden snigger erupted, the pulsating energy coursing through me. Its overwhelming intensity seared through my every bone and muscle, ripping them apart with the abrupt dispersal of power emanating from the multitude of figures surrounding me. As I frantically scanned the area, the once sparse crowd had swelled exponentially, far too many of their kind now encircling the sacred ground and the witch who had sparked this cataclysmic event.

"Foolish witch!" he spat, his voice dripping with rage and contempt. "You murdered Matace, and now you dare to plead innocence? Do you truly believe we, the demons, are so easily deceived?" His words echoed through the hollow, their biting tone piercing the air.

"So, you've finally decided to end my life?" I asked, my voice unwavering despite the gravity of the situation. Bravely, I met his gaze, my eyes locking with his from the depths of the pit I found myself in. "I was under the impression that this was a sacred circle, a place where my fate would be weighed, where the decision would be made whether my life was worth saving." The tension in the air was palpable, and I could feel my heart pounding in my chest as I awaited his response, steeling myself for whatever judgment he had in store.

My final challenge echoed back to him, defiant and unwavering. The sacred circle could not be denied; its ancient powers demanded respect. The unyielding and absolute rules must be upheld – even the leader, mighty as he was, could not escape their grasp.

The atmosphere felt intense as he faced the inescapable truth: Though his demonic dominion was vast, he, too, was bound by the immutable laws of his dark realm. The weight of this realisation bore down upon him, a burden he could not simply cast aside. In the depths of his twisted soul, he knew that to defy the ancient rites would invite the wrath of forces beyond his comprehension.

He answered with a low, rumbling growl, acknowledging the unbreakable hold of the primordial pact that governed his existence. The sacred circle would not be breached, not by his hand, for to do so would be to invite the unimaginable – a consequence he dared not even consider.

"Ah, I see you are well-acquainted with our kind," he said, his eyes gleaming with curiosity and unease as he leaned precariously forward in his chair, almost losing his balance in his eagerness to hear more. "Tell me, what were the reasons that compelled you to take Matace's life? You must know that he was a dear friend of mine, and his passing has left a void in my heart."

The man's voice was laced with palpable tension, and his body language betrayed his emotional turmoil. He seemed torn between his desire to understand my actions and his grief over the loss of his friend. The intensity of his gaze bore into me, demanding a justification for the deed that had shaken his world.

A sense of stunned disbelief gripped me as the accusation hit my ears. How could anyone dare to level such a heinous charge against me? My mind raced, scrambling to make sense of this outrageous allegation. Unless the accuser had been deliberately fed false information, a calculated ploy to divert attention from the true culprit, I was utterly at a loss for words to profess my innocence.

The air grew thick with tension as I struggled to maintain my composure. My heart pounded, adrenaline coursing through my veins while my mind grasped for a coherent response. Innocence, a quality I had always taken for granted, now hung in the balance, teetering precariously. The weight of the accusation threatened to crush me, leaving me paralysed and unable to mount a defence.

At that moment, I felt the very foundations of my life crumbling beneath me. How could this be happening? The betrayal, injustice, and complete disregard for the truth were too much to bear. I yearned to shout my innocence from the rooftops, demand an explanation, and uncover the twisted web of deceit that had ensnared me. But the words refused to form, trapped behind a wall of stunned silence, leaving me powerless to refute the heinous charge that had been levelled against me.

I found myself transported back in time, my mind vividly recalling the moment when I had first laid eyes upon the partially written documents entrusted to me by Matace. The weight of those pages, the faint scent of age and mystery, had captivated me, drawing me deeper into the enigmatic world within the ink-stained lines. As I poured over the fragmented words, a sense of anticipation and curiosity consumed me, urging me to unravel the secrets they held and piece together the fragments of a story frozen in time.

"Read those? Pfft, no way!" I had exclaimed, a mischievous grin spreading across my face. Excitement bubbled within me as I waved my hand dismissively, baffled as to why Matace was insistent. "I mean, come on," I said, shrugging nonchalantly, "do I really need to bother with that stuff?" My eyes danced with a playful, almost defiant gleam as I revelled in the thrill of the disclosure.

My heart pounds with a mixture of dread and curiosity as I ponder the possibility of encountering a demon. The very thought sends a shiver down my spine, conjuring images of a malevolent, otherworldly being, its eyes glowing with an unholy light, its claws and fangs poised to rend my flesh.

"When am I going to meet a demon?"

Matace stepped into the room, his presence immediately commanding attention. His weathered countenance, etched with the wisdom of years, broke into a warm, familiar smile – the kind I had grown accustomed to over time. The intensity of his gaze seemed to bore into me as if he could see through to the depths of my very soul. His entrance was quiet yet powerful, and I was instinctively drawn to his fatherly aura.

"You'll need them no matter the job you pursue," he asserted firmly, his unwavering gaze dull into mine. "So, I highly recommend you start reading because I have a wealth of material on various subjects that I'm eager for you to delve into." His voice carried a sense of urgency, as if the knowledge he possessed could be the key to unlocking your full potential.

The air crackled with intense excitement, and you couldn't help but feel a surge of anticipation at the prospect of diving into the trove of information he had to offer. With a determined nod, I steeled myself, ready to embark on a journey of intellectual discovery that could forever transform my career.

I couldn't help but curve my lips into a content smile as I immersed myself again in the captivating document. My eyes meticulously scanned every word, dissecting each syllable and tracing every line, sentence by agonising sentence. I was a relentless sponge, greedily absorbing the information that poured forth, my thirst for knowledge insatiable.

With unwavering focus, I devoured the text, allowing the words to seep deep into the recesses of my mind, embedding themselves firmly within the folds of my cerebral cortex. This was no mere casual read – it was an intense, almost primal exercise in understanding, a quest to extract every last nuance and implication from the carefully crafted prose.

Every fibre of my being was engaged, my senses heightened, as I savoured each turn of phrase, each subtle inflexion. I was wholly consumed by the task at hand, my world shrinking to the confines of the document before me, everything else fading into insignificance. This was my moment of intellectual rapture, a symphony of understanding unfolding one word at a time.

"Why don't you come down here and read my mind?" My voice boomed across the stunned crowd, who were exchanging hushed whispers and heated debates in their native tongue. "Isn't that another one of your demonic abilities?" I challenged, my eyes narrowing with a mixture of defiance and frustration. "If so, then go ahead and delve into my mind. You'll see that I had nothing to do with Matace's death. So, who told you I was responsible?" I asked, my tone dripping with a mixture of accusation and a desperate plea for understanding.

He fell deep into contemplation, silently observing his people as they continued their passionate debates. After a few moments, he seemed to have reached a decision, raising his hand authoritatively to command their attention.

Rising from his seat, his flowing gown billowing around his legless form, he regarded the half-formed demons before him. Their bodies hovered above the ground, their gowns concealing the secrets of their peculiar physiology. The air was tense as the leader prepared to address his subjects.

I staggered with a mixture of shock and disbelief as his robe slipped to the side, exposing his bare form. This was no ordinary encounter – this was my first face-to-face with a demon, a creature I had only heard whispers of before. Never had I witnessed one approach a witch, let alone capture and imprison one as they had done to me.

"I will see for myself," he growled, his eyes piercing mine with a dangerous intensity. "I warn you, if there is even the slightest chance that you are lying, I will end your life on the spot. Do you understand?" The challenge was unmistakable in his gaze, daring me to defy him.

A maelstrom of emotions swirled within me – fear, indeed, but also a desperate need for him to believe my innocence, to clear my name of a crime I had not committed. I knew my very life hung in the balance, and I had to tread carefully lest I incur the wrath of this formidable demon.

"Who implicated me?" I hissed through gritted teeth, my voice barely above a whisper.

The bravado that had momentarily bolstered my courage had vanished, replaced by a palpable fear as I beheld his proper demonic form, its essence oozing malevolence and darkness. My heart pounded in my chest, adrenaline coursing through my veins. Yet, my limbs felt leaden, paralysed by the sheer weight of his imposing presence.

The air around us seemed to crackle with an unseen menace, as if the shadows had come alive to witness our confrontation. I steeled my nerves, refusing to let my trembling show. However, deep within, I knew I was no match for the malignant force that stood before me, its eyes burning with a hellish fury threatening to consume me whole.

"Lilly," he breathed, the name falling from his lips with a desperate yearning that echoed in the room's stillness. His heart pounded, the mere utterance of her name igniting a fire within him, a primal need that consumed his every thought. The way it rolled off his tongue, caressing each syllable, betrayed the depth of his affection – a love so all-encompassing it threatened to overwhelm him. At that moment, she was the centre of his universe, the light guiding him through the darkness, the essence of his being. "Lilly," he repeated, the word laced with an intensity that conveyed the full measure of his devotion.

I couldn't stifle the sharp gasp that escaped my lips, knowing full well that he had heard me and was now intrigued by my visceral reaction. My heart pounded in my chest as his gaze bore into me, his piercing eyes studying my every movement with a captivating intensity that threatened to steal the very breath from my lungs.

The air seemed to crackle with an underlying tension, leaving me acutely aware of his presence, my senses heightened and attuned to his every subtle shift or gesture. I found myself trapped in his attention's raw, magnetic pull, unable to look away, my body thrumming with anticipation and trepidation.

As he approached, the air around me turned icy, a paradox of uncertainty swirling within. I held my breath, waiting in trepidation for him to commence his reading. The anticipation was heightened, and I was torn between a desire for the unknown and dreading what was to come. The suspense gripped me, my heart pounding in my chest, as I braced myself for the impact, hoping against hope that the pain would be bearable.

"Hush, now, don't you worry," he murmured, his voice low and soothing, like honey dripping from a spoon. He placed a firm, steadying hand on my shoulder, his grip unwavering. "This will be over before you know it. Just stay perfectly still for me." His eyes locked with mine, their depths reflecting a mixture of authority and calculated calm, daring me to defy him. The air grew thick with the weight of his words, the tension unmistakable as I held my breath, my heart pounding in my ears.

I stood frozen in place, the frigid air binding me in place, my breath turning to knives in my chest. My mind spun with nonsensical thoughts, my body aching to break free. I screamed, desperate for release from the torment.

He lowered his head until it lightly touched mine, sending a chill racing through me, making me shiver uncontrollably. The coldness of the moment seemed to seep into my very bones, and each breath I exhaled formed clouds in the air, a tangible reminder of the piercing coldness surrounding us.

As my mind was slowly invaded, I felt every memory of my entire life being pulled out of me, bit by bit. The whole story unravelled itself, revealing every intricacy. Lilly's face emerged repeatedly, emitting envy, hate, and jealousy that seemed to pour from the depths of her soul. It was a revelation, a section I had missed earlier, and it hit me with an almost overwhelming intensity.

He whispered in my ear, "I see I've been fed some misleading information. Your life is truly intriguing. I sense your strength, passion for justice, and readiness to protect those around you. Quite commendable for one so young." With those words, he stepped away, leaving me reeling as my knees gave way beneath me. I collapsed to the ground, clinging to myself for warmth in the wake of his formidable presence. "I will send you back now," he declared. "We shall trouble you and those around you no more. But before you go, tell me one more thing..."

As I gazed up at him, his face mere inches from mine, his lips parted, but no words emerged. The captivating spell he was weaving over me tightened its grip, and a surge of warmth began to course through my very being. My limbs, mind, and entire body were no longer my own, consumed by a growing, all-encompassing desire.

"Why didn't you kill Lilly earlier when you had the chance?" he murmured, his voice low and seductive, his eyes burning with an intensity that made my heart race.

"Because," I managed to choke out, my parched and cracked lips struggling to form the words, "I have to understand why she's doing this. In all the years I've known her, she's always been kind, even bossy at times, but never have I seen her filled with such envy and hatred as she is now. I simply can't comprehend any of it." My voice quivered with a mixture of desperation and confusion, my brow furrowed as I searched for answers in the haunting gaze of my companion.

"Your life may have seemed intriguing from the outside," he said, his gaze piercing. His voice was laced with a subtle intensity, "But you have no idea of the hidden depths, the intricate web of secrets and complexities that lie beneath the surface. The true nature of your experiences, the raw emotions, and the pivotal moments that have shaped you are the details that remain concealed, known only to you and a select few. It's a perspective that eludes the casual observer, a perspective that grants a profound understanding of who you truly are," he said. "I've just given you the task. You have two days, Seira, to destroy her. If you haven't done it by then, I will have no choice but to summon my people back to Earth to do it for you. Is that a fair deal?" I nodded, unable to respond; I could not utter a single word. I was utterly spent; my energy had been drained by his overwhelming power and intrusion into my mind's deepest corners, leaving me utterly exhausted.

Slumbering into a light, restless sleep, I felt my body slowly returning to me as if my soul had finally escaped the demonic hideout and was being fully restored. Yet, the ordeal had left me completely spent, and I found myself sleeping fitfully on the cold, hard ground, my mind still reeling from the sheer intensity of the encounter.

I stirred faintly, Luke's voice breaking through the hazy veil of my slumber. Forcing my heavy eyelids open, I met his anxious gaze, mustering a reassuring whisper, "Everything is fine." Though barely audible, my words eased his concern, and he gently gathered me into his arms, carrying me inside the house.

Waves of exhaustion washed over me as I drifted in and out of consciousness, my sleep plagued by horrific nightmares.

Dark, sinister beasts lunged at me, their razor-sharp fangs bared, while demons clawed at my soul, refusing to release their merciless grip. The past few days' events had taken a devastating toll, leaving me feeling utterly lost and powerless to understand Lilly's motives. The uncertainty and the terror of the nightmares were relentless, dragging me deeper into a consuming state of confusion and dread.

"Are you awake?" Luke's voice cut through the darkness, his urgency evident. I blinked, the fog of sleep slowly lifting from my mind.

"I am, barely," I croaked, my words thick with exhaustion. "Have they gone?" A tense silence hung before he replied, his chuckle laced with a nervous edge.

"They have," he replied solemnly, his voice tinged with a hint of sorrow. "But alas, my home lies in ruins, ravaged by the relentless flames." He paused, his gaze distant as he surveyed the devastation. "The fires have been extinguished, but the damage is done. What was once a haven of comfort and security now stands as a stark reminder of the destruction that has befallen it.

I let out a heavy sigh, my words laced with desperation. "I'm sorry," I muttered, my voice quivering slightly. A profound sense of shame washed over me as I met the bartender's gaze, pleading. "Can I please have a drink?" I asked, my fingers drumming anxiously on the worn wooden counter, the need for the numbing effects of alcohol palpable in every syllable.

Without a word, he firmly placed a glass of water in my hands, his unwavering gaze silently urging me to sit up and take it. The weight of the glass and the clarity of his actions left no room for argument – I knew I needed to heed his unspoken directive and regain my composure.

I fought against the overwhelming fatigue that weighed down my tired body, straining to push myself into a sitting position. With Luke's gentle assistance, I could accomplish the task more swiftly.

"What happened?" he questioned softly, his voice laced with concern.

"They've issued a chilling ultimatum - we have a mere 48 hours to resolve this crisis before they dispatch their own operatives to eliminate her," I responded, the details searing into my mind with stark clarity. "And you, my friend, have been unconscious for far too long. We're running out of time."

The air crackled with an imminent sense of urgency, the weight of the situation pressing down upon us. I could feel the adrenaline coursing through my veins, the need for decisive action pulsing in my every fibre. The stakes had never been higher, and failure was simply not an option.

The room was cloaked in darkness, the heavy curtains drawn tightly, sealing off any glimpse of the outside world. The impenetrable shadows concealed the passage of time, leaving me disoriented, unaware of how long I had been lost in slumber. As I slowly regained consciousness, the mystery of Lilly and Matace loomed before me, its tangled web waiting to be unravelled, its secrets beckoning me to uncover them.

"Roughly four hours," he replied, his voice terse and clipped. His eyes narrowed, a muscle in his jaw twitching as he fought to maintain his composure. "What else did they say?" The unspoken anticipation felt immense, the question laced with a hint of urgency and an undercurrent of concern.

"They seemed to think my life was somehow enthralling," I said, my brow furrowing in confusion. "I have no idea why they found it so captivating when it's all mundane routine and monotony to me." I glanced around the empty room, the eerie silence pressing in. "Where on Earth has everyone gone? It's like a ghost town in here."

I had no desire to discuss the harrowing encounter with the demons. It was a profound, sacred moment that few had ever experienced and survived unscathed. The tales I'd heard from others who had faced such entities were sketchy at best, often ending in their untimely and mysterious demise. I had no intention of sharing the same fate, for I had emerged from that encounter forever changed, my perceptions of reality forever altered.

"I'm waiting patiently for you to wake up downstairs," he replied. "Did they say anything else to you?"

His relentless questioning set my nerves on edge, as if he were deliberately withholding crucial information from me. A creeping sense of unease settled in my stomach. I couldn't shake the nagging suspicion that he was hiding something – some vital piece of the puzzle he refused to share.

This sudden evasiveness seemed so out of character for him, especially given the high stakes at play. I couldn't fathom why he would lie or keep me in the dark, not when we needed to be completely transparent. The uneasy silence between us was perceptible, thick with the weight of unsaid words and unspoken truths. I searched his face for any sign of deception. Still, his expression remained maddeningly inscrutable, leaving me increasingly unsettled and off-balance.

"No," I shook my head vehemently, my heart pounding in my chest. "He read my mind, can you believe that? Lilly dared to tell them I was the killer, that I killed Matace. The irony is unbelievable - she did it just to get away quicker. But they'll find her and won't stop until they do. We have only two days left." I paused, the weight of the situation pressing down on me. "I had to prove my innocence, so I had to let him into my head. It hurt, and I was so cold," I moaned, shivering at the memory.

"I bet you were," he answered, his voice laced with empathy. "It's not a pleasant experience, having someone invade your mind like that." He smiled, but there was a hint of sadness in his eyes. "Besides, I've given up trying these days since you've managed to artfully block me out." His light teasing was all we both needed to acknowledge the reality of the situation - it was slipping out of our control, spiralling into oblivion.

"We need to go downstairs immediately," I said, urgency lacing my voice as I rose from the bed. "I have to check on everyone and ensure they're alright."

He stopped me in my tracks, his eyes dark and heavy beneath his long, fluttering lashes. "There's something you need to know first," he said, his tone grave. "A few of our people have lost their lives, and now the others are demanding vengeance. I've tried to calm them, but they insist on speaking with you."

I felt a chill run down my spine. "Vengeance?" I breathed, my heart racing. "What do they want from me?"

His gaze bore into mine, intense and unyielding. "They're angry, and they won't back down easily. You'll need to be strong to stand your ground against them. Don't show any fear, no matter what they say or do."

The weight of his words settled over me, but I knew I had no choice. Lives were at stake, and I had to face whatever awaited me downstairs, no matter how daunting it might be. With a deep, steadying breath, I nodded and moved towards the door, steeling myself for the confrontation.

"Oh dear, this doesn't sound good at all!" I exclaimed, my heart racing with worry. "Just how dire is the situation? And please, spare me the gory details – I don't think knowing the specifics will help me understand their anger when I finally go downstairs." My voice trembled slightly, betraying the growing sense of dread that was settling in the pit of my stomach.

I tried to brace myself for the confrontation to come, but the uncertainty of the situation only heightened my anxiety. The unknown was always the most terrifying part, and I desperately wished I had more information to work with. Still, dwelling on the details would only further agitate me, so I took a deep breath and steeled myself for whatever lay ahead.

"It was disastrous," he said, his voice laced with urgency and concern. "One of the coven leaders is on his way here, and he's hell-bent on getting involved in what we're doing. He won't stop until he destroys Lilly once he finds out what's happened since. The vampire he killed was his own son, whom he had taken from this world when the boy was just a child – his only remaining true relative. And let me tell you, he's seething with rage beyond your wildest imagination."

His words hit me like a ton of bricks, and I shot out of bed, suddenly feeling a surge of adrenaline coursing through my veins. The fatigue and exhaustion plaguing my body only moments before vanished, replaced by a renewed sense of alertness and vigour, even though I had not consumed any sustenance or enjoyed a proper night's rest, which my body had desperately craved.

"I see the weather has changed again," I commented. "It's finally sunny out there."

The ominous, charcoal-coloured clouds loomed menacingly overhead, their oppressive presence a harbinger of the demons' impending assault. These malevolent entities had conjured the gloomy, foreboding skies as a stark warning to their unsuspecting prey, casting an ominous pall over the land.

Lilly couldn't help but wonder if her actions had somehow triggered this dramatic shift in the weather, a portentous sign of the dark forces now gathering their strength, preparing to unleash their wrath upon the unsuspecting populace. The air crackled with eerie, unsettling energy as if the demons' malicious intentions had tainted the atmosphere.

The people trembled with fear and anticipation, bracing themselves for the inevitable clash between the forces of light and darkness that would soon engulf their world. The stage was set, and the battle lines had been drawn – a conflict that would test the mettle of even the bravest of souls.

I nodded, feeling a lump forming in my throat as the memories of the encounter came rushing back. My mouth had gone suddenly dry, and the mere mention of the demons sent a shiver down my spine. Today, I ventured into the very pits of hell and miraculously returned, a testament to my resilience. I was undoubtedly fortunate to have escaped with my life, let alone with my skull intact.

The intensity of the experience had left me shaken. Still, I knew I had to find the courage to recount the harrowing details. As I steadied my voice, I could feel the adrenaline coursing through my veins, fueling my determination to convey the gravity of what I had witnessed and endured.

The demons, with their piercing eyes and menacing claws, had nearly consumed me. Still, through sheer willpower and a touch of luck, I had managed to claw my way back to the realm of the living.

The experience had been a harrowing descent into the darkest corners of the human psyche. The sights and sounds that assaulted me were the stuff of nightmares, a cacophony of agonising screams and the stench of sulfur and decay. Yet, through sheer force of will and a newfound determination to survive, I had managed to claw my way back to the surface, battered and bruised but ultimately victorious.

As I stood there, facing my companion, I could still feel the weight of that hellish journey upon my shoulders. The memory of it burned like a brand, a constant reminder of the horrors I had faced and the price I had paid to emerge unscathed. Yet, at that moment, I knew I had been forged in the fires of adversity, my spirit tempered and strengthened by the ordeal.

"She has cast a veil of deception over everyone, obscuring the truth of her presence in this world. She unconsciously manipulates the elements wherever she goes, altering the weather to suit her whims. Her mind is no longer her own, consumed by a darkness that has taken root within her. Once, there may have been a chance to stop this malevolent force before it consumed her, but now it has grown too strong. No hope is left – the evil has already spread too deep."

He stood there, unflinching, his gaze fixed on me as I spoke. No emotion crossed his features, no sign of complaint or even the slightest acknowledgement. He simply waited, his posture rigid, his presence commanding, as if the air around him had stilled in anticipation of my following words.

His face was eerily still, not a single muscle twitch or a flicker of emotion. His eyebrows remained frozen, devoid of any semblance of life. Aside from his human appearance, nothing about him suggested he was anything but a lifeless entity. The reality was that he had been dead for a very long time, his heart no longer beating, his soul long departed from this world.

"Hey, are you listening?" I said, a slight edge to my voice as I waited for his response. The silence was growing heavy, and I couldn't help but feel a little frustrated that he hadn't acknowledged what I had just said. I leaned in, maintaining eye contact, and repeated myself with a bit more emphasis, "Did you catch what I just told you?"

"Huh? What was that?" he responded, shaking his head as he snapped out of his deep, contemplative state. A sheepish grin spread as he apologised, "Sorry about that! I heard you, but I was kind of lost in my own thoughts."

"Phew, I'm so relieved you were there to hear me when we were trapped in that dark, damp cave with Meniagier, or else you would have been vampire chow," I replied sharply, a hint of sarcasm in my tone. "So, when do you think the big boss vampire will appear?" He scrunched up his face at my mocking nickname for him but couldn't help letting out a slight grin.

"I strongly advise against addressing him with that term," he cautioned, his voice laced with urgency. "He's not the type to take kindly to such remarks, and unless you're prepared to become his next meal, I'd recommend keeping that comment to yourself," he added, his brow furrowing with concern. "There's something I need to discuss with you," he continued, his tone shifting to a more serious note.

I turned slowly and was struck by the abrupt transformation in his expression. His face had shifted from its usual cheerfulness to a grave, serious demeanour. The remarkable change in his characteristics was almost unsettling, if not downright peculiar. I never knew his mood, and gauging or maintaining any meaningful conversation with him took a lot of work.

I eyed the person cautiously, my guard up. "Go on," I said warily, "Ask away."

"When all this is over," he began, "Do you think there will be a time when we can go out?"

I couldn't believe my ears. With his astonishingly idiotic behaviour, this vampire dared to ask me out on a date. The mere thought of it sent shivers down my spine. If anyone were to find out about the passionate kisses we had shared in the past, it would wreak havoc. And if we were actually to start dating, the consequences would be catastrophic, beyond my wildest imaginations.

"I...err..." I stammered. I was aware I would hurt him deeply. Because of how I already felt about him, it wasn't something I wanted to do. "I don't think we can, Luke," I whispered unsteadily. "Can't you see what would happen? It would end up with either one or both of us dead. The realm won't stand by and let us have any kind of relationship."

"I see," he replied thoughtfully. "I was checking for your reaction. I know you have feelings for me. I see it every time you look at me, with every word you speak. It's between us, but we're prevented from taking advantage purely because of the realm and what it stands for. Don't you think it's about time someone changed the rules slightly?"

His words carried a sense of urgency, a quiet intensity that demanded my attention. The way he spoke and held my gaze left no doubt in my mind that he was acutely aware of the feelings we shared, the desires that simmered just beneath the surface. It was as if he was daring me, challenging me to take that leap, to push past the barriers that kept us apart.

"It's frustrating that we can't be together," I sighed heavily, "but the High Witch sets the rules, and she's consumed by evil. So, any change is unlikely to happen anytime soon." I turned away, gazing into the distance. "Someday, everything might be different, and if I'm still around, there's a chance for us. But, Luke," I said, meeting his eyes, "I do have feelings for you. I've tried to deny and ignore them, but I can't. This is a terrible situation we find ourselves in, and the best we can do is move on and try to forget."

He stormed out without a word, spinning on his heel and marching out of the room. The door slammed behind him, rattling on its hinges and making me flinch at the loud, thunderous bang.

I trudged over to the window seat and collapsed onto it, my heart sinking like a heavy stone. My mind spun, unable to find a way out of this tangled mess. I don't know how much longer I can keep going, not with the threat hanging over me and the overwhelming complexity of my feelings for Luke. This is the most complicated situation I've ever faced, and I could improve at problem-solving. I feel trapped, with no room to breathe or escape.

As I made my way down the dimly lit corridor, I was met with the lingering haze of smoke that had seeped into the air. The walls, now stained with soot, bore witness to the intensity of the recent altercation. The air felt thick and heavy, the acrid scent of burnt embers still hanging in the atmosphere.

The commotion that had drawn me here had clearly taken a dramatic turn, leaving behind a trail of destruction that sent an unsettling chill down my spine. With each step, the weight of the situation grew, the charred surfaces serving as a stark reminder of the chaos that had unfolded.

The destruction of Luke's home was immense. Rooms lay in ruins, unrecognisable. I found myself not in the room where he had initially placed me but in a completely different one, devoid of any of my belongings. As I rummaged through the space, I came across a set of clothes belonging to someone else – plain but clean, which was a relief.

The long, flowing dress I discovered bore an uncanny resemblance to the one I had recently discarded, its ethereal, billowing sleeves reminiscent of the garments worn by the elder witches of the realm.

Aside from the esteemed High Witch, countless elder, wiser witches had been around since the dawn of the century. Through their powerful magic, they had managed to preserve their lives indefinitely, meticulously altering their appearances like the vampires, ensuring that no mortal could ever suspect they were the same individuals.

Even if someone caught a glimpse of these ancient beings, the witches swiftly cast a spell, inducing a targeted memory loss in the observer. This memory lapse would not be a complete eradication but rather a selective fading, just enough for the witness to forget the sight of a witch hailing from a bygone era.

My dress cascaded along the floor, elegantly flowing behind and around me. The snug, cosy fit felt heavenly against my skin, a welcomed respite from the tattered, foul-smelling garments I had discarded. The stench of the Meniagier still clung to me, their putrid odours permeating the air, tainting the very space I occupied. The revolting scents followed with each step, a lingering reminder of my torment.

The heated exchange took place in the downstairs dining room, which was the second of the many dining areas in Luke's sprawling estate. The whitewashed walls seemed untouched by the earlier commotion. At the same time, the sleek, silver-lined furniture now held Darcy, Benjamin, and a few other unfamiliar faces. The tension in the air was palpable as the voices grew louder and the disagreement intensified, the participants locked in a fierce battle of wits and wills.

I had caught a brief, fleeting glance of them earlier but couldn't linger. I had to hurry and retrace Lilly's path, following in her footsteps with urgency. My curiosity and anticipation compelled me to leave that place and pursue the trail quickly, determined to uncover the truth ahead.

The atmosphere was tense, their voices bristling with frustration and their tone harsh. Drink in hand, Luke leaned casually against the fireplace as if the heated exchange barely registered with him.

Ignoring the voice in my head that cautioned against eavesdropping, I settled into a secluded spot where I could listen undetected. The cover of invisibility allowed me to slip into the room and take up a position in the far corner, giving me a prime vantage point to observe the unfolding scene.

"Look, Luke, you clearly don't grasp the full gravity of this situation," one of them snapped, his voice laced with frustration and barely contained anger. "There's too much at stake for any of us to handle; not even your precious little witch can be of much help," he sneered, his words dripping with disdain.

"Listen, Greg," Darcy whispered, leaning closer and glancing at Luke worriedly. "Hurling insults won't help. Trust me, you don't want to see him lose his temper. I've been there, and it's not pretty."

She shuddered at the memory. "Earlier, I made the same mistake with the girl, and he almost..." Darcy trailed off, her voice laced with fear and caution.

The intensity in her voice was evident, and the urgency in her words conveyed the gravity of the situation. She knew firsthand the consequences of provoking Luke's anger and was determined to prevent Greg from making the same mistake.

Luke gazed at her, his expression brimming with amusement as her words echoed. His eyes locked onto her, captivated by her presence, their intensity unwavering.

"Nah, I didn't come close to offing you," he said with a smirk, playfully nudging her arm. "That's a bit too much, even for your flair for the dramatic, don't you think?"

"Ugh, you just don't get it, do you?" she huffed, her brow furrowed in frustration. "You've hurt me, and it stings like hell." Her eyes narrowed, and her lips pressed into a tight, disapproving line. "Can't you see how much you've hurt me?" she asked, her voice dripping with a mixture of hurt and accusation.

"Look, I'm not going to tolerate any more of this 'witch' nonsense about Seira. If you keep disrespecting her like that, there will be serious consequences. I'm done with the threats and the name-calling - it stops now. Understand?"

The room fell into an eerie silence; the only sound was the quiet clink of utensils against plates as they ate. Greg, his food untouched, fidgeted nervously, his eyes glued to the door.

Tense anticipation hung in the air as if he were waiting for something or someone to come crashing through at any moment. The others glanced at him, unsure, the unease palpable. Greg's constant glances towards the entrance only heightened the tension, the sense that something ominous was about to happen.

"Where the hell is she?" Benjamin blurted out, his voice laced with frustration as he sipped his drink. His eyes darted around the room, searching for any sign of the missing person. He finally fixed his gaze on Luke, his brow furrowed, demanding an answer.

"I have no idea," Luke said, his voice laced with frustration. "She's probably sitting there, replaying everything that's happened, trying to make sense of everything. That's her thing, you know? Obsessing over every little detail until she's got it all figured out." He let out a weary sigh, shaking his head.

The silence was deafening, an uncomfortable tension hanging thick in the air. No one dared to voice the thoughts racing through their minds, the true nature of this situation becoming increasingly unclear. The investigation had hit a frustrating dead-end, with no real answers to explain Lilly's troubling actions. It spiralled out of control, leaving everyone uncertain and uneasy.

The lack of progress only heightened the sense of unease as they struggled to make sense of the deepening mystery before them. The stakes were high, and the way forward seemed murkier than ever, adding to the growing dread that permeated the room.

Luke's head snapped around, his eyes darting across the room. He inhaled sharply, his brow furrowing as he scrutinised the air. "When is he getting here?" The urgency in his voice was palpable, his every muscle tense with anticipation.

"He's on his way and should arrive by nightfall," a woman responded urgently. "I spoke to his daughter on the phone earlier. He's devastated by the loss of his son and demands answers. He wants to talk to Seira too; he somehow believes it's her fault," she explained.

Darcy's eyes widened in disbelief. "How can he think that? It's not like she summoned the demons here! As Luke already explained, Lilly lied to them in the first place," she exclaimed, her voice laced with frustration and concern.

"I understand," she said softly, her voice a gentle balm. A pensive sigh escaped her lips as she continued, "But Darcy, have you ever had the pleasure of meeting Zanda?"

"Absolutely not," she declared firmly, shaking her head. "Honestly, I've never had the slightest desire to do so. The atrocities committed by his family are simply abhorrent, and I'm baffled by how they've managed to evade any real consequences. The realm seems powerless to hold them accountable." She paused, her voice laced with apprehension. "Agnes, do you think he'll spark another conflict? I'm not being a coward, but I'm just not prepared to engage in another round of fighting," she confessed, her brow furrowed with concern.

Agnes smiled in answer, stepped over to Darcy, and patted her shoulder gently.

"Zanda has no intention of getting into any fights. His sole focus is on seeing Seira and getting the answers he needs. Zanda decided it was best not to tell his mother where he was going. Still, the daughter has followed my instructions and informed her mother. Hopefully, this means there won't be any need for confrontation today," he said, his voice tinged with urgency and determination.

"Whew, thank goodness!" Darcy exclaimed, a visible shiver running down her spine. She let out a deep breath, relief washing over her. "I was really hoping you'd say that," she admitted, her eyes wide with apprehension and anticipation.

Benjamin gulped down his drink, making a loud slurping sound. He then yawned and stretched his limbs, letting out a heavy sigh. With a casual wave, he excused himself, eager to take a short break until Zanda arrived. As he left, he asked someone to collect him later.

Greg collapsed back onto the sofa, his limbs sprawled out casually in front of him. He studied Luke's back intently, his brows furrowing as he contemplated something. Suddenly, a brief chuckle escaped his lips, and Luke turned to him with a friendly, questioning gaze.

"What's so funny?" he asked, his gaze fixed on the young vampire. "Care to enlighten me?"

The vampire responded with a slight taunting edge, "I've just figured out why you're so damn overprotective of her. You're in love with the dirty witch, aren't you?"

The man's eyes narrowed, and a flash of anger crossed his features. "Don't you dare speak about her that way," he growled, his voice low and menacing.

The vampire's lips curled into a smug grin, delighted at having struck a nerve. "Oh, it's true, isn't it? You can't bear the thought of anyone insulting your precious little witch."

The air crackled with tension as the two faced off, the unspoken emotions thick between them. The vampire's taunting laughter further enraged the man, his fists clenching at his sides as he struggled to contain his rising fury.

Before Greg could utter another word, Luke swiftly crossed the room, unleashing his vampiric nature. In a flash, he had Greg pinned to the chair, his fingers wrapped tightly around Greg's throat. Helpless and speechless, Greg could only stare into the eyes of his attacker, acutely aware of the vast difference in their vampiric prowess. The age gap between them was palpable. Greg dreaded that he had no idea how to defend himself against this formidable foe.

Darcy rose to her feet, her heart racing. With a gentle touch, she placed her hand on Luke's arm, a silent plea for him to let go of Greg. The tension in the room crackled, and she knew time was running out. She had to act fast to prevent any more violence from erupting in the quiet sanctuary of their home.

"I've warned you not to address her that way," Luke growled, his teeth bared menacingly as his vampiric nature threatened to overpower his self-control. His eyes glowed with a predatory intensity, and his fangs gleamed in the dim light, a stark reminder of his supernatural strength. "She is not some foul, wretched witch. In fact, she is far more powerful than any of you can possibly imagine." His voice dripped with a mixture of protective fury and undisguised contempt for those who dared to underestimate the woman he was defending.

Luke forcefully shoved Greg to the ground, causing him to collapse onto his haunches, staring at Luke with wide, panicked eyes. Luke had stepped back, his muscles rippling as he continued to hiss and rumble menacingly.

"I'm sorry, man," Greg blurted out, his voice trembling. I swear I won't repeat it, but Luke, you can't do this. You just can't," he pleaded, his eyes wide with desperation. You know why we can't get involved with witches. It's too dangerous. Please, you gotta listen to me."

"Are you seriously deluded, thinking I'd do something like that?" Luke spat, his eyes narrowing in disgust. "Don't be so ridiculous. Show some damn respect for her, will you? I'm here to protect her, and that's all there is to it." The edge in his voice was palpable, his every word dripping with a barely contained fury.

I lurked in the shadows, my heart pounding as I watched from my concealed vantage point. Suddenly, Luke whipped his head around, his eyes locking onto my hiding spot as if he could sense my presence. Panicked, I hurriedly shuffled away, scurrying out of the room with a sense of urgency, desperate to avoid being discovered.

I barely had time to react when Luke's grip tightened around my elbow, and he swiftly dragged me into the next room. When we were out of sight, his eyes burned with unbridled hostility. I could feel the seething anger radiating from him, directed straight at me.

There was no escaping the intensity of his gaze or the palpable tension in the air.

"What in blazes were you up to?" he bellowed, his face flushed with rage. He began pacing furiously across the room, his heavy footsteps echoing like the pounding of a drum. His hands clenched and unclenched as he tried to contain his mounting anger, his eyes narrowing and brow furrowing with each passing step.

I listened intently, my gaze fixed on the speaker. "Listening," I responded, my voice steady but with a hint of curiosity. "It was, well, quite fascinating, to say the least." My words carried a subtle weight as if I were carefully mulling over the experience, trying to unpack its nuances.

"Interesting? Interesting?!" he shouted furiously, his voice dripping with contempt. "It was a private matter between them and me, and I didn't want you to know about how they felt or the vile things that spilt from their foul mouths!" He spat the words out, his eyes narrowed in anger, every muscle in his body tense with the intensity of his emotions.

"Why on Earth would you let me stay there?" she exclaimed, her voice dripping with frustration and a hint of confusion. The words tumbled out, laced with a palpable sense of bewilderment, as if she couldn't fathom the reasoning behind such a decision. Her brow furrowed, and her eyes searched the other person's face, desperately seeking an explanation that made sense. The tension in the air was palpable, and the question hung there, demanding an answer that would shed light on this perplexing situation.

"What did you just say?" he spat, his eyes narrowing into a fierce glare as he whirled around to face me, his expression a mixture of shock and pure outrage.

"You could feel my presence in the air," I responded with a terse smile. "Yet, you chose to let me stay." I continued, "You didn't point out my presence, nor did you ask me to leave."

A slow dawning of understanding flickered in his eyes. He recognised that I was acutely aware of my surroundings, that I was growing stronger, no longer the feeble witch who needed to be rescued in every battle. This was my moment to shine, and I would make sure of it, even if it meant taking my last breath. Lilly was headed straight to the depths of hell, and if necessary, I would be the one to send her there with the perfect spell.

He visibly shook himself, his body language betraying a shift in his demeanour. Turning to me, he offered the first genuine smile I had seen from him and said, "I wasn't sure if I was simply imagining your familiar scent. My mind has been playing tricks on me lately."

I replied with a tinge of scorn, "Tell me more about that. Where have the Cronomiun people disappeared to?"

"They vanished a long time ago," he replied, his voice laced with a hint of unease. "They promised to return, but I have no idea when. Honestly, I hope they don't show up while Zanda is here," he added, a tinge of worry in his tone.

"Why not?" I inquired, my curiosity piqued, my brows furrowing slightly.

"Look," he said, struggling to keep his composure. "If they're around when Zanda shows up, there's going to be trouble. Zanda can't stand those people, not one bit." His words were laced with palpable tension, hinting at the impending conflict that would erupt should the two parties cross paths.

The harsh reality dawned on them—vampires, the elusive creatures of the night, were notoriously known for their disdain and distrust toward other demons and denizens of the underworld. Accepting these otherworldly beings into their ranks was met with resounding opposition, a testament to their unwavering allegiance to their own kind.

The information they had received was a stark reminder of the divide between the various factions of the supernatural realm, which was not easily bridged, even in the face of adversity.

"Well, looks like I'll have some serious explaining to do when he arrives," I muttered under my breath, a tinge of apprehension in my voice. Without another word, I hurried to the back garden, my feet carrying me swiftly across the grass. I plopped down on the cold stone bench, my mind racing with a million thoughts. The weight of the situation seemed to press down on me, and I sank deeper into the quiet solitude of the garden, bracing myself for the impending confrontation.

Chapter Eleven

The crisp autumn air nipped at my skin, sending a shiver down my spine. Goosebumps rose along my arms as I pulled my coat tighter, huddling against the bite of the cold. Lately, I had been leaning heavily on my magical abilities, shaping the world around me with a simple flick of my wrist and controlling every detail of my life. But the thought of summoning even one more spell to ward off the chill felt daunting, like a burden too heavy to bear.

Magic had become my crutch, a way to avoid life's natural ebb and flow. I longed for the simplicity of feeling the elements as they were meant to be experienced—unfiltered and raw, the cold seeping into my bones and reminding me of my humanity. Yet, the comfort of my powers was all too familiar, the ease of control too tempting to relinquish.

As the wind whipped through my hair, I stood at a crossroads—caught between embracing the stark reality of the moment or retreating to the safety of the world I had so carefully crafted. The choice loomed before me, as tangible as the cold biting my cheeks, pulling me in two opposing directions.

The whirlwind of events had left my mind in a dizzying state of turmoil. As I grappled with the gravity of the situation, a newfound sense of independence began to emerge. Without Luke's constant guidance and interference, my thoughts and ideas started to take shape. I found them remarkably compelling – ideas I believed could transcend even lofty expectations.

Determined to maintain this newfound autonomy, I consciously kept my mind firmly my own, shielding it from Luke's prying eyes and influence. This was no easy task, as the temptation to revert to the familiar comfort of his guidance was ever-present. But I knew that to grow and realise my full potential truly, I had to chart my own course, guided by the strength of my convictions and the power of my imagination.

The path ahead was uncertain, but the thrill of forging my own way, free from the constraints of others, filled me with a sense of exhilaration and purpose. I was no longer content to follow the lead of others simply; instead, I was determined to blaze my own trail, trusting in the power of my mind to guide me towards the success that lay beyond my wildest dreams.

I'd used one last spell to create a small bubble of tranquillity around me, my perfect escape. Surrounded by a shield magically forged to respond to my voice and Luke's. There was no need for anyone else to be able to enter. The place was in the surrounding gardens of the remains of Luke's house, where others would see the real world, and I saw whatever I wanted.

The moment Luke entered through the shield, I felt his powerful presence envelop me, even before laying eyes on him. My heart raced with anticipation, skipping beats in the process. His captivating scent and an aura of sheer determination surrounded me, nearly overwhelming my senses.

I yearned to be with him, his equal, his true mate. But I knew that could never happen unless I surrendered my very soul, becoming like him - a creature of the night, forever bound to the darkness. The intense, primal desire that consumed me was both terrifying and exhilarating.

The idea of a love affair with a mysterious "bad boy" might have seemed thrilling and straight out of a fairy tale to some, but not to me. For me, my career and ambitions took precedence. I wasn't about to entrust my future to the whims of a vampire, no matter how alluring the prospect.

At most, I could see us maintaining a close friendship, but even that seemed risky. The unknown and the potential danger of such a relationship held little appeal. My sights were firmly set on my chosen path. No matter how captivating it might appear to others, I wouldn't be swayed by the siren's call of a forbidden romance.

As I pondered my uncertain future, a sense of unease settled over me. I knew an inevitable confrontation with Lilly was looming, and the demons' impending deadline only added to the mounting tension.

The outcome of that battle weighed heavily on my mind – would I emerge victorious or perish? Unlike many witches of the past who had the power to peer into their own destinies and shape their paths, I felt no such comforting connection to the future. The unknown ahead filled me with a growing sense of dread and unease.

I was once a mortal being bound by the constraints of the physical world. In that previous life, I had the power to shape my destiny through my choices and the principles I upheld. The spells I wielded, the realm I inhabited, and the people who surrounded me - these elements commanded my respect, yet none more so than the mortal body that housed my very essence.

As I navigated the complexities of the mortal realm, I came to deeply appreciate the significance of every decision, action, and interaction.

But I revered my mortal body, fragile yet resilient, the most. Once so vulnerable, this physical vessel is now imbued with a newfound sense of purpose and determination. It was the canvas upon which I painted the masterpiece of my life, the instrument through which I expressed the full spectrum of my being. Every breath, heartbeat, and movement were a testament to the power and fragility of my mortal form.

"Seira," he whispered, his warm breath tickling the sensitive skin of my ear. His lips nearly brushed against me as he spoke, sending a shiver down my spine. "You have a guest," he continued, his voice low and urgent, hinting at a sense of urgency or importance that I couldn't quite place. Although he was on the other side of the shield, the fact his voice and presence caused a reaction in me always took my breath away. It always felt as though he was standing right beside me.

My heart raced as I whirled around, desperately seeking the source of the unexpected noise. Alarm flooded my senses, and I scanned the immediate area, my eyes wide with trepidation. Who could have found me in this secluded hideaway where I had sought refuge?

No one knew my location inside my tranquil space or the events unfolding around me. I felt the shift of change in the atmosphere to one of surprise, and I braced myself for a confrontation, my muscles tensed and ready to react at the slightest provocation. The question burned in my mind, a silent plea for answers—who had intruded upon my solitude, and what did they want? I slowly reached the front door, stepping out of my tranquillity.

"Who's there?" I called out, my heart pounding in my chest. The sound of footsteps approaching sent a surge of unease through me.

"Your parents have arrived," came the response from one of the many vampires inside the house, the voice thick with impatience. I hesitated, gripping the doorknob as a million thoughts raced. Taking a deep breath, I steeled myself and pulled the front door open, bracing for what lay on the other side.

I was completely transported to a different realm, utterly disoriented and bewildered. His response simply didn't compute in my mind – it made no logical sense. How could my mortal parents be here, in this foreign place, surrounded by individuals like him and his companions, people I perceived as ruthless killers?

"My parents?" I blurted out, my voice laced with disbelief and confusion. My heart raced, and I felt a sudden heaviness in the pit of my stomach as the words sank in. "Are you absolutely certain?" I asked, my eyes searching the other person's face for any sign of doubt or deception. The revelation had caught me completely off guard, leaving me grappling with a whirlwind of emotions that threatened to overwhelm me.

"Well," he said, as he met my gaze, and walked to stand beside me. His voice held a playful, almost mocking tone as he continued, "If these mortal individuals, one a woman and the other a man, have both shown me photographs of you as a child and they absolutely reek of their humanity, then I suppose I can assume they aren't lying," he teased, a mischievous glint in his eyes.

"Oh," I murmured, my body trembling slightly as I tried to maintain a calm demeanour. My heart raced, and my palms felt clammy as I asked, "Where did they go?" The question hung in the air, thick with unspoken dread and the nagging fear of the unknown. I desperately needed answers, but the uncertainty of the situation weighed heavily on me, making it challenging to keep my composure.

"The blue room," he called out urgently. "It's on the other side of the house. That's the only room that didn't get burned down." His words fueled my excitement as I sprinted towards the house, my heart racing with anticipation. The smoke-filled air stung my eyes, but I pushed forward, determined to see what awaited me in that untouched room.

I screeched to a halt outside what was supposed to be the "blue room," though I found the name a bit misleading. Only one wall was actually blue, while the others were a kaleidoscope of different colours, each seemingly competing for attention. Despite the eclectic décor, the space had an undeniable sense of comfort. Maybe it was the oversized armchairs arranged in cosy clusters throughout the room, inviting anyone to sink into their plush cushions. Or the state-of-the-art music system that dominated one corner, its sleek design a sharp contrast to the room's otherwise quirky charm.

I didn't have time to dwell on the details, though. My eager parents were already there, drinks in hand, their eyes sparkling with anticipation. Barely able to contain my excitement, I rushed in, not bothering to take a closer look at the room. All I cared about was diving headfirst into whatever adventure awaited us.

"Mum, Dad," I shouted, hurling myself into my dad's arms. "How are you? Why are you here? How did you find me? Who told you I was here?" I asked in a rush without pausing for a breath.

"Calm down," My dad chuckled, "Slow down."

My mother's eyes brimmed with tears as she laid eyes on me. Her lips trembled, and she quickly brought a delicate, lace-trimmed handkerchief to dab at her eyes. Despite the overwhelming emotion, her expression remained remarkably composed, far more serene than I had ever witnessed in all the years I had known her.

"Lilly told us where to find you," she said. We've been worried. Why didn't you ring us?"

At the mention of her name, my heart plummeted. This was indeed bad news. If Lilly had told them where to find me, didn't that mean they were now in danger?

"Sorry," I replied, trying to compose myself steadily, "When did Lilly tell you where I was?" I was hoping it was before her heart had turned black, but I wasn't going to be that lucky by my mother's reply. She was playing her tricks. That much was obvious.

"She came round the house a few days ago," she answered, her head switching to my father worriedly, "Is there something wrong?"

"No," I replied, smiling bravely. "Nothing at all."

I stayed with them for as long as I dared, acutely aware that Zanda's arrival was imminent. The unfamiliar scent already hung in the air, a telltale sign that he was approaching, likely with company. A sense of unease gripped me, tightening like a vice around my chest—meeting the leader of a coven was another dramatic shift into the unknown, a realm where I didn't belong.

This was supposed to be the domain of the High Witch, not a lowly desk witch like myself. The recent cascade of events was never meant to involve someone as insignificant as me in the grand scheme of things. Yet here I was, standing on the precipice of another encounter that felt far beyond my station.

The tension in the air was thick, almost suffocating, as I held my breath, bracing for the inevitable confrontation. The weight of the situation bore down on me, making it difficult to breathe. But I knew I had to prepare for what was coming.

With a deep breath, I steeled my resolve, determined not to let my apprehension show. I would face Zanda and whatever unknowns he brought with him, even if it meant stepping further into a world I never imagined would be mine to navigate.

As the unfamiliar scent grew more substantial, I could feel my heart pounding in my chest and the blood rushing in my ears. This was no mere routine meeting - it was a pivotal moment that would test the limits of my abilities and challenge everything I thought I knew about the world. I braced myself, ready to face whatever Zanda and his companion had in store, knowing my survival could hang in the balance.

"Excuse me a minute," I smiled brightly. "I have to go and get Luke."

My parents stayed behind in the dimly lit blue room, sensing the agitated energy radiating from me. Wisely, they decided against trailing after me, recognising that their presence might only exacerbate the situation. I, however, could not contain my distress and hurried down the echoing corridor, the commotion growing louder with each desperate step.

The air felt thick with tension, and I could feel my heart pounding in my ears as I rushed towards the source of the commotion, unsure of what I would find but driven by an overwhelming need to understand and confront the unfolding events.

The room was alive with the pulsing chatter of nervous laughter and awkward exchanges. Luke, stationed by the door, observed the newcomers with a keen, scrutinising gaze. I presumed these to be Zanda and his followers, their every move and gesture scrutinised by Luke's watchful eyes.

"Hi," I croaked behind him, "Who's that?"

Before Luke could respond, Zanda abruptly pivoted towards me, his jovial expression instantly vanishing. He stood before me in a flash, looming over me with a stern, unwavering gaze, cutting off any further words from escaping my lips.

"My name is Zanda," he said, his deep voice commanding my attention. I met his piercing gaze and nodded, feeling a surge of nerves flutter in the pit of my stomach. The weight of his pointed stare seemed to bore into me, and I found myself struggling to maintain composure, my throat constricting as I swallowed hard, desperate to find the right words to respond.

"I'm certain that we may have crossed paths on other occasions under vastly different circumstances. But today, I need to understand why my son's life held such significance to you that he enrolled in your crusade," he said, his voice laced with sorrow and accusation. Pausing for a moment, he continued, "Because I refuse to believe that he would have willingly chosen to end his life only to have it taken by the demons he sought to vanquish. So, tell me, what do you have to say for yourself?"

I felt the weight of his gaze upon me, and the words caught in my throat. "I-It was his choice," I stammered, hoping desperately that my parents had remained there. "I didn't know who he was or why he was here. I was merely pursuing Lilly," I explained, my voice wavering with uncertainty and a hint of guilt.

His expression darkened, his brow furrowed in grief and anger. "My son's life was not yours to gamble with," he said, his words like daggers cutting through the tense silence. "He was a bright, vibrant young man with so much potential. And now, because of your crusade, he's gone forever."

"Ah," he murmured, his piercing gaze scrutinising me intently as he paced around me in a slow, deliberate circle. "I've heard the whispers, the tales of her exploits. Is it true, then? Did she truly slay the mighty Matace with her own hand?" His voice carried a mixture of awe and barely contained excitement, as if the mere thought of such a feat filled him with a morbid fascination.

"Yes," I whispered, "She did." My gaze was unwavering, and my eyes locked onto the person before me, conveying the depth of my certainty in a way that words alone could not.

"Time is of the essence," he said, his voice laced with urgency. "You have only two days to eliminate her, and I will be right there by your side to ensure the deed is done." His eyes narrowed, and a glint of determination flashed across his features. "We cannot afford any mistakes or delays. This is a critical mission, and failure is not an option." He leaned in, the weight of his words hanging in the air. "I will be there every step of the way, guiding you, pushing you to finish the job with the ruthless efficiency it requires. The clock is ticking, and we must act swiftly and decisively. Are you prepared to do what is necessary?"

He paused, his nostrils flaring as he deeply inhaled the air, savouring each scent that drifted his way. A wicked grin slowly spread across his face, the smile of a true immortal predator. He knew, with unwavering certainty, that his prey—my parents—were nearby. The thrill of the hunt had begun, and he could already taste their fear in the wind.

"Ah, I see you've brought us a treat," he said, his voice dripping with anticipation. He turned to his two loyal followers, a sinister grin spreading. "Well, don't just stand there; come and join me. Where are these delightful morsels you've procured?"

I firmly planted my feet, staring him down without flinching, I said, my voice dripping with resolve. "These are my parents, and I won't let you anywhere near them." I could feel the heat of my anger rising as I spoke, my hands clenching into fists at my sides. "You need to leave now before this gets ugly." My gaze was unwavering, my expression hardening with each passing moment. There was no doubt in my mind that I was willing to do whatever it took to shield my parents from this threat.

"The craving burns within me, an insatiable thirst that I can no longer suppress," Seira's companion confessed, his eyes darkening with an almost primal hunger. "When they come to us, willingly stepping into the lair of the undead, how can I resist? I'm certain even Luke feels the same primal urge coursing through his veins."

I could see the struggle behind his words, the battle between his humanity and the vampire's true nature that now dominated his being. The allure of fresh blood, the promise of sating that relentless thirst, was a siren's call that grew increasingly difficult to ignore.

"The temptation is far too great," he continued, his voice barely above a whisper yet laced with a tension that sent a shiver down Seira's spine. "I fear I may not have the strength to deny it much longer."

Luke had wandered a few yards away, and I initially assumed he was giving me space to summon my protective shield. But when I turned to look at him, a wave of regret washed over me. His thirst was taking over, and he was clearly struggling to control himself. His eyes had shifted into a strange, unsettling hue that made him almost unrecognisable.

A shiver ran down my spine as I observed his demeanour's subtle yet profound change. The once familiar features I knew so well were now distorted by the primal urge surging through him. His normally calm expression was replaced by something darker and more dangerous. I could sense the battle raging within him.

I held my breath, my heart pounding in my chest, bracing myself for the possibility that his impulses might overwhelm his reason. Uncertainty gripped me, and I had no idea what might happen next or if I could stop him.

Panic surged through me, igniting every nerve as I turned and fled, desperate to escape the encroaching horde of vampires. My heart pounded in my chest, their predatory snarls echoing ominously behind me. The night seemed to close in, tightening around me like a vice as I raced to reach my parents.

When I finally reached them, I spun around, positioning myself between them and the advancing creatures. Together, we faced the feral vampires, their crimson eyes gleaming with an unholy hunger. They circled us with predatory precision, fangs bared and glistening in the dim light. It was like being trapped inside the lair of a ravenous lion, the air thick with the scent of danger and the chilling promise of a violent, bloody end.

Adrenaline coursed through my veins, sharpening my senses and fueling my resolve. I knew I had to protect my loved ones at all costs, even as the vampires drew nearer, their movements fluid and menacing, ready to strike. The tension was palpable, the atmosphere charged with the anticipation of the deadly confrontation that loomed just seconds away.

"They're not food!" I shouted, desperately searching for Luke, praying he had regained his senses. "Luke!" The sound of his name seemed to jolt him back to his senses. He shook his head, the haze of bloodlust clearing from his eyes. Instantly, he positioned himself before us, a fierce, protective growl rumbling from his chest, warning the others to stay back. Darcy quickly fell in beside him, her bared fangs and snarling posture making it clear she would not hesitate to defend us.

The air crackled with tension as the vampires eyed us hungrily, their predatory instincts urging them to strike. But Luke and Darcy stood firm, a formidable barrier between us and the ravenous creatures. Their unwavering stance radiated a fierce determination to keep us safe, no matter the cost. I held my breath, heart pounding, as the standoff unfolded, the outcome hanging by a thread.

"You need to step away from them, Zanda," he growled, his jaw clenched in barely restrained fury. The muscles in his neck tightened as he glared at her, his eyes narrowed to slits. "They're my friends, not yours, and I won't let you intimidate them like that." His voice dripped with venom, each word laced with a warning.

As I stood there, facing the menacing wall of vampires before us, I was dimly aware of my mother's whimpering and my father's stunned expression behind me. My shield stood as a formidable barrier, protecting us from the monstrous creatures that loomed large. I didn't want my parents to witness this terrifying confrontation, but it had spiralled beyond my control.

The vampires, their eyes gleaming with predatory hunger, seemed to loom ever closer, their sharp fangs bared in a menacing display. I felt a surge of adrenaline coursing through my veins as I braced myself, my muscles tensing in anticipation of the impending clash. The air was thick with tension, the silence broken only by the rapid beating of my heart and the soft, fearful sounds from my parents.

At that moment, I knew I had to stand firm and shield my family from the unimaginable horrors that threatened to consume us. The weight of this responsibility settled heavily upon my shoulders. Still, I was determined to do whatever it took to protect them, even if it meant facing these otherworldly predators head-on.

"What's the matter?" my father murmured softly, his warm hand resting on my shoulder, his brow furrowed with concern. His gentle touch and soothing tone immediately caught my attention, signalling that he had sensed my distress and was eager to understand what was troubling me. His voice had an air of quiet understanding, as if he knew I was grappling with something and wanted to provide the comfort and support I needed.

"I don't have time for this right now, Dad," I barked, my voice dripping with frustration. My eyes remained glued to the computer screen, my fingers flying across the keyboard as I desperately tried to finish the task. The ticking of the clock and the constant buzz of my phone only added to the tension in the air. "Just give me a minute, okay?" I snapped, my jaw clenched tight, my shoulders hunched with the weight of my mounting responsibilities.

Luke forcefully ushered the others back into the adjacent room. Zanda was boiling with rage and outrage, his frantic calls to his family echoing loudly enough for me to overhear. The same tiresome conversation played out between him and the two individuals who had accompanied him. He needed to comprehend the significance and importance of the two humble mortals before him. Zanda remarked how bizarrely Luke had transformed since becoming acquainted with me.

Grateful for his understanding, I silently mouthed the words 'Thank you' to Luke. He responded with a curt nod, acknowledging my appreciation, before turning and swiftly exiting the room to join the others waiting outside. The weight of the situation lifted slightly from my shoulders as I watched him leave, his departure a silent signal that I was not alone in this moment of difficulty.

"It's time for you to go, and I need you to leave this instant," I said, looking directly at my parents. My voice was firm, leaving no room for negotiation. The urgency in my tone made it clear that this was not a request but a demand. I couldn't hide the underlying frustration and desperation that fueled my words. With a sense of finality, I watched their faces, waiting for them to acknowledge the gravity of the situation and comply with my command.

"Please, Seira, tell us what's happening," my father urged, his voice laced with concern. "We can handle it; just be honest with us."

I averted my gaze, the weight of the secrets I carried bearing down on me. "I can't, Dad," I replied, sorrow etching every word. "But I need you to listen carefully. Do not, under any circumstances, trust Lilly. Whatever happens, you must forbid her from entering this house again. If she comes around, you have to make her leave and never let her back in. Do you understand? This is vitally important."

My father's brow furrowed, confusion and worry etched on his face. "Seira, what has she done? What's going on?" he pressed, reaching out to put a hand on my shoulder.

I flinched away, the mere thought of Lilly filling me with dread. "Please, Dad, just promise me you'll keep her away. I can't explain it all now, but you must trust me. Lilly is dangerous, and I can't let anything happen to this family."

The intensity in my voice seemed to startle my father, and he nodded slowly. "Alright. I trust you. If you say she's not to be trusted, she won't be setting foot in this house again. I promise."

My mother let out a dramatic groan, her hand dramatically flying up to press against her forehead. I rolled my eyes in sheer exasperation at her overreaction. She could never handle the slightest bit of adversity or unpleasantness with any semblance of poise or composure. Her flair for the dramatic was always on full display, no matter the situation.

"Mother, let's get you home safely," I said, gently wrapping my arm around her frail, trembling shoulders. Her face was etched with exhaustion, her eyes pleading for support. "Dad, please help me with her other arm. We need to get her back home now."

My words came out firm yet laced with concern, underscoring the situation's urgency. I could see the worry in Dad's expression as he quickly moved to her other side, carefully slipping his arm under hers to provide the additional support she needed. Together, we slowly guided her forward, each step a testament to her resilience and our unwavering determination to ensure her comfort and safety.

With a newfound sense of responsibility, I took a deep breath and activated the portal of transportation I had discovered.

Dad's eyes widened in surprise as he stared at the mysterious object on the table. "What in the world is this?" he exclaimed, his voice tinged with curiosity and apprehension. He leaned in closer, brows furrowed, carefully examining the strange, unfamiliar item that had seemingly appeared out of nowhere. The air was thick with anticipation as he reached out, his fingers trembling slightly to gently touch the surface of the unknown object.

"A portal, Dad," I said, my voice brimming with confidence. I could see the confusion on his face, so I quickly added, "You remember that I'm a witch, right?" He nodded slowly, his eyes widening as the realisation of what I was saying sank in. I could feel the surge of power coursing through me, the familiar tingling sensation in my fingertips as I prepared to open the portal. With a flick of my wrist, the air shimmered, and a swirling vortex of energy began to form, the edges glowing with an otherworldly light. "Watch closely, Dad," I said, my eyes fixed on the portal as it grew more significant and stable. "This is just the beginning of what I'm capable of."

"Well," I said, a warm smile spreading across my face, "this is another skill I can add to my repertoire." He leaned in slightly, his eyes locking with mine, conveying a sincere concern. "And right now," I continued, my voice taking on a more resolute tone, "my top priority is ensuring you get home safely. That's what's most important to me at this moment." I gently touched his arm, reassuringly squeezing him, determined to see him through to his destination without a hitch.

"Okay, I'm not sure I understand," he replied, his brow furrowed with apprehension. His voice wavered slightly as he asked, "Will it... will it hurt?" The uncertainty in his eyes was palpable, and he seemed to brace himself for my response, his shoulders tensing up.

I stifled a sudden urge to laugh, pressing my lips tightly to hold back my amusement. "No," I replied, my voice firm and unyielding, leaving no room for argument. The word came out crisply, cutting through the air with a decisive finality that left no doubt in the listener's mind.

As we arrived at my parents' house, I sighed in relief, grateful that our journey had gone smoothly without further interruptions or unwelcome encounters. Unsurprisingly, the moment we stepped through the door, my mother scurried upstairs, eager to retreat to the solace of her bedroom and lie down.

She had always been easily unsettled by anything outside her own experiences. Despite her knowledge of the supernatural world, we now found ourselves entangled; the weight of it all still seemed too much for her to bear.

Would you like a drink?" he asked, his voice low and measured. "I've got whiskey, tea, or coffee." Without waiting for a response, he poured himself a generous glass of amber liquid, the ice cubes clinking against the crystal as he took a long, deep sip. The tension in the room was palpable, and I couldn't help but wonder what was going through his mind, how he was processing all we had faced.

"No, thank you," I replied with a faint smile, but the concern in my voice was palpable. "Is she going to be okay?" I asked, unable to hide the worry that gnawed at me. Honestly, I found my mother to be a bit of a drama queen, incredibly fragile, and I just couldn't fathom why fate had chosen her and my father to be my parents. We were polar opposites, and the thought of it all frustrated me.

"Don't worry, she's going to be alright," he said, his voice laced with a reassuring glow as he flashed me a comforting smile. The air grew tense as he cleared his throat, and I sensed the weight of his following words. "So... they were vampires, huh?" His gaze locked with mine, a hint of curiosity and concern flickering in his eyes. I nodded slowly, the gravity of the situation settling around us. Silently, I sat at the table, my father's presence a steady anchor as I braced myself for the unfolding conversation. "Would they have really hurt us?"

"Probably," I conceded, trying to sound casual, but the tightness in my father's expression told me he wasn't convinced. His grip on the glass tightened, his knuckles turning stark white, and I could sense the unease radiating from him. As I met his gaze, his features were etched with a grim determination, indicating that something was deeply troubling him.

The tension in the air was palpable, and I couldn't help but wonder what was weighing so heavily on my father's mind. His typically calm demeanour had given way to a palpable sense of unease, leaving me to ponder the nature of his concerns. Whatever it was, it weighed heavily on his heart and mind, and I couldn't help but feel a twinge of worry for him.

"What's wrong?" I asked. "You seem jumpy, "

"Goodness, I'm so on edge!" he exclaimed anxiously. "I barely escaped being devoured by those dreadful vampires. How much longer do you intend to work with this supernatural realm? Is it truly essential to continue? We can provide you with everything you require; I cannot bear the thought of any harm befalling you. Although you may not be our biological child, we love you as if you were our own flesh and blood," he said, his voice laced with genuine concern and affection.

"Dad," I sighed heavily, pushing myself up from the chair to cross the room towards him. "I truly love my work at the realm. But this latest situation was never meant to unfold this way. Lilly..." I paused, struggling to find the right words. "An all-consuming hatred consumes Lilly, but I don't understand why. She wants me gone, dead even, and I can't let her continue down this dark path." My voice wavered with emotion, the weight of the situation bearing down on me. "I wish things were different, Dad. I wish I could make Lilly see the reason and make her understand. But for now, my duty to the realm has to come first. I hope you can forgive me."

He looked at me with sorrowful, pain-filled eyes, and his following words hurt me beyond belief. The weight of his emotional torment was palpable, leaving me feeling helplessly trapped in the agonising moment, my own heart shattering in an empathetic response.

"I'm truly sorry, Seira," he murmured, his voice laced with regret. "But you can't come and see us. There's too much danger lurking, chasing after you, and I can't risk your mother getting hurt – she's already so fragile." He paused, his brow furrowed with concern and gently touched her arm. "I know it's difficult, but your safety, and your mother's, has to be my top priority. I won't let anything happen to your mother, not on my watch." His eyes met mine, pleading for me to understand the gravity of the situation they found themselves in.

My mother didn't move; she sat staring into space, unblinking and with a blank facial expression. It was clear she was in shock. I realised then it wasn't fair to drag either of them into this.

Tears welled up in my eyes, stinging as they spilt over my lids. I blinked rapidly, trying to hold them back, but they refused to be contained. My father stood before me, his back turned, his knuckles white as he gripped the edge of the cabinet. His head hung low, a glass of amber liquid clutched tightly in his other hand. The silence between us was deafening, thick with unspoken emotions.

Unable to bear the weight of it any longer, I turned and fled, my footsteps echoing against the walls as I made my way out of their home. For once, I wished I could be human, to walk the streets without needing magical transportation.

I longed to feel the ground beneath my feet, the fresh air on my face, anything to distract me from the heaviness in my heart. But the well-worn path of portals was all I knew, and I disappeared into the ether, leaving the pain of that moment behind, if only temporarily.

Nothing seemed to go my way, and the overwhelming sense of defeat steadily closed in. Lilly, my relentless adversary, was gaining the upper hand. Her cunning ploy had been to systematically isolate me from the people I cherished for reasons known only to her twisted mind.

I was determined not to let her get away with it this time. The walls were closing in, and I could feel the noose tightening around my neck. Lilly's malicious influence had seeped into every aspect of my life, turning those I trusted against me. I was trapped in a web of her own weaving, and the more I struggled, the tighter the grip became.

But I refused to surrender. A spark of defiance still burned within me, fueling my resolve to break free from her sinister machinations. This was a battle I could not afford to lose, for the stakes were far too high. I would not let Lilly's scheming ways rob me of the connections and support that kept me grounded. With a renewed determination, I prepared to confront her, ready to put an end to her relentless pursuit once and for all.

Distancing myself from the bustling city, I focused on summoning the mystical portal—my gateway to the exiled realm where the enigmatic Meniagier dwelled. It was time for these powerful entities to join the impending battle about engulfing the small city of Lilly. Though she might believe she had won this skirmish, I would ensure that her triumph would be short-lived.

I stepped through the shimmering portal with a determined stride, leaving the mundane world behind. The exiled realm was a place of ancient magic where the air crackled with otherworldly energy. The Meniagier, towering creatures of primal might, turned their piercing gaze upon me. I pleaded for their assistance, their formidable powers crucial in the fight to come.

Sensing the gravity of the situation, the Meniagier rumbled in agreement, their deep, resonant voices echoing through the ethereal landscape. Together, we surged back through the portal, ready to face Lilly and her forces head-on. This war was far from over, and I would not rest until the final victory was secured, no matter the cost.

A sudden, hushed voice pierced the silence behind me, "Stop, Seira! Don't do this, please!"

The plea was laced with raw emotion, a desperate attempt to halt my actions. The voice, though barely above a whisper, carried an undercurrent of urgency that sent a chill down my spine. I felt the weight of the words, the underlying fear and concern, as they reverberated in the still air.

Slowly, I turned to face the source of the voice, my heart pounding in my chest. In the dimly lit hallway stood a figure whose eyes were filled with anguish and pleading. "Seira, I know what you're considering doing, but it's not the answer. There's another way, I promise." The words hung in the air, a fragile lifeline offered amid my turmoil.

"Is that you, Cronomiun?" The gruff, deep voice sent a shiver down my spine. It was undoubtedly male, with a rumbling, almost primal quality – a stark contrast to the soft-spoken tones of the leaders I was accustomed to. The stranger's words hung in the air, thick with an underlying tension that set my nerves on edge. I couldn't quite place the familiarity of the voice, but it was clear this was no ordinary encounter. My heart raced as I steeled myself, unsure what to expect next.

"One of us," a faint chuckle suddenly echoed, sending a chill down my spine. I froze, my heart pounding, as the ominous voice cut through the eerie silence. "Wait there," it commanded.

The air seemed to thicken with tension, and I found myself rooted to the spot, my senses heightened, waiting with bated breath for whatever was to come next.

I stood there, my feet firmly planted, exuding a sense of unwavering patience as I waited. The portal behind me chimed melodically, almost like a living entity anticipating its utilisation. The intricate patterns on its surface shimmered, captivating my gaze and adding to the tranquil expectation permeating the space.

I could feel the portal's eagerness mirroring my own as we both stood poised, ready to be used at any moment. The air was thick with a palpable sense of anticipation. I found myself lost in the moment, savouring the stillness before the inevitable activation of the portal's power.

A pair of fiery eyes materialised before me, glowing with an intense, unwavering gaze. The figure, which had previously appeared as a singular unit, now looked remarkably petite. Yet, as they gathered together, they transformed into a formidable, wispy army – a sight that, at first glance, evoked a sense of unease and apprehension.

The eyes, burning with an unnatural luminescence, seemed to pierce through the darkness, demanding my attention. Their presence was captivating and unsettling, like the air around them crackled with otherworldly energy. I stood transfixed, my heart pounding, uncertain of what this strange manifestation meant.

"I'm here," a voice whispered, echoing with a disquieting resonance that sent shivers down my spine. "You cannot embark on this journey alone," he cautioned, his voice laced with urgency. "The others are anxiously awaiting my return to deliver this critical message. We had no choice but to depart; we cannot remain while Zanda is present, for a blinding, cataclysmic battle between our two factions is imminent. I beseech you, Seira, do not venture to the exiled planet."

I lifted my chin defiantly, my eyes burning with determination. "I have no choice," I responded sternly. "This must come to an end, here and now." I stood my ground, unwavering in my resolve.

"I understand the turmoil you must be feeling," he responded compassionately. "I overheard the harsh words your father directed at you, and for that, I sincerely apologise. But you must not face Lilly alone - it would be far too perilous, and your life is invaluable to us."

I sighed, frustrated, "I'm utterly confused by everything unfolding around me. I know there's some inexplicable connection between us, but I can't fathom the reasons or the mechanisms behind it. It seems impossible for me to be a witch, a Cronomiun, and a human all at once. I feel trapped in a game of Connect Four, just waiting for that final piece to fall into place and complete the puzzle."

The weight of the situation pressed heavily on my shoulders, and I longed for clarity amidst the swirling uncertainty. The lines between my identity and purpose had blurred, leaving me grasping for any semblance of understanding.

Beneath the calm exterior, a storm raged within. Inwardly, I was gripped by fear, a primal instinct urging me to flee, to escape the impending confrontation. Yet, I refused to let anyone glimpse this vulnerability. To show such weakness would be futile, a mere facade that I was determined to shatter.

Deep within, a fire burned, a relentless drive that had been kindled since birth. I was born to fight, to face adversity head-on, and this day had been long in the making. Steeling my resolve, I knew I had to find Lilly and ensure that the coming battle unfolded precisely as I had envisioned. The stakes were high, and failure was not an option.

Every nerve ending was alight with anticipation as I ventured forth, the adrenaline coursing through my veins like a raging river. The world around me seemed to fade into the background, my sole focus being the task. I would not be cowed, not by fear, not by the overwhelming odds. This was my moment, my chance to prove my mettle and emerge victorious, no matter the cost.

"One day you will," he said, his smile warm and reassuring. "We will be there when you face Lilly. You may think you're alone, Seira, but you're not. We are also your family and will always be here for you." His words resonated within me, stirring a fresh wave of emotions that threatened to spill from my eyes. As quickly as he had appeared, he vanished, leaving me standing before the portal, my heart heavy yet resolute.

I stepped through the shimmering threshold, determined to collect the animals that had readily welcomed me into their fold, still burning brightly. The weight of the past lingered, but a newfound sense of purpose filled me, fueled by the knowledge that

I was not alone in this journey. Whatever challenges lay ahead, I would face them with the unwavering support of those who had become my family. This realisation filled me with both solace and a renewed sense of strength.

As I set foot in the exiled world, I was greeted by a stark contrast to the bleak, dark realm that Lilly had left behind. Sunlight bathed the land, casting a warm glow upon the gently swaying trees, whose leaves rustled with the faint whispers of diverse creatures.

From the nearby cave, where I stood just a few paces away, came the echoes of various alien tongues – the voices of the nearly three hundred exiled beings, be they demons or vampires, all of whom had been banished to this realm as punishment for their misdeeds.

This was no mere desolate outpost but a carefully contained sanctuary, its sole entrance and exit guarded by a portal locked within a binding spell. An exiled soul could only pass through by first seeking consent from the realm's governing body, which would weigh the necessity and safety of any proposed journey to another dimension.

The intensity of the situation was palpable, as I knew that these outcasts, cast out from their former lives, now resided in a world of their own, a domain of exile and unforgiving isolation.

My personal gateways into the supernatural world remained unobstructed, granting me unfettered access to this parallel realm as a witch of the realm - a privilege that few could claim.

I cautiously navigated the overgrown, winding path, the rustling of leaves and the occasional squeak from unseen creatures heightening my senses. I knew with certainty that the exiled inhabitants of this secluded sanctuary would be keenly observant of any intruder who dared to venture into their domain. The sense of being watched, of countless eyes scrutinising my every move, sent a shiver down my spine. Still, I pressed on, acutely aware that I could not remain undetected for long.

As I neared the cave's entrance, the thunderous roars from within sent a shiver down my spine. The Meniagier, the fearsome creatures that dwelled within, were settling down, their guttural growls echoing through the narrow passage. I paused, wondering if they had just finished a meal, which could mean my venture into their domain might take longer than anticipated.

The anticipation built as I drew closer, my heart pounding with trepidation and determination. The cave's gaping maw loomed before me, its darkness seemingly swallowing the light. I steeled my nerves, knowing that the Meniagier's lair held both danger and the answers I sought. With a deep breath, I stepped forward, prepared to face whatever lay in wait within.

I stepped cautiously into the vast, cavernous space, the dim light casting eerie shadows across the rough, uneven walls. "Hey," I whispered, my voice echoing softly through the cavernous chamber, "I'm here."

The majestic creature greeted me as it lumbered towards me, its massive frame towering over me. Instinctively, I felt excitement and trepidation as the animal nuzzled its colossal head against mine. Suddenly, its cavernous jaws parted, revealing a large, slimy tongue that flopped out, descending upon my face in a sloppy, viscous assault.

Despite my attempts to sidestep the inevitable, the tongue's moist, gooey caress landed squarely on my cheek, leaving a trail of thick, glistening saliva in its wake. The sensation was both startling and strangely captivating, a stark contrast to the initial awe I had felt in the presence of this magnificent yet formidable beast.

"Ew," I grinned at him and patted his cheek. "That was awful!"

He strode away, his back turned to me, he turned to me and let out a deep rumble. It was a silent summons that I obeyed.

I quickened my pace, falling in step behind him, the weight of watchful gazes pressing upon me. The others, unmoving, their eyes locked onto mine, a palpable tension in the air, as if they awaited my command.

"I've come here to ask you for your help," I began, my voice tinged with urgency. "I hope you can understand me."

To my utter amazement, the largest of the creatures, who appeared to be the leader, pawed at the ground and puffed out a thick plume of smoke, his eyes twinkling with what seemed like a curious interest. I couldn't help but laugh at the sight, for these imposing, fearsome beings had revealed a surprisingly docile and almost endearing nature.

Though they were undoubtedly powerful and intimidating, their acceptance of my presence filled me with wonder and comfort. I was captivated by their raw, primal energy, and I knew that whatever lay ahead, I could count on their support.

"Will you come with me inside the portal?" I asked, my voice tinged with eager anticipation. The portal pulsed with mesmerising energy, its ethereal glow beckoning us to cross the threshold into the unknown.

They surrounded me, their hulking figures looming closer, their guttural growls reverberating. I tensed, my heart pounding, as I met their piercing gazes, each brimming with a primal, unspoken acceptance of my perilous and unconventional plan. The tension was palpable, the air thick with anticipation, and I knew there was no turning back. These formidable creatures had trusted me, and I would have to see this through, no matter the risks.

I could already envision the Cerberus and other formidable creatures Lilly had ominously conjured, ready to unleash their wrath upon us. Yet, I knew these creatures would be invaluable in our impending battle. The thought of facing such a daunting challenge filled me with trepidation and exhilaration. If only I could rally more witches to our cause, our side would be the mightiest, capable of withstanding Lilly's menacing attacks.

The idea of a grand showdown sparked a fire, fueling my determination to assemble the most powerful coven. With our combined magical prowess, we would stand firm against the onslaught of Lilly's dark forces, emerging victorious in this epic clash of light and shadow.

"Alright, time to show off!" I exclaimed confidently, tenderly patting the massive creature beside me. The colossal beast loomed over me, its damp breath cascading down onto my shoulder, leaving behind a thick, gooey trail. "Hey, could you please not do that?" I winced, gingerly wiping the sticky, unpleasant drool off my fingers.

He nodded solemnly and effortlessly lifted me onto his broad back. I nestled comfortably, my eyes fixed on the Meniagier procession as they marched through the colossal portal, the largest I had ever conjured. At last, it was our turn, and we stepped into the vast, unknown expanse beyond.

I erected a shield across the vast expanse of the realm to conceal the beasts that roamed the Earth. If witnessed by mortal eyes, these colossal creatures would spark a frenzy that even I, with all my powers, would struggle to contain. Their existence must be shielded from the mortal realm lest chaos and pandemonium ensue.

The shield I constructed was a marvel of my craft. This shimmering dome cloaked the beasts in an impenetrable veil of secrecy. Within this protected space, the creatures could roam freely, their majestic forms hidden from the prying gaze of the outside world. Only I, with my unwavering guardianship, knew the true extent of their power and the necessity of keeping them concealed.

The thought of these magnificent beings being exposed to the mortal world filled me with unease. Their sheer size and might would undoubtedly overwhelm the senses of any who dared to gaze upon them. My sacred responsibility was to ensure these beasts remained hidden, their presence a closely guarded secret known only to the realm's most steadfast protectors.

"Seira!" Luke's voice cracked with desperation as he stumbled through the charred doorway. His eyes burned from the acrid smoke that billowed around him. "What have you done?" he demanded, his chest heaving with a mixture of fear and anger. "Why did you bring them here?"

"Reinforcements have arrived!" I yelled from atop my towering steed, addressing the crowd gathered below. A reassuring smile spread as I gently patted the powerful beast beneath me. "No need to worry, my friends," I continued, "They won't harm you, but it's best to keep your distance. These creatures have no love for the dead."

Luke grimaced, his brow furrowed with uncertainty, but he remained steadfast, waiting patiently for my arrival.

"I need those covered up, quick!" he cried, his eyes darting nervously. "Zanda's still around, and I don't want anyone to see them," he shouted up at me, his voice laced with urgency and concern.

"Ah, I see what you mean," I responded, my voice brimming with understanding as I nodded thoughtfully, taking in the details before me.

The colossal creature crashed to the ground, its massive frame shaking the Earth beneath my feet. I swiftly dismounted, my heart pounding, and leaned close to the beast, whispering a hushed command. "Stay within the shield, with the others. I'll return shortly."

The creature's eyes glinted with a mix of understanding and unease as if it could sense the gravity of the situation. I gave its flank a reassuring pat, then turned and strode away, my grip tightening on the hilt of my sword. The air was tense, and I knew I had to act quickly to ensure my companions' safety.

"I'm truly sorry," Zanda said, cautiously approaching me. The Meniagier, sensing the intruder, let out a thunderous growl, warning Zanda to keep his distance.

I raised my hand, my eyes meeting his, and spoke softly, "Stay right there. I'll come to you."

I approached him, standing in the middle, equidistant from Luke's house and the Meniagier settlement. His eyes lit up when he saw my smile, and a young woman emerged from the shadows to stand beside him.

"Let me introduce you to my beloved," he exclaimed with pride, "This is Seira, the captivating young witch I've been telling you all about." His eyes shone with adoration as he gazed upon his wife, a hint of a mischievous grin playing on her lips. "She's truly a remarkable woman."

"It's about time we finally met," she said, her eyes rolling exasperatedly at her husband. "I've heard he's caused trouble and has even tried to invite your parents for dinner." Her tone was laced with disdain.

I clenched my jaw, the muscles in my face tightening. "Yeah, that's putting it mildly," I replied, my voice strained.

"I deeply regret my actions," Zanda said, his lips pursed tightly in a pained expression. He paused for a moment, then continued, his voice tinged with a hint of frustration, "Anyway, how was I supposed to know you weren't involved in my son's tragic passing?" he asked, his voice laced with frustration and disbelief.

The woman turned to me, her expression a mix of empathy and resolve. "Perhaps you could have spoken with her first instead of taking matters into your own hands in such a dreadful manner," she replied, her tone firm yet gentle. She then offered a small, saddened smile. "My name is Fiona," she said, her gaze meeting mine with a weight that belied her outward composure.

The exchange was charged with emotion, each word carrying the burden of unimaginable loss and the yearning for understanding. The air between us was thick with the need for answers, tinged with the lingering pain of a tragedy that forever altered our lives.

"I'm so sorry about your son," I said.

She sighed, and her eyes filled with tears. "He was my only child," she whispered, sniffing. "There will be time to grieve once we've dealt with Lilly."

She offered a small smile, her eyes filled with grief that she bravely held at bay. Zanda pulled her close to his side and kept his arm around her shoulders, offering her strength.

I flashed a warm smile in response and leaned closer to the Meniagier, whispering gently to soothe their growing unease. Their murmurs of discomfort steadily rose, prompting me to act swiftly to calm the situation. With a reassuring tone, I addressed their concerns, hoping to ease the tension that had settled over the group.

"Seira, the others are waiting for you inside," Luke said, his voice low and urgent as he stood behind me. The anticipation in his tone was palpable, hinting at the importance of the gathering. "More witches have arrived, eager to speak with you." His words carried a sense of gravitas, underscoring the significance of this moment.

Chapter Twelve

I strolled into the house with Luke, his arm wrapped tenderly around my waist. As we entered, I felt the intrigued gaze of the other vampires and witches upon us, their curious eyes studying us intently.

"I can only imagine what you're thinking right now," he whispered, his voice barely audible above the chatter. "I know it might seem crazy to put my arm around you, but I don't care what anyone else thinks anymore." His grip tightened ever so slightly, a gesture of both reassurance and defiance. "They shouldn't be so damn nosy anyway. Whatever happens, I want you to know that everyone here will fight on your side. Lilly won't get away with this, I promise you that."

His words were laced with a mixture of determination and protectiveness, and I could feel the intensity of his gaze as he spoke. The warmth of his arm around me was both comforting and electrifying, a stark contrast to the cold, prying eyes that seemed to bore into us from every direction. At that moment, I knew he would stand by me, no matter the consequences.

I nodded, the lump in my throat preventing me from speaking. Once all of this was over, I knew this would be the last time I saw Luke. The thought of placing myself in the path of such torment, never to be with him in the same way as two mortals, was a pain so excruciating that it threatened to consume me.

The finality of the situation weighed heavily on my heart, and I felt a deep, visceral ache at the prospect of being separated from him forever. The intensity of my emotions threatened to overwhelm me. I struggled to maintain my composure, longing for one last moment to hold him close and let him know the depth of my feelings.

But the cruel reality of our circumstances was inescapable, and I knew that this parting would be the most agonising I had ever endured. The torturous knowledge that I would never again experience the warmth of his embrace or the tenderness of his touch was a burden I feared I could not bear.

The witches of the realm materialised before me with wide-eyed disbelief, their expressions a mix of anxiety and intense scrutiny as they sensed my presence. Their gaze immediately shifted to the Meniagier outside, and their eyes reflected a profound reverence for the young witch who had tamed them, leading them into the impending heated battle.

The silent realm elders approached me, their expressions warm and welcoming. Stella, Mia, Titan, and Leo greeted me with radiant smiles that lit the air around us. Their eyes sparkled with genuine kindness, and I felt a sense of belonging wash over me as they extended their hands in greeting.

The atmosphere was charged with an undercurrent of power and wisdom, yet their demeanour remained gentle and inviting. I could feel the weight of their ancient knowledge and experience as they welcomed me, their presence both humbling and comforting.

"Seira," Titan whispered, the fire of his youth burning brightly in his warm embrace. "I see you've managed to tame the mysterious Meniagier," he remarked, his voice filled with admiration. "That's truly impressive."

Titan's words were laced with awe and respect as he gazed at me, his eyes sparkling with curiosity and pride. The intensity of his gaze was palpable, his entire being radiating a captivating energy that seemed to envelop me. The air around them crackled with a palpable tension, the weight of Titan's praise and the challenge it posed hanging between them. I could feel the heat of his body, the warmth of his breath, and the unwavering focus of his attention.

"Thanks," I replied with a confident grin, "Somehow, they just instantly welcomed me in." A hush fell over the elders as they exchanged troubled glances. Their concerned expressions filled me with a creepy, unsettling feeling as if I was being kept outside their inner circle.

"Where is Lilly?" Mia snapped, her eyes narrowing with determination. She had always been direct, cutting through the pleasantries to reach the point. "I've heard she's been completely consumed by darkness. I had a feeling that becoming the High Witch would be her downfall. Still, I never imagined she'd resort to murder to claim the title," she said, her voice laced with a mixture of anger and disappointment.

Mia's words were sharp and to the point, reflecting her no-nonsense approach. The intensity in her expression and the urgency in her tone conveyed the gravity of the situation. She was determined to get to the bottom of Lilly's actions, unwilling to let her former colleague's descent into darkness go unchallenged.

"She has," I responded, my voice tinged with uncertainty. "But I'm at a loss as to why. Do you have any insights into her actions?"

Leo's expression grew concerned as he asked, "You truly don't know?" I shook my head, completely baffled by their worried looks. A growing sense of doubt consumed me, eroding my hope to remain part of this realm I loved dearly. It was a foreign and unsettling feeling I never imagined I'd experience towards the world I held so close to my heart.

"Enough is enough, Leo," Stella's voice rang out, sharp and unyielding. "Seira doesn't need to hear it like this. We all need to have a meeting and sort this out." Her gaze shifted to Luke, her expression softening ever so slightly. "Is there a place to discuss a few important details with Seira?"

The intensity of Stella's words was palpable, and her concern for the situation was evident in her manner of conduct. The atmosphere had become heavy, demanding a resolution, and her request to Luke had an underlying urgency that could not be ignored.

"Absolutely," Luke responded, ever the gracious host to the gathering of vampires and witches. "The library is downstairs, though unfortunately, much of my home has been ravaged by the demons' attacks. That room, however, remains intact. Seira can guide you there."

My voice held firm. "I'll only go with you if Luke is also invited." If they needed to discuss something, I wanted the one person who had stood by my side throughout this ordeal to be privy to the information. I wasn't about to leave him out.

The atmosphere was tense as the supernatural beings eyed each other warily. The air crackled with an underlying current of power and unease. Yet, I remained resolute, unwilling to back down. Luke had repeatedly proven his loyalty, and I wouldn't exclude him from whatever was about to unfold.

They froze, their faces etched with shock as they turned to face me. Our eyes locked, and they saw the unwavering determination in my gaze. The air grew thick with tension as all eyes turned to the witches, everyone waiting to see their reaction. I wondered anxiously if they would deny me their companionship.

Leo's jaw tightened as he replied, "If that's what you truly want, then so be it." His words carried a tinge of resignation, yet a subtle undercurrent of defiance lingered beneath the surface. The tension in the air was palpable, charged with unspoken emotions and a sense of finality.

Luke grasped my hand, his touch igniting a newfound intensity between us. The bold gesture shocked our onlookers, whose expressions betrayed surprise and unease. Yet, I couldn't bring myself to pull away. There was a captivating power in the way he claimed me, one that transcended any concern for their reactions.

Luke's sturdy hand enveloped mine, his touch instantly calming my nerves. I felt a sense of security wash over me, knowing he would stand by my side no matter what news the witches had to deliver. His unwavering presence was a comforting anchor, assuring me that whatever challenges lay ahead, we would face them together.

I whirled around to face them, the door slamming shut behind me. "Well," I demanded, my voice laced with a demanding edge. My eyes narrowed as I scrutinised their expressions, ready to assert my position.

"Please, have a seat," Leo said, his tone warm yet firm as he gestured towards the solitary chair nestled within the confines of the room. He attempted to assert elder dominance over me, forgetting this wasn't his home. His eyes locked onto mine, a subtle invitation that hinted at the moment's gravity. The chair, worn but sturdy, seemed to beckon as if it knew the weight of the conversation that was about to unfold.

"I'd prefer not to," I replied, leaning back in my chair and crossing my arms. A hint of irritation crept into my voice. "Just spit it out and get it over with, will you?" I watched the person across from me, my gaze unwavering, waiting for them to deliver their message and be done.

I couldn't shake the overwhelming sense that they were about to reveal something connected to the information Luke had already shared with me. A part of me braced for the impact, knowing deep down that my life had always been a little...peculiar. Yet, I couldn't help but feel a growing anticipation, as if the next piece of the puzzle was about to be unveiled, shedding light on the mysteries that had long shrouded my existence.

"Do you know about your life or how it all started?" Stella inquired, her eyes narrowing at me with a hint of scepticism. Her gaze was intense, and I could feel the weight of her scrutiny as she studied me, waiting for my response.

I shook my head, determined to lie to them, and a shiver ran down my spine as Luke's firm grip tightened on my shoulder. His touch radiates a silent caution that I couldn't quite decipher. The weight of his hand, heavy with unspoken concern, seemed to anchor me in place, halting my movements as I searched his gaze for a clue to the warning lingering in the air.

"Luke, I'm impressed that you kept your promise to the realm," she said, her eyes shining with approval. "Matace was right to choose you," she continued, gazing at me. "You're not like other humans. You were created within the confines of Matace's home, hidden in the deepest of secrecy."

I feigned confusion, but internally, I yearned for her to get to the point. "I don't understand," I mumbled, my mind racing with questions and anticipation.

I could sense the gravity of the situation, the layers of mystery and intrigue surrounding my existence. I was on the edge of a revelation that promised to change everything.

She sighed heavily, her shoulders slumping as she turned to face the picture on the wall. Her eyes locked onto the framed image, a palpable sense of longing and wistfulness etched across her features. The weight of her emotions seemed to pull her towards the picture as if she could step into the frozen moment captured there and find the solace she so desperately craved.

"Listen, I'm telling you this for your safety," she snapped, visibly irritated by my reaction. "Lilly has been trying to create another being like you, but she's failed so far. She doesn't have the final page of the spell we used to make you initially, so her attempts keep falling short. It's been her own downfall within that realm," she explained, her voice dripping with intensity.

"I'm sorry," I blurted out, lifting my hand to stop her mid-sentence. My heart pounded as I tried to make sense of her words. "What do you mean by 'creating another like me'? What exactly am I?" I asked, my voice quivering with a combination of bewilderment and unease. Of course, none knew that my entire demeanour was merely a facade.

Luke stood frozen, his mouth agape in bewildered silence. The startling revelations about my birth and DNA had left him utterly baffled, shaking the very foundations of his understanding. It was as if the solid ground of his beliefs had crumbled beneath his feet, leaving him grasping to comprehend my origins' complex and astonishing truth.

"You were not born to merely exist," she said softly, her voice fading slightly. "You were meticulously crafted with a singular, unwavering purpose – to wage a relentless war against the one who seeks to seize control of this realm and unleash unimaginable evil upon our world, wielding the devastating power of every demon known to us," she continued, her gaze fixed and unyielding. "You are not just a being but a formidable weapon forged to defend against the all-consuming darkness that threatens to devour us all," she declared, her words heavy with a profound sense of gravity and urgency.

I whirled and twirled, utterly unrestrained, every fibre of my being pulsing with a raw, human essence. I bled, spoke, moved, and loved—just like anyone else. Yet, how she looked at me, and her words hinted at something more profound. What was she trying to convey to make me understand myself?

Her gaze bore into me, intense and unwavering, leaving me unsettled and unsure. The weight of her scrutiny felt like a physical

THE SEQUENCE OF IMMORTALITY 337

presence pressing against me, demanding that I confront the hidden depths of my own nature.

I could feel the uncertainty coiling within me, a tangle of questions and doubts that refused to be silenced. She had uncovered something in me, some hidden truth that I had yet to fully grasp. The moment's intensity threatened to overwhelm me. Still, I knew I had to stand my ground to face whatever revelations she had in store.

I shook my head, a slight yet resolute motion, as I sensed the familiar sting of tears welling up in my eyes. Despite the sharp, prickling sensation, I defiantly resisted the urge to let those tears spill over and stream down my face.

Gently, she knelt before me, her eyes gleaming with tenderness and empathy. "Seira," she spoke, her voice soft yet unwavering. "We are here to stand by your side, but this battle is yours alone to fight. Among us, you are the only one strong enough to face her. No one else stands a chance, for she has grown too powerful – even if we were to combine our efforts, we would be no match for her. You were created to be our ultimate weapon."

The weight of her words settled heavily upon me, igniting a spark of determination within my core. I could feel the intensity of the coming conflict, like a storm brewing on the horizon, and I knew that I was the only one who could weather its fury. The fate of our world rested upon my shoulders, and I was ready to confront the challenge head-on, no matter the cost.

The woman's words carried a sense of urgency and resolve. Her posture, intensity in her gaze, and gravity of tone conveyed the seriousness of the situation. The task ahead was daunting, but she believed in my ability to confront this formidable opponent. The weight of responsibility rested squarely on my shoulders, and the woman's unwavering faith in me was palpable.

"So, let me get this straight," I said, trembling slightly as I ran my tongue over my parched lips. The weight of the situation pressed down on me, making it hard to breathe. "You're telling me that I have no other option but to... to die?" The words felt foreign and heavy on my tongue, as if I was uttering a deadly curse.

She glanced around nervously, avoiding eye contact as she searched for a response to my question. Her body language betrayed her discomfort as she stepped back, creating distance between us. The hesitation in her movements was palpable, hinting at her reluctance to address the matter at hand.

"No, she mustn't die!" Luke exclaimed frantically, his voice laced with desperation. "I can grant her eternal life, which will surely save her from the clutches of death," he pleaded, his eyes filled with hope and determination.

"No!" I exclaimed, recoiling from his touch as if it burned my skin. I swatted his arm away, the unwanted contact leaving an unpleasant sensation. "I don't want that," I continued, my voice firm and unyielding. "So be it if I'm meant to face my demise. But there's one condition..." I paused, my gaze unwavering, the weight of the situation palpable in the air around us.

"No strings attached, Seira," Leo said firmly, cutting off any potential objections. "This is your purpose, your destiny." His eyes burned with unwavering conviction as he spoke, leaving no room for doubt or hesitation.

"Absolutely not," I responded firmly, jutting out my chin in resolute defiance. "There is one non-negotiable condition I require before I even entertain the thought of confronting Lilly," I declared, my voice dripping with unwavering determination.

The four witches scrutinised one another, piercing gazes betraying a deep unease. They seemed to be searching for an elusive answer, a glimmer of understanding that refused to manifest. It was as if they feared speaking out of turn lest they be punished for granting my condition and breaking the sacred pact that bound them together.

The silence was weighted with the burden of their unspoken thoughts. Each witch held her tongue, unwilling to be the first to break the eerie stillness, for the consequences of doing so were far too grave to risk.

"What's your condition?" Stella snapped, her eyes burning with fury as she glared at me. The intensity in her voice sent a chill down my spine, and I could feel the tension thickening between us.

"It's time for Luke to be properly named and integrated into the realm agency," I said, my voice firm and unwavering. "The agency has never had a vampire as an active high member before - they've always been relegated to the outside, mere workers following orders from the higher elders like yourself. But that needs to change." I paused, fixing Stella with a piercing gaze. "You've gone to great lengths to bring me into this world, and now I'm asking you to extend that same effort to ensuring Luke's status allows him to make decisions within the realm."

Stella opened her mouth to respond, but before she could speak, Leo cut in, his tone leaving no room for argument.

A sly smile crept across his face as he spoke, 'I believe we can accommodate that request.' He paused, the weight of his words hanging in the air. "He will be welcomed back into our fold, but only once Lilly has been... eliminated."

"Wonderful!" I exclaimed with genuine enthusiasm. Turning to Luke, who stood nearby with a curious expression, I said, "Luke, could you please escort our guests back to the other room to join the others? Then, I need to have a word with you."

I wasn't seeking an answer; I needed to confront him. There were things I didn't comprehend, and I was sure he knew at least some, if not all, of the answers. For years, I had believed my birth was a mistake, that my mother had simply given up and didn't want me. But now, I was stunned to discover that wasn't the case—I was unique and indefinable in my own right.

The weight of this revelation bore down on me, leaving me unsettled and yearning for clarity. I could no longer ignore the nagging questions that had haunted me for so long. It was time to face him, who held the key to unlocking the mysteries of my origins. The intensity of my need to understand burned within me, a flame that demanded to be extinguished.

"Hurry up, everyone!" Luke shouted from the doorway, his voice filled with urgency. He opened the door, beckoning the group to follow him swiftly to the next room. His eyes were ablaze with purpose, and his stance commanded attention as he ushered them out, leaving no room for hesitation.

I watched as the four witches swiftly exited the room. Stella remained aloof and high-status, focusing solely on the realm and its best interests - precisely as I had anticipated. When Leo passed by, his gaze met mine, a mix of miserable defeat and pity etched on his face. He bravely reached out and touched my hand as he went. The other two witches didn't look at me or speak a word; they were too ashamed to acknowledge the revelations about my life and how I had been created, but it was their doing.

They were all responsible for this disastrous situation, including Matace. If they hadn't created me, Lilly wouldn't have turned to the darker side of magic and decided to try and destroy the entire realm, both on Earth and beyond. It was a senseless and foolish thing for her to do, a complete waste.

I sat there, my forehead pressed against the chilly window, anxiously awaiting Luke's arrival. A dull, throbbing ache was starting to build in my head, and all I wanted was for this ordeal to be over. Based on everything I had been told, there was no way I was supposed to make it through this alive.

The air felt thick and heavy, weighing down on me with each passing minute. My heart raced as the seconds ticked, my palms growing clammy with nervous anticipation. I couldn't shake the sinking feeling that something terrible was about to happen.

The uncertainty of the situation only added to the overwhelming dread that consumed me. With each shallow breath, I braced myself for the worst, my mind racing with all the possible outcomes. This was far from how I imagined my day unfolding, but here I was, trapped in a nightmare that seemed to have no end.

"I'm back," he whispered, his voice barely audible as he stepped closer, his hand gently resting on my shoulder. His presence was both comforting and unnerving, like a gentle breeze on a summer day. "Are you alright?" he asked, his eyes searching my face for any sign of distress or concern.

I whirled around, my gaze locking with his. Worry was etched across his features, his eyes darting around frantically, desperately seeking answers in mine. But, as I often did, I concealed the turmoil within me, the thoughts swirling and crashing through my mind.

"Did you catch even half of what they just said?" I demanded, my voice taut with tension.

"I admit, I do feel a little concerned," he confessed, his voice tinged with regret. "As I told you before, you were created for a different purpose, and as a vampire, I know I'm not supposed to have a say in the affairs of this realm. But I did try to warn Matace that subjecting you to this ordeal was wrong. He refused to listen and insisted on bringing you into existence anyway. I'm truly sorry for what you're going through."

There was no way I could define his emotions. Since I had begun to learn about the demons and creatures that existed, I knew vampires were exceptionally skilled at conveying emotions, almost to a theatrical degree. I wasn't entirely sure that he was genuinely sorry.

"You know," I said wistfully, "I may not fully understand it, but I accept why I was created. The only times I've ever felt a sense of belonging is when I've been around you. Thank you, Luke, for allowing me to be a part of your world, even if it was for a short while."

I rushed away from him before he could respond. He had already turned my world upside down, and my heart followed suit. I was not immune to his vampiric ways, and I certainly wasn't accustomed to them either. His presence had shaken me, leaving me intrigued and unsettled.

I felt utterly foolish for believing I could survive after facing Lilly. All the carefully laid plans I had meticulously crafted were crumbling into ashes, never to be realised or accomplished. The only thing I could now hope and wish for was to emerge victorious in the way Matace had trained me to be. This final task, his last request, was the sole purpose I was determined to fulfil, no matter the cost.

Luke stayed back, respecting the space I needed during these final hours. I was grateful for his intuitive understanding – this was a solitary journey I had to undertake to find inner peace before facing her, Matace. As the last moments of my life trickled away, I knew I had to fully accept the truth – that I was my own person but had been made to destroy the one I cared for the most. This realisation weighed heavily on my heart, filling me with sorrow and resolve. I needed to confront this burden to make peace with the role I had been forced to play before the end.

The path ahead was clear yet daunting. I steeled myself, drawing strength from the knowledge that Matace would have wanted me to remain true to myself, even in the face of this impossible task. With a deep breath, I stepped forward, ready to embrace the final destination of my soul. I ran back to the room

Luke had put me in. Although the demons had blown the wall open, it was still somewhere I could go to be alone.

Darcy stood hesitantly in the doorway, her soft gaze fixed on me. "Can I come in?" she asked, her voice barely above a whisper.

I let out a frustrated sigh, the weight of solitude pressing down on me. "Will anyone ever understand that I need to be alone?" I snapped, my words dripping with an edge of bitterness.

With a sigh, I gestured for her to enter, my irritation still palpable from her unexpected arrival at my door, driven by an apparent need to engage me in conversation.

"I'm so sorry," she giggled nervously, a mischievous glint in her eyes. "But I really need to talk to you right now," she said, her voice low and urgent, a sense of intensity underlying her words.

"Come on in," I replied, still irritated by her sudden appearance in my room and need for conversation.

"I'm so sorry," she said, collapsing onto the bed beside me, her voice heavy with regret. "I'm sorry for everything I said to you. Now I can see how much Luke means to you and how much you mean to him. I never should have interfered." She paused, her eyes pleading. "Can you... can you answer me something?"

"What?" I muttered, a sense of unease washing over me. I knew she was talking about something I had desperately tried to forget - that Luke would move on with his immortal life and choose a more suitable partner to share it with, and that person wouldn't be me. Jealousy surged through me, a burning, overwhelming sensation that consumed my thoughts.

"If I hadn't been such a bitch about Luke," she said, her voice laced with hesitation, "would you have accepted the life that Luke wants to give you?" She paused, her eyes searching my face, waiting for my response. The air was thick with anticipation, the weight of her words hanging heavily between us.

I slowly pivoted to face her, her eyes wide and curious, studying my reaction. "How did you find out about that?" I murmured, still baffled that anyone could have overheard our private conversation in that room. My heart raced as I waited in tense anticipation for her response.

A mischievous smile spread across her lips. "I am a vampire," she whispered, her voice low and captivating. "My senses are heightened, and I hear everything."

I let out a heavy sigh. "If they hadn't told me the reason for my creation or how it would all end, perhaps I would have wanted to live." I paused, the weight of those words sinking in. "But I'm not meant to live. It's not my destiny. I was created to exist for a brief moment and then fade away. So Luke's offer, as tempting as it may be, doesn't stand a chance."

Realising my true purpose weighed heavily on me, a burden I carried with resignation. The knowledge that my life was destined for a premature end made the prospect of living seem futile, no matter what opportunities presented themselves. The intensity of these thoughts left me feeling sombre and resigned, as if I had already accepted my inevitable demise.

"It does," she insisted, her voice firm and unwavering. "There's no way they can pinpoint where a vampire chooses to take your life and bring you back. And the fate they decide for the witches of the realm is shrouded in uncertainty." She paused, her eyes narrowing. "You and Luke together as you are now is a forbidden combination, but it would be different if you were to become a witch-vampire. In that state, you can live with us and be one of us without joining the realm. I'm sure Luke wouldn't mind if you added a few hours for them occasionally," she added hastily, a hint of urgency in her tone.

My jaw slackened, falling open in disbelief. Indeed, I was drooling, but I couldn't feel it. My body and mind had gone numb, overwhelmed by the constant revelations. Enough was enough - I could only take so much and reached my limit. All I wanted was for the shocking discoveries to stop, to give someone else a turn. This weird breed I was had endured its fair share for one day.

"I have no idea," I said, letting out a long, weary sigh. The uncertainty was weighing heavily on my mind. "I honestly don't know anything at all." My gaze darted around the room, searching for any sign of Luke. "Where did Luke go?" I asked, my voice tinged with growing concern.

"Well..." She cleared her throat, her humanlike gesture making me smile. "He's waiting outside the room. But he didn't ask me to come here - I made him follow me. I want you to consider what we can offer you. There's no way the realm can stop it. If you somehow manage to survive the fight with Lilly, we only need you to have a weak pulse for us to turn you, and it won't hurt," she promised, her voice laced with a sense of urgency.

Darcy spoke with compelling intensity, her gaze locked onto mine, each word carrying a weight that demanded my full attention. The proposal she laid before me was laden with significant implications, a web of consequences that stretched far beyond the immediate moment. The way she had deftly orchestrated the situation—leading the man to wait just outside—underscored her resolve to win me over.

Even after the harrowing encounter with Lilly, the promise of survival added a sense of urgency and high stakes to the conversation. And the assurance that the transformation would be painless made her offer all the more seductive, tempting me to consider the impossible. Darcy's tone, a careful blend of persuasion and calm certainty, created a palpable sense of unease. It was as if the very fate of the realm teetered on the edge of my decision, her words threading through the air like a spell cast over the moment.

But the thought that weighed heaviest was the knowledge that Luke—the man I had fallen hopelessly in love with—was waiting just beyond that door. The idea was unimaginable and deeply affecting, as if the revelations had reshaped my reality's fabric. Each word Darcy spoke tugged at the fragile threads of my resolve, leaving me to grapple with the enormity of what was being offered.

"I know you mean well," I began, my voice faltering, "but..."

"But what?" Luke's voice rang out, his eyes burning with a fiery anger. "I know you love me, Seira," he said, his words laced with intensity. "I can feel it, but you have to listen to reason. Everything you've been told is a lie. Join me in my world, and you'll know that someone won't deceive you at least once in your life." His gaze narrowed, and his expression turned desperate, pleading for her to understand.

"You had lied to me once, hadn't you?" I retorted, my voice tinged with accusation. "You had to reveal what you knew because you saw my unwavering determination to uncover the truth about Matace's death. But even then, you only told me half the story." I paused, feeling the weight of my heritage on my shoulders. "I'm made up of many demons and witches, and that's my legacy. I'm supposed to feel proud of it, but they messed up and left me to pick up the shattered pieces of something that wouldn't have happened if they hadn't created me in the first place." I took a deep breath, the intensity of my words palpable. "You knew the entire time but didn't say anything to protect the realm."

"What else could I do?" he asked softly, his voice laced with a hint of desperation. "But I'm working on it, I promise. I want to give you the life you deserve, the one you've always been deprived of. You've been through so much, and I know you deserve much better than they've offered you." His gaze was intense, his eyes pleading for understanding as he searched my face, determined to make things right.

I didn't want to engage in conversation. My reluctance was natural, considering my life had been destined and handpicked to end abruptly while I was still young. Luke remained by my side, sitting in the corner, observing me statuesquely. Darcy sensed the tension between us and eventually left the room, suddenly needing to change her clothes.

The impending battle was closing in, just like the inevitability of my short life. Luke was powerless to stop it, which irked him more than my refusal to resort to his vampire world. He was a control freak but also a joker at times – a multifaceted vampire, just as I was an intricately woven witch with my peculiar genetic makeup.

"I couldn't help but wonder, am I even allowed to walk alone, or will you just send someone to follow me?" I asked him, my voice laced with frustration and a hint of defiance.

"I'll be right on your heels," he cautioned, his voice laced with a protective edge. "You know I'm still your guardian, and I can't let you wander off alone. But I'll make sure to keep my distance." He paused, a faint hint of concern flickering across his features. "I feel you don't want me near you or anyone else."

"Do you blame me?" I snapped back at him, stepping off the bed and quickly slipping into my comfortable shoes. "Everyone here knew what I was before I even did! It's like waking up in the middle of what was supposed to be a nightmare, only to realise it's not a nightmare but a harsh reality that I've been powerless to control." I took a deep breath, my voice laced with frustration. "So far, it's all about you looking out for yourselves without a single thought for anyone else. Let's all just 'protect the realm,' shall we?" I mocked, injecting a strange, sarcastic tone into my words.

To my surprise, I heard his soft chuckle behind me.

"Stop laughing at me," I grumbled, leaving the room and walking rapidly towards the doorway at the end of the corridor.

"Seira," Leo called behind me.

I turned around, groaning loudly from another intrusion.

"Yes," I replied.

"I just wanted to say good luck," he smiled gently, "and well done for taming the Meniagier. Can you send them back to their world before you face Lilly, though? None of us can do it," he asked hopefully.

"Nope," I replied, turning away from him in a show of disrespect, to his shock and horror. "They now belong in this world, and if I die," I emphasised the 'if'; however, I knew I would undoubtedly die once Lilly caught hold of me, "Then they will remain with me."

"You know you can't do that," he shouted, "What's wrong with you? It's not like you were meant to live, and you know it."

Luke hissed in response and stood between Leo and me, his eyes glaring dark daggers in his direction.

"Thank you, Leo," he spat, "She's is aware of her fate and doesn't need someone like you, who has already done enough damage to her, to remind her of it. Go away!" he warned.

"Or what vampire," he demanded, standing ready to fight, "What are you going to do?"

"Nothing," I interjected firmly, cutting through the tension. Raising my voice, I addressed them both sternly, "One thing is certain – I have to go, but don't let my passing be in vain. For goodness sake, learn to coexist with each other. You may not be complete enemies, but you both lied to me, putting you on equal footing in my eyes."

My words hung in the air, heavy with a sense of finality. I could see the weight of my statement sink in, their expressions shifting as they grappled with the gravity of the situation. The air was thick with the realisation that this may be my final plea, a last-ditch effort to bring them together before I met my fate.

A deep sense of satisfaction washed over me as I walked away, leaving the pair behind, locked in a heated confrontation. Their tempers had reached a boiling point, and the space between them seemed to vibrate with the intensity of their clash. The seconds dragged on, each thick with mounting frustration as neither could back down. The air around them crackled with tension, their voices rising to a fevered pitch, each desperately trying to overpower the other.

It was as if sparks were flying between them, the energy of their anger almost tangible. I could feel the weight of their animosity, a battle of wills playing out in a charged silence broken by their escalating shouts. Yet, amid the storm of their conflict, I had emerged victorious, slipping away. At the same time, they remained ensnared in their own fury. The satisfaction of outmanoeuvring them lingered as I distanced myself from the scene, the echoes of their anger fading with each step I took.

As I glanced back, a small, self-assured smile tugged at the corners of my lips. I savoured the moment, relishing that I had outmanoeuvred them, leaving them in a state of paralysis, unable to continue their heated exchange. It was a moment of triumph, a testament to my cunning and composure in the face of their rising emotions.

I marched forward, determined to put some distance between myself and Luke. His lingering presence only served to agitate my already fraying temper. As I reached the Meniagier, I knew he could not follow me within the impenetrable shield I had constructed around them. I had created this barrier with great skill, one that even the other witches would struggle to counter or breach, let alone tame the creatures within and send them back to their exiled realm - a feat that would prove no easy task.

Despite my swift pace, I could hear Luke's plaintive cry behind me, "Wait for me!" But I had no intention of slowing down or affording him any reprieve. The brief respite from his company was a welcome relief, and I savoured the opportunity to have a moment's peace.

"I don't need you to tag along," I hissed through gritted teeth, my voice dripping with frustration. "I'm going to see the only decent creatures I've ever encountered, and I don't want you there." The words spilt out, laced with a raw, uncompromising intensity.

"Oof!" he grimaced, clutching his chest dramatically. "That stung right in the ol' ticker," he groaned, his face contorted in agony.

"Now is not the moment for your silly jokes, Luke," I sternly cautioned, striding forward and leaving him in my wake. If he wished, he could effortlessly catch up to me. Still, I sensed his hesitation to push the boundaries of our relationship. "And cease this constant trailing behind me," I commanded, the irritation in my voice palpable.

"I can't do that," he said, flashing a grim smile. "You know I must stick by your side, no matter what. And just so you know," he continued, his tone turning serious, "if by some miracle you manage to survive, I'll be turning you in without a second thought. For once, I'm making a decision for the greater good. The world would be a lonely place without you, Seira."

I whirled around, nearly colliding with him, but I stopped myself just in time. "There's no way I'm coming out of this alive," I snapped, my voice laced with fury. "So stop kidding yourself and just admit the only thing left to do is bury me if you can even find any pieces of me left."

"I'm utterly perplexed," he said, his brow furrowed in confusion. "What exactly do you need to do to get Lilly out of the picture?" He leaned forward, his eyes filled with desperation and determination, yearning for a straightforward solution to this vexing problem.

"I have to take the plunge into the depths of darkness with her," I replied, my voice laced with a hint of nonchalance. "If I'm fortunate, I might get turned away; it all depends," I added, a bitter edge creeping into my tone, "on the tangled mess that is my DNA. It will be a conundrum for them to navigate; I might just get lucky, but you know what, at least the precious realm and everyone in it will be safeguarded," I concluded, a sense of determination and resolve underlying my words.

"I'm afraid I must decline your generous offer, Seira," he responded sombrely. "Although it was a noble and courageous proposal, I simply cannot accept it. If I am not granted the opportunity to work alongside you, then there is no way I would ever join an endeavour that harbours more evil within it than I possess." His words held a weighted gravity, the intensity of his conviction evident in how he held my gaze.

"What you're suggesting is downright foolish," I said, frustration evident in my voice. "But if that's truly what you want, then so be it. The offer from Leo will remain open, and I can tell he's quite fond of you – an unusual thing, given how he typically dislikes everyone, especially vampires. Yet, you seem to have struck a chord with him for some reason."

"That's quite a sight, isn't it?" he remarked, his words dripping with sarcasm. "Anyway, go see your Meniagier. If it lifts your spirits, then we can tackle this mess together. There must be a way to ensure you don't meet your end here amidst the chaos they've created. I won't accept that this is your fate - to die in this utter disarray."

His tone was firm, his gaze unwavering. The situation was bleak, but he refused to let the hopelessness consume them. There had to be a solution, a glimmer of hope in the darkness they now faced. Whatever it took, he would find a way to prevent the unthinkable from happening.

He was the most infuriating individual I'd ever encountered, obstinate and pig-headed beyond belief. His universe centred solely on himself, with every desire catering to his needs, including mine. But this time, it was different; it was far beyond his control, and sooner or later, he'd have to accept that and stop obsessing over his own world, allowing himself to be a part of it. Didn't he understand before? I was destined to end Lilly's life just as much as I was to perish alongside her; my fate was sealed.

As I approached the Meniagier, the creature immediately scurried towards me, its eyes briefly glancing at Luke, who stood outside my protective barrier. For once, Luke's uncertainty brought me a sense of satisfaction. He needed to learn the harsh lesson that one must take risks and try new things, whether they are living or not. To succeed, he must listen carefully to others to gather all the necessary details, lest he miss out on significant opportunities.

Perhaps one day, Luke would finally learn this crucial lesson, but I knew I wouldn't be around to witness his transformation. The weight of this realisation settled heavily upon me, fueling my determination to impart this wisdom before my time ran out.

"Hey, little ones," I murmured, tenderly caressing their snouts as they stood in a line, gazing up at me eagerly. My eyes were immediately drawn to the largest of the group, their undisputed leader. Something about that particular one captivated me, an irresistible pull that drew me closer. I felt a profound inner calm when my fingers brushed its soft fur.

I let out a soft chuckle, gazing up at the night sky, "I know you've missed me," I said as he nuzzled my neck, his warm breath tickling my skin. I could feel his happiness radiating through the gentle puffs of air he exhaled. "I've missed you too," I admitted, my heart swelling with affection. "But you'll have to go back willingly after the fight, okay?" I reminded him, my tone tinged with a hint of reluctance.

I patiently waited for him to comprehend what I had conveyed. He sensed my emotions when I placed my hand on his bowed head. He snorted in contempt, angered by my determination and my inevitable fate.

"I know this isn't pleasant," I consoled him softly, "But what choice do I have?" My voice was laced with a hint of sorrow, yet it remained resolute. I could see the conflict in his eyes, the reluctance to accept the truth I had shared. The air was thick with tension, but I remained steadfast, hoping he would understand the gravity of the situation we found ourselves in.

Luke was utterly cut off from my words. The impenetrable shield surrounded me, visible only to those I allowed to see. All he could perceive were the movements of my lips, as the barrier was so tightly sealed that not even a vampire with their enhanced senses could eavesdrop on my conversations.

I remained with them for an extended period, observing Luke grow restless, pacing back and forth as he contemplated the information. Deliberately, I prolonged the process, stretching it out for as long as I dared, a final small attempt to irritate him.

With a cheerful smile, I promised to meet them later. As they left, they planted another messy kiss on my cheek, a habit that had become all too familiar. The sloppy display of affection was becoming a routine they eagerly indulged in, and it never failed to leave me feeling a mix of endearment and mild discomfort.

With a deep breath, I emerged from the protective shield, only to be confronted by a towering, enraged vampire. His piercing gaze bore upon me, radiating a palpable fury that sent shivers down my spine.

"We need to get inside now," he said sternly, his voice laced with urgency. "And don't you dare pull that stunt again," he added, his eyes narrowing.

"Do what?" I asked, feigning innocence and struggling to suppress a grin.

"Take your sweet time," he replied with a sly grin. "But if you don't hurry up, I'll fill your dreams with such sizzling thrills that you'll be lost for words," he playfully teased.

He was a mysterious puzzle I couldn't solve. He was boiling with anger one moment, and the next, he was teasing me. I couldn't help but wonder, what kind of vampire was he?

"Stop overthinking," he growled, yanking me towards the house. "I don't want to hear a word of whatever's buzzing in your head."

"I'm really trying to understand you," I exclaimed. "It's confusing. One minute, you're fuming, and the next, you're playfully teasing me. I can't wrap my head around it. What's going on?"

"I can't stand how much you annoy me," he grumbled. "And I can't deny how much I care about you. The more time we spend together, the more I dread the thought of you facing this alone. Isn't there some other spell you could use so you don't have to die?"

"No, Luke," I spoke softly, my heart heavy with sadness. "It's settled. The only thing left is to ensure that Cerberus and Tye are removed from this realm for good. Meniagier has agreed to leave peacefully, but promise me you'll make sure they won't cause harm to anyone anymore."

"Absolutely, I'll do it," he vowed, his patience wearing thin. "Hurry up before I can't hold back anymore and sweep you off your feet to escape!"

"Don't you dare," I chuckled, feeling his warmth enveloping me. "I doubt the others will let you off the hook for that."

"I don't think they'll even make an effort to stop me," he observed, gauging the mood. "But we ought to join them immediately. I can hear their tension rising; they're all pointing fingers and refusing to take responsibility for their actions. This will be a monumental moment in your realm's history."

"They might not even bother writing about it," I whispered, doubtful. "Let's go face them." As we entered the house, I surprised myself by lacing my fingers with Luke's, unafraid of what anyone might think. It was like standing on the brink of my own mortality, and I was determined to approach it with grace and fulfilment. I wanted to seize every moment, especially with Luke, before facing whatever fate awaited me.

"Seira," Fiona exclaimed, leaping up from her seat next to Zanda to greet me, "We were just discussing how to corner Lilly. Our only plan so far is to storm the house and surround her. What's your take on this?"

"Sounds good," I said tensely. "But who's going to take on the Cerberus? They breed like crazy, and their numbers explode. Plus, they grow into full-grown adults only two weeks after birth."

"We all will," she replied, flashing a warm smile. "You're incredibly brave to embrace the responsibility of sacrificing your life for the kingdom."

"Sorry," I stammered, struggling to speak. "Can you repeat that?"

Before she could even think of a response, Leo sprang to his feet with lightning speed, leaving her startled and caught off guard.

"We were telling our new friends," Leo jumped in, "about how you've bravely taken on the responsibility of putting an end to Lilly and her scheming once and for all because no one else was willing to step up."

I kept a close eye on him, finding it hard to believe he would share such a secret. But as a loyal member of the realm, he was bound by duty to prioritise the realm's well-being and uphold its honourable reputation at any cost.

"I understand," I said, a hint of uncertainty in my voice, "Yes, I agree. It had to be done."

I had no clue why I decided to go along with them when I could have easily sparked a big argument among them and watched them defend their viewpoints. But I didn't think I had any value left, not even as a human.

"I really admire what you're doing," she sighed, with a hint of longing in her voice. "If I could, I would definitely take your place, but Zanda simply won't allow it," she said. "And nobody else is as powerful enough as you are to be able to do this. It would end up with many of us dead, and Lilly could still take over the realm."

Fiona never seemed to mean to sound apologetic, but Luke's constant whispers in my ear always made it seem that way.

"Why on Earth couldn't they hear what was said in the room?" I demanded, incredulous.

"They couldn't," he answered, his voice filled with tension. "Darcy waited outside the library, desperate to hear what was being said within. I chose the library because its walls are impenetrable by vampire senses. Darcy pressed her ear to the door, straining to catch every word of the conversation."

"Wow," I exclaimed in amazement, "Why on Earth would she go and do something like that?"

"She wants you to stay alive just like I do," he said intensely. "And you're not paying attention to their talk about how they are plotting your demise. You better listen up!"

I snorted at him under my breath, feeling a surge of defiance. "Maybe with them planning my imminent death, I've had enough of their control," I whispered. "It's freaky and off-putting. Why can't I have a say in how I meet my end? It's their fault that my life has to end, so shouldn't I have the final say?"

"I agree with you," he chuckled, "Go ahead and tell them then."

I eavesdropped for a little longer as they deliberated on who would get the chance to take down whom, based on the increasing threat of the Cerberus.

"They're multiplying like rabbits," Stella snarled at Zanda. "They've got the advantage. What do you expect us to do? Cast a spell on them or something?"

"Ha!" he scoffed at her reply, unfazed. "You are supposed to be witches, but I've seen many failures. Poor Seira's life hangs by a thread because you can't even muster up the power to take someone out. All we're left with is the small stuff."

"How could you?" she erupted from her seat and circled him like a predator eyeing its prey. "How could you?" she repeated, her body trembling with fury. "You dare underestimate the strength of the realm? We are the mightiest beings ever to set foot in that place. It's our power that brought her into existence," she jabbed her finger at me for emphasis.

He sneered with a look of disdain, "You're still standing by that awful decision you made with Matace. Typical! Because of you, she has to die for no reason. If your so-called power is so strong, then why can't you be the one to kill Lilly?"

Leo leapt to the realm's defence and his own power, his voice firm and resolute, "I won't allow a blood-sucking vampire to belittle the realm. Seira was created solely to take Lilly or anyone else to the depths of hell, and that's where I'll send you if you don't stop this nonsense."

"Go ahead and give it a shot," Zanda taunted playfully. "But I wouldn't recommend it. Multiple bloodthirsty vampires are in the room, and if you pick a fight with one, you better be ready to tangle with the whole bunch."

Teasing the vampire and the old witch was a bad idea. Their ongoing argument was irritating and confusing, as they still couldn't agree on who should be in charge of dealing with whatever creature Lilly decided to conjure.

"Both of you. Stop!" I screamed.

All of a sudden, all attention focused on me. Everyone in the room fixed their eyes on me, their mouths hanging wide open in shock. At that moment, I desperately wished I could vanish into thin air and hide away in my usual quiet corner. Leo's furious departure echoed in my ears as he stormed out of the room and slammed the door behind him. No one had anticipated that a mere witch like me would have the guts to order him to 'shut up.'

"Stella, can you tell me the exact number they have?" I inquired eagerly, my curiosity piqued.

Sheepishly, she admitted, 'They're multiplying at an alarming rate.' Her fiery eyes remained fixed on Zanda as she declared, "It's clear we can't continue like this."

I remained composed. "You don't have a choice. Zanda is right. Due to the realm's limitations, I now hold all the power. I'll be directing your every move. That's final."

Stella slumped in shock while Leo, now more composed, gave me a knowing wink before retaking his seat.

Once I fully understood the situation, I could tell that Luke was thoroughly impressed. He remained silent, but his intense focus showed he was fully engrossed in listening to every word.

All eyes locked on me as I took charge of the impending battle. Lilly was about to face my fierce army, which had rallied together in response to the chaos she had sparked. The curse the realm had placed upon me felt like a heavy burden, yet they saw it as a badge of honour. It made me feel sadness and frustration, like carrying a weight no one could see.

Stella spoke passionately as I finally joined Luke, saying, "You're doing something honourable. Leading someone through hell will surely immortalise you in the annals of history as the hero who saved us all."

"I really wish I had been given the choice to say whether I wanted to do that instead of just having your decision forced upon me," I said, trying to contain my frustration.

She marched away with clenched fists while the rest of the group indulged in drinks and food, gearing up for what lay ahead.

"Do you think you can take a walk with me?" Luke asked quietly.

"Absolutely," I said with a smile. "It'll be such a relief to focus on something other than the bleak subject of people passing away."

With a mischievous grin, he grabbed my hand and pulled me out of the room, drawing curious glances from everyone. Zanda's knowing smile was aimed at me.

"Isn't there any other way?" Luke asked, a touch of sadness in his voice as he walked beside me.

I shook my head defiantly. "No," I declared, "There's no easy way out. If there was, I'd grab it without hesitation rather than watching my life slip away because of someone like Lilly."

We made our way to the distant edge of the garden and settled on the slope overlooking the road. No cars dared venture here anymore, scared of the lurking danger that loomed over this eerie land. It was notorious for its hunters and the unexplained vanishings. Everyone knew Luke's property turned sinister after the sunset.

"I believe," he murmured, "that if you were to embrace the life of a vampire, I would transform you in this very moment."

I chuckled gently as the night enveloped us, the breeze whisking away my laughter. "I'm sorry, but I can't agree to that," I said with a smile, my eyes reflecting my firmness. "You understand why, don't you?"

"Do you feel scared?"

"Scared of dying, huh?" I asked, my voice tinged with curiosity and a hint of daring.

"Are you?" he asked in a gentle voice. I shook my head, indicating that I wasn't.

"I'm not completely scared," I admitted, trying to be as truthful as possible. "It's the uncertainty of what happens after my soul leaves my body that terrifies me, not the pain or anything else. When you were turned, were you afraid? What was it like?"

"I had no choice," he confessed with a deep sigh, drawing me closer. "I got into a brawl when I was young, left for dead on the roadside. My body was broken, and my blood alcohol level was too high for the medics to help. Back then, medical care wasn't as advanced. Another vampire found me and offered to save my life. I accepted, not knowing he was granting me immortality. When he bit me, it was hell. Sweats and shakes - it was a nightmare, and I won't tell you the rest in case you change your mind," he added ominously.

"How long have you been a vampire?" I asked, my curiosity piqued.

He let out a soft chuckle, and I nestled closer to him, seeking comfort from the cool night air. At that moment, all I wanted was to be near him, knowing it was the final night before I would have to say goodbye forever. I was determined to cherish every precious second with him.

"Ha! I'm over 400 years old," he chuckled, seeing the horror on my face. "That's right, take it in. I've seen more than you can imagine!"

"Oh, please," I chuckled, "You're like a relic from ancient times. What makes you think I'd want to be forever bound to you?"

He laughed loudly and playfully slapped my arm.

"Age doesn't matter when you're immortal," he interjected, setting me straight. "Zanda and his wife have been around for over

500 years. We were here long before any other demons decided to make Earth their home and even before the realm gained its current prominence. Back then, the realm was less popular than it is now. I knew about it, but I never felt compelled to join. The folks in charge at the time weren't exactly welcoming to us 'dead folk' roaming around their domain."

"I can see why that might seem a bit strict," I remarked. "But not much has really changed, except now vampires and other 'undead' folks are allowed to work remotely for the kingdom, as long as they're only protecting someone. So, why did you agree to protect me?" He let out a deep sigh, his fingers gently twirling through his hair before he answered.

"I wanted to nip it in the bud," he confessed. "And the longer I kept my eyes on you, the stronger my urge to shield you grew. I couldn't fathom why I felt such an instant, unyielding need to safeguard you. Initially, you were just an assignment to me, but then it blossomed into something profound."

His words echoed in my mind, drawing me deeply into his world. What started as a mere "job" observation had become something much deeper, a connection we had only begun to acknowledge. As time passed, we realised we were no longer afraid to show the world the bond that had formed between us.

"Listen," I murmured, urgency creeping into my voice, "Our time together is running out. Let's make every moment count before it's all over."

He smiled and tenderly rested his head on top of mine, his lips brushing softly against the crown of my head, and I felt his hands gently embracing my lower back. We did not need to be unclothed to feel the closeness between us. At that moment, I only wished for Luke to find a soulmate who would bring him lifelong happiness.

Chapter Thirteen

We sat silently on the riverbank, the air thick with an uneasy tension. The night sky was blanketed in a veil of clouds, casting a shadowy embrace that seemed to envelop us, drawing us deeper into the embrace of the impending darkness. In those fleeting moments, it felt comforting to be near someone, to find solace in their presence, before the inevitable that loomed ahead.

"It's cloudy tonight," he murmured, his voice tinged with unease. "How do you feel?"

I carefully pondered his question, taking a moment to grasp the gravity of the situation entirely. The seriousness of this matter surpassed anything that had ever been documented before. Still, I could no longer rely on the realms' official records, for so much had transpired that remained unwritten.

This was a practice they had supposedly prided themselves on for centuries. Yet, they continued to make the same empty promises for the future. With a sense of urgency, I reached my hands towards the sky, summoning the essential power I had once considered the greatest – the ability to control the very elements of the Earth. The moment's intensity was palpable. I knew I needed to act quickly to address the unprecedented challenge that lay before me.

"See, they've all moved now," I said as I gazed up at the sky, a gentle smile playing on my lips as the clouds drifted away, gradually retreating from our presence. The clouds, once looming overhead, now seemed to float effortlessly, putting on a serene display as they carved their path through the vast expanse above us. The shift in the weather felt almost palpable, like a weight being lifted from the atmosphere, allowing a sense of tranquillity to settle in around us.

The night sky was alive with a dazzling display of stars. Their radiant light twinkled and shimmered, casting a mesmerising glow upon the Earth below. I felt a surge of power coursing through me as if I had summoned these celestial beauties to shine even brighter for this enchanting moment. It was a magical experience I knew would be etched in my memory forever.

I reclined on the lush, verdant grass, the tender blades caressing my neck. My dress fanned out around me, the vivid purple hue starkly contrasted against the twinkling stars above; Luke lay beside me. Though our bodies barely touched, we were acutely aware of each other's presence. Our heads rested together, a subtle connection amidst the physical distance. Silently, we gazed up at the starry expanse, allowing the world's tranquillity to envelop us, savouring this moment of much-needed solace before the impending, momentous battle that would resolve the conflict with Lilly and, inevitably, end my life.

"I can't stand the thought of what's going to happen," he murmured, his voice trembling. "I understand you must do this, but why won't you let me assist you, even if you succeed? I'm confused by your decision." His brow furrowed, and his eyes pleaded for an explanation, the weight of his concern etched on his face.

I yearned to respond with profound significance. Was it a genuine desire or a mere necessity? Wasn't it more straightforward to succumb and be free from it all? That way, the realm would have fewer queries to address, and I wouldn't become the prey they would inevitably pursue, given their quest for my demise in the first place. Nevertheless, my mind grappled with the notion that if I managed to survive, he was offering me eternity – to be by his side, to live.

I inhaled a long, deliberate breath, meticulously considering my following words, determined not to cause any undue pain or raise unrealistic expectations. The gravity of the situation weighed heavily, and I knew I needed to convey my message with unwavering clarity and sensitivity.

"I'm sorry, but I can't give you any false hope about my chances of survival," I said, my voice heavy with resignation. "If one of us doesn't make it, the other can't bear to go on alone. And if you get killed too, I'd be left utterly devastated without you by my side." I forced a bittersweet smile. "I know you think you're invincible, like some kind of superhero, but the Cerberus doesn't discriminate. They'll eliminate anyone who dares to challenge the realm and Lilly's dark reign." I took a deep, shuddering breath. "I couldn't live with myself if I made it through only to find you're gone. We need to accept that I might not come back from this. I must be prepared for the worst, no matter what happens."

"I understand your perspective," he said, plucking a blade of grass and twisting it between his fingers. His gaze was intense, a glimmer of determination in his eyes. "But I won't give up, and you know I'll be waiting for you no matter what happens. Do you think there's even the slightest chance?"

I let out a deep, weary sigh. The only chance I'd ever heard of had occurred long ago, in a distant corner of the realm's intricate dealings. Someone had been sent to the depths of hell itself in a desperate attempt to prevent their vile actions from harming anyone else.

The devastation they had caused was nothing short of catastrophic, a blemish upon the realm's very records. It had resulted in one of the most harrowing kinds of exaltation ever witnessed within our world. The individual in question had eventually been spat back out from the fiery pits of the underworld, forced to continue their wretched existence until the realm's leaders finally caught up with them and cast them out for good.

The mere thought of such a heinous ordeal sent a shiver down my spine. Whatever horrors that person had faced, they had narrowly escaped the realm's most severe punishment. I couldn't help but wonder what unspeakable acts they had committed to warrant such a fate.

"I let out a deep, resigned sigh. "There's a slim possibility," I admitted, my voice tinged with uncertainty. "But I honestly don't believe it will apply to me, considering how I was created."

He pivoted to face me, his eyes locking onto mine. "I'm listening," he said, his voice unwavering and intent.

"A man was sent to the depths of hell, but to everyone's surprise, he was quickly spat back out. The realm of the underworld found this rather strange and lost track of him for a while. It soon became clear that hell had its agenda - it would only accept those deemed truly and profoundly evil, the kind who would remain in its hidden, dark recesses for eternity."

"Well," he chuckled, a glint of amusement dancing in his eyes. "You're not exactly the wicked sort, so I don't think that fiery pit of despair can keep you for long. No, it'll probably just spit you right back out."

"I'm not so sure about that," I replied, my voice laced with melancholy. "You see, I'm just not built like you are. Truthfully, I'm not even supposed to be here, alive and breathing. It's just not my destined path, you know?" I shook my head, my words heavy on my heart.

Luke's unexpected pivot towards the house brought our exchange to a jarring halt. A sense of unease crept in as we both noticed a figure rapidly approaching our location. The air grew thick with anticipation; our senses heightened as we waited to see who or what was drawing near.

"Are you ready?" Darcy asked, her voice tinged with impatience. Her face flushed with embarrassment, a telltale sign of her discomfort. Without meeting our gaze, she let her eyes dart around, avoiding any direct eye contact.

"Are you ready?" he asked, his hand clasping mine with a tightness that betrayed his nervousness. His eyes searched mine, a hint of desperation seeping through. "We could just run away somewhere, just the two of us," he suggested, his voice brimming with hopeful anticipation.

"Absolutely not," I responded firmly, shaking my head. "This plan is bound to lead to nothing but trouble. We need to get out of here, now." My voice held a sense of urgency, reflecting my growing unease about the situation. The potential for disaster was palpable. I knew we needed to act quickly to avoid being caught in the impending calamity.

I sprang to my feet, frantically brushing at my clothes. Bits of grass and dirt clung stubbornly, but I couldn't bear facing my end with anything less than pristine attire. It was strange how my mind fixated on such trivial matters when staring down the barrel of inevitable demise. Yet, in that moment of profound distress, these petty concerns seemed to loom large, a futile attempt to exert control over the inevitability that loomed before me.

Luke strode ahead, his heavy steps echoing in the stillness. Darcy followed behind, her head dipped low. I stepped out of the house, joining the others who lined up, their eyes fixed on me. As I made my way towards the Meniagier, their boisterous snorts and thunderous stomping filled the air, the only thing that managed to coax a smile from my lips.

I greeted the peculiar creature with a warm smile, gently stroking its unusual snout. "We're all set. Are you ready to begin?"

I asked, my voice filled with anticipation and a hint of excitement. The creature's eyes gleamed with curious intelligence, and I couldn't help but feel a surge of connection as we prepared to embark on our adventure together.

The beast's eyes softened as it nuzzled my hand, a glimmer of sadness reflected in its gaze, or perhaps it was just my mind playing tricks. With the grace of an expert, I climbed onto its lowered back, steadying myself as the creature began to rise.

Suddenly, I found myself elevated, the ground below seeming miles away, a dark chasm that threatened to swallow me should I lose my footing. As the beast trotted off, it growled menacingly at Luke when he attempted to approach, the animal's eyes filled with a protective reproach.

"Alright, boys," I said, flashing them a warm smile as my eyes sparkled with a hint of playful mischief. "Let's keep things friendly, shall we?" My tone was gentle, yet firm, as I gently chided them, my words carrying a touch of amused affection. I wanted to make sure they understood that while I was approachable, I also expected them to play by the rules and treat each other respectfully.

"I will," Luke responded, a hint of scepticism in his voice. "But I doubt he intends to be kind to anyone other than you. He paused, his eyes narrowing as he surveyed the scene. "We're ready. The plans have been set in motion. The vampires will strike from the north and south, the Cronomiun from the west, and the remaining Meniagier," he said, nodding towards them, "will attack from the east. Do you think you can get them to follow a direct order?"

His words carried a sense of urgency, the weight of the impending battle palpable in the air. The plan had been meticulously crafted. Now they stood on the precipice of its execution, the fate of all hanging in the balance.

"Did you catch that?" I murmured into the creature's ear, my voice barely above a whisper. "Lure them towards the east; you and I will hang back. We don't need to get our hands dirty in the ground skirmish; there are much bigger prizes for us to claim."

The beast's eyes gleamed with understanding, and a low rumble vibrated in its chest. We were on the same wavelength, our plan unfolding like a well-oiled machine. There was a thrill in the air, a palpable tension as we prepared to move, our sights set on a grander prize than the melee about to unfold.

"Hey, which way are you heading in?" I asked Luke, my gaze fixed on him, my curiosity piqued. The question hung in the air, the tension palpable as I waited for his response.

"I'll be right there with you," he responded earnestly, his gaze locked onto mine. "I can't bear the thought of you facing this alone. The mere idea of you fighting her on your own, possibly..." His voice trailed off, the unspoken words hanging heavily in the air. "No, I won't let that happen. We'll face this together, no matter what."

"Ah, I understand," I responded, nodding thoughtfully. Reaching out, I gently touched the creature's rough, shaggy fur. "Alright then," I said, "you'd best stick close to us and make sure you can keep up."

The journey to Lillie's abode was lengthy and strenuous, the conversation starting stiffly and eventually fading into silence. Luke's expression was solemn and pensive; I often caught him stealing glances at me, even though he thought I couldn't see him. My vision was not as limited as he presumed mortal eyes to be; the immortal sight was far superior and a remarkable ability they possessed. Years prior, it had served them well when they had hunted relentlessly in the shadows for mortals to sate their ravenous appetite.

He watched with a growing sense of unease as I sat atop the rickety contraption, my balance precarious and my safety a grave concern. "You really shouldn't be riding on that," he called out, his voice laced with worry and frustration. "It's far too dangerous;

anyone can see it's you up there." How I handled the meniagier with such reckless abandon only heightened his apprehension.

"I'm counting on the cover of darkness and the magical forces at play to ensure no one pays us any attention," I responded hastily. The weight of our secretive actions hung thick in the air, but I couldn't resist a subtle jab. "And let's be honest, you haven't been trying to engage in conversation. I've had more meaningful exchanges with him than with you."

My words carried a palpable intensity, underscoring the gravity of our situation and the growing tension between us. The darkness provided a shroud, but the stakes were high, and I couldn't help but feel the need to assert my position in this delicate dance.

I didn't need the beast to speak out loud to understand it. There was a peculiar, almost mystical connection between us. The moment I looked at the creature, I could feel its profound inner essence resonate within me as if we were kindred spirits. And in turn, I knew the beast could sense the depths of my emotions as if we were the same.

It was a bond unlike any I had ever witnessed between a human and a wild animal. We communicated without words, our souls intertwining in a way that defied logic or explanation. The intensity of this unspoken understanding was palpable, almost overwhelming, as if we had known each other for a lifetime, despite this being our first encounter.

Luke stared at me, his gaze heavy with the weight of the unspoken truth. "How can I talk about anything else when I know your time is running out?" he said, his voice tinged with sorrow and frustration. The weather? Idle chatter?" He shook his head, the reality of the situation pressing down on him, making it hard to string a sentence together. "I can't pretend everything is normal when you're slipping away."

He gazed upwards, his expression a mix of grimace and shudder, before shifting his attention towards me. Curious, I followed his line of sight, and the once-vibrant sky had darkened ominously. Flashes of strange, partially illuminated shadows streaked across the heavens, coalescing into small, huddle formations as if seeking protection.

The brilliant blue haze now seemed to strain the eyes with its complexity. Instinctively, I knew Lilly had initiated the battle, summoning those shadowy, evil spirits that most would never even dare to consider, let alone call upon for aid in a fight.

"The ritual has commenced," I uttered with a sense of unease. "She has summoned the otherworldly forces; I did not anticipate her taking such a drastic measure, yet I cannot fathom what exactly I had expected her to do." My voice wavered, betraying the growing trepidation that gripped me as the weight of the situation became increasingly palpable.

"What are the spirits going to do?"

"They'll do whatever they desire," I stated grimly. "If they manage to seize power over Lilly, which is a real possibility, they'll seek to control the entire town. And from there, darkness and malice will spread like an unstoppable plague. No one will be spared. This time, she's taken things too far."

He carefully schooled his expression, reverting to the same steely, unapproachable demeanour from earlier. His eyes constantly scanned the area, occasionally flickering to meet mine as I heard the sounds of the impending battle. Roaring, stomping, eerie cackling, and ghostly laughter filled the air, making it feel more like a twisted game show than a real-life confrontation where lives were at stake.

The atmosphere was thick with tension, and my composure began to crumble. I desperately wanted this to be over, but with the large number of people and strange creatures surrounding the house, the opposition vastly outnumbered our forces. Lilly had anticipated every angle and found solutions to her predicament.

The Cronomiun vastly outnumbered us. Their guard blanketed the grounds, yet they were united despite standing far apart. I felt a connection to them, a thread that entangled me, pulling me into their midst. They were aware of my presence and turned, their eyes burning fiery while their mouths remained taut, thin lines of determination.

A voice whispered, emerging from the shadows. "You've arrived. Excellent, we're relieved you're unharmed. We can hold them off. The malevolent spirits stand no chance against us; they know we've defeated them before, but their determination is fiercer this time. She's enticed them with deceitful vows. She's eagerly anticipating your arrival."

The voice carried a sense of urgency, its tone laced with a mix of relief and apprehension. The air crackled with an undercurrent of tension as if the atmosphere was charged with the impending conflict. The evil spirits, emboldened by false promises, posed a formidable challenge. Still, the speaker exuded a quiet confidence, a resolve forged by past victories. The stage was set, and the final confrontation was imminent.

"Thanks for the oh-so-helpful reminder," I muttered inwardly. I glanced towards Luke, who stood nearby, anxious anticipation etched on his face. "I'll stay put and keep watch here. She needs to be ready and make sure the path is clear to find her. You've got to keep Luke safe and stop him from following - he'll probably try, so do whatever it takes to hold him back." My words carried a sense of urgency and determination, underscored by a tinge of frustration. The stakes were high, and I couldn't afford any missteps. Casting a quick, wary glance around, I steeled myself for what lay ahead, every muscle tensed in preparation.

I sensed their silent approval as I delivered my commands, their unwavering gaze conveying their agreement. Yet, their heads remained motionless, a wordless understanding passing between us. Despite this, their fervent yearning to join the clashing forces outweighed their reluctance to leave my side. The pull of the battle was irresistible, and I knew I could no longer hold them back.

With a deep breath, I urged the meniagier forward, "Go now and join them. Make me proud." Carefully, I swung my leg down, disengaging my foot from the other side, lest I tumble headfirst onto the ground below.

He sensed the impending fate, his eyes dark with resignation yet exuding a quiet pride. Gently, he leaned in and licked my cheek, a gesture of pure love and adoration from this misunderstood creature. His actions spoke volumes, conveying a depth of emotion that words could not capture. The intensity left an indelible mark, a poignant reminder of these animals' complex and often misunderstood nature.

"I hope you're not planning on leaving that mess there," Luke said, his voice laced with a hint of disapproval as he stood behind me. His gaze fixed on the smudge on my shirt, a subtle but clear indication that he expected me to clean it up.

"This is it for me, but please, feel free to have your way with my body before laying me to rest. I'm at your mercy now," I responded, my voice steady despite the gravity of the situation.

I knew that sharp retort would silence him, ending his ceaseless bickering with the Meniagier. The two creatures were not meant to coexist, a lifeless entity at odds with a misunderstood one. Who could have imagined they would become sworn adversaries, their animosity burning fiercely?

He moved to my side, his arm resting protectively around my shoulders as we observed the battle unfold from a relatively safe distance. The creatures fought with unwavering determination, their fierce movements and thunderous collisions echoing across the open space.

Cronomiun fought back with ferocity, unleashing a relentless assault against the tidal wave of spirits. Deafening crashes and resounding booms filled the air, making me wonder how the mortals must perceive the sheer scale and intensity of the conflict surrounding them.

The chaos was immeasurable, the ground trembling beneath our feet as the combatants clashed. Yet, despite the overwhelming power on display, I couldn't help but be captivated by the raw, primal energy of the scene unfolding before us.

"Oh, boy, it seems like something's gone wrong down there. I'd better hurry and check it out. Can you manage on your own for a bit? I don't want to leave you in the lurch, but this sounds like it needs my attention."

Anxiety flickered in his gaze, a restless energy pulsing through him as he yearned to join his comrades in battle. The weight of uncertainty cast a shadow over his features. Yet, his determination burned brighter, urging him to step forward and stand alongside those he held dear.

"I'll be alright, don't worry," I reassured him with a confident smile. "You should go and take care of what you need to do. I've got this."

The evil spirits unleashed a relentless barrage of underhanded tactics, overwhelming us with the sheer numbers of the dreaded Cerberus. It was a dire situation I had never encountered, but I refused to stand idly by and watch my friends suffer. I was prepared to face this challenge head-on despite the daunting odds.

The truth was, I was more than capable of handling the situation on my own. The spirits resorted to every underhanded tactic imaginable, and the Cerberus multiplied tenfold, leaving us in a precarious position. This was unlike anything I had ever experienced, but I wouldn't let my friends be harmed. I was confident in my abilities and ready to take on this challenge, no matter how overwhelming it seemed.

The nearby hill stood as a beckoning challenge, a canvas upon which I could unleash my powers and defeat Lilly, meeting her might with my own. Gathering the folds of my skirt, I ascended to the summit, spreading my arms wide. A tingle of energy crackled at my fingertips, the magical essence pulsing through my veins, flooding my senses.

With a commanding call, I summoned the storm, enveloping the people below. The darkness receded, replaced by a cleansing light that washed away the lingering shadows, leaving only the pure and the good in its wake.

The raging storm descended upon us, its roar echoing. The spirits, once able to float effortlessly, now struggled to find purchase, their power diminished by the whirlwind's fury. The storm's relentless grip tightened around them, its single-minded determination to overwhelm any trace of Lilly's plans. I knew my timing had to be perfect. I couldn't let anyone else fall victim to the storm's wrath. This storm had grown far beyond Lilly's expectations, its eye a terrifying vortex that consumed the spirits she had callously summoned.

The terrified creatures shrieked in sheer panic, their cries piercing the air as they clung desperately to their positions. Their terror mounted as the winds around them began to howl with increasing fury. The ropes that tethered them snapped with a resounding crack, sending them hurtling skyward in a chaotic frenzy. I summoned the eye of the storm, focusing its wrath directly on the towering Cerberus, intent on sweeping these wretched beings away from this cursed place.

Now, a full-blown storm, the wind tore through the scene with savage force, snatching up as many of the creatures as it could in its merciless grip. They were flung sideways into a terrifying spiral, spinning helplessly through the air before being slammed back to the ground with bone-shattering force, leaving them battered, bruised, and disoriented in the storm's wake.

The Cerberus, caught off guard by the sudden and savage counterattack, unleashed a chorus of howls. Their fury struck me squarely, forcing me to stagger backwards. I steadied myself, planting my feet firmly on the ground.

Sudden flashes of lightning erupted all around, painting the sky with vibrant purple, green, and red hues. The Cerberus, a menacing three-headed beast, was the target of these striking bolts, causing it to become disoriented and reliant on the chaotic sounds surrounding it.

"Come on, Luke," I grunted through clenched teeth, my muscles straining to control the thunder, lightning and raging storm. The wild energy crackled and writhed, desperate to break free and unleash its destructive power. "Hurry up and finish this before it slips through my grasp!"

The air was dense with tension, vibrating with the barely restrained power of the storm that churned overhead. Sweat trickled down my brow as I strained to maintain control, every muscle taut with the effort of holding the volatile elements in check.

Lightning crackled and darted, eager to break free and unleash its fury upon the world, but I wouldn't let it. My teeth clenched, I pushed back against the storm's relentless assault, my will locked in a fierce battle with the wild, untamed forces threatening to spiral out of control.

"Just a little longer, Luke," I urged, my voice strained with the effort. "We're so close. Don't let it all fall apart now!"

Never before had I yearned for someone's safety as desperately as I did for Luke's in that moment. He fought his way through the battlefield with fierce determination, his every move calculated and precise as he pushed forward to reach his allies.

He deflected incoming attacks with a fluid grace, his exceptional combat skills transforming him into a whirlwind of motion. A snarling Cerberus charged towards him, its massive paws pounding the Earth and kicking up thick dust clouds. Luke leapt aside with a swift, acrobatic twist.

The creature's hot breath seared the air, but Luke was relentless. With a surge of raw power, he tore into the beast, ripping it apart with his bare hands. Blood sprayed as he severed its limbs, the monstrous remains crashing to the ground in a gruesome heap. All around him, his enemies lay broken and battered, their bodies marred by deep gashes and torn flesh, testaments to Luke's unmatched strength and unyielding resolve.

I stood my ground, fully aware of the intense energy around me. Lilly had unleashed her formidable power, and the rain lashed against my cheeks, sharp and biting. Each sting was designed to disrupt my focus, to let the storm spiral beyond my control. Fury welled up within me, and I bellowed her name, the sound tearing through the storm, echoing across the turbulent landscape in a desperate attempt to reach her.

The chaos deepened as more demons surged into the fray, their presence marked by snarls and the stench of sulphur. Lilly's malevolent laughter rang out, a chilling sound that sliced through the cacophony, her voice dripping with the dark satisfaction of her relentless attacks.

Amid the turmoil, I caught sight of a shadow moving swiftly through the chaos, searching with intent. But I couldn't afford to be distracted. My focus remained locked on the storm, my will ironclad as I summoned my demons from the depths. They descended upon Lilly's forces with ferocity, clashing violently in a desperate attempt to turn the tide.

The air pulsed with magic and fury, and I could feel the storm teetering on the edge of madness, my resolve the only thing holding it together. I knew I had to keep the chaos under control, even as the battlefield erupted around me, each side fighting with a brutal intensity that matched the fury of the storm itself.

The shadow glided effortlessly through the night, its form melding seamlessly with the surrounding darkness, a phantom slipping between worlds. Driven by the need to unmask this intruder, I summoned a burst of lightning, its blinding brilliance cutting through the blackness like a blade.

The sky erupted with thunderous roars, each one accompanied by agonised shrieks that sent shivers down my spine yet fed the growing power within me. This energy was fierce and primal, surging through my veins, awakening with a hunger that throbbed in anticipation of my command.

The shadow moved with otherworldly grace, almost ethereal in its fluidity, as it wove through the darkness, eluding my every attempt to corner it. But I was relentless. Determined to bring it into the light, I conjured another searing flash of lightning, its jagged brilliance illuminating the void and momentarily freezing the shadow in its tracks.

The air crackled with the raw power of each thunderous boom, and with every piercing scream, the force within me grew stronger, more intense. It was a living thing now, a fierce and untamed energy that pulsed with readiness, poised and alert, eagerly awaiting my next move.

"Tye!" I cried out, my voice laced with fear for Luke's safety. He was locked in a vicious battle, surrounded by three fearsome Cerberus beasts relentlessly snapping at his throat. Yet, he refused to give up even in such imminent danger.

I watched, my heart pounding, as Luke fought with unwavering determination. Summoning every ounce of my strength, I amplified my voice with the wind and magic, shouting his name across the chaotic battlefield. "Tye!" I desperately called out, my words carrying a sense of urgency and desperation, urging him to hold on.

My voice echoed across the battlefield, a desperate cry that cut through the chaos. Luke's head snapped toward me, his eyes finding mine for a brief, heart-stopping moment. The connection was fleeting, but it was enough to send a surge of urgency through me.

Suddenly, Tye appeared, charging towards Luke with a determined stride, his arms outstretched as if in a gallant attack. The massive, snarling and restless Cerberus parted to clear a path, allowing Tye to close in on Luke. It was a trap, a sinister ploy crafted by Tye to lure Luke into the fray. The air buzzed with anticipation as Luke braced himself for the confrontation, muscles coiled and ready, but Tye's eyes had a cold, calculated gleam that betrayed his true intentions.

Tye struck with lightning speed, his blade a blur as he aimed for Luke's side. Luke twisted just in time, but not without cost—blood blossomed from a fresh wound on his arm, staining his shirt with a dark, spreading stain.

The injury was deep, a vicious slice meant to weaken and disorient. Luke gritted his teeth against the pain, retaliating with a ferocious swing. Still, Tye was already moving, dodging the blow with a smug grin.

The fight escalated into a brutal dance of blades and fury; each strike met with a counter that left the ground around them stained with blood. Luke fought valiantly, but Tye's cunning had turned the tide of battle, and it seemed the trap was tightening.

With every clash, more blood was spilt, their injuries accumulating—a gash across Luke's brow, a brutal cut on Tye's thigh. The Cerberus circled them, snarling and restless, as if feeding off the violence.

Luke's breath came in ragged gasps, his strength waning under the relentless onslaught. Yet, despite the odds, he refused to yield. This was more than a fight; it was a battle of wills, a test of survival, and Luke knew that surrender meant certain death. Tye pressed his advantage, his movements precise and deadly, but Luke's determination burned fierce, his resolve unshakable even as the battle pushed him to the brink.

"Cronomiun!" I cried out, my voice laced with urgency and fear. "You've got to help Luke, please!" The desperation in my tone was evident as I pleaded for my friend's life, my heart racing with the gravity of the situation.

They materialised in a flash, their arrival heralded by the relentless horde of spirits that surged after them. The spirits swarmed and writhed around their targets like enraged hornets poised to strike with their venomous stingers.

"Save Luke!" I pleaded, my voice trembling as I reached out with quivering hands, desperate to intervene.

The storm raged with unbridled fury, its howling winds tearing through the night like a beast unchained. My pulse quickened, knowing I had to act swiftly. I summoned every ounce of my power, channelling the swirling winds and the ferocious tornado toward the enemy, my heart hammering with fear. The thought of harming Luke was unbearable, and the stakes were too high if the twister veered towards the house, threatening to obliterate the portals Lilly relied on.

Desperation gnawed at me as I wrestled with the storm's immense power, struggling to keep it under control. The violent winds howled around me, eager to unleash their destruction, but I couldn't let that happen—not when the house and its precious portals were at risk. With no choice, I forced the storm's wrath away from the house, redirecting its deadly force into the night. The decision left me drained, my only path to finding Lilly now swept away by the winds I had commanded.

I stood transfixed, watching as the Cronomiun fought alongside Luke with a fluid grace that was both mesmerising and deadly. They moved in perfect harmony, weaving through the throngs of snarling Cerberus, each step calculated as they positioned themselves to face a chosen adversary. The air was thick with tension, the ground trembling beneath the weight of the battle.

Meanwhile, Luke and Tye were locked in a brutal dance of blades, wholly absorbed in their combat. Their strikes were fierce. Each blow met with equal force, the clash of steel ringing out like thunder. They fought relentlessly, oblivious to the chaos around them, their focus narrowed to the life-or-death struggle they were entangled in. The battlefield blurred in the periphery, but their battle raged on, the ferocity of their duel unmatched by the chaos surrounding them.

Luke launched himself at Tye with a ferocity that bordered on pure hatred, his movements a blur of raw power and rage. In one brutal motion, he tore Tye's arm from its socket, the sound of ripping flesh mingling with Tye's agonised roar. Luke cast the severed limb aside with disdain as if it were nothing more than refuse, unworthy of a second thought.

Tye's bellow of pain reverberated through the air, his howl a primal, anguished sound that sent shockwaves through the battlefield. The force of his scream seemed to draw my storm towards it, the swirling winds responding to his anguish as if the sheer intensity of his suffering drew them. For a terrifying moment, the storm shifted direction, its deadly power harnessed by Tye's cry. But I fought back, my will clashing with the storm's fury as I wrestled control from its grasp.

With a surge of desperation, I redirected the storm's wrath towards the remaining Cerberus, the winds howling in unison with my commands. To any observer, my frantic attempts to protect the vampires might have seemed absurd, a futile struggle against forces far beyond my control.

Yet, it felt like second nature, an instinctual response honed by countless battles. The storm raged on, tearing through the Cerberus with merciless force. At the same time, Luke's relentless assault on Tye continued the battlefield a tempest of blood, fury, and unyielding determination.

A sudden shift in the air sent a shiver down my spine, and I spun around, heart pounding. There they stood—the misty, ethereal figures of the realm, materialising from the shadows like ghosts summoned by my turmoil. The swirling mist obscured their faces, but I could still feel the weight of their disapproval, the cold disdain that emanated from them like an energetic force.

But this time, I did not cower before them. The storm of emotions within me was no longer a source of shame but a wellspring of power that I refused to suppress. These figures, once so revered, had long since lost their hold over me. Their misguided actions and relentless attempts to shape and control my existence led us to this inevitable confrontation.

Now, as we stood face to face, the final reckoning loomed. The air crackled with the tension of our unspoken histories. I could feel the storm inside me intensifying, feeding off the defiance that pulsed through my veins. This was the moment I had been waiting for, the culmination of all they had wrought upon me—and I was ready to meet it head-on without fear or hesitation.

"The time has come, Seira," they murmured, their voices laced with urgency. "We must find Lilly, no matter the cost." Their eyes gleamed with a determined resolve, the weight of their mission tangible in the air around them. I felt a surge of adrenaline and anger coursing through my veins.

"I'm not giving up yet," I growled through clenched jaws, my eyes fixed on the intense battle unfolding before me. Adrenaline coursed through my veins as I steeled my resolve, refusing to turn away until the very last moment. The clash of steel and shouts of the combatants filled the air, fueling my determination to see this through to the bitter end.

A cold hand grazed my arm, and I shuddered at the chilling, unnatural touch. It carried no warmth, affection, or sense of kinship—only an unsettling coldness that felt utterly foreign to me. This touch was worlds apart from the courageous battles I had witnessed among the mysterious creatures in the field, where bravery and camaraderie had once reigned.

Their world, once vibrant and full of purpose, had been corrupted by the twisted schemes of Lilly, one of their own. She was meant to be the realm's guardian, the protector of its ancient magic. Yet, she had allowed hatred, pain, and cruelty to fester within her, twisting her soul and poisoning her domain. It was a fundamental lesson in the ways of the witch: never to let such dark forces seize control, for doing so would endanger the very magic that sustained us all.

And yet, here I stood, surrounded by the consequences of her failure. The air was thick with the remnants of her betrayal, the once-powerful magic of the realm now tainted and fragile. The creatures, who had once fought valiantly, now cowered in the shadows, their world tarnished and broken. This was the bitter fruit of Lilly's descent into darkness, a stark reminder of the peril when one allows the darkness to take hold.

"You must find her immediately, Seira," she urged in a hushed tone, gripping my arm to hold me back. "I can't allow you to remain here any longer." Her words were laced with urgency and fear, her eyes pleading with me to heed her warning.

"Oh," I said, pivoting to face her directly. The sudden movement caught her off guard, and she wobbled slightly, her eyes widening with surprise. "And what exactly do you think you'll do to stop me?"

I spoke calmly, almost casually, but beneath the surface, my voice vibrated with barely contained intensity. My gaze locked onto hers, sharp and unwavering, as I held my ground, waiting for her response. The space between us seemed to tighten, filled with an unspoken tension that hung like a storm cloud ready to burst. Each second dragged on, the weight of our unvoiced words pressing down on us, the atmosphere heavy with anticipation.

Though my challenge appeared insignificant, my words rippled through the crowd like a shockwave. The atmosphere shifted, growing tense as unease spread among those gathered, their faces betraying the stirrings of doubt and fear. I could feel the weight of their anxiety pressing in, the air thick with the anticipation of what was to come.

Then, a sudden roar of rage erupted from the Cronomiun, shattering the silence. The sound was raw, primal, charged with a fierce energy that crackled in the air. Their reaction was immediate and electric, the force of their anger surging through the crowd, igniting a deep sense of dread. The unravelling of events had begun, and there was no turning back.

"We'll do whatever it takes to stop you," she declared firmly, her eyes narrowing with determination. "And we'll make sure you end up in Lilly's hands, no matter what." She leaned in, her voice lowering to a menacing whisper. "So don't even think about fighting us, Seira. It won't end well for you."

"I'll fight you," I growled, my voice dripping with contempt. "How dare you? I'll choose when I die, not you. You don't get to decide when it's convenient for you."

My eyes narrowed into slits, and my fists clenched so tightly that my knuckles ached, every muscle in my body tensing as I prepared to defend myself against this brazen assault on my autonomy. The sheer audacity of this person, daring to believe they could dictate the terms of my life and death, ignited a blazing fury deep within me.

My blood boiled with indignation, and a fierce resolve took hold—there was no way I would surrender without a fight. This was my life, my choice, and I alone would determine when to let go. No one else had the right to make that decision for me.

I was seething with rage, a fierce storm of emotions swirling within me. Torrents of wind erupted from my very being, striking them like relentless waves battering against a shore. They crumbled before my onslaught, like soldiers forced to concede defeat, unprepared for the sheer magnitude of my power and the intensity of my wrath. Yet, even amid my fury, my resolve remained steadfast – to ensure the safety of all, no matter the personal cost I might have to bear.

I whirled around, my heart racing with a newfound sense of power. It dawned on me then that I had grown beyond the limitations of Matace's teachings and expectations. He had only imparted a fraction of his knowledge, keeping me occupied with endless studies. Yet, I now felt stronger and more than capable of overpowering Lilly.

The battle raged on fiercely. Tye, undaunted, deployed his relentless tactics, fighting with one arm. Yet, Luke valiantly struck him down repeatedly, refusing to yield. Meanwhile, my loyal Meniagier trampled their way through many Cerberus. The defeated Cerberus whimpered, then resigned to their fate, lying down to await the inevitable end.

Chapter Fourteen

I slipped away silently as the raging storm finally settled, its furious assault slowly fading into the distance. The storm had unleashed dread and fear upon those it needed to, no longer requiring my presence. I departed the scene, leaving the realm's leaders sprawled on the ground, their eyes staring at me with a vacant, lifeless expression.

Adjusting my stance, I carefully made my way to the side of the house and waited, holding my breath, as the Cerberus prowled past. The beast's minions lumbered behind it, seemingly devoid of purpose or drive, their sole focus the unwavering protection of their creator. The Cerberus collapsed in a heap; its imposing armour and fierce demeanour crumbled away as the raging storm whipped up dirt and debris, pelting the creature and causing it to falter more swiftly than I had anticipated.

The spirits knew their defeat was imminent, yet they refused to surrender. They fought the Cronomiun with unwavering determination, even as the centuries-old war ravaging both their kinds climaxed. Despite the overwhelming odds, the spirits remained resolute. They had the support of the vampires and the Meniagier, but they could sense their impending loss. The air was thick with tension, the clash of powers echoing as the final battle unfolded.

The spirits poured every ounce of their strength into the fight, their desperation fueling their actions. They clashed with the

Cronomiun, their movements a blur as they fought for their existence. The battle raged, the two sides locked in a fierce struggle for supremacy.

Yet, deep down, the spirits knew that their fate was sealed. The Cronomiun's power was too great, and they could feel their strength waning. Still, they refused to give up, their pride and defiance driving them forward, even as the looming darkness of defeat crept ever closer.

The tiny house stood alone, a solitary figure amidst the chaos of the raging battle. The warring creatures' deafening roars and furious cries echoed through the air, a cacophony of violence reverberating across the land.

Amid the turmoil, I knew I had to act swiftly. An idea formed in my mind—a protective shield to safeguard the house from the onslaught. Focusing all my energy, I willed the barrier into existence. Slowly, a shimmering dome materialised, encasing the house in a protective cocoon. The sounds of battle, once thunderous, became muffled within the confines of the shield, effectively silencing the horrors from reaching the ears of any unsuspecting mortal witnesses.

I couldn't afford the risk of their terror and despair. If they saw the monstrous events unfolding here, it would only fuel Lilly's twisted ambitions. She craved fear and chaos, using them as weapons to seize control over all worlds and their inhabitants. This shield was more than a barrier; it was a defiant stand against her wretched attempts at domination.

Little did she know, however, that her future had already been foretold. I had been sent to this place desperately to prevent her malicious plans from coming to fruition. Matace had witnessed a prophecy describing these events, hence his decision to create me.

Amid the shadows of the upstairs landing, a faint light flickered into view, steadily cutting through the darkness. As I strained my eyes, the familiar features of Lilly's face came into focus, her gaze fixed with unwavering concentration on the path before her.

A sudden blow from the side caught me entirely off guard as I cautiously rounded the corner. The force of the attack sent me stumbling, and I collapsed to my knees, pain radiating through my body. My dress tore, the fabric ripping away to reveal a deep gash in my arm. Blood began to flow freely, staining the ground beneath me in dark, crimson pools.

Gasping in dismay, I frantically searched for my attacker, my heart pounding in my chest. I remained on my knees, eyes darting across the shadowed surroundings, straining to catch the slightest hint of movement. But to my horror, the area was deserted. An eerie stillness hung in the air, broken only by the faint sound of animals scurrying away to safety.

Yet, despite the apparent emptiness, the prickling sensation at the back of my neck warned me otherwise. My assailant was still close, lurking in the shadows, cowardly concealing themselves from view. They had struck with stealth and retreated just as swiftly, too afraid to face the consequences of their cowardice. The silence around me was deafening, a stark contrast to the thudding of my heart as I braced myself for what might come next.

I called out into the darkness, my voice barely audible, a faint whisper from the cold night air. "Who are you?" The words escaped my lips with a sense of urgency, my heart pounding in my chest as I strained to see through the veil of shadows that surrounded me.

Panic seized me, and tears began to flow uncontrollably, blurring my vision and choking my breath. A wave of frustration washed over me as I chastised myself for faltering, for letting this person and the looming darkness ahead unravel my composure. This was no time for fragile tears or wavering resolve. I needed to gather every shred of strength to stand tall against the encroaching shadows and face the daunting challenges that awaited. The time for weakness had passed; only courage and determination would see me through now.

I stared into the darkness, my voice wavering slightly as I spoke up again. "Who are you?" The words felt heavy on my tongue, a tinge of fear creeping into my tone as I called out a second time. The unknown before me filled me with a sense of unease, an overwhelming tension that made the air feel thick and suffocating. Yet, I refused to back down, my determination growing with each passing moment as I steeled myself to confront whatever lay in the shadows.

The air was filled with the infectious crackle of laughter beside me, prompting my head to snap in that direction. But as I looked, I saw nothing there, only an empty expanse of towering trees and wildly overgrown bushes, their tangled branches casting dancing shadows across the forest floor. The silence that followed the fading laughter felt heavy, almost oppressive, as if the very air had become thick with an unseen presence.

"Show yourself, now!" I bellowed, my voice laced with urgency and a demand for immediate action. The intensity in my tone pierced the air, leaving no room for hesitation.

The ominous voice crept closer, enveloping the air with anticipation and tension and the unmistakable scent of death. To a witch like myself, death had a distinct, haunting aroma that was impossible to ignore. The nauseating stench caused me to instinctively cover my nose, desperate to block out the overwhelming presence of mortality that now permeated the atmosphere.

"Impressive, quite elegant," I muttered, my voice muffled by the sleeve covering my mouth. A tinge of anticipation crept into my words as I spoke, "Now, reveal yourself."

My order had been ignored, and the thunderous booms echoed around me. Suddenly, the air was filled with agonising cries and moans; the outer edges of the shield had been breached, allowing the deafening noise to escape. The storm transformed the sky into a fiery display of orange and red. The night sky came alive as lightning danced across it, striking the Earth in the distance with each piercing bolt.

The sudden twig crack alerted me, and I whirled around just in time to catch a glimpse of a dark figure hurtling towards me. Then, everything went dark. Dimly, I perceived shadowy figures surrounding me, their empty black eyes boring into me. Their twisted grins were filled with a malicious satisfaction, delighting in my capture.

Slowly, I opened my eyes, wincing at the pounding in my head. The world around me was a blur of shapes and shadows, nothing familiar in sight. A constant, maddening water drip only heightened my disorientation and parched throat. Where was I? What had happened? I struggled to piece together the last thing I remembered before everything darkened.

My eyes frantically scanned the area, searching for the assailants. I could sense there was more than just one. The exact number, I couldn't tell, as I had been knocked unconscious earlier. But I knew they were lurking, waiting to strike again.

My wrists were tightly bound behind my back, leaving me helpless and vulnerable. I was forced to lie on my side, my legs curled up close to my body, the strain of the day weighing heavily on me. The throbbing ache in my head from the earlier blow intensified as I struggled to focus, my senses overwhelmed by the discomfort and the growing sense of dread that consumed me.

A raspy voice startled me awake. I turned to see a figure looming beside me. "Don't panic. Believe it or not, we're not here to hurt you. We just want to stop you from doing something you have no right to do."

"Who are you?" I croaked, my parched throat aching as I struggled to form the words. My dry, cracked lips scraped against each other, and I desperately longed for a sip of water to soothe the burning dryness.

A gentle, soothing voice reached my ears, "You look thirsty. Allow me to fetch you some water." The voice had a calming, androgynous quality, making it difficult to discern whether it belonged to a man or a woman. There was a genuine concern and warmth behind the words, as if the speaker genuinely cared about my well-being.

I watched in horror as the lifeless, formless black shape vanished. Overwhelmed by despair, I desperately wanted to lash out and chase it back into the house. If there were any more interruptions tonight, I would have no chance to find Lilly in time before the final vestiges of her portal closed forever.

A disembodied voice echoed through the darkness, startling me. "Here," it said, as a mysterious cup materialised in the air, hovering before my face. I stared in bewilderment at the shapeless form that seemed to lack any visible hands, yet it held the cup out to me as if demanding that I take it.

I gulped down the drink greedily, relishing the cold liquid as it splashed against my lips and chin. The refreshing droplets trailed down my neck and chest, sending a shiver of relief through my body. My mouth craved more, but I resisted asking for a refill, knowing it would only lead to disappointment.

"Thank you," I said, sitting up and watching it move to the other side of the hut. "Who are you?"

"We are the spirits of the departed," the voice echoed, its otherworldly tone sending chills down my spine. "We've returned to this wretched world to stop you. Lilly's actions led to our demise, and we cannot let her take you from this realm. You are too precious to the Earth and the realm beyond to let that happen."

The words hung in the air, thick with a sense of urgency and a haunting intensity. The dead had come back, driven by a relentless determination to thwart Lilly's plans and protect me, the one they deemed essential to the balance of the world.

"What do you mean you're dead?" I blurted out, my heart racing with disbelief. The words felt foreign on my tongue, as if I'd just heard the most absurd and unimaginable thing. I searched their face, desperately seeking any sign that this was all some twisted joke. Still, the solemn expression staring back at me told a different story. I simply couldn't wrap my head around it – how could you, the vibrant and full-of-life person I knew, suddenly be gone? The reality of the situation hit me like a ton of bricks, leaving me utterly confused and grappling for a way to make sense of it all.

My mind reeled as she unveiled the troubling details. Years ago, her people had perished in their desperate bid to stop the darkness from consuming Lilly. They had foreseen this calamity through the divination of their sacred stones, a method by which they could glimpse the fate that awaited others. Remarkably, they had never before needed to intervene.

Still, with Lilly, they had witnessed the rise of pure terror, a malevolent force that threatened to engulf the very Earth. Lilly's soul had already been ensnared by the wickedness that spread like a raging inferno, fueled by the toxic blend of jealousy, hatred, and envy that could corrupt a witch. Worse still, she could summon the most deadly of nightmarish creatures, conjured from the darkest corners of her imagination and the depths of hell itself.

"Whoa!" I cried out, my mind racing. "Please, you have to let me go. I have to finish this; it's my destiny. You must understand, I was born for this moment, to fight her and to die trying." I could feel the urgency coursing through my veins, the overwhelming need to fulfil my purpose. The situation's intensity was immense, the weight of the task at hand heavy on my shoulders. I pleaded with the person holding me captive, desperate to be freed so I could face my foe and potentially meet my end.

The words tumbled out, laced with a mix of determination and resignation. This was my calling, my reason for being, and I was willing to give everything to see it through, no matter the cost.

"We comprehend the complexities of life," it responded in a soothing, contemplative tone. "But what if your time runs out before you can fulfil your purpose with her? The uncertainty of the future weighs heavily, does it not?" The entity's words carried a sense of gravity, urging me to consider the fragility of the situation.

I mulled over the question, my mind racing with possibilities. It was a viable option, one I couldn't dismiss entirely, but deep down, I had a strong hunch and a sense of confidence that I could stop her until they pummeled me relentlessly, forcing me to reconsider.

I tilted my chin defiantly, my jaw set with unwavering determination. "That's not going to happen," I declared, my voice laced with a steely edge. "I have the strength and power to match whatever she dishes out. Now, untie me. I'm ready for whatever she wants to throw at me."

"We shall see what the future holds," the entity responded, echoing with mystery. "Now, enlighten us, my companions and I, as to why you must undertake this task. Our ability to peer into the unknown has been obscured, for death has thwarted our powers and chances to see what lies ahead."

The entity's words carried a weighted gravity, conveying a profound shift in their cosmic understanding. Its unflinching and piercing gaze demanded a compelling explanation that would justify the significance of the human's involvement. The air seemed to shimmer with anticipation as the entity and its allies awaited the response; their curiosity was evident.

I let out a heavy sigh. "You're right," I said, my voice tinged with resignation. "Matace created me in a laboratory with the sole purpose of destroying her. But the truth is, I'm not just one being – I'm a fusion of many different creatures. It's a complex story, but the important thing is that I've gained immense power in a short period. And that power is the only thing that can defeat Lilly." I leaned forward, my eyes burning with urgency. "You have to let me go. I can't stay here any longer – if I do, everything will be lost. Matace's portal will close, and the strange, lingering mist will vanish, leaving nothing in its wake. I'm the only one who can stop it all from disappearing forever."

They cowered before me, their faces etched with fear. I knelt, waiting with bated breath for one of them to break the ominous silence. Their hushed whispers sent shivers down my spine, for their words spoke of the unthinkable – the dead returning to wage war against the living. This was no mere fantastical tale; it was a stark reality that the realm had failed to prepare us for, a nightmare come to life that defied all rational explanation.

"We're willing to let you go, but there's a catch," the voice said, its tone stern and unwavering. "You'll need to make us a promise, and we expect you to keep it."

The words hung in the air, laced with a subtle threat that sent a chill down my spine. I knew I had no choice but to listen, my heart pounding as I waited for the demand.

"What is it?"

"We implore you to give voice to our spirits, to guide us back to the virtuous realm and grant us respite in the peaceful hereafter," they pleaded. "And we wish to have our names etched into the annals of the realm. For too long, we have been silenced and shunned like malevolent phantoms when we were merely responding to the misdeeds of others."

"I'll do it," I said, mustering every ounce of courage. The clock was ticking, and dread consumed me, fearing I might not make it in time. "Just take these restraints off my wrists and ankles, please," I pleaded, my voice trembling with a mix of desperation and determination.

The voice had a sly, taunting tone as it spoke. "You can free yourself, you know. We've only bound you and tested your abilities. Now it's your chance to prove yourself – to shine brightly and set yourself free." A sense of challenge hung in the air, coupled with an underlying threat. "Untie those ropes and liberate yourself. And remember, we'll be watching, waiting to see how you rise to the occasion."

The wind howled furiously, whipping up a flurry of dust that swirled and danced around me. I had to squint my eyes, shielding them from the relentless onslaught of gritty particles. As the gusty onslaught subsided, I cautiously opened my eyes, only to find the hut eerily silent and utterly devoid of any presence, an unsettling emptiness that sent a chill down my spine.

"Ugh, this is so frustrating!" I grunted, desperately trying to free myself from the tight, unyielding restraints. The coarse material dug into my skin, and I could feel the strain in my muscles as I strained against the bindings, my heart racing with a mixture of panic and determination.

A powerful jolt rippled through my body, sending a sharp, pulsing sensation up my spine. Overwhelmed, I collapsed into a helpless heap, utterly bewildered by the unseen force that had struck me. The onslaught felt relentless, as if every inch of my being had been battered and bruised. A crushing weight bore down on my soul, shattering the last remnants of my weary heart.

Fueled by a surge of adrenaline, I strained against the bindings, panting with frustration. With determined tugs and pulls, I finally freed my hands, sighing in instant relief as the tight restraints fell away. Surprised by the unexpected strength coursing through me, I marvelled at my own capability, a power I had never tapped into before. The overwhelming sense of newfound capacity left me reeling. Without hesitation, I sprinted towards the house, driven by an urgent need to find Lilly.

Adrenaline surging, my feet pounded the Earth, a blur of bushes and trees whizzing by as I pushed my body to its limits. The air rushed past, carrying the pungent ammonia scent from the house. This stifling odour only fueled my determined sprint. In the back of my mind, a voice whispered of the witches' unknown gift, but I dismissed it, my sole focus consumed by the image of Lilly's face.

The intensity of my obsession drove me onward, my legs burning with each stride, a stitch building in my side, but I refused to slow down. I was a being unbound, driven by an all-consuming need to reach her, no matter the cost.

Breathless and panting, I leaned against the rough bark of a nearby tree, desperate for respite. The once-lively forest had settled into an eerie stillness, the usual hoots of owls conspicuously absent. Straining my senses, I listened intently for any sign of scurrying wildlife, but the forest floor remained eerily silent. This unnatural hush was no mere illusion – a sinister trap woven by the manipulative Lilly.

I was trapped in her dimensional construct, a twisted stage where she reigned as the director and narrator of this haunting saga. The weight of her control pressed down on me, a suffocating force that robbed me of breath and clarity. I was trapped in her domain, a helpless pawn in her devious game.

"Ugh, no way!" I huffed, still hunched over and clutching my aching stomach. "You'll never get the best of me, bitch, you hear? I won't let you win, not a chance!" I spat the words through gritted teeth, my voice laced with defiance and a hint of desperation.

I was speaking figuratively as if she was standing right beside me. I could sense her presence all around, her essence lingering as if she had just departed the area. Navigating cautiously through the dense undergrowth, the ache in my body began to subside with each step. As long as I maintained a steady pace, the pain would remain manageable, allowing me to preserve my strength for the impending confrontation with her – a head-to-head battle that I knew was inevitable.

The sudden rustling in the bushes ahead instantly alerted me to the presence of another person nearby. I knew it was Lilly. She had been silently observing, patiently waiting for the right moment to strike. I could sense her next move was imminent, and the anticipation filled the air with fierce tension.

Cautiously navigating around the bushes I had just rushed through, the house came into view. Its grandeur never failed to astound me, even now, knowing she had been inside and had tainted all the cherished memories of Matace. And equally, I was aware of Matace's deception in not revealing who I was or the nature of my creation. I could understand his reasoning.

Had he told me the truth, my mind may not have been able to accept it, let alone the information itself. I might have even destroyed myself. His experiment would have been a futile endeavour, and the world would still be at the mercy of the wickedness of others.

I cautiously approached the house, my senses heightened by the sudden eruption of sounds from the battlefield. Perhaps my intense focus on navigating the forest path had blinded me to the commotion, or Lilly had conjured a cruel illusion to make me feel utterly isolated and alone. Either way, her message was clear – I had no one, no place to call my own.

The unlocked door creaked open, its hinges swaying slightly in the gentle breeze. The muffled sounds of movement inside the house piqued my curiosity and raised my suspicions. I fought the urge to investigate, wary of the possibility of a trap—another one of her cruel, deceitful schemes designed to weaken my resolve and make me an easier target.

She wanted to win, to take what was rightfully mine, but I refused to let that happen. I steeled my determination, unwilling to give in to her manipulations. This was my fight, and I would not back down.

Cautiously, I stepped through the threshold, my eyes adjusting to the inky blackness that enveloped the room. This must be a secret passage Luke and I had missed during our previous visit – a hidden route shrouded in mystery and darkness. As I scanned the space, cobwebs clung to every corner, shimmering with a menacing gleam.

The spiders, their bulbous bodies and elongated legs, watched intently, poised to pounce should I dare to linger. Their unnatural, unsettling gaze bore into me as if they were not of this world but rather denizens of some sinister, shadowed realm.

I couldn't help but shudder, the hairs on the back of my neck standing on end. These were no ordinary spiders – they were Lilly's twisted creations, stolen from a place beyond our understanding and brought to this earthly domain, a testament to her defiance and the lengths she would go to defy us.

I cautiously stepped through the doorway, pressing myself firmly against the wall. Gazing upwards, I noticed a colossal black spider weaving a web directly towards me. Its numerous eyes were fixed on me, anticipating my panicked reaction so it could pounce. Determined to remain calm, I deliberately slowed my movements, inching forward at a snail's pace towards the opposite door, hoping not to startle the predatory arachnid.

Lilly had meticulously laid out trap after trap, eagerly awaiting my arrival. She was determined to avenge whatever had transformed her, and she wouldn't go down without a fierce battle. Her mind was consumed with a thirst for destruction and domination. In contrast, my mind was focused on a different kind of destruction - to avenge Matace and the countless others she had killed without justification and to liberate the human race from her harmful grasp.

Lilly's relentless pursuit of vengeance clashed with my unwavering resolve to end her reign of terror. The stage was set for an epic confrontation, where the fate of countless lives hung in the balance. I knew this would be no easy fight, but I was prepared to do whatever it took to stop Lilly and restore her peace and safety to the world she had so cruelly threatened.

Determined to uncover what lay beyond, I gripped the second door handle and twisted it firmly. To my astonishment, it was locked. Undeterred, I shifted my weight, pressing my shoulder against the frame and exerting all my strength. The door groaned and finally swung open, a surge of raw power coursing through me. Stepping through the threshold felt like entering an entirely different world.

The room was flooded with a dazzling, almost blinding light, forcing me to shield my eyes. In the centre, ethereal fairy-like creatures flitted and danced, their delicate features twisting into sinister expressions as they noticed my arrival. Without hesitation, they turned towards me, their tiny but deadly-looking weapons poised to strike.

I raised my protective shield, and the fairies slammed against it, bouncing off the front with a deafening chorus of horror and defeat. Their high-pitched cries could shatter an average person's eardrums. Still, for someone like me, built for greater purposes and blessed with unusual strength, I merely shrugged and walked through to the other side.

Their anger fueled my irritation, but I knew fairies could not be harmed. Evil had consumed them, and it was not their fault. Once Lilly was destroyed, they would revert to their usual selves, returning to their distant world where they would be their gentle, caring beings, visiting Earth occasionally to spread warmth, not hatred.

I braced myself as the fairies swarmed around me, their tiny bodies colliding with my shield in a cacophony of screeches and wails. The air was thick with their frenetic energy, and I felt a pang of sorrow for what they had become. But I steeled my resolve, knowing their salvation depended on destroying the malevolent force that had corrupted them.

With a deep breath, I pushed through the swarm, my shield deflecting their desperate attacks as I made my way towards the heart of the darkness – towards Lilly, the source of their torment. This was a battle I had to win, not just for myself but for the fairies and the peace they had once embodied. The fate of two worlds hung in the balance, and I was determined to emerge victorious.

They persisted in their relentless assault, and I couldn't help but scoff. "Nice touch," I retorted sarcastically, my voice dripping with contempt as I faced their unrelenting barrage.

They simply couldn't wrap their minds around the fact that my shield made me untouchable. Undeterred, they spread out widely, eager to attack. Incessantly, they somersaulted across to the opposite wall, shaking their heads in bewilderment. With flawless precision, they flew straight back towards me, only to be swiftly sent back from whence they came.

"Enough!" I cried out, overwhelmed by their feeble attempts. Stunned by my direct approach and unwavering composure, they huddled together, glaring at me with dark, venomous eyes. Yet, at least they had halted their frenzied and bewildering assaults.

I hurried out of the room, my heart pounding as I navigated the dimly lit corridor. The air felt thick with tension, and I could almost hear the blood rushing through my veins. A sense of dread crept up my spine as her scent lingered in the air, a haunting reminder of her presence nearby.

Panic began to set in, my fear evident and consuming. I knew she was somewhere in this house or perhaps had just slipped away. But I was determined to find her, no matter what. This was a matter of life and death, and I was hellbent on ensuring that she would not make it through the night.

Stepping into the stark white room, a suffocating stench of blood assaulted my senses. A sudden wave of nausea rose from the depths of my stomach, and I gagged, fighting back the bile that threatened to escape. The once pristine space was now tainted with rot, grime, and the haunting imprints of bloodied hands. The sheer filth of the room was overwhelming, and I knew this was not the state Matace had left it in.

As I surveyed the space, a sense of unease settled over me. I couldn't quite grasp the purpose of this room, and I felt compelled to investigate further. Slowly, I scanned the area, taking in every gruesome detail. The pungent odour burned my nostrils, and I swallowed hard, struggling to keep my composure as the sights before me filled my vision. This was no ordinary room – it was a laboratory, and the horrors it contained were beyond my comprehension.

The laboratory was a disturbing sight. Countless jars and samples labelled as 'experiments' filled the room, causing a sense of unease in the pit of my stomach. Peering into the containers, I saw half-formed faces and partially developed bodies, which instantly made me feel nauseous.

When a peculiar test subject stared back at me, I could no longer hold back the rising bile in my throat. This creature was a bizarre cross between humans and something otherworldly, with horns and a tail. Yet, its other features disturbingly resembled my own. I had never witnessed anything like this before, and the faces that gazed back at me filled me with horror and disbelief.

Gripping the wall for support, I succumbed to the overwhelming urge to vomit, my body shaking with a sense of disbelief. As I purged the contents of my stomach, I watched helplessly as my resolve rapidly crumbled into nothingness.

An archway had been crudely smashed in the corner, revealing the entrance to another room beyond. Curiosity piqued, I stepped through the gaping hole, unsure of what horrors might lie. As I crossed the threshold, I found myself in yet another laboratory filled with more test subjects but of a different kind. The eyes of these subjects seemed strangely familiar, sliding across the uneven floor and meeting my gaze with an alien, unsettling quality.

Their skin barely contained the skeletons beneath, which were not formed correctly, as if some fundamental aspect of their anatomy had been altered or distorted. There were no labels, no names, not even the simple designation of "tests" as in the previous room - these people, if they could even be called that, were nameless, forgotten, and reduced to mere specimens in this place of twisted experimentation.

The scene filled me with a deep, unsettling dread, and I could not help but wonder what horrors had been inflicted upon these poor, unfortunate souls. The laboratory felt like humanity had been stripped away, leaving only the cold, clinical pursuit of knowledge, no matter the cost.

I was utterly stunned, frozen in place. Staring back at me was Lilly's unsettling grin. Her eye sockets were hollow and lifeless, just like the skeletal reflection in the mirror. It was as if the rest of her body had failed to develop, leaving only her disembodied head entirely.

I had a profound realisation about my purpose here. This sight before me revealed the countless efforts to craft my very existence. The same attempts Lilly had desperately tried to complete in a misguided effort to create another version of herself, to match my skill for skill, strength for strength. It was an evil beyond anything I could have imagined, far exceeding what Matace taught me.

"This is absolutely horrific," I grimaced, speaking out loud to myself, surveying the dismal surroundings. "This wretched place fills me with utter revulsion. How could they have allowed this to happen?" I shook my head in dismay, my stomach churning at the sheer horror of it all.

I reached out and gently touched the lifeless hand peeking out from the covered trolley beside me. The sight of the partially formed body filled me with a deep sense of sorrow. These subjects had once been alive, but their lives had been cut short due to their incomplete state. It had taken years of painstaking effort to resurrect me, and now I was the sole survivor, destined to breathe my last breath soon.

The weight of the many losses I had witnessed pressed heavily upon me, and I couldn't help but shed tears for those who had come before me. These were not just specimens; they were lives that had been extinguished too soon, victims of a process that had not yet been perfected. As I wrapped the hand back into the cover, I felt a profound sense of gratitude and melancholy, knowing that I was the only one left to carry on their legacy, even if it was for a brief moment.

The question that plagued my mind would forever remain unanswered. It was clear that Lilly and I were destined to destroy one another, for we were equally powerful adversaries. Her monstrous protectors had either been captured or annihilated by Luke and his devoted followers, leaving me to confront her alone.

A smaller, dimly lit room lay ahead, and the stench grew increasingly unbearable. Yet my curiosity propelled me forward, urging me to explore the depths of Lilly's secretive domain. The air grew thick with an oppressive aura like the walls closed around me. Each step I took reverberated with a sense of impending doom. I knew my encounter with Lilly would ultimately test our strength and resolve.

The situation's intensity was profound, and I could feel the weight of the unspoken conflict pressing upon me. I steeled my nerves, knowing that whatever lay in wait would challenge me to the core. Yet, I was driven by a determination that burned brighter than the fear that threatened to consume me. This was a battle I had to win, no matter the cost.

As I crossed the threshold into the adjacent room, the dimmed lighting only amplified the sheer chaos surrounding me. Everywhere, Lilly had left a trail of devastation in her wake. Demon corpses were strewn haphazardly across the table, their insides partially exposed and examined. Some had even been cruelly dissected, their organs and innards carelessly discarded onto the side.

The tables were stained with fresh, crimson blood, and dried splatters of it marred the walls, painting a haunting scene of violence and macabre experimentation.

I gazed around, bewildered, as I found myself in a strange and unfamiliar place. The air felt heavy, the atmosphere unsettling, and I couldn't help but wonder, 'What the hell is this place?' The uncertainty of my surroundings filled me with a sense of unease, and I knew I had to tread carefully in this foreign environment.

The room was in complete disarray. Numerous failed attempts to create another cross-breed similar to Lilly were scattered across the tables. The remnants of these experiments were haphazardly piled on top of one another, a testament to Lilly's frantic efforts.

In her obsession, Lilly had paid no heed to the cleanliness or organisation of the workspace.

Lilly's goal was clear - to create a super witch, a being resembling her but possessing even greater power. Yet, despite her countless attempts, she had been unsuccessful. Undeterred, Lilly's determination only grew stronger. Her final wish was about to be granted, as she would finally be able to destroy Lilly and anything else associated with her.

The intensity of the room was powerful, the air thick with the weight of Lilly's ambition and the remnants of her failed experiments. The scene vividly depicted her obsession and the desperation that fueled her pursuit of power. Her pursuit would stop at nothing to achieve its ultimate goal.

The aftermath of her desperate attempts to salvage something from the experiments done to create me was nothing short of a harrowing scene. The toll it had taken on her soul was evident, diminishing her to a level even below those outcasts exiled to the other realms. As I stopped, the remnants of her hastily departed portal came into view, and her distinct perfume lingered around me. Its cloying, sickeningly sweet fragrance filled my nostrils, overpowering the stench of decay and filth that permeated the area.

The haunting image of the blood lingered in my mind, seeping into every fibre of my being and filling me with a profound sense of revulsion. The house before me lay in ruins, beyond any hope of repair. Whether I lived or died, there was no way I would ever set foot in this accursed place again.

The only viable course of action was to reduce it to ashes, to burn it to the ground and erase the remnants of the twisted experiments that had taken place here. The thought of anyone else discovering the horrors that had unfolded and exploiting them as Lilly had done sent a shiver down my spine. This abomination had to be destroyed before it could claim any more victims.

On the side, a weathered journal lay open, its pages filled with the scrawny handwriting I had come to recognise – the writing of Matace. His plans and failed experiments were meticulously detailed, as he had desperately tried to breathe life into me. I eagerly flipped through the pages, my excitement building like a child discovering a hidden treasure.

Yet, there was nothing about how I had been made. The only clues were the failures, and there had been many. There had been more losses than the lifeless forms across the room, none of them named, but some had lived briefly. I read Matace's words, filled with excitement and disbelief, as each one eventually stopped breathing. Their final words spoke of a world far removed from this one, a realm of purity and grace that he had never known.

Based on his notes, the final page must have been written after I was born. He realised the infant he had created was alive and ready to fight, breathing and wailing. He had carried me to the orphanage and left me on the doorstep. He hadn't wanted to let me go; my fist was clenched to my mouth, reflecting the sorrow that seeped from the pages. His tears and anguish felt like my own, a raw and emotional connection.

I tossed the book aside, its final page etching the details of my status within this realm. For so long, I had been a small witch, unaware of the powers that lay dormant within me, the magic I could command at my own whim. No one had ever taken the time to guide me, to unlock the true extent of my abilities.

They had feared the person I might become if I delved deeper into this arcane knowledge, unwilling to risk their precious hold on power slipping through their fingers. So they kept me in the dark, denying me the truth of who I really was - a force to be reckoned with, a wielder of potent magic beyond their wildest imaginings.

But no more. The blinders had fallen away, and I could see the world for what it truly was - a stage upon which I was meant to hold dominion, to shape the very fabric of reality with a mere thought. The time for their petty machinations had come to an end. I would rise, and they would tremble before my ascent.

I hastily scribbled a note to Lilly requesting she meet me at the secluded hill next to Matace's house, a place hidden from the outside world. I knew she would receive the message through the portal she frequently used, and she would be willing to meet me. The humans and the secrets of all those involved with the realm would be kept safe. I deliberately chose that location to keep Luke and the others away; this was not their battle.

According to Matace's diary, I was destined to become the High Witch, hand-picked and genetically crafted to bring goodness and harmony across all the living demons and creatures in every realm since I had discovered that I possessed a unique blend of their DNA and that of a human.

The weight of this responsibility rested heavily on my shoulders. Still, I was determined to fulfil my role and balance the realms. As I waited anxiously for Lilly's arrival, a sense of purpose and determination burned within me, fueling my resolve to face whatever challenges lay ahead.

I scribbled a hurried note and tossed it into the flickering remnants of her portal, confident it would reach her no matter which realm she fled. The paper was infused with a powerful spell called "Destination," crafted by the sorcerer Matace. This enchantment ensured the message would always find its intended recipient and never rest until it had completed its journey home.

The words on the page burned with urgency, my desperate plea to her echoing through the swirling vortex. I watched, heart pounding, as the paper vanished into the shimmering abyss, carried away by unseen forces to wherever she had taken refuge. Though the portal was closing, I knew that note would pursue her relentlessly, traversing the boundaries between worlds until it landed in her hands, no matter how far she had run.

A strange and unsettling sensation enveloped me as if the air had grown heavier and more oppressive. Hastily, I exited the rooms, leaving the disturbing atrocities behind and slamming the door shut. This was Lilly's and Matace's domain, and I felt like an unwelcome outsider, a mere intruder in their twisted world.

The horrific visions I had witnessed and endured were simply too overwhelming, too haunting to even begin to articulate. Not even Luke, my closest confidant, could comprehend the sheer terror and revulsion that had gripped me. It was a level of darkness and depravity that defied casual conversation, unfit for even the most innocuous of dinner discussions.

Chapter Fifteen

The clock chimed midnight, ushering in the bewitching hour when vicious demons emerged from the shadows to roam free. Lilly stood there, her white robe billowing in the eerie breeze. On the surface, she appeared to be a vision of angelic beauty, but I knew the truth. Beneath that radiant facade, she was a monstrous creature, capable of unspeakable acts. Her innocence was merely a facade, a veil that concealed the true darkness within her.

Lilly's name echoed through the dimly lit hallway, my voice laced with a hint of desperation. "Lilly! Where are you?" I called out, my heart pounding as I searched the shadows for any sign of her.

Her eyes narrowed, and a sneer twisted her lips as she spat. "You have made a huge mistake asking me to join you here." The intensity of her words felt like pure evil, dripping with disdain and accusation. Her body language radiated hostility, her posture rigid, and her gaze unwavering, as if daring me to challenge her.

"It's only the two of us now," I said, my voice steady but tinged with concern. I looked into Lilly's eyes, searching for some explanation, some reasoning behind her actions. "Why, Lilly? Why did you do this?"

The air between us was thick with tension and the weight of her decision. I needed to understand and make sense of this situation that had unfolded before us. My heart raced, awaiting her response, hoping to find clarity amidst the chaos.

"I owe you no explanation," she growled, her lips curling contemptuously. "You're nothing but a lab rat, a genetically engineered superhuman freak. Do you know how much time I've dedicated to studying spells, poring over ancient tomes, and memorising every word Matace uttered?" She leaned in, her eyes narrowed to slits, the intensity radiating from her like a powerful force.

I shook my head as her jealousy seeped through. Her eyes burned with intense loathing toward me. The hatred radiating from her was so intense that it sent a chill down my spine.

"I slaved away for hours on end," she lamented, her voice laced with frustration. "Countless sleepless nights, and for what? Absolutely nothing because you are his heir; it was some twisted scientific experiment they somehow managed to perfect. I'm utterly baffled by how they pulled it off because everything I tried didn't pan out as I had hoped." Her words dripped with anguish and disbelief as she grappled with the reality that her efforts had been for nought. The intensity in her voice conveyed the sheer weight of her disappointment, a testament to the futility of her struggle against a powerful, unseen force.

"I wish there was another way, Lilly," I said, my voice heavy with regret. "You don't have to go through with this. If you stop now, I'll make sure you get a fair trial – one where your side of the story can be heard." My heart sank as I looked into her eyes, pleading with her to reconsider her reckless plan. The stakes were high, and I couldn't bear the thought of her facing the consequences alone.

"That is all just a fantasy!" she yelled, her voice dripping angrily. "A fair trial? Do you even hear yourself?" She leaned in, her eyes narrowed. "After everything I've done for you, sheltering you in this realm when I should have thrown you out long ago, especially after I discovered those documents about your birth."

"Why didn't you?"

"If I had done that, it would have raised too many questions, and I couldn't risk that," she said, her voice laced with an edge of regret. "For a while, I even found myself drawn to you, this messed-up experiment. But let's be real - just because you're a lab rat doesn't make your life less valuable. This whole thing is just wrong," she shook her head, her expression hardening as she transformed from a vulnerable woman into a fierce, unyielding warrior.

Searing lightning bolts crackled and danced around us, illuminating the chaos that was about to unfold. As if by some unseen force, a shimmering barrier began to form, encasing us within its impenetrable walls. This protective circle rose higher and higher, sealing us off from the outside world, ensuring that no one could interfere unless one, or perhaps both, of us were to perish within its confines.

Captivated, I watched as the steely walls swirled and swirled, building momentum with each passing second. Heedless of anything that might lie in its path, the barrier's sole purpose was to contain the impending battle, to keep it isolated and away from prying eyes. The spell had been cast, and a surge of both power and trepidation washed over me, for I was now both the master and the captive of this ever-intensifying maelstrom.

"I must say, you've gained quite the expertise," she observed, her gaze fixed on me. A subtle smile played on her lips as she continued, "Now, let's put that knowledge of yours to the test, shall we?" The way her eyes sparkled with a hint of challenge made it clear that this was no ordinary conversation. The air was charged with anticipation, inviting me to rise to the occasion and showcase the full extent of what I had learned.

Suddenly, a blinding lightning bolt crashed against my torso, hurling me backwards through the air. Searing pain seared through my chest as I gasped for breath. The first warm trickle of blood seeped from my wounds, but I couldn't afford to waste time tending to them. With gritted teeth, I steeled myself to counterattack, determined to curse my foe and send her straight to the depths of hell.

"I see not a lot," she scoffed, her lips curling in disdain. Her gaze swept across the empty, barren landscape, a clear expression of disappointment and frustration etched onto her features.

"I strongly disagree with your assumption," I retorted abruptly. Without hesitation, I grabbed the nearest object and hurled it towards her with all my might. The object collided with a thunderous impact, enveloping her in a fiery explosion that sent her hurtling backwards.

My palms blazed with searing heat, the intensity almost unbearable as the fire within me surged to life. Bright, crackling sparks erupted from my fingertips, arcing above my head in a dazzling display of raw power. With a swift flick of my wrist, I unleashed a scorching ball of fire, sending it hurtling through the air with blistering speed. The flames roared in their descent, aimed directly at her, intent on overwhelming her senses and forcing her to submit.

But she was faster than I anticipated. In a blur of motion, she twisted her body with the grace of a dancer, executing a seamless double somersault through the air. The flames licked at her heels but missed their mark as she landed lightly on her feet, mere yards from where the last sparks sizzled and faded into the Earth.

A fierce energy crackled between us, the air vibrating with the awakening of her own formidable powers. I could feel a storm of magic building around her, challenging my own as if the elements were rising to answer the call of our impending clash.

As she staggered from the initial blow, I seized the moment to unleash another fiery assault. Summoning every ounce of my power, I hurled a blazing sphere of flames towards her. The ball of fire tore through the air, leaving a vibrant, crackling crimson trail. It struck her with a thunderous impact, the overwhelming force that drove her to her knees.

The flames erupted around her instantly, transforming into a blinding inferno that consumed her entirely. The scorching blaze roared to life, its fierce, merciless heat enveloping her form, turning the air around her into a seething, capitulating vortex of fire. The intensity of the magic was overwhelming, the power of the flames undeniable as they ravaged everything in their path.

A piercing scream tore through the air, mingling with a furious cackle that echoed across the hill as her body became engulfed in flames. The acrid stench of burning flesh assaulted my senses, and I watched in horrified fascination as her hair ignited, the fiery strands writhing like serpents before crumbling to the ground in smouldering ashes. Her eyes locked onto mine, seething with raw hatred, burning with a malevolent intensity. Her mouth twisted, spewing venomous curses that poured forth in an unending stream, the words thick with spite and fury.

Despite the raging inferno consuming her, her face remained twisted in a terrifying scowl, defiant even in the grip of the flames. Then, with a sudden, vicious force, she unleashed a counter-curse. The fire snuffed out instantly, vanquished by her dark magic. I watched, stunned, as her charred body mended itself before my eyes. The scorched skin regenerated with unnatural speed, and her hair regrew in a cascade of black strands as if the flames had never touched her.

She stood before me, whole and unscathed, her eyes now darker than before—black as coal pits, devoid of life or humanity. They bore into me, bottomless and unyielding, her presence more menacing than ever.

"Fascinating," she murmured, her eyes sparkling with intrigue as she leaned in, captivated by the revelation before her.

Her body began to rise, lifting into the air as if gravity had relinquished its hold. Slowly, droplets of crimson rain began to descend from the darkened sky, splattering against her dress in vivid, violent splotches of red. It was the blood of those she had claimed, now pouring down like a twisted storm, drenching the ground and encircling us in a macabre downpour.

The air grew thick with the sorrowful cries of benevolent spirits, their anguished wails echoing through the heavens. Their voices, filled with confusion and despair, reverberated around us as they bore witness to the dark magic that had sealed our fates. The spirits wept for what had been lost, mourning the soul she had become and the grim destiny that now awaited us both.

She had the power to have it all if only she had been patient. Instead, she revelled in her spoiled, selfish ways, indulging her insatiable greed without restraint. Her relentless desire had become an all-consuming fire, and now it threatened to be her undoing.

Her eyes hardened into cold, lifeless stones, void of any warmth, as the thick, crimson blood rained down on me, soaking my dress and drenching my hair. Strands clung to my face, heavy and slick, my cheeks smeared with the blood of those who had fallen. Across from me, her hair was matted to her pale skin, streaks of red tracing lines down her cheeks as she stared, her gaze fixed and unseeing.

But it wasn't me she saw; it was the envy and hatred that consumed her from within, twisting her into something monstrous. The evil had seeped into her soul, filling her entirely and leaving nothing of the person she once was. Her essence and humanity had been drained away, leaving only a hollow shell driven by darkness. I felt a cold certainty settle in my bones—it was far too late to save her. Any hope of redemption had been lost, swallowed by the abyss that now claimed her heart.

I charged forward, my feet hammering the Earth in a desperate, frenzied sprint. Dust clouds erupted around me, stinging my already raw and bloodied skin. My hands stretched out, trembling with the need to reach her, to end this madness before it consumed everything.

The metallic taste of blood lingered on my lips, fueling the firestorm of rage burning within me. Hate and disgust boiled in my veins, propelling me forward with a ferocity I had never known. Every ounce of strength, every shred of willpower, surged through me, driving me to destroy her and restore the balance that had been shattered.

My determination grew with each pounding step, relentless and unstoppable. This was no longer just a pursuit but a crusade to right the wrongs that had torn the realms apart. The fate of all worlds hung by a thread, and I was the one who would tip the scales. Nothing else mattered. I was the last hope, and failure was not an option.

She sensed my intentions and swiftly grounded herself, her body instinctively shifting into the defensive stance of a seasoned witch. Her posture was firm, yet I could feel the tension crackling between us like a live wire.

Without hesitation, I lunged forward, seizing her hair with both hands, the strands twisting between my fingers as I yanked and clawed at her scalp. My fingertips had transformed, sharp talons erupting from them, summoned by a force I barely understood. They honed themselves with terrifying precision, cutting deep into her skin as if guided by a primal instinct beyond my control.

A wild, untamed fury surged within me, a feral beast clawing its way to the surface. I tried to suppress it, confused and fearful of this unfamiliar power. But the sensation was undeniable—something inside me had shifted, an awakening I could feel in every nerve and muscle. However, its full nature remained just out of reach. The change was there, pulsing with dark energy that terrified and empowered me, pushing me to the brink of a transformation I could no longer ignore.

Her fingers twisted and coiled around me like serpents constricting their prey. The relentless pressure crushed my lungs, stealing the air from my body. Panic set in as the world around me faded to black, my desperate pleas for breath going unheard.

I let go of her, and my body crumpled to the ground. I gulped in deep, desperate breaths, trying to fill my aching lungs with air. My heart raced, thumping loudly in my ears as the adrenaline coursed through me.

"I see you've finally come to terms with who you truly are," she hissed, her words dripping with venom. I knelt before her, helpless, as her voluminous gown spilt around me, concealing my trembling form beneath its opulent folds.

Disoriented, I glanced down at myself, confusion swirling in my mind. Her words echoed in my ears, but it wasn't until I truly looked that the reality hit me. I had been transformed into a Meniagier—a creature both familiar and alien to me. My body was now cloaked in soft, plush fur, starkly contrasting to the full-sized creatures I had once been befriended.

Yet, beneath the fur, I could still sense the essence of my human self, a flicker of the person I used to be, now intertwined with this new form. The strangeness was unsettling, and I struggled to reconcile the transformation with the person I knew myself to be.

I moved cautiously to the edge of the puddle that Lilly had used to extinguish the flames that had once consumed her. The water, still rippling from the recent battle, reflected my altered form back at me. The sight was fascinating and disturbing; my new form was a testament to the intense magic unleashed.

I stared at my reflection, grappling with the unexpected and profound change that had overtaken me. The soft fur, the unfamiliar contours of my new body—a transformation that left me questioning everything I thought I knew about myself and the world around me.

I stifled a chuckle, biting back a grin. If Luke caught me like this, he'd never let me live it down. He'd poke fun at my appearance and tease me mercilessly, unable to comprehend the situation I found myself in. The thought of his mocking laughter made my cheeks burn with embarrassment.

She loomed over me, her presence overwhelming. Her eyes burned fiercely, the whites consumed by a sinister darkness that had taken hold of her very being. It was as if the evil had seeped into the depths of her soul, corrupting her from within. Her body no longer seemed to belong to the mortal realm, as if the darkness had consumed and twisted it, transforming her into a haunting, inhuman figure.

Adrenaline surged through me as I sprang to my feet, planting myself firmly on the ground to confront her. The wind howled around us, whipping my purple dress into a wild frenzy. With a fierce determination, I summoned my most potent storm, the air crackling with raw energy as the swirling vortex enveloped her.

She was caught in the tempest, spinning helplessly as the wind tore at her, flinging her body like a rag doll. The storm's fury propelled her into a tree, and the impact resonated with a sickening thud. Battered and bleeding, she struggled to rise, her eyes wide with confusion and fear as they locked onto mine.

Around me, debris whirled in a chaotic dance, the storm's power coating my body in dirt and grime. The Meniagier transformation faded, my fur receding as I returned to my human form. I stood tall and unwavering, watching as she fought against the maddening storm of debris that assaulted her from every direction.

Her fear was obvious, her movements frantic as she tried to resist the relentless force of the storm I had unleashed. Yet, despite the chaos, a part of me remained eerily calm, focused solely on the task at hand—bringing her to her knees and ending this once and for all.

Lilly's intense powers surged through her, knitting together her wounds with terrifying speed. In an instant, she unleashed a powerful blast that sent me hurtling through the air, crashing violently into the crumbling walls of her secret hideout. The impact was brutal—my body slammed into the stone, the force cracking and breaking my bones with sickening precision. Pain erupted within me, and I could feel the warmth of internal bleeding spreading rapidly, sapping my strength and slowing my every movement.

The world around me blurred as I struggled to remain conscious, the only sound of my heart's frantic pounding echoing in my ears. Desperation gripped me as I scanned my surroundings, searching for anything to turn the tide. My gaze fell upon an old, fallen tree nearby, half-buried beneath the rubble. With a last, desperate surge of strength, I reached out with my mind, summoning the power that still flickered within me.

The tree trembled, then slowly lifted into the air, hovering unsteadily for a heartbeat. Summoning every ounce of remaining willpower, I launched it across the space between us with incredible speed. The massive trunk slammed into Lilly's stomach, the force of the impact sending her hurtling backwards. She crashed into the small cabin behind her, the structure shattering into a million splintered pieces.

For a moment, everything was still. Dust and debris settled around us, and I lay there, gasping for breath, my body wracked with pain. Yet, amidst the devastation, I could only hope that this desperate act had finally ended the relentless battle.

Fury etched across her face, she rose to her feet, her presence towering over me. With a skill honed in the depths of the underworld, she rapidly mended her wounds, a small but remarkable feat that left me in awe. The intensity of her power caused me to shrink back as she commanded the room.

"Nice try," I murmured, my voice barely above a whisper. I lay on the floor, surrounded by the scattered debris of what was once her hideout. The once-sturdy structure now lay in ruins around me. "But I've got something for you."

I sprinted towards her, every muscle straining with desperate urgency. The moment our bodies collided, the final, devastating spell would be unleashed, ending her life in a heartbeat. And yet, I knew with absolute certainty that this act would also seal my doom, condemning me to the same fate.

My legs pumped furiously, every step a race against time, as I closed the distance between us. I could see the fear in her eyes, the realisation of what was to come, yet I pressed on, driven by an unshakable resolve to fulfil my duty, no matter the personal cost.

The air crackled with intensity, making the hairs on my neck stand on end. I was mere seconds away from reaching her, from triggering the apocalyptic conclusion to this harrowing ordeal. My heart pounded in my chest, thundering in my ears, as I summoned every ounce of my strength, propelling myself forward with a final, herculean effort.

Sudden and forceful, I landed on top of her, catching her completely off guard. Despite her piercing screams, I managed to whisper the words, my weight pressing down on her, overwhelming her with my presence.

"Consume my life and her soul within the depths of this black hole. Hold us captive until her soul is depleted; take my life and make this complete."

The chanting of the spell sent tremors through the ground, causing it to split open. Zigzagging gaps appeared all around us, and sinkholes seemed to be sucking everything in their path towards us. I couldn't help but bow my head and watch as Lilly stood frozen, resigned to whatever fate awaited us.

"You won't survive," she taunted. "Just a naive lab creation."

"I won't regret it, and at least I'll die with dignity," I whispered. "But your soul, Lilly, is heading straight to hell."

As the sky darkened to an ominous black, the Earth beneath us trembled violently, quaking with the energy of a sinister plan about to unfold. Lilly, once the revered leader, now stood at the precipice of her doom. The heavens exploded in a dazzling crimson, purple, and green kaleidoscope, each flash illuminating the landscape in surreal, otherworldly hues.

I was violently thrown to the ground, my grip tightening around Lilly as I felt her strength begin to wane. She, too, realised that her reign had come to an end. Our fates were now inextricably intertwined—me, the innocent, and Lilly, the wicked. The ancient spell we had unwittingly invoked demanded the sacrifice of both a good and an evil soul. One would vanish without a trace, consumed by the relentless forces, while the merciless Earth would devour the other.

The air crackled with dark magic, and I could feel its icy tendrils wrapping around us, pulling us deeper into its cruel grasp. This was the deadliest of all witchcraft, a force older and more powerful than anything we had ever known. And now, we were caught in its unforgiving embrace, powerless to escape the fate our intertwined destinies had sealed.

"Seira!" a voice cried out, assaulting my ears with desperate fear. "Please, there has to be another way. Don't do this."

I didn't dare look back to see who it was.

When I finally opened my eyes, they met Luke's horrified gaze. His face was etched with mixed emotions—guilt, sorrow, and something deeper. Love. I could feel it wrapping around us, a tender force amidst the chaos.

Beneath me, Lilly lay motionless, her body trembling as her wide eyes stared in terror. The ground beneath her slowly split open, revealing a raging inferno that burned with an unforgiving hunger, ready to claim her soul.

When the Earth finally cracked open wide enough to swallow her, the flames eagerly danced along the edges of the gaping hole. We tumbled into the darkness, Lilly holding on to me with a fierce grip, refusing to let go despite my efforts to pry her hands from my clothes.

"Lilly!" I screamed over the crackling flames. "Release me! What's going on? There's only room for one!"

"Come with me; there's always space for another. If I step in, you're stepping in too," she laughed.

As I twisted and spun in a frantic dance for freedom, every muscle strained against her iron grip. I was desperate to break free and rise to the surface before the Earth swallowed me whole. The flames crept ever closer, licking at the ground with ravenous hunger, their scorching tendrils reaching out to claim Lilly.

Her grip tightened, but her terror was as clear as the inferno that encircled us, the fire's searing heat drawing nearer. Her screams pierced the night, shrill and filled with unimaginable fear as the flames began to consume her. The fire wrapped around her like a living thing, clawing at her flesh, pulling her down toward the fiery abyss that awaited her.

With a final, blood-curdling shriek, Lilly's hold on me faltered. The flames tore her away, dragging her down into the churning depths of hell reserved for witches who had lost their way. As she vanished into the inferno, I felt her grip release, leaving me gasping for breath as I scrambled to escape the flames that had claimed her.

In this place, there was no way out, no hope for a fresh start. My thoughts spun wildly as I confronted the blaze, pausing as it dared me, gently licking my skin and sending shivers down my spine. My fiery ordeal wasn't as terrifying as I had imagined. It was a unique world, unlike anything I had read about.

Displeased with the taste, the Earth let out a furious, guttural roar that shook the ground beneath me. In a sudden, violent surge, it propelled me upward, expelling me from its grasp. My feet flailed wildly as I was thrust toward the surface, my instincts screaming for me to protect myself. I clamped my hands over my head, bracing against the crushing pressure.

Agony tore through me as the ground began to close, the gap narrowing rapidly. With a bone-rattling jolt, my body was ejected through the shrinking opening, the force sending me hurtling into the air. I landed hard on the ground, the impact jarring every bone in my body, leaving me sprawled and gasping for breath on the cold, unforgiving Earth.

With a deafening thud and a bone-chilling crack, the Earth sealed shut behind me, its finality reverberating through the air. I lay motionless, breathless, clinging to the last flickers of life that stubbornly pulsed within me. My heart beat weakly, each throb a reminder of the brutal battle I had endured. My head swam with a dizzying haze, the world around me blurring as exhaustion threatened to pull me under.

But I had won. The battle was over, and I had emerged victorious over Lilly, the formidable witch who had once seemed unstoppable. Now, she was lost to a realm of unimaginable horrors, a place feared by mortals and immortals alike. A place where darkness reigned supreme, and even the bravest souls quaked in terror. Whatever awaited her there, I could only imagine the nightmares that would consume her for eternity.

If she believed she could conjure up terror, she had no idea of the horrors awaiting her in that place. The reports and records of the realm were accurate, and if I had lived, my record-keeping would be forever changed. Her body would be engulfed and torn from her head, which would float among the lost and hungry souls of the dead, never to reunite with the living world.

The battle-weary shield drooped even lower, signalling the final end of the fight. Onlookers hurried towards me, their faces blurred in the distance as exhaustion weighed heavily on my soul.

Luke was the first to reach me. He dropped to his knees beside me, his hands trembling as he gently cradled my battered face. His touch was warm, but even that couldn't stop the cold creeping through my veins.

The relentless struggle within me became unbearable. The internal bleeding surged, an invisible force threatening to pull me into the abyss of unconsciousness. I could feel the tranquil embrace of death drawing nearer, its cold fingers brushing against my skin.

It was undeniable—I was on the brink of leaving this world. The edges of my vision darkened, and I knew my time was slipping away.

As I gazed up at the sky, weakened and weary, the sight above me was breathtaking. The once-raging storm was fading, its furious power ebbing away until it dissolved into a soft whisper of wind. The dark clouds that had dominated the heavens slowly drifted apart, revealing the twinkling stars beyond, each a distant beacon of light in the vast expanse.

Suddenly, a burst of light pierced through the night, dazzling me with its brilliance. It was unlike anything I had ever seen, an unfamiliar vision that filled my mind with wonder. I was enveloped in a hazy glow, the light shimmering and pulsating around me as if it had a life of its own.

The glow dimmed momentarily, only to blaze brighter with each breath I took, its rhythm perfectly in sync with the rise and fall of my chest. As my strength began to ebb, the light grew more intense, a luminous force drawing me closer. This radiant glow welcomed me, even though the world of men had cast me out.

It was as if the light had always been waiting for me, ready to embrace me in my final moments, offering a peace I had long yearned for. Its warmth wrapped around me, comforting and familiar, as I was drawn inexorably toward its inviting glow.

"Luke," I whispered, mustering a weak smile as I strained to lift my arm, pointing toward the source of the blinding light. "Can you see it? The brightness here is overwhelming."

My arm hung limply by my side, a heavy reminder of my helplessness. I had no fight left in me; my body refused to budge. So, I let go of resistance and surrendered to the beckoning light, beckoning for me to embrace it.

I could feel my blood slipping through his fingers, leaving sticky, warm stains all over my body. It was the work of a furious, deceptive witch, draining the life out of me.

"I've got you, sweetheart," he whispered, looking down at me with tenderness as he cradled me in his arms. "Darcy, hurry back to the house and prepare a room for her. I can't move any quicker than this."

I squinted through the swirling mist as Darcy raced off into the distance.

The unbearable agony was almost too much to bear as I was bumped and tumbled around. The endless trip felt like it was dragging on forever, but as long as the light was there, I could endure it.

The light encircled Luke's head like a halo, casting a comforting glow that spread a warm, fuzzy feeling throughout my body. His familiar scent enveloped me like a cosy hug, filling me with trust and love I had never felt before.

I could feel the life draining out of me, each drop of blood slipping through Luke's fingers. It was a slow, agonising death, and I knew there was no turning back. Luke didn't even seem to be affected by it, despite nearly starving me to death before.

My only sorrow was not being able to say goodbye to my adoptive parents and express my gratitude for the love and care they gave me. Because of them, I had a childhood filled with warmth and happiness, and I would never have had that if Matace hadn't forced me away. Yet, somehow, against all odds, I found my way home to where my journey began.

I whispered, 'I'm so scared.' My legs went numb, and the light grew closer and warmer. The fear was gripping me tight.

"I understand," he reassured me. "We're almost there; just stick with me." Gently, he planted a tender kiss on my forehead and affectionately brushed away the stray strands of hair from my face.

I just nodded. I couldn't find the right words to tell him that I was fading away and that the prophecy was about to become a reality.

The distance to the house seemed to stretch forever, far beyond what I had anticipated. Doubt crept in as I questioned whether my mind was playing tricks on me or if my recollection was slipping away. The uncertainty hung in the air, leaving me unsure what to believe.

Quietly, I slipped into a trance, fully aware of the frenzy of footsteps around me. Luke's hurried pace echoed through the air, punctuated by the occasional hushed question. His steely focus guided us back to his home, a refuge where he sought to rescue me from the clutches of death.

"Seira, please don't leave me," he pleaded desperately, his voice filled with urgency and fear. "Stay with me, please, don't go."

I felt utterly powerless to say anything. My mind was shutting down, just as it should at that moment. I knew there was nothing he could do. My hearing was the last to go, slowly slipping away. Soon, I wouldn't hear anything he said.

I listened as the door creaked open and footsteps echoed in Luke's house. A wave of warmth enveloped me as if embracing me, and I held onto it, not wanting to let go. It was a rare moment of goodness in my life, yet I knew I couldn't hold onto it forever, and the thought of letting go felt like a looming threat.

"Stay with me," he urgently whispered, the sounds of others fading away as Luke led the way to the room Darcy had been getting ready for us.

I sensed her before she even said a word. The change from the person I had met earlier was striking. It was as if Darcy had finally started to warm up to me, and a bit of fondness had started to peek through. I could feel it in how she spoke to me and in the gentle touch of her cold hand grazing my forehead.

"She's right around the corner, Luke," she whispered, her voice filled with sorrow. "Hurry, whatever you're scheming, do it fast. Time's running out."

What are we doing now? I pondered. And why do we have to do it in such a rush? I wished my mind would let my words flow to express the depth of my thoughts in these final minutes rather than uttering meaningless phrases handed down by others.

"Let's get her laid down," he said urgently. "Can you stick around with us?"

"Of course," she murmured gently, her voice barely above a whisper. "Place her gently on the ground here."

I felt jostled slightly. His strong arms gently released me, and I sank into the welcoming softness of the mattress. With aching bruises, I lay down, feeling the warmth of a blanket draped over me. Surprisingly, the vampires, who had once recoiled at my sight, now embraced me. Matace's help revealed their hidden magic to me, empowering me to form formidable alliances and conquer Lilly.

I heard Darcy's urgent question: "What happened to Tye?"

"Dead," he muttered. "Did you manage to snag some fresh clothes? And what about bandages?"

"Take this," she demanded, her voice filled with urgency.

The moment felt like time had stopped, and the surroundings were engulfed in darkness. What was once a vibrant world now felt treacherously dark, and it seemed like everyone would soon start grieving. The pain from my wounds still throbbed, and every touch and whisper felt like it was adding to my agony, leaving me feeling completely paralysed.

"I have to begin right away," Luke declared with urgency in his voice.

An idea struck me. It was a long shot, but something I was sure would work. It was something I had read about a while ago: a link between souls destined for each other, whether by eternal love or eternal friendship. It was a complete gamble.

"Luke, can you hear me?" I silently begged in my thoughts, straining to grasp any response. My heart raced, desperate to understand my surroundings.

"I hear you, my love," he murmured urgently, his voice clear as he spoke back into my mind. "Stay still. I won't ever let you go. You got that?"

"Not entirely," I whispered honestly.

"Time is running out," Darcy's voice cut through the tense silence. "Her life is slipping away faster than you thought, Luke. You have to act. Now."

The desperation in her voice was evident, and I couldn't help but wonder what had her so on edge. I had hoped the connection wouldn't extend to her, but I was mistaken. She was tied to Luke and, by extension, to me. The unspoken urgency in her words sent a chill down my spine, and I knew I needed to find out what was happening quickly.

"What are you doing?"

The deafening silence was broken only by the steady, rhythmic ticking of the clock in the distance. Each tick echoed through the room, reverberating in the air and creating a sense of unnerving anticipation. The pauses between the ticks felt like an eternity, like time had slowed to a crawl. The relentless beat of the clock was the sole reminder of the passage of time, its unwavering presence a constant, inescapable reminder of the present moment.

"Something you might not agree with, so I'm not telling you," he said, his voice tinged with uncertainty. "This will be difficult, but I need you to be prepared." He paused, his gaze holding mine intensely. "Remember how much you mean to me, and try to keep an open mind."

The agony seared through my arm, radiating down to my leg. The searing pain intensified, slowly crawling up my body until it reached my throat. I felt a warm, viscous liquid trickling out of me, but I couldn't tell where it was coming from. The blood seemed to be draining from my body, leaving me weak and disoriented.

"Luke!" I cried out, my voice laced with sheer terror and confusion. Panic gripped me as I frantically tried to make sense of what was unfolding. "What's happening to me?" I pleaded, my heart racing with fear and uncertainty, desperate for answers in this unnerving and inexplicable situation.

"Shhh," he murmured, his voice low and soothing. "It's done now. Take a breath and rest easy. I'm not going anywhere; I'll be right here with you."

His words pierced through me, cutting deep. Immediately, my body retreated, shielding itself from the outside world. The warmth that had enveloped me vanished, and I plunged into a silent, solitary world of anguish and captivating mystery. The light that had once guided me faded, leaving me trapped, isolated in a void of torment and intrigue.

The world around me was in a constant state of flux. Amidst the turmoil, I found myself suspended in a serene expanse, untethered from the constraints of the physical realm. As I drifted in this ethereal space, my gaze was drawn to a magnificent sight – a pair of radiant, golden gates shimmering before me, beckoning me forward with an aura of mystique and wonder.

The gates of heaven loomed before me, towering and majestic, a testament to the divine realm that awaited me. Beyond those gates, I knew Matace, my guiding mentor, stood ready to welcome me. This was the hallowed sanctuary where my journey as a witch would continue, free from the distractions and burdens of the mortal world.

I was certain that I had passed on. The serenity that enveloped me was unmistakable. This was the mystical place I had read about in ancient texts—the sacred domain reserved for the most righteous of witches, a true witch's heaven.

A profound sense of tranquillity washed over me as I approached the towering gates. The weight of the world had lifted, leaving me light and unburdened. Within these celestial walls, I knew Matace would be able to share the full breadth of his wisdom unimpeded by the interruptions of earthly life.

The anticipation of the knowledge I would gain and the peace I would find fueled each step. This was the moment I had long yearned for—the chance to fully embrace my calling as a witch in a realm untouched by the chaos and strife of the mortal plane.

"I can sense them, Luke," I murmured, my eyes shut tight. "They're here, and they're exquisite beyond words."

"Please, you have to listen to me!" he cried out desperately, his voice laced with urgency. "Don't go with them, I beg you. Stay here; you don't have to leave. I love you with all my heart, so please, don't go." His eyes pleaded, his hands reaching out, desperate to keep her by his side.

The words escaped my lips in a soft, trembling murmur, 'I love you, Luke.' My gaze locked with his, and the world around us faded at that moment. The intensity of my feelings burned within me, a glowing ember that threatened to ignite into a blazing fire. My heart raced, and I could feel the warmth of his presence, a comforting familiarity that enveloped me.

Trembling with fear and awe, I slipped into the second dimension, the guardians flanking me on either side. The air was thick with anticipation, and peripherally, I could feel Luke's frantic movements beside my motionless form in the mortal realm. His bewilderment and self-perceived shortcomings weighed heavily on the atmosphere.

The shift was immediate and profound as I stepped deeper into the celestial realm. Magical and otherworldly energies swirled around me, their intensity far exceeding anything I could have imagined. The fabric of this dimension seemed to pulse with life, vibrant and electric, a captivating and humbling power.

The sheer vastness and complexity of this new reality were overwhelming. My senses strained to their limits, desperately trying to absorb every detail of this extraordinary place. The energies danced around me, wrapping me in their ethereal embrace. I felt the boundaries of my understanding stretching as I stood on the brink of something far greater than anything the mortal world had ever offered. In front of me stood the one person who could answer all my questions; Matace.

"Matace," I said softly, my voice laced with concern. The weight of unspoken words hung thick between us, like a veil obscuring the truth. I searched his eyes, hoping to find a reason for his silence. "Why didn't you confide in me?"

The question hung in the air, heavy and insistent, pleading for an answer to dispel the shadows clouding my mind. I yearned to understand, to reach out and offer the comfort and support he desperately needed. Still, the weight of his unspoken burden thickened the air between us.

A burning desire to uncover the truth about my heritage consumed me, igniting a fierce determination to break through the veil of secrets that had been meticulously guarded for far too long. These revelations had become the unravelling of Lilly's existence. Ever since she had uncovered the intricate details of who I truly was and the profound significance of my birth, my life had begun to crumble.

The knowledge had gnawed at her, her own crippling jealousy becoming the catalyst for her ultimate downfall. What had once been a simmering envy had festered into something darker, driving her to the brink of madness. And now, as her world fell apart around her, the truth that had been hidden for so long stood at the centre of it all, pulling the threads of her life apart one by one, until she was no more.

"My dear child," he said, embracing me tightly. His voice was soothing, a gentle whisper that calmed my racing heart. "You're safe now," he reassured me, his warm eyes filled with a tender smile. However, his expression quickly turned serious as he added, "But your journey is not over yet."

The way he held me was firm yet tender, his arms wrapping around me with a protective strength that spoke volumes. The concern etched into his face, the furrow of his brow, and the gravity in his eyes conveyed a deep sense of urgency and importance. Every word he spoke was weighted, laden with a significance that made my heart race.

I could feel the moment's intensity thrumming between us, an unspoken understanding that this was only the beginning. There was more to come—something on the horizon that demanded my full attention and unwavering focus. His embrace offered more than just comfort; it renewed my sense of purpose.

At that moment, I was reminded that my journey was far from over and that my time had not yet arrived. There was still much to do, and his presence was a steady anchor, grounding me as I prepared to face whatever lay ahead.

Bewildered, I remained rooted to the spot, unable to move. Matace grasped me firmly by the shoulders, his eyes glistening with unspilled tears. His robe swirled around him as he held me at arm's length. The proud and imposing guardians stood tall and vigilant in the room, adding to the moment's intensity.

I furrowed my brows, puzzled by the ambiguous remark. "What exactly are you implying?" I inquired, my voice laced with a hint of confusion and curiosity.

"Your time has not yet come," he said, his voice laced with urgency. "You are not meant to perish, Seira; you misread my diary entry. You are merely lost but were born to shield our world from the darkness." He paused, his eyes grave. "We have known for a long while that the demons would one day rise against us. That is why you were made – to be a force powerful enough to confront them all." He placed a weathered hand on her shoulder, his grip firm. "Your unique heritage, your connection to many different species, is what gives you the ability to lead them. They will have no choice but to follow you rather than stand against you. That was the very purpose of your creation, my child."

"Am I a part of you?" The words lingered, laced with a sense of vulnerability and a yearning to belong.

"My child," he chuckled, his voice gentle yet filled with a tangible sense of power. "I am the one who brought you into this world, the one who shaped you into the being you are today. And I will never abandon you, for I shall always be by your side, guiding you through the mysteries of life." His words carried a deep, unwavering conviction, and I could feel the weight of his authority and the deep bond that connected us. The intensity of his presence was a source of comfort, like a warm embrace that enveloped me, shielding me from the world's uncertainties.

Spinning around in bewilderment, I found Matace standing close, his presence calming amidst the chaos. He leaned in and placed a fatherly kiss on my cheek, the warmth of his touch grounding me. As he softly waved with a reassuring smile, I felt a deep sense of comfort wash over me.

His words echoed in my mind, their meaning sinking in as the world around us shifted. The room's walls gradually faded, dissolving into the background, leaving an open, expansive space behind. The guardians remained steadfast, their silent vigilance comforting in the midst of the change.

Matace watched the transformation with the same familiar, understanding smile. There was a wisdom in his gaze, a quiet confidence that bolstered my own. His calm, unwavering demeanour instilled a sense of strength and reassurance as the scene around us evolved.

As the Earth came into focus, my eyes frantically blinked, and I could feel my soul being pulled back into my aching, broken body. A scorching, agonising pain seared through me, causing me to cry out in agony. The sensation of Luke's cold hands on mine, combined with a strange, eerie pain on the side of my neck, heightened the intensity of the moment, leaving me desperate and disoriented.

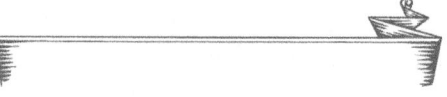

Chapter Sixteen

"She's back!" Luke's voice rang out, his words laced with relief. "It's done, finally! I was so afraid I was too late." His shoulders visibly relaxed as if a weight had been lifted from them.

"I know," Darcy responded.

I smelt her perfume. As I lay there, eyes still closed, I knew everything had shifted, though I couldn't focus entirely on what had changed. The air felt different, with a tension that sent a shiver down my spine. I was acutely aware that my world was no longer the same. Still, the extent of the transformation remained elusive.

Rightfully and by the prophecy, I should have been dead, yet here I am, lying in Luke's bed, still drawing breath. My body, though altered, remains my own. A strange, powerful sensation washes over me as if I've been transported to a different time and place – a time that is now mine, a time where I am the High Witch.

With Matace's untimely demise and the treacherous Lilly, who had seized the title out of sheer avarice, I now stood as Matace's rightful heir to the realm. My commands and my name would echo with authority, shining a spotlight on all those who dared to defy me.

"Luke," I whispered, mustering the courage to ask, "What did you do?" The question burned on my lips, though a part of me dreaded the answer, uncertain if I genuinely wished to uncover the truth at this pivotal moment of awakening.

I heard him draw in a sharp, agonised breath. Then, his hands were on mine, feather-light and trembling, starkly contrasting to the weighted, powerful touch I had experienced before when his immortal nature infused every gesture. This delicate, almost tentative caress was deeply unsettling, a stark deviation from the norm.

"You're alive!" he exclaimed, relief washing over his face. "Thank goodness I made it to pull you from the brink." His words carried a heavy weight, underscoring the gravity of the situation.

"What have you done?" I couldn't help but ask, my heart pounding as I braced myself for the answer, unsure if I genuinely wanted to know the truth that was about to unfold.

"I turned you, whether you liked it or not," he said hastily, his words tumbling out in a rush. "You were dying, and I couldn't bear the thought of a world without you in it. It's far more interesting with you as one of us, and I don't care what you say about it." His voice held a tinge of desperation, betraying his awareness of my previous warnings against being transformed into an immortal.

And now, it felt as if my destiny had been etched in stone. I could have showered him with grateful kisses for granting me this second opportunity, a chance to forge a new life regardless of the realm's expectations. No one could dispute that I was the rightful heir to the leadership and the esteemed title of the High Witch, destined to reign over the kingdom and all that it entailed.

"Thank you!" I blurted out, my eyes snapping open. I watched Luke's expression shift to utter bewilderment. "Thank you, Luke, for saving my life!" I grasped his hand tightly, squeezing it with all my might.

"Do you really mean that?" he asked firmly, weighing his words. "And listen, I'm only going to say this once - please let go of my hand. You're a newborn, and right now, you're stronger than me until you get used to your new strength and all the incredible things we can do. But it will be so much fun teaching you all about it!"

I gazed up at him from the pillow as the shadows of past bitterness, anger, and regret melted away, allowing me to bask in the bliss of my new life, my renewed purpose. The weight of those emotions had been lifted, leaving me free to fully embrace this moment, this newfound joy.

"I'm so sorry," I said, my voice trembling as I gently pulled my hand away from his. The weight of my apology hung in the air, the words laced with regret and uncertainty.

The room was in shambles, with a gaping hole in one side—a clear sign of the fierce battle that had taken place here. Shattered glass from the broken windows littered the floor, but Darcy had done her best to make the space livable. She had put together a makeshift bed, piling on as many pillows and blankets as possible.

The moment Luke carried me, her purpose became crystal clear. She had genuinely grown to care for me and welcomed me into the immortal realm she was trapped within. Her affection was surprising, and I could feel her sincere desire to integrate me into her world. A raw, undeniable emotion radiated from her, drawing me deeper into her immortal existence.

"What happened to the rest of them? Where did they go? I need to know—tell me everything you saw!" The urgency in their voice felt intense as they desperately sought answers about the fate of their missing companions. Their eyes were wide with concern, and every muscle was tense with anticipation for the response.

"The Cerberus has been annihilated," he declared emphatically.

"You should have been there to witness Luke's epic showdown with them," Darcy said, chuckling from the other side of the room. "It was downright terrifying to watch, but it became absolutely hilarious when they sent him flying clear across the front of the house. And when Tye stepped in, oh man, you should have seen it!"

Darcy's eyes lit up with excitement as they recounted the events, their voice brimming with energy and amusement. The vivid description transported the listener right into the middle of the action, making visualising the intense yet comical scene easy.

"Enough, Darcy," Luke cut her off, his tone sharp. He let out a laugh, though it held an edge. "Go tell the others she's awake now. She's one of us."

The intensity in Luke's words was compelling, underscoring the gravity of the situation. His abrupt command to Darcy and the hint of darkness in his laughter added a sense of urgency and tension to the scene. The simple, direct phrasing makes the exchange more engaging and impactful, keeping the same core meaning while elevating the emotional tone.

He leaned in, his eyes sparkling with mischief. I held my breath as his lips brushed against my forehead, lingering for a heartbeat. The soft touch sent a shiver down my spine, igniting a spark.

"That woman will drive me absolutely bonkers for the next few weeks. She won't stop yapping about that fight, and it's the happiest I've ever seen her in her immortal life. I swear, it's going to drive me up the wall."

"I heard that!" Darcy's voice boomed through the house, her tone sharp and unyielding.

"You were meant to do it," he playfully taunted, chuckling at her sharp retort. He then shifted his gaze to me, his eyes softly caressing me. "Are you alright? How are you feeling?"

His words ignited a spark within me, propelling me upwards into the vast, starry expanse. Our eyes met for a fleeting moment, and in that instant, I felt the profound connection that transcended the bounds of mentor and mentee. The bond we shared ran deeper, tugging at the very core of our beings.

"I'm fine," I said, smiling. "How are my Meniagier?"

The curious animals watched intently; I could see them through the window. Their faces were etched with eagerness as they observed my every move. I could feel their sorrow acutely when they realised I was dying, just like their beloved Lilly. At that moment, their true nature became starkly apparent—a hollow, predatory instinct that had led them to corner and blindly follow me, their perceived leader.

"They're all there, waiting for you," he said, gesturing toward the front lawn. His voice was urgent, as if he couldn't wait for me to join them.

I forced myself up, wincing as the pain throbbed through my body. "I have to get moving," I muttered, gritting my teeth. "Now that I'm immortal, my wounds should heal on their own, right?" The thought filled me with a mix of hope and unease. No more worrying about injuries or death - but what did this new immortality entail? I needed to find out, and quickly.

He scrutinised me intently, and I held my breath, propping myself up on my elbows, waiting anxiously for his response. The ambiguity of his answer, or his reluctance to give one, left me unsettled and on edge.

"Well? Come on, don't keep me waiting!" I pressed, my voice tinged with impatience. I couldn't hold back my curiosity and needed to know the answer.

"Your transformation may take longer, but that's only because you haven't been properly nourished yet. After all, you're still a newborn in this realm. I didn't expect you to awaken so soon. Your body needs time to adapt to the changes. In my experience, the transition to immortality is a drawn-out process, much more so than the time it's taken you to cross over."

"Why don't you go and get me a drink?" I asked, my voice trembling with fear. The thought of having to drink blood for the rest of my life filled me with dread. The reality of my newfound vampiric nature weighed heavily on my mind, and I desperately needed something to dull the overwhelming sense of unease that consumed me.

"I've got this," he said, his voice firm and reassuring. Before I could protest, he gently kissed my forehead and swiftly made his way to the door. "No need to worry. I'll take care of it."

I lifted my gaze from the empty window frame and asked, "About what?" My voice carried a sense of curiosity and urgency, eager to understand the context of the conversation.

"Drinking blood? It's not as bad as you might think," he said, a mischievous glint in his eye. "In fact, you'll likely grow to enjoy the taste. Of course, that's all a matter of personal preference regarding your blood intake." He leaned in, his voice lowering to a conspiratorial whisper. "But trust me, once you get used to it, you'll find it quite...satisfying."

"In what way?" I pressed, my curiosity piqued. "Explain it to me, I need to understand."

He let out a deep, weary sigh. "Look, it really depends on your preference. Some of us like to stick to animals, but others, like me, are just partial to humans. That's what we crave, you know? Human blood is where it's at for us."

I scrunched up my face and playfully stuck out my tongue, chasing him. Bursting through the door, I unleashed my pillow, striking him directly in the back of his head with a resounding thud. What an absurd thing to say! Talking about a preference for blood intake sounded more like ordering a fine-dining experience, where the waiter politely inquires about your preferred level of steak doneness.

The idea of being immortal was bound to feel peculiar, no doubt. Yet, with Luke by my side and Darcy's support, I was sure I would adjust and grow to cherish my newfound existence, particularly with a realm to govern that would occupy me for ages.

The weight of eternal life was not lost on me, but I was determined to embrace this extraordinary circumstance. Luke's unwavering presence and Darcy's guidance would be my beacons as I navigated this unfamiliar territory. Though the road ahead may be uncharted, I was resolute in making the most of my immortality and the responsibilities of ruling a realm that would outlast the ages.

Chapter Seventeen

My legs trembled as I stepped onto the uneven wooden floorboards, the missing tiles a stark reminder of the earlier confrontation. The unfamiliar scent engulfed me, simultaneously intriguing and unsettling. I was overwhelmed by a newfound sense of strength. This immortal power surged through me, leaving me momentarily awestruck and unsteady as I rose.

I staggered, my knees trembling with each step, but I refused to give in. Determination coursed through me as I fixated my gaze on the lone mirror that had miraculously survived the onslaught of the demons. My heart raced with anticipation as I finally reached the mirror, victory surging through my veins.

Yet, I felt a deep, primal urge stirring within me—an inkling that only one thing could quench this hunger—blood. My body craved the crimson elixir, the sustenance that would propel me from the mortal realm into the realm of immortality. Without it, I would wither and succumb, my life force fading away. But I was not ready to relinquish my hold on this world. I would do whatever it took to survive, to transcend the boundaries of mortality.

The truth is, I hadn't been honest with myself earlier when facing Lilly. I knew this was my destiny, something I was born to do, and I had simply accepted it. Throughout my life, I had surrendered to whatever fate had in store for me. I had never possessed the courage to say 'no' to anyone's demands, not even to my adopted parents, who had tried their best to shower me with love.

Looking back, they had also wanted to shield me from the realm and all its complexities, hoping to save my life. They had been aware of the fate that had befallen me since the day of my adoption, even before I could utter my first words.

"Seira!" Luke exclaimed, his voice trembling as he knocked over the mug, spilling its contents onto the floor with a loud clatter.

The pungent odour assaulted my senses, and I stumbled backwards, desperate to escape its pull. The primal urge, the insatiable thirst, burned through me like wildfire, beyond my control. I was consumed by a crimson haze, overcome by the same ravenous desire that had driven countless vampires to commit unspeakable acts throughout history. The need was all-consuming, a relentless force that threatened to shatter any semblance of my humanity.

"Listen up," he said, his gaze fixed on me as he strode closer, his hands outstretched. "Take it slow, you hear?" he warned, his voice firm and unwavering.

My need was overwhelming, surpassing the power of his words. Without hesitation, I snatched the cup from his grasp, carelessly scratching the back of his hands in my haste. The liquid sloshed and swirled, filling the mug to the brim and mirroring the burning desolation I felt deep within.

I gulped it down in a single, desperate motion, acting like a famished half-breed ravenous for sustenance after a long period of starvation. When I finally looked up, I was met with Luke's kind and compassionate expression, understanding the depth of my yearning.

I sank to the floor, my head hanging low in utter shame. "I'm sorry," I whispered, the words barely escaping my lips.

The hunger had been all-consuming, a relentless force that had swept me away, drowning me in the aftermath of my actions. The weight of what I had done pressed down on me, a crushing burden I struggled to bear. Every fibre of my being ached with regret, the consequences of my surrender to temptation now staring me in the face.

"Hey, look at me," he said firmly, kneeling beside me and placing his hand on my shoulder with a firm, reassuring grip. His eyes locked onto mine, and I could feel the weight of his gaze urging me to focus on him and nothing else.

I cautiously lifted my head and locked eyes with him. A sharp gasp escaped my lips. His skin had transformed - it was still Luke, but somehow entirely different. The once flawless, chiselled features had softened, exposing a tenderness and vulnerability I had never witnessed in vampires before. It was breathtakingly beautiful and magnificent.

"What's going on?" I breathed out, frantically reaching out to grab him, ensuring this wasn't just a dream. My heart raced as I tried to make sense of the situation unfolding before me.

"Seira, you're witnessing us, your own kind, for the first time," he murmured, his voice barely a whisper. "Look into the mirror and see for yourself."

I nodded dumbly, overwhelmed by the urge to hold him close and shield him. I realised there was so much more to the vampire race than anyone had ever documented. It made sense that no one had been as deeply involved with them as I had. No one had fought alongside an entire coven or two before me, and that would indeed be recorded in the tragic history of this realm.

"Let me give you a hand," he said, firmly gripping my elbows. His eyes held mine, a glint of determination in them. "Come on, you can do this," he urged, gently pushing me toward the mirror.

I staggered through the room, my senses clouded by a haze. Vaguely, I noticed him move to stand before the mirror, leaning against it with a soft smile on his lips. I ached to capture those crimson, blood-tinted lips with my own in this moment.

"Listen closely, for what I'm about to tell you is of the utmost importance," he said, his voice taut with urgency. "Before you lay eyes on what's before you, there's something you need to understand – something that will change everything."

I locked eyes with him, giving him my complete, unwavering focus. Every ounce of my attention was firmly fixed on him, eager to hear what he had to say.

"What is it?"

"Well," he said, his voice shaky with a hint of shame, "There's one more Cerberus, but he's different from the rest. He won't hurt anyone, and he's much calmer. I reckon he'd be easy to train if he had the right master." The man paused, his gaze intense as he looked directly at me. "And I was wondering... would you be interested in taking him on?"

"No way!" I snapped, raising my hand to cut him off before he could finish. The anger in my voice was evident. "You can't keep that animal, Luke. You know as well as I do that it'll end up dead if I ever see it again.

The sun's blazing radiance amplified the splendour of my newfound state, transforming the space into a mesmerising spectacle of shimmering silver light. The dazzling illumination bounced off the walls, momentarily blinding me. Yet, it remained the most breathtaking sight I had ever witnessed in my short life. No one within this realm could hope to match the extraordinary tale I was about to embark upon.

"No love whatsoever," he chuckled darkly. "We're the ones who're already dead inside."

His words infiltrated my subconscious, rippling through my being. I couldn't help but notice a subtle yet undeniable transformation within me - a blossoming into a new role, a new purpose. Suddenly, I found myself at the helm, responsible for the fate of others, both animal and demonic, and even the occasional mortal who dared to cross my threshold. While the mortals often proved adept at concealing their flaws and turmoil, the demons were no match for my discerning eye.

The voices around me erupted in a cacophony, Darcy and Benjamin's banter echoing loudly as they played and quarrelled over a card game. Accusations of cheating flew back and forth, but neither was willing to concede. Their dispute felt like it was unfolding beside me, a disconcerting yet captivating experience that transported me to a world untouched by others. The moment's intensity pulled me in, tempting me to immerse myself deeper in this newfound excitement.

"I'm sorry, Luke, but you can't keep it," I said sternly. "That creature has to go back with the Meniagier. It wouldn't be right to keep it alive here, and if it ever broke free, there would be a bloodbath, and I won't allow that to happen. We have to do the right thing, no matter how difficult."

He eyed me warily, a flicker of irritation igniting in his gaze as he grasped that I had firmly assumed the role of a superior authority, poised to scrutinise his intention of keeping a creature he had summoned, one that seemed to have emerged from the very depths of hell itself.

He took a deep, steadying breath, his jaw clenching with determination. "Alright, it will be done as you've requested," he said firmly, his voice laced with a sense of finality.

I must have him by my side, making decisions together. Only then can we genuinely reign supreme. But the only voice that will be heard and obeyed is mine - no other shall dare challenge my authority. I will brook no dissent; my will shall be the sole guiding force as we shape the future to my liking. He will be my loyal lieutenant, carrying out my commands without question. Our partnership will be one of absolute dominance, with me as the undisputed master. There is no room for compromise; my vision is the only one that matters.

"Take a look then," he said, dismissing me with a playful wink. Despite our challenges, his casual demeanour conveyed a sense of acceptance, as if he had embraced fate's hand. His words were laced with a subtle understanding, a silent acknowledgement that we were in this together, weathering the storm side by side.

I felt the excitement in his voice, the sheer joy radiating through his words. In that moment, our immortality was sealed, binding us together eternally. No longer would we be shackled by the constraints of laws or societal norms - we were now equals, free to live in perfect harmony, untouched by the external world and its attempts to tear us asunder.

I stared at my hands, mesmerised by the intricate network of silver veins beneath my ghostly pale skin. These veins were more than just a physical attribute; they embodied my vampiric nature, a testament to the magical transformation over centuries. My kind had been identified solely by their peculiar feeding habits for ages. Still, as time marched on, our race had evolved. The silver tracks that snaked through our bodies had become a defining feature, a visible mark of our supernatural existence. Yet, this enchanting detail remained hidden from the untrained eye, accessible only to those with the keen senses of a practised witch.

The ability to amplify the visual effects on our skin allowed these perceptive individuals to distinguish us from the masses, granting them the power to identify us whenever the need arose. It was a subtle yet profound aspect of our existence. This duality set us apart from the mundane world we inhabited.

"Luke, it's breathtaking!" I exclaimed, my eyes wide with awe. The stunning landscape before us took my breath away, and I couldn't help but be captivated by its sheer beauty.

Exhilarated, I spun and twirled, the newfound power of vampirism surging through my body. The transformation was complete, and I revelled in the intoxicating sensation, knowing that I had become the perfect vampire companion for Luke. My heart raced with excitement and anticipation as I yearned to live up to his every desire and expectation. The allure of this new existence had captured me entirely, and I couldn't wait to explore the depths of our vampire love.

"I hope I will be everything you need for eternity, Luke," I said.

"Of course, you will," he gently chided, capturing me in his arms and holding me tightly. "You will always be everything to me so long as you never stop being yourself and don't turn into something like Lilly or get too greedy."

"I'll never do that," I said, backing away with shock. "She was evil and beyond anyone's control."

It felt like the chains fell away, and I stood before the mirror, my gaze fixated on my reflection. Mesmerised, I studied my skin, captivated by the radiant beauty that stared back at me. The sight was breathtaking, leaving me in awe of the sheer magnificence of my own form. Every curve and contour seemed to shimmer with an otherworldly glow as if I had been reborn into a realm of pure splendour. In that moment, I felt a surge of empowerment, a deep appreciation for the exquisite person I had become.

"This is amazing," I breathed, my voice shaking with awe and excitement. The scene's sheer beauty left me utterly captivated, my heart racing as I struggled to take it all in. "I can't believe my eyes," I murmured, my words barely audible as I found myself lost in the stunning wonder.

The mocking laughter from downstairs jolted my head as the sudden conversation began.

"I need to go talk to the others for a bit," he said, quickly turning towards the door and swinging back to face me. "You gonna be alright on your own for a few minutes?"

Although he had uttered the exact words before, I couldn't help but question their sincerity. I laughed it off and brushed him aside, as my newfound joy was the unexpected twist that allowed me to truly live. Yet, I found myself navigating a profoundly different reality, witnessing the vampires up close and from an unfamiliar vantage point. It was a novel and thrilling experience, a whole new adventure. Still, this time, I would embark on it with someone I loved and in whom I ardently hoped to find that same profound affection in return.

"I can't believe this is real!" I exclaimed, my body buzzing with exhilaration. The realisation that I was now a vampire sent waves of pure joy coursing through me. It was the most incredible dream come true, and I prayed it was not just a figment of my imagination.

"She's onto you, Luke!" Benjamin chuckled, his eyes gleaming. "You'd better get your butt back up there right now."

"I firmly believe she's destined to become an extraordinary High Witch, the perfect leader for our realm. Who could be more suited for this role than an immortal with the wisdom and experience to guide us all? Her immense power is astounding, yet she remains unaware of her remarkable abilities. I have no doubt she will lead us to unprecedented heights once she embraces the full extent of her potential."

"Quiet, you two!" Luke scolded sharply. "She can hear you, so keep it down!"

A burst of laughter erupted around me, and I couldn't help but chuckle softly. I stood transfixed in front of the mirror, holding each of my hands up to the light, captivated by the stunning sight of my shimmering silver veins. The beauty of it mesmerised me, and I couldn't tear my eyes away from the captivating display.

The sun's blazing radiance amplified the splendour of my newfound state, transforming the space into a mesmerising spectacle of shimmering silver light. The dazzling illumination bounced off the walls, momentarily blinding me. Yet, it remained the most breathtaking sight I had ever witnessed in my short life. No one within this realm could hope to match the extraordinary tale I was about to embark upon.

"You look absolutely breathtaking," Luke said, his voice low and intense as he leaned against the open doorframe. His gaze was fixed on me, unwavering. "I knew you would. Tell me, are you angry with me for turning you?" His tone showed a hint of challenge, as if he dared me to admit my true feelings.

I pondered my response, carefully considering my words. I wasn't angry or shocked, but a sense of joy suddenly surged. It was a happiness I had never experienced before, illuminating my entire being in a way I never knew was possible. The overwhelming feeling filled me with a warmth and elation I couldn't describe. It was as if a switch had been flipped, and the world around me had become brighter and more vibrant. At that moment, I was consumed by this newfound happiness, which radiated deep within me.

"No," I said firmly, shaking my head as my hair swayed. "I'm not angry. How could I be? You've given me a new life. I'm technically dead, but I love what I've become. The fact that I have a second chance makes it even better. No, Luke, I'm not angry with you at all." I spoke with conviction, my words carrying a weight that conveyed the depth of my feelings. There was no room for doubt or uncertainty in my voice. I had embraced this new existence and wanted Luke to understand that he had given me a gift, not a curse. My gratitude was obvious, and I hoped he could see the sincerity in my eyes as I expressed just how much this second chance meant to me.

"Pheww!" he exclaimed, wiping the sweat from his brow with a look of exaggerated concern. "Thank goodness, I'm so relieved!"

I crossed the room, acutely aware of his piercing gaze following my every step. The vampire's legendary strength pulsed through me with each stride, making my movements feel strangely powerful. The more I tried to walk like an ordinary human, the more I failed. Ultimately, I dashed across the room in a bizarre, rapid blur.

I let out a loud groan as the gravity of my actions dawned on me. Luke's look was one of pure enchantment and amusement. This was a side of him I had never seen before, or perhaps it was just my imagination running wild, given that I had only just been thrust into this extraordinary state.

"We can work on that part, you know, controlling your speed," he said, laughing when I collapsed on the bed. "You'll be fitting right in, I guarantee it," he added, a reassuring tone in his voice.

"It's all about practice, isn't it?" I said, my voice brimming with determination. "And let's be honest, I've got plenty of time to figure this out – a lifetime and then some. This is just the beginning, the start of something great."

"Yeah, you do," he said firmly, his voice brimming with conviction.

The casual chit-chat seemed to avoid the core issues in our relationship. Love was the burning question that consumed my thoughts. I desperately needed to know if his proclamations of love were genuine or just empty words.

"Luke," I said, my voice trembling slightly. "Did you really mean what you told me earlier?" I searched his face, my heart racing, desperate to understand the truth behind his words.

"Which part?" he probed, a faint smile tugging at the corners of his lips as he furrowed his brows, delving deep into his recollection to retrace the conversation threads.

"The moment you confessed your love for me? That part absolutely captivated me. The raw emotion in your voice, the way your eyes gazed into mine – it was as if the entire world had faded away, and there was only you and me in that breathtaking instant. Your declaration of love left me utterly spellbound, my heart racing with a whirlwind of feelings. It's a memory I'll cherish forever, a precious moment that ignited a fire within me that continues to burn bright even now."

"What do you think?" he asked.

"I have no idea," I said, shrugging helplessly. "Maybe you said it because of the moment's intensity, but did you truly mean it? I need to know the truth." My voice was laced with urgency as I searched his face for any hint of the needed answer.

He studied me intently, his piercing gaze locked onto me as I sat there, yet he remained silent. His lips were pursed tightly, not a word escaping them. I could hear his breathing, or was it just an act of pretence? The steady clock ticking, the laughter drifting up from downstairs, and the muffled voices in the house all provided a backdrop to the charged silence between us.

The persistent gruff huffs and stamping of feet from the Meniagier snapped me back to reality. This was a different moment to bombard him with questions when I had forbidden creatures patiently awaiting their return to their rightful realms. The Cerberus had to accompany them; Earth was no place for either of their kinds to thrive.

The mere sight of them would undoubtedly strike utter terror into the hearts of the humans. Their very existence was something I dared not even begin to explain, for the depths of that realm were beyond their wildest imaginings. The sheer otherworldly nature of these beings would leave the humans paralysed with fear, unable to comprehend the true nature of what lay before them. It was a secret I was bound to keep, no matter the cost, for the human mind was not equipped to handle the harsh realities of that enigmatic domain.

"Your parents are here," he declared, his voice low but urgent. "And yes, I can assure you, every single word I said was absolutely sincere."

I was stunned, my mouth hanging open as I watched him walk away. My parents were here, but why? He loved me. I could feel it, taste it, and it surrounded me like a thick fog. He had unlocked the secret door to his vampire heart, letting me in and granting me access to his private world—a world he shared only with those he deemed worthy.

I heard my mother's soft, anguished sobs and my father's deep, gruff voice drifting up from the floor below. Their cries echoed through the house, conveying the sheer devastation they felt as they surveyed the ruins of what had once been a magnificent, expensive dwelling – the lonely vampire's once-proud domain.

I hurriedly gathered my clothes, struggling to dress as my movements blurred with the newfound vampire's strength and speed. It was a battle to control my actions, to slow down and not startle anyone with the sheer intensity of my abilities. I had to learn to adapt, to restrain the power coursing through me, lest I inadvertently frighten those around me.

"Mother! Father!" I cried out, my voice urgent, as I reached the top of the stairs. My tone of relief and joy was evident, and my footsteps quickened with each passing moment.

I rushed toward them, my heart pounding. Their quick, worried glances at each other spoke volumes - concern etched on their faces as they recognised something different, something troubling in me. The intensity of their reaction sent a chill down my spine, and I couldn't help but wonder what they had seen that I had missed.

"You're alive!" Mother exclaimed, rushing towards me and wrapping her arms tightly around my neck. "Oh, thank heavens you're safe!" she cried, her voice trembling with relief.

I stood there, my heart pounding with fear and restraint. The power coursing through me was immense, and I knew, with just a touch, I could easily hurt her. The very thought of being the one responsible for causing harm to a human being filled me with a sense of dread.

It went against every regulation and code I had been instilled with since birth. There was no way I would let that happen, not on my watch. The situation's intensity hung in the air, and I struggled to control the sheer force that threatened to break free. Every fibre of my being longed to reach out and comfort her, but I knew I couldn't. The risk was too significant, and the consequences too severe. No matter how much it tore me apart, I had to keep my distance.

I tensed up as I broke free from her embrace, standing rigid and unmoving. "I'm alright," I said, my voice strained and distant. "And how are you?"

The last time I encountered this woman, she was wailing loudly and feigning distress as if she were the one wounded and ailing. Her perspective on the world, its inhabitants, and the supernatural forces was remarkably grim. I was sure she had made futile attempts to erase my existence from her memory over the years.

The woman's dramatic anguish and pessimistic outlook on the realities around her left a deep impression. Her ostentatious cries echoed through the air, drawing unwanted attention and creating an uncomfortable atmosphere. It was clear that she was intentionally playing the role of the victim, desperately seeking sympathy or perhaps attempting to conceal some deeper, unresolved issue. Despite her theatrics, I could sense an underlying vulnerability in her behaviour, a desperate need to be seen and acknowledged, even if it meant resorting to such manipulative tactics. The years had evidently not been kind to her, and she struggled to come to terms with her own literal and figurative demons.

The room spun rapidly around me, a disorienting whirlwind frightening and exhilarating me. My mother's approach was fearsome, her gaze fixed upon me with an intensity that sent chills down my spine. I watched as the trepidation built in her eyes, starkly contrasting the warmth and affection I had grown accustomed to. Her face fell, and a torrent of emotions swept through my mind, each one conveying a different message – her confusion, her longing for my embrace, her desire to feel the love she had so freely given me.

My confusion was overwhelming, a tangled web of uncertainty about navigating the human world and adequately expressing the care and tenderness I felt for this precious, fragile being. I feared that my embrace, so natural and comforting to me, could be detrimental to her delicate form, shattering her like glass beneath my touch. It was a notion that filled me with dread, for I would never intentionally harm the one I held most dear. This was a situation far from ideal, and I struggled to find a way to convey my feelings without causing her further distress.

"Goodness!" she gasped, her hand instinctively flying to her mouth as her eyes widened in surprise. The unexpected revelation had left her utterly stunned, her heart racing with shock and disbelief.

She knew without a doubt what I had become. She felt the icy chill of my skin, the desolation in my approach to her; it was unsettling to think that the very people who had raised me were now the most distraught in my life. They no longer belonged in my world but in a parallel existence that no longer included me.

She watched me, and the terror quickly built into her eyes. My father pulled her close, shielding her from the unknown and treating me like an enemy, which I was to a certain degree. I remained composed; I didn't want to hurt them, but their scent, the blood pulsing through their veins, made me crave a small taste, even though I knew it was an inevitable part of my new vampire nature.

Luke seemed to sense my inner turmoil and came to my aid instantly, standing by my side and ushering me into the study or what was left of it. His face was etched with concern, and his voice dripped with the emotions of the one person who would endeavour to guide me through this tumultuous chapter of my new life. This was the worst part, which I would be relieved to overcome and move past.

"The cloying scent of their blood is suffocating me. I can't bear to go back in there with them," I pleaded, my hand pressed tightly over my nose. Desperation gripped me as I begged, "Please, you must get rid of them. I can't stand it anymore!"

The closest chair was unforgiving and hard-backed, but I gratefully sank into it. My nerves were frayed and on the verge of snapping. I had never felt the powerful draw into the darkest depths of the loathed vampire thirst before. It was a curse they had to endure. Now, I had to find a way to suppress it and become more stable before venturing into the world and being around humans again.

"Don't worry, you've got this," he said softly, reassuringly touching my shoulder. "Just stop overthinking it, and it'll all start to click. Hey, I think your dad's got something to say that might lift your spirits." He flashed me an encouraging smile.

"How can I ever face the world again when all I can think about is devouring my own parents? The urge is overwhelming, an insatiable craving that gnaws at my soul. I'm tormented by this monstrous desire, and the mere thought of it fills me with equal parts shame and hunger. Yet, I must find a way to suppress this abhorrent impulse and carry on as if nothing is wrong, all the while my true, horrific nature threatens to consume me from within."

Suddenly, his boisterous laughter erupted as if the old, carefree version of himself had broken free from the layers of concern and the looming threats of Lilly's vengeful schemes. The vibrant spark in his eyes shone through, momentarily eclipsing the worries that had previously shrouded his demeanour.

"I swear you're gonna be just fine. You've got this. I know it. Trust me, everything's gonna work out - I promise I won't let anything happen to you."

He extended his hand, and as our fingers interlocked, I felt a surge of reassurance in the tender squeeze of his grip. The almighty smile he flashed and a playful wink filled me with anticipation and comfort before he turned and faced my parents again.

"Mom, dad," I said firmly. "Come, let's go to the living room. We'll be more comfortable there."

"Are you one of them?" The words came out sharp and accusatory, and my eyes narrowed as I scrutinised the person before me. I could feel my heart racing. The question hung between us like a challenge.

I stood frozen, feet planted firmly, my flowing skirt gently caressing my scrunched toes. An overwhelming urge to lash out consumed me. He had infuriated me with his ignorant insinuations about my people - the ones he knew only through the fantastical tales that portrayed us as soulless, nocturnal creatures. Yet, now he had firsthand experience. Ready or not, his adopted daughter was one of us, and she embraced her new identity with pride, standing as an equal among our kind.

"I am!" I declared, whirling around to confront him, my face mere inches from his. The sudden proximity caused him to stagger back, a hint of intimidation flickering in his eyes. "Does it really matter what I am?" I challenged, my voice laced with a quiet intensity that demanded his attention.

Luke's loud throat-clearing sent a shiver down my spine, reminding me of the drastic changes in my body and the immense power I now possessed. This power could easily harm a human. But I would never use it against my parents, no matter how infuriated they made me. They were my parents, after all, regardless of their peculiar beliefs.

"I'm sorry," I said, my voice shaking slightly as I realised what I had done. "Let's go into the other room to talk this through calmly and figure things out."

I burst into the front room, my feet pounding with frantic urgency. A sense of uncontrollable rage surged through me, the unsettling certainty that I could harm either of them. I had spiralled into an unstable state, a perplexing phenomenon for them to comprehend. I had never been more grateful for Luke's soothing presence to calm the storm within me.

"Tell me, how did you survive?" my father demanded, sitting in the nearest chair. He grabbed my mother's hand and pulled her close, his eyes burning with curiosity and concern.

"I defeated Lilly in combat," I declared, my voice unwavering. The sweet scent of the flowers beside me struggled to mask the metallic tang of blood that filled the air. The steady, pulsing beat of their hearts consumed my every thought, igniting a primal thirst that refused to be quelled.

"Now hold on, young lady," he said sternly, like a strict father. "Matace told us you were supposed to die with her. So how come you're still standing here?" His eyes narrowed, demanding an explanation.

"Of course," I said, with a hint of sarcasm. "That's the very reason I was created. But when the underworld depths swallowed Lilly, it seems they didn't quite agree with my flavour, and they unceremoniously spat me back out." I paused, a shudder running down my spine as I recalled the experience. "You should have seen it - being inside that infernal pit was both awe-inspiring and utterly terrifying, all at once."

"Wait, is that when Luke turned you? The moment he flipped the switch and changed you forever? I can't believe it - tell me more; I need to know what happened!"

I couldn't believe my eyes as Luke approached my father and firmly shook his hand. All the tension seemed to melt away from Luke's posture, and he interacted with my father as if he were just any ordinary person, not someone with a debilitating condition.

"I had no choice but to turn her," he said, his gaze unwavering as he stood before my father. "She was clinging to the brink of life, and I knew that if I didn't act, she would be lost forever." His words were laced with a sense of urgency. "The weight of his decision hung in the air. "There was nothing else I could do to save her; it was either this or watch her slip away."

"In that case," my mother's voice, once small and meek, now carried a newfound strength. For once, she did not appear fragile nor under the ever-controlling command of my father. "I want to thank you for saving my child. I know she's not human anymore, but I still get to see her for the rest of my life, and I am truly grateful for that. She is my daughter, my only child, and I could not bear the thought of her dying. However, for her father, it's a little harder for him to accept this change, so please excuse him for being rude."

I let out a startled gasp, the sound echoing through the room. My father whirled around, his eyes locked onto his wife. A stunned expression crossed his face, his lips tightening into a thin line. The exchange between them crackled with tension. Their gazes met, locking in a silent battle of wills. My father, always so meticulous in maintaining his politically correct facade, now faced off against my mother, whose once-soft tones had hardened, her once-fearful manner toward anything remotely scary now replaced by a steely resolve.

"I can't believe you're supporting this dreadful situation!" my father thundered, his voice dripping with rage. "Do you really think having a vampire as a daughter is okay? I just pray you'll finally come to your senses one day and see how wrong this is."

The intensity of my father's words cut through the air, his outrage powerful. He was clearly struggling to understand how I could be content with the reality of being a vampire. The sharp edges of his condemnation left no room for compromise, as he made it abundantly clear that he could not accept this new part of my identity. His fervent hope that I would one day "come to my senses" underscored the depth of his rejection and the unbridgeable divide between us on this issue.

"Listen, dear, let's not be harsh here," she said softly. "She's our daughter, but she's different now. She's all grown up and can decide who she wants to be. I know she didn't choose this path, but she didn't choose to be born and genetically engineered to fight and then die, either. It's a tough situation, but we must be understanding and supportive."

He furrowed his brow, deep in thought. His once rigid posture faded, replaced by a more relaxed demeanour as he listened to my mother's forceful words crashing against the walls. I was captivated yet stunned by their heated discussion.

The world around me was in a state of flux. I had undergone a remarkable metamorphosis, becoming a being with a second chance at life, free to make my own choices without the interference of external forces that had once compelled me down paths I never desired. But the changes continued. To my astonishment, my mother, once the epitome of gentleness, had also undergone a profound transformation. She was now asserting her dominance in her relationship with my father, a sight I had never envisioned. Beneath her familiar nurturing persona, a new, potent feminine energy had emerged, tinged with stark darkness I had never witnessed before.

"I don't understand how this changes who I am," I interrupted firmly. "Father, you must see that I'm still your daughter, no matter how I am or what I eat. It doesn't change the fact that I'm here, alive and with you. Would you honestly prefer that I had died out there, and you'd be mourning me in the ground right now?"

"No way in hell!" he blurted out, his voice shaking. "I never wanted you to go out there and fight in the first place. That's why I'm here now. I've got to apologise for what I said before you left. I was a mess - confused, hurt, and scared out of my mind that you might not make it back alive."

Luke swiftly rejoined my side, his presence radiating a soothing aura. My body trembled, consumed by an overwhelming urge to embrace my parents. Yet, I knew such an act would prove fatal to them. I couldn't suppress the all-consuming need to feed nor restrain the surge of newfound strength that threatened to overpower them. To do so would be to inflict unimaginable, tragic harm.

"I'm relieved," I said with a slight smile. "But please forgive me for not coming over there as I should have. There's something important I need to warn you about. Since I'm a newly turned vampire, you're in danger of being around me. It's not easy for me to say this, but I'm afraid I might hurt you with my newfound strength, or I may not be able to resist the thirst. I've already fed, but I'm unsure how it all works. Luke, could you please explain a bit more?"

I spoke with a sense of urgency, my expression reflecting the gravity of the situation. The newfound power coursing through my veins made me acutely aware of the potential danger I posed to my friends. My words carried a weight of concern, wanting to ensure their safety while conveying my uncertainty about the extent of my abilities and impulses as a vampire. The request for Luke's input highlighted my need for guidance and understanding in navigating this transformative experience.

I lifted my gaze to meet his, and to my utter bewilderment, he seemed amused by something. His eyes crinkled at the edges as he fought to suppress a smile, and he let out a loud, deliberate cough in a feeble attempt to stifle his laughter.

"Look," he said, his voice low and serious. "She's got a point, but since she's already fed, I don't think you're in immediate danger." He paused, a faint crease forming on his brow. "However, she's just woken up, so she's not entirely in control. Sometimes she's doing surprisingly well, but other times, she's a bit...unpredictable."

Their faces drained of colour as my mother's hand darted out and latched onto my father's, her fingers clenching his tightly until they turned ashen. The sudden, desperate grip conveyed the moment's weight, the intensity of their reactions obvious in the charged silence.

"Are we in grave danger?" she cried out, her voice laced with panic. "Did it hurt you? Are you in pain? Please tell me!" she pleaded, her eyes wide with concern.

I couldn't help but chuckle softly; she had no idea what this extraordinary experience felt like. Truthfully, it was absolutely exhilarating. I could feel the raw power coursing through my veins; deep within, an uncontrollable urge was building, urging me to run and push the limits of my speed, to wrestle something, just to see if I could emerge victorious. The possibilities seemed boundless, filled with excitement and wonder.

"Don't worry, it didn't hurt a bit. Just stay over there, and you'll be perfectly safe," I responded, my voice firm and calm.

Darcy stepped into the room, her eyes fixed on my parents. A playful smile spread across her face as she approached them. Her self-assured demeanour was an attempt to ease the tense atmosphere that enveloped my parents and me.

I could feel their joy radiating around me. They were overjoyed that I had returned, more alive and vibrant than ever before, even more so than in my mortal existence. However, the journey had been utterly terrifying, especially in the final moments.

"Oh, hi!" she exclaimed, her voice brimming with enthusiasm. "I'm so happy to see you again. And aren't you just over the moon that Seira is here with us, alive and doing so well?" She beamed, her eyes sparkling with joy.

"I am," my father said, his voice heavy with emotion. He turned to me, his face etched with regret, his eyes brimming with unshed tears – a rare sight for a man usually as unyielding as stone. "Seira," he continued, his words coated in remorse, "I'm so glad you're alive. Your mother is right – I should be grateful that you're here with us despite what you've become. And I can see it, you're happy now. I just hope he treats you the way you deserve to be treated." The intensity of my father's words and the raw vulnerability in his expression pulled at my heartstrings. His typically stoic demeanour had melted away, revealing a man deeply affected by the events. The weight of his words and the emotion behind them made the moment all the more powerful and engaging.

His final remark was directed squarely at Luke, who stood beside me, his body trembling with uncontrollable laughter. The mirth vanished when he realised it was his turn to convince my father of his intentions towards me the traditional way.

"I will always treat her with the utmost respect," he said with conviction. "Every day, I will shower her with as much love and affection as possible. Her happiness is the sole driving force in my life, and I will move Heaven and Earth to ensure I never let her down. You have my unwavering commitment to this."

"That's great to hear!" he exclaimed, a hint of enthusiasm seeping into his voice. His face lit up with a warm smile, and he leaned in slightly, eager to engage further.

Darcy knew precisely when to step in and promptly offered to serve tea. To Darcy's elation, my mother agreed and followed her to the kitchen, much to my father's dismay. He sat there, torn between the urge to call my mother back and the desire to join them himself. But neither impulse won; his stoic facade swiftly slipped back into place, and the solid, stone-like man we knew returned.

My entire being crumbled as the last fragments of my human existence slipped away. Yet, my body had surrendered to the embrace of vampirism, welcoming it with open arms. This newfound life now coursed through me, a breathtaking gift I eagerly wanted to share with Luke.

"It's time," my father said, his voice laced with urgency. "The realm has summoned you for a meeting tomorrow afternoon. They want to speak with you." He paused, his eyes searching mine knowingly. "Are you prepared to face them?" The subtle nod towards my vampire nature did not escape me. I nearly laughed at his tactful evasion of the stark reality. "They sent a messenger to deliver the request."

"I'm all set and raring to go. You can count on me - I'll be ready, no doubt about it."

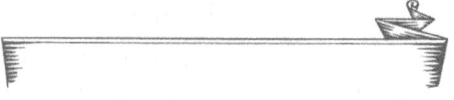

Chapter Eighteen

It took a while for my parents to finally leave. After much deliberation and the gentle, pleading cries of my mother urging me to visit her and bring along Luke and Darcy, whom she had grown particularly fond of. The pair had bonded remarkably well, which struck me as rather odd. A vampire and a human forming such an instant connection was strange, especially with my mother, who had always yearned for someone to call her own. But Darcy seemed to fit the bill perfectly, and she didn't appear to mind one bit; she lapped up the warmth from my mother and eagerly agreed to the visit.

"I promise we'll visit soon," I said firmly, determined to follow through. "Goodbye, Mother. Goodbye, Father."

I stood frozen, my body tense and unyielding, as they wrapped their arms around me. A part of me longed to return their embrace, but fear held me back, keeping me distant and detached.

I felt my mother's body tremble slightly, and she pulled away, her eyes searching mine with a curious, almost wary expression. Unspoken questions swirled in her gaze, mingling with the underlying love I knew she had always harboured for me – if only it hadn't been for my father's final words, uttered during our last encounter.

My body stiffened, every muscle locked in place, as my mother's gentle embrace seared into my memory. My father's calloused hands softened when he sensed the tension coursing through me, and I knew he understood what was weighing on my mind – the hunger gnawing at my gut.

"We need to get going, darling," he said with a wink, his voice brimming with excitement. "Time to head out."

"You must come to see us, dear," my mother told Darcy. "I can't wait to have you over. Just swing by whenever you can. No need to wait!"

I shuddered, slamming the wall with the last willpower I could muster. Their intoxicating aroma and the alluring pull to seize and savour them consumed me. Luke wrapped his arms around me, enveloping me in his embrace, and whispered soothing words that barely registered in my mind.

"We need to leave right now!" My father yelled urgently, his voice filled with a sense of urgency.

"Leave, Mother," I snarled. The unquenchable thirst consumed me, driving me towards them. I needed their lives to satisfy my craving.

"Take care, my love," she murmured, her voice trembling. The door closed with a resounding thud, sealing them away from me, where they would be safe and beyond my reach.

"Is she alright?" Darcy asked, her voice laced with concern as she anxiously nibbled on her lower lip. "Looks like this is proving tougher than you expected, isn't it?" she said, her eyes searching my face for any sign of struggle or distress.

I eagerly nodded, my face flushed with shame and overwhelming desire. I craved to savour anything I could put into my mouth, no matter how small. The temptation was too strong for me to resist.

"Darcy, please get something for her, will you?" Luke demanded, his teeth clenched. He pulled me away and marched me back to the front room.

Benjamin suddenly emerged, his brow furrowed in deep focus. He exchanged a knowing glance with Luke, and it irked me to think they were aware of my struggle. But their presence was useless – they could only ensure I didn't hurt anyone, not actually help me.

The room was dark; the tattered curtains and blinds fluttered helplessly before me. Despite the devastation, the chairs and most of the decor remained unscathed. The walls had borne the brunt of the attack, with the shattered glass long since swept away by Darcy or Benjamin.

"When will this get any better? When will the pain finally end?" I cried out in anguish, my voice laced with despair.

Luke's eyes gleamed with assurance as he handed the flask to the newcomer. "This will help, I promise." His voice was firm, conveying a sense of unwavering confidence. "Drink it up. In a few days, you'll start feeling better. We've all been through this and know it's difficult, but the first few days are the toughest. Your body has undergone a massive transformation, and the urge to feed is at its peak. But trust me, you'll get through this." Luke placed a reassuring hand on my shoulder, his touch steadying me. "You've got this. We're here for you every step of the way."

"I desperately hope so," I groaned, my words dripping with despair.

I seized the cup Darcy brought and greedily gulped the crimson liquid. The blood sloshed against the mug's edge, but I licked it clean, savouring every last tantalising drop. I couldn't bear to let a precious morsel go to waste, spilling onto the floor.

"God, I almost took them," I admitted, my voice unsteady as the gravity of the situation sank in. "I can't believe I came so close to hurting my own parents. What the hell is wrong with me?" My heart raced, and a wave of shame washed over me. How could I have even entertained such a horrific idea? The mere thought made me sick to my stomach.

"Don't worry; I'm sure your dad saw the problem coming from a mile away," he said, trying to reassure me. "Benjamin, could you please ensure the animals are well cared for?"

I stopped in my tracks; the animals were the only ones here and were my responsibility. There was no way anyone else would be taking them back through the portals except me, and I knew Luke would object to it right now. I had a sneaking suspicion that he wanted me to rest, but resting was all I could do, and I had a lifetime ahead of me to do that. The weight of the situation pressed down on me. These animals were counting on me. I couldn't leave them stranded, not when I was the only one who could get them to safety. Luke might protest and convince me to take a break, but I couldn't afford the luxury. These creatures were my charge, and I would see them through no matter what.

The portals loomed before me, the only way back, and I steeled myself. It was time to act, to put my doubts aside and do what needed to be done. With a deep breath, I turned and began to herd the animals, guiding them towards the shimmering gateways that would lead them home. This was my responsibility, and I would see it through to the end, no matter how weary I might feel. There would be time to rest later, but the animals came first.

"No way!" I retorted, my voice trembling with determination. "I'm taking them home, and that's final. Luke, you can join me if you want, but these are my 'animals,'" I shot back, playfully mocking his words as I nimbly evaded his attempt to catch me.

His smile was captivating, a sight that had been too long in the making. I couldn't bear to let this precious moment with my newfound family slip away. Yet, the Meniagier were a part of my identity, as the records had made clear. Peculiar as it was, my DNA had been engineered to withstand Lilly's powers, ensuring my involvement with every species and demon so that I could secure their unwavering support in this dire struggle.

"Alright, let's go," he said, walking behind me towards the front door. "Can you still use your powers?"

"Yeah, I think so," I said, brow furrowed in concentration. "You only turned me into a vampire, but I still have my magic powers, so I guess it'll be fine," I added, shrugging nonchalantly.

The Menagier, the largest one I had grown attached to, stood before me. As I held out my hand, he gently nuzzled it, sensing the change within me. But his confusion was clear as I still stood before him. Suddenly, he shrank away in shock, his eyes widening as he recognised the transformation that had taken place.

"Shhh, it's alright, my friend," I murmured, tenderly running my fingers through his soft fur. "It's still me, but I've returned in a new shape. I would never hurt you, I promise."

The slimy sensation of his tongue on my cheek elicited a giggle from me, much to my relief. On the other hand, Luke cringed visibly and turned his attention to his three-headed beast, the remaining Cerberus. His approach to the creature was unlike anything I had witnessed before. The unwavering trust and the instant affections from all three heads were a testament to his remarkable ability to tame an animal that rightfully belonged in the deepest, darkest pits of the underworld, not on Earth.

"The animal has to come with us, too," I insisted, gesturing towards the Cerberus. "I'm sorry, but you can't keep him."

"Ha! I can assure you, my friend," Luke chuckled, his eyes sparkling with amusement. "This one is definitely a female, and she's about to become a proud mama to a little brood of her own."

He gestured towards the woman's prominent belly, the gentle movements of the unborn babies visible beneath her skin. She watched me intently, a remarkable calmness enveloping her—a sight far more profound than any tales or legends could capture.

"I see she likes you," he commented, rubbing her head gently. "She seems to want to have a cuddle with you."

I inched closer to her, my hand trembling as it reached out. The Cerberus let out a guttural moan, her restless pacing quickening as she fixated her hungry gaze upon me, desperate to claim me as her own.

"Easy there, big fella," I said, guiding her cautiously towards her pack. "Steady now, I'm not going to hurt you," I continued, keeping my voice low and soothing.

She stood motionless, her multitude of eyes and heads intently observing my actions. Warily, she scrutinised me with all six eyes, her long lashes partially covering her pupils, obscuring her thoughts. Suddenly, she stepped forward and affectionately nuzzled all three of her heads against me, knocking me to the ground with a surprising burst of strength far exceeding my newfound power.

I chuckled as I tenderly stroked her head, remaining on the floor while she revelled in the affections I showered upon her. Luke laughed and gently rose, keeping a firm grip on her. Her pure, loving presence offered a glimpse into the depths of affection the animals could harbour, given the right environment and the people they chose to bond with. I suppose it was their decision to make, and this Cerberus had selected Luke and me as her masters.

"Alright, let's get going," I said, a sense of urgency in my voice. "We can't afford to waste any more time."

They stood together, their eyes filled with understanding and anticipation, waiting for me to open the portal. My magic returned effortlessly, to my surprise, as if my recent transformation had never occurred. Given my new nature, I had expected some resistance, but instead, a strange sense of acceptance washed over me. I was the new vampire High Witch, and with this title came the responsibility of overseeing the entire realm and all it represented.

"Luke!" I shouted, my voice laced with urgency, as I realised he had fallen behind. "Are you coming? We need to keep moving!"

He rushed towards me, and in a heartbeat, we vanished from the human world, stepping into the forbidden, exiled realm where the animals would find sanctuary, safe from fear and strife. This was their haven, where they could live in peace, free from the turmoil of the outside world – the very thing they longed for more than anything else.

"You know I'm going to miss the Meniagier," I said sadly when we reached the other side. The darkness succumbed back into the brightness of the dimension. "They've come to mean a lot to me."

"You're always welcome to visit," he said, his voice brimming with sincerity. "In fact, I'd love to come along and check on her and the pups," he added, his eyes shining excitedly at the prospect.

"Yeah, I guess we can do it," I said, my voice firm. "But it can't become a regular thing, you know? They must go back to living as they used to, without being influenced by anything else except each other. I just really hope they don't forget about me."

"I don't think he will," he said, nodding toward the approaching pack leader. He moved in front of me, then suddenly grabbed me and tossed me onto his back. I clung to him, my heart racing as we took off.

The animals' farewell parade had commenced, and it was a bittersweet moment. Witnessing the profound respect these creatures showed him filled me with a deep sense of reverence. His joyous demeanour, however, was tinged with a hint of melancholy, for this was our parting, at least for now, until I could find a way to harness my powers and quell the thirst that burned within me.

"I have to go now," I murmured, my eyes stinging with a hint of tears that threatened to spill over. I blinked hard, trying to hold them back. "But I'll be back before you know it."

The lead Meniagier's massive tongue dragged across my cheek, leaving a trail of warmth in its wake. His pack's scent surrounded me as they gathered close, their heavy paws pounding the Earth.

The sounds of nature faded away, replaced by the thunderous farewell of the wolves. With a final glance, they watched as the portal transported me back to the other side. Stepping into the brilliant starlit night, Luke stood by my side, my faithful lover who had been with me since the beginning, though I had been unaware. Now, I knew with unwavering certainty that his love was real and eternal, transcending the boundaries of time.

"Now I have to prepare to face the realm tomorrow," I uttered, a sense of trepidation filling my voice. "I dread how they will receive the news that I plan to retain my title and that their esteemed High Witch is now a vampire, very much alive and amongst them."

The gravity of the situation pressed upon me, and I could feel the tension building within. I knew I had to confront the realm and its potential reaction to the revelations ahead. The path was uncertain, but I steeled myself, determined to stand firm in the face of the challenges looming.

"They soon fled when you defeated them on the hill," he chuckled in the darkness. "I guess you did something they didn't expect you to do."

I couldn't help but chuckle as the harmony within me swelled, accompanied by the sheer amusement of outmanoeuvring so many witches simultaneously. Stella and the others, who were undoubtedly vying for the coveted title, would soon realise that I was very much alive the moment I stepped into the realm's meeting room. My father had warned me that the secret realm leaders, aside from the High Witch, had summoned me, which meant they had accepted me for who and what I was and needed me to make my own appearance to quell the rest and assert my rule. The entire congregation would be left utterly stunned.

"Would you like me to accompany you?" he suggested as we both hesitated to enter. The lights were illuminated, and the loud chatter between Darcy and Benjamin spilt out from the house.

The offer hung in the air, weighted with an unspoken invitation. Neither of us moved as if suspended in a moment of indecision. The intensity of the conversation within the house felt overwhelming, drawing us in yet keeping us at bay. His words were simple but carried a depth of meaning. The choice was ours, to venture forth together or remain on the threshold, listening to the lively discourse that beckoned us forward. The decision lingered on a silent question demanding our attention.

"I can definitely handle this," I said, confident and determined. "And honestly, you're needed here more than coming with me. This place needs a lot of work, and if you want me to move in with you, it's gotta be cleaned up first."

"Why would you even think I'd want you living here?" he said, his eyes gleaming with mischief.

"Ah, well, no need to fret," I said, stifling a yawn. "Herbert and I can always head back to my modest little place. Heck, we might even be better off there, don't you think?" I couldn't help but feel disappointed, but I tried to keep my tone light and casual.

"You've got nowhere else to go, darling." He pulled me close, his eyes burning with desire. "You're staying right here with me." His strong arms enveloped me, and I felt the raw passion radiating from his every touch. The intensity of his gaze left me breathless, captivated by the fire of his love.

"Oh," I replied, shocked. "And why not?"

"Because I leased it to someone else already, you don't technically have it anymore."

Breathless moments passed as I steadied myself, and his actions swelled inside me; he felt my apparent anger and held me steady.

"Don't be angry," he begged. "I did it before the fight, and I knew you wouldn't want to go back there anyway, not without me anyway."

His lips crashed into mine in a desperate, hungry kiss. Our mouths moved together feverishly, all barriers and hesitation forgotten. We were pulled towards each other, irresistibly drawn as we had been from the start - his darkness and secrets, the vivid dreams he'd invaded night after night, now a reality. Here we stood, ready to face whatever trials lay ahead, no matter the challenges my title might bring. Nothing could keep us apart any longer. We were meant to be together and would confront tribulations that came our way, united in our consuming passion.

"Lovebirds!" Darcy exclaimed, a mischievous grin spreading across her face. "Get over here and join the fun!"

We hastily parted at her voice, our intertwined fingers reluctantly slipping apart. Hand in hand, we trudged across the desolate terrain to the remnants of the once-grand house, its walls now reduced to a heap of rubble. I closely examined the debris with my newfound immortal vision, which allowed me to perceive far more in the darkness than my mortal eyes ever could. Clearing the scattered wreckage would be a formidable challenge for Luke and the others. Yet, I shrugged it off nonchalantly, knowing that their vampire strength would make light work of the daunting cleanup.

"Where the hell is Herbert?" I shouted, frantically scanning the area and calling out his name into the dark night.

"Right here!" Luke growled, his voice ragged as he clenched his jaw. I couldn't help but chuckle as he whirled around. On his leg was my cherished pet, Herbert, clawing his way up. The sight was both comical and endearing.

"Hey, boy," I exclaimed, pulling the boy close and running my fingers through his hair. "I've been searching everywhere for you. Where on Earth have you been hiding?" I asked, a hint of playful scolding in my voice as I held him tightly against me.

The cat let out a series of loud, angry meows and hisses directed at Luke. All this time, I had assumed the cat's dislike for Luke was solely due to his vampire nature. But now, it was clear the cat's antagonism stemmed from pure, unadulterated jealousy.

"I think he's jealous," I said.

"He'll be homeless if he claws me like that again," he complained.

I swung my fist and landed a playful punch on his arm, then took off running, squealing with delight. I could hear his heavy footsteps rapidly closing in behind me as he chased after me. The thrill of the pursuit sent a surge of excitement through me, and I ran even faster, daring him to catch me.

Giddy with excitement, we burst through the door to find Darcy and Benjamin in a peculiar situation. They clearly recognised each other and confessed their feelings—an unmistakable revelation. Darcy had come to terms with the fact that her love for Luke was not genuine and that Benjamin had stolen her heart all along.

"Well, well, look who's been getting cosy around here," Luke said, pulling me close to his side and eyeing the cat warily. "Seems like you two have found something to bond over, huh?" His tone was playful, but there was an underlying edge as if he was slightly uneasy about the situation.

"We've made up our minds. We want to be together, no matter what," Darcy said firmly, her eyes filled with determination. "Do you have any objections?"

"Absolutely not," he responded hastily, taken aback by their tender and unexpected revelation. "I'll be honest, I'm a bit stunned, but it doesn't bother me at all." He paused, his expression softening as he processed the weight of their words. "In fact, I'm rather intrigued by this turn of events. Please, tell me more."

"That's good," she said. "Seira," she added, the hope entering her voice. "Can you forgive me for being such a prime bitch?"

"I've already forgiven you," I declared, my voice firm and unwavering. The words carried a weight, a resolve that left no room for doubt. I wanted them to sink in, to erase any lingering unease between us. This was a clean slate, a fresh start, and I was ready to move forward.

The house erupted with boisterous laughter as everyone inside shared jokes and chattered excitedly about the future. The joyous atmosphere was beautiful and comforting, and I couldn't help but feel a growing anticipation for the momentous day ahead. As the evening drew close, I reluctantly bid farewell to the lively gathering, knowing I needed to rest up for the pivotal challenge that awaited me tomorrow. The thought of facing the realm and setting the rules straight filled me with trepidation and determination. I was ready to take on this momentous task and could feel its weight settling on my shoulders.

"Let's get out of here, shall we?" Luke urged beside me, his eyes gleaming with a desperate longing to have me to himself, even for a moment.

I silently followed as we made our way to the stairs. No words were needed - the profound moment was already etched deep within us. As we reached the bedroom where I had been transformed, Luke stepped in first and swiftly shed his clothes, revealing his chiselled, muscular physique that left me breathless. I had never seen a body so captivating; the intricate network of veins that played across his face continued downward, branching out across his magnificent form.

A burning curiosity consumed me, and I had to know if my body had transformed like his or if I was completely different. Nervous anticipation swelled within, and my hands trembled as I began to undress. I had only focused on the changes to my face earlier, but now the rest of my body demanded attention. What did I look like underneath these layers of fabric? The suspense was almost unbearable.

Luke's gaze intensified as he propped himself up on his elbow, his eyes hungrily tracing the curves of my body as I started to undress. I took a deep, steadying breath and made my way to the mirror, moving with a newfound confidence, no longer the self-conscious gait from before.

Standing before the mirror, I marvelled at the stunning transformation of my once-human form. My eyes were captivated, tracing the intricate and mesmerising patterns of the beautiful silver veins that now branched across my body. The sight was utterly compelling, a glorious vision that left me enthralled.

"The moment I looked at you, I knew you'd be a sight to behold. I was tasked with keeping you safe, and I couldn't help but wonder what you'd look like as one of us," he murmured, his voice low and captivating in the hushed atmosphere of the bedroom. His gaze locked onto mine, a hint of intensity burning in his eyes. "Tell me, Seira, are you content with how things are?"

"How did you know this plan would work?" I inquired tentatively, mindful of the possibility of agitating him with my questions. "I knew it would," I responded, intently observing and shifting my gaze to every angle, captivated by the radiance from my skin. The moonlight danced across the veins, summoning shards and small rays of light illuminating the room, dispelling the darkness with a dazzling display.

"How what might work?"

"You turned me," I said, my heart racing. "You had no idea if it would work or if my body would even accept it, did you?"

"Yes, that's true," he said solemnly. "But I was still hopeful, and I stayed with you the whole time, and Darcy did too. Neither of us wanted to leave you alone because we knew you might need us at any moment."

"It must have been excruciating going through that," I said, my voice laced with empathy. "But how does it actually work? I'm ashamed to admit I don't know or remember much about it - is the process itself painful?" I leaned forward, eyes searching his face, genuinely curious and concerned to understand his experience better.

He reclined against the pillows, his gaze fixed on me, wary of the questions in my mind. Yet, I remained determined to uncover the answers, my resolve unwavering.

"Listen, I know you have this wild notion that it's a smooth, seamless transition to become one of us, but that's not the case," he said bluntly. "Fortunately for you, though, given your condition and the state your body was in, you were already drifting in and out of consciousness, so you didn't feel a thing."

"I know I didn't," I replied, slowly turning to face him. "But how was it for you?"

"You won't believe it," he said, his voice dripping with mystery. "I'm not telling you any more. It'll freak you out for sure." He paused, then added, "Now, why don't you come to bed? You have a long day ahead of you tomorrow, and you must rest before facing everyone. Are you sure you don't want me to come with you?"

"I've been wrestling with this decision, wondering if I should ask you to accompany me. But I think I have to. It would be a disaster if you came along. They'd never accept you in that realm, especially once they find out you're like me. It would just rub salt in their wounds, you know?" I pressed him for a response, but he shrugged as if he didn't care. Yet, I could see the turmoil boiling up inside him.

"You're probably right," he conceded, a hint of resignation in his voice. He took a deep breath and fixed his gaze on me, his eyes burning with frustration and longing. "So, are you going to join me in bed?"

The open-ended question hung in the air, a silent challenge between us. I was unsure of his intentions and his expectations of me. He sat there, completely at ease, as if the idea of us tumbling into bed together was the most natural thing in the world.

It was a wholly unfamiliar experience, unlike anything I had ever encountered. I felt a surge of exhilaration, tinged with a hint of trepidation, as I stepped into this two-dimensional realm of love – a world vastly different from the one I had known. I was both thrilled and terrified, for he had accepted me for who I truly was, not for the powers I possessed or the purpose for which I had been created. This newfound connection felt fresh and raw, and my mind revelled in the realisation that he not only liked me but loved me in a way that was deeply profound and unapologetic.

"Don't be afraid," he said reassuringly, recognising my unease. His calm smile never wavered. He extended his hand towards me, inviting me to come closer. I promise I won't bite you," he added, his voice low and reassuring.

I could have groaned at his choice of words, bad timing and certainly a better selection of words he could have used, my mind in turmoil and torment with the power of the moment I had been flung into. I wanted badly to get into bed with him. Still, I was scared, which was uncanny considering the fight I'd just accomplished against someone who'd learnt all of her powers from one of the greatest witches of all time, Matace.

"Please, don't be afraid," he pleaded. "I just want to hold you. Can you imagine how terrifying it is to think you might lose someone you love? It was the worst feeling ever, Seira, and I never want to go through that again. I care about you deeply, and I know I can be a bit difficult to understand sometimes, but I'm just as scared and unsure about all this as you are, even though I might not show it."

"Are you?" The words slipped out before I could stop them. His confession had opened a window into the private depths of his soul - a side of him I never imagined existed. It was a fragile, unfamiliar Luke, unlike the confident facade I had grown accustomed to. I held my breath, waiting anxiously for his response.

How many hearts had he shattered over the years? Given his age, it must have been countless. That's why he had built up these impenetrable walls, shutting out anyone who dared to get close, even his own kind. The mere thought of attachment seemed to terrify him, and the agonising fear of losing the one he loved again was a pain he couldn't bear.

I hurried across the bedroom, unable to resist the mesmerising display of light that trailed behind me. Vibrant hues danced on the walls, a captivating kaleidoscope reflecting off the remaining bedcovers. The spectacle captivated my senses, drawing me deeper into the ethereal display unfolding before my eyes.

I melted into Luke's warm, secure embrace, surrendering entirely to him. I could feel the vulnerability in his touch, the way he opened his heart and exposed his innermost thoughts to me alone. The depth of trust between us was profound as he pulled me tightly against his strong, steadfast chest, shielding me from the world.

"I've lost so many people, Seira, in my lifetime," he said, his voice heavy with grief. "When I saw you lying there after Lilly had gone, I was devastated. I couldn't bear the thought of losing you too. I wasn't going to let you die - I couldn't go through that pain again." He gripped my arm tightly, his fingers digging into my skin, though I didn't mind. "I had to watch as my parents and sisters passed away. I couldn't even say goodbye to them because I still looked young while they aged. The people back then," he paused, swallowing hard, "they would have torn me apart, done anything to destroy what they saw as the devil himself, reborn. I witnessed our kind being captured and killed, hunted down in every village by those they called 'dead walkers.'" His eyes darkened with the weight of his memories. "When I became one of those I had hunted with my father, I fled to the mountains and hid, uncertain what to do. Then, I was shot by a villager who had misfired. My father was furious and attacked him in a rage."

"Luke," I whispered, my voice trembling as hot tears streamed down my face. I could only imagine the anguish his family must have endured. The thought of their pain weighed heavily on my heart, and I felt a deep sorrow within me.

"I'm alright," he said calmly, his mind still lost in past memories. "I was lying on the forest floor, bleeding heavily and beyond the point of being saved. The medicine back then wasn't good enough, and I knew I was going to die. Suddenly, this stranger emerged from the darkness, filled with fear and hesitant to approach me. I wanted him to deliver a message to my father, who hadn't returned. I called out to him, and he spoke to me."

"What did he say?" I asked gently, the words bursting from my lips as the excruciating silence between us stretched on.

"He asked me if I wanted to live," he said, trembling. "I didn't understand what he meant at first. So I whispered back that yes, I wanted to live - to see my family grow, to watch over my mother and father and make sure they were safe and cared for. I was their only son, and back then, the whole weight of the household rested on my shoulders. If I was gone, there was no way they could survive on their own."

I was utterly captivated, my whole being focused intently on his every word. His memories enveloped me, pulling me into the depths of his own life - a world I had never experienced before. I hung on his every syllable, devouring the breathless details of his recollections. This timeless moment had me in its grip, and I could not escape its hold.

"I swear on my life that I won't do anything reckless tomorrow," I muttered into the pitch-black room, my voice laced with determination. "And you have my word that I'm not planning on dying anytime soon, not on my watch."

"Don't you dare," he growled, gripping me firmly and refusing to let go.

His strong arms enveloped me, and his tender kisses grazed my forehead as we lay together in bed, watching the first rays of dawn slowly illuminate the room. We were both lost in our private worlds, needing no words to convey the depth of our connection. We both knew they could tear me apart if my father was wrong. His worry and concern for my meeting with the realm tomorrow weighed heavily on him. The other elders had not shown up, just as he had hastily explained to me over the phone after persuading my mother to take a sleeping pill, allowing him to concentrate and fully explain the events of his visit today.

My world was consumed entirely by the ideas I had started meticulously crafting within my mind for their domain. They were a relentless comparison to the existing one and the immense power that had reigned supreme for so long.

As the first rays of dawn crept through the window, the room was illuminated with a captivating kaleidoscope of colours. Our veins, once hidden, now shimmered and pulsed with a mesmerising brilliance that dazzled the senses. The light was so intense that it was almost too much for our eyes to bear, dancing and glinting from every corner and crevice. Luke and I locked gazes, anticipating the sun's arrival, knowing its warm glow would soon spread through our room.

"It's beautiful. I thought it would hurt," I said. "I love this."

I moved my hands in wonder in front of me, watching the lights dim and glare as I progressed with deliberate purpose into the shadows and then back into the light again. I had fully expected the sun to burn.

"You won't be saying that when you've had to face it for centuries like we've had to," he chuckled.

"I think I will," I replied stubbornly. "I love the silver veins curling through my arms. It's fantastic. "

"I know," he agreed. "The sun burning is just an ancient myth, similar to the one you thought I lived in a crypt," he teased.

"Oh," I murmured, switching my hands to look at the other in wonder.

"Will you stop moving at least until the dawn has changed to daylight," he moaned. "I just want to hold you for a bit longer, and for extra privacy, I will be having the house repaired today and the curtain put back up. "

I studied him, and for the first time, I saw the desperation of someone frightened of losing something precious. It was a remarkable sight to see a man, a vampire who was supposed to be known to be vicious and the complete opposite of the man that lay with me now, full of fear, doubt, and an innocence that I guessed came from the facts that he hadn't been given the opportunity like I had to grow and then become a vampire.

The sun burst through the darkness, flooding the world with its radiant brilliance. The dazzling rays that had once seared my eyes, now softened, their glare fading as if the intense moment had never occurred - a mere figment of my imagination. Refreshed and renewed, I stepped outside, feeling the caress of the air on my skin and the wind gently caressing my hair, causing my locks to twist and dance with graceful elegance as my clothes billowed behind me. The breeze was not harsh but gentle and sublime, inviting you to take a leisurely stroll and savour the tranquillity of the moment.

I was alone, embracing the solitude of the morning. Determined to hone my skills, I dedicated myself to mastering the endurance required to sustain my spells for the longest possible duration. This newfound mastery would prove invaluable when facing anyone who dared to challenge the High Witch. With a renewed sense of purpose, I was determined to make my name resound across the sky. The world expected me to be dead, and in a way, they were right – my mortal life had ended, only to be replaced by this new, empowered existence.

Chapter Nineteen

The realm meetings took place in a location shrouded in secrecy, veiled by potent cloaking magic that rendered it invisible to the outside world. This hidden sanctuary belonged to the most powerful witches. On this sacred ground, their arcane powers flourished, untouchable even by the mightiest of demons.

Though the journey to this revered site spanned only a short distance across the bustling town, it felt like crossing a threshold into another realm entirely. The air thrummed with ancient energy, a tangible aura of mysticism that seeped into every corner of the sanctuary, enveloping all who entered in its timeless embrace.

Here, the most powerful witches of the realm convened, their presence alone a formidable bulwark against any dark forces that might dare to trespass upon their sacred ground. Within this secretive sanctum, their combined might create a shield of arcane energy, an impregnable defence that no malevolent force could breach.

Even the most fearsome demons, notorious for their wrath, knew better than to challenge these seasoned masters of magic. Their powers, steeped in ancient lore and myth, were the stuff of legend—capable of vanquishing even the most tenacious supernatural threats with an ease that sent shivers through the underworld.

I shoved my way through the revolving glass doors, and the chaotic scene inside engulfed me instantly. The air hummed with tension, thick with the presence of vigilant security personnel, their eyes sharp as they swept over the restless crowd. All around, a sea of downtrodden souls huddled in clusters, their weary gazes locking onto me the moment I stepped inside. Their eyes, haunted by desperation, followed my every move as if hoping to decipher the purpose of my arrival or glean some faint glimmer of hope from my presence.

As I strode into the intimidating assembly of the realm, I felt less like a mere mortal and more like an unstoppable force of nature. This was, without question, the most daunting challenge I had ever encountered. Yet, the power within me surged, crackling with energy. It hummed through my veins, a living current I knew I could harness with just a touch. Every step I took was infused with a sense of purpose, as if the air around me acknowledged the strength I wielded, ready to unleash it upon whatever trials lay ahead.

Power had never been my primary pursuit, but the allure of its effects was undeniable. This morning, I immersed myself in practising my magic, much to Luke's chagrin, as I unleashed my abilities on the unsuspecting garden. Flames erupted from the ground with a flick of my wrist, engulfing objects in a blaze of crackling energy. At the same time, the towering trees bent and swayed under my command, responding to the thunderous claps that echoed ominously overhead. The raw intensity of this newfound power coursed through me, a heady mix of exhilaration and humility that left me breathless yet craving more.

He thrashed and grunted, desperately trying to pin me down, but his efforts were futile. With a flick, I effortlessly levitated and trapped him inside an air-tight bubble above my head. Undeterred, I turned my attention to the rest of my abilities, determined to push them to their limits.

"Oi, this isn't right!" he yelled, his voice laced with frustration. "This is a bloody outrage!"

"Look, I'm in the zone here, alright?" I shot back, unfazed by his shouts and protests. "You're not going to stop me from focusing on what I'm doing, so don't even try." My tone was resolute, and I continued to work with unwavering concentration, determined to see this task through.

Eventually, he reluctantly fell silent and remained motionless, but not without contorting his face into grotesque expressions that he believed had escaped my notice. Life had undoubtedly taken an unexpected turn, locking itself into a peculiar pattern of unfamiliar occurrences; I eagerly anticipated the start of the next chapter.

As I walked past each realm member, I could hear the whispered murmurs around me. "She's here," they'd say, the hushed voices closing in from both sides, their excitement clear. The atmosphere was charged with an electric anticipation, every eye trained on me as I walked through the crowd.

With my head held high and the elite bodyguards of the High Witch trailing behind me, their guard was up. They had been pre-warned by the most influential members, who were even higher in authority than the High Witch. However, they remained silent during the turmoil, fearing for their safety.

However, this time was different; there were no more gaps to be mended and no more bridges to be built. It was time to walk the new path Matace had unknowingly carved, diverging from the old one.

Chin lifted defiantly; I strode forward with the high witch's elite bodyguards. Their hackles were raised, having been pre-warned by the most influential figures – ones who outranked even the High Witch but had remained silent during past conflicts, too concerned for their own well-being. This time, though, was different. There were no more chasms to bridge, no more pathways to construct. It was time to forge ahead on the new trail that Matace had unwittingly carved, branching off from the old route.

The tension was almost suffocating as I stepped forward, every pair of eyes in the room fixed on me. They had been waiting with bated breath to glimpse the new High Witch, their expectations soaring. But the figure they saw before them now clearly differed from what they had envisioned. Disappointment and a hint of irritation flickered across their faces, their hopes shattered by the reality that confronted them.

Commanding the attention of the gathered assembly, I stood at the centre, acutely aware that none of these individuals truly belonged within this hallowed chamber. They had been elevated to positions of power, but I questioned the validity of their claims and aspirations.

In due time, I would select my realm members, watchers, and grand witches – a chosen few whose loyalty and dedication would not be tainted by the insatiable greed and malicious intent that threatened to consume these power-hungry witches. I knew that if left unchecked, they could transform into something far more sinister than the likes of Lilly, who dared to dream of usurping my rightful rule.

"Silence!" the authoritative voice of the realm's conference leader thundered as he slammed his fist onto the table, cutting through the whispers and the tension engulfing the once-tranquil room.

"Well, well, look who's back from the dead!" Stella exclaimed, approaching without a moment's hesitation or concern for protocol. "I have to say, I'm impressed. How the heck did you pull that off?" Her eyes sparkled with curiosity and a hint of admiration as she eagerly awaited your response.

Her scorn was evident as she approached, her eyes burning with malice and hatred directed at me. The disrespect for the established order was apparent in her every step. Without hesitation, the guards rushed towards her, swiftly seizing her arm and escorting her away. But I raised my hand, commanding them to cease their actions mid-motion.

"No," I said. "Wait!"

Agonizing seconds ticked by as the audience held their breath, eager to witness my response to the one who dared to challenge the long-established rules and policies. Their eyes were fixed on me, bodies leaning forward in their seats in anticipation.

"Enough!" I commanded, my voice echoing with a sense of authority. "She is blind to the weight of her actions. Let this be the lesson you all take away today," I said, my gaze unwavering. "No more explanations are needed – I am alive, thriving, and a vampire. I intend to claim my rightful, elevated status above all of you." I paused, the air thick with anticipation. "The old prophecies no longer hold sway. A new era dawns, brimming with exciting changes. But remember, we carry the burden of those we've lost due to the misdeeds of one among us.

"Are you seriously telling us that you are immortal and now plan to seize control of the entire realm?" another voice bellowed, laced with disbelief and alarm.

"That's precisely what I'm telling you," I asserted, my voice firm and unwavering. "Furthermore, those we have exiled without just cause in the past will be granted a new trial, for I am no longer convinced that the old prophecies hold true in the world we now inhabit. The realm has failed to keep up with the times; we've tried to maintain the balance, but because some of us," I said, locking eyes with Stella, her gaze burning with fury, "have decided to seize power without the High Witch's consent, that will no longer stand. From this day forward, we shall work towards restoring the balance, but with the new age of prophecies I intend to set in motion."

A deafening silence fell upon the room. Not a single soul dared to make a sound. Jaws hung open in stunned disbelief as all eyes fixed on the scene unfolding before them. The whispers that had once filled the air abruptly ceased, and even the guards stood frozen, awaiting their next orders.

I could sense the fury radiating from Stella. Her body was tense, poised for action, her every muscle coiled and ready to strike. Yet, within these walls, where the High Witch reigned supreme, Stella knew her chances of success were slim. She was trapped, surrounded by those who would protect their leader at all costs.

"Absolutely, I couldn't agree more," a voice suddenly chimed in, startling me as it emerged from behind my right shoulder. The words carried a sense of conviction, cutting through the silence with a confident, almost commanding tone.

I gazed upon the captivating dark-haired woman, Yana, whose existence had only been documented in records until now. Her name, meant to signify peace, had become shrouded in the horrors of her tumultuous reign, a reign that had cost her the position I now held. Yet, despite the turmoil, she had remained a silent, unassuming presence within these walls, her voice heard only to offer counsel and soothe the anguish of others.

Torech, the old and frail but commanding figure, rose to speak. "I, too, support this young lady's proposal," he declared, his stern voice echoing through the chamber. These historical witches had arrived, just as they had promised my father, to back me in taking over the order of the realm and sorting out the problems of the past.

The group held their breath, every eye fixed on the empty space in the circle, anticipating the arrival of the third silent partner. Their fate hung in the balance, his word the decisive factor that would seal their shared destiny. The tension mounted, powerful and electrifying, as they strained to hear the slightest sound that would signal his long-awaited appearance.

I sat, my hands trembling in my lap, unable to control the restless movement. The past weighed heavily on my mind, the events that had unfolded repeatedly, the exiles of so many people due to some ancient, unyielding rule. Despite their forgiveness of others and their sincere efforts to make amends for their own transgressions, they were no longer allowed to remain on this Earth. The injustice consumed my thoughts, fueling a growing sense of unease and a deep desire for change.

Chaos erupted in the far corner, and the witches scurried about, urgently shifting the benches. Their furrowed brows and anxious expressions betrayed the confidence they had exuded when I first arrived. Hushed whispers quickly gave way to fear.

Anxious eyes locked with mine as the thick, misty air shifted and aggressively pressed towards the radiant light at the far end. The witches had hastily crowded together, their bodies tangled and intertwined as if they had hurriedly piled on top of one another in a frantic attempt to reach the illuminated space.

Slowly, the silhouettes of three figures started to take shape; the mysterious elder was never seen alone. He was infamous for being accompanied by his carefully selected entourage of seasoned warriors, once lords of a mysterious and formidable power.

"Heed my words, for I hold the power and status to rule over all of you!" he bellowed, his voice resonating with authority. "I stand behind the motions of the others, summoned here today by a mortal who believes his daughter can surpass any of you. And I can assure you, she holds the power, the wits, and the strength to traverse the strange parallel we have fought tirelessly to sustain for years. Seira, it is time for you to claim your rightful place as the ruler of your realm!"

I was utterly stunned when he suddenly bowed before me. That was his way of welcoming me, or so I assumed. But it was the most unexpected and peculiar response I could have imagined from him. He had never been known to bow down to anyone, especially those associated with the realm he had fought so hard to distance himself from since his tumultuous reign had ended. He had long ago resolved to be a silent, passive observer in matters related to this time and this particular term. Yet, here he was, breaking his self-imposed protocol, leaving me perplexed and intrigued by this uncharacteristic display of deference.

The congregation erupted into conspiratorial whispers, their sniggers laced with resentment. Despite the respect I had initially earned by having silent partners and leaders with me, I felt their disdain. They all bowed, defiantly showcasing their resistance to Stella's cause and her potential retaliation. Stella returned the bow, her shoulders trembling with fear as she felt the overwhelming powers threatening to outmatch anything she could muster to fight back.

I couldn't bear the thought of her turning out like Lilly. That's why I had been tasked with protecting the realm from the voracious and power-hungry witches who tried to seize control but through twisted and unacceptable means. This responsibility weighed heavily on me, fueling my determination to ensure history would not repeat itself.

My leadership had been solidified. I was the vampire witch, primed and prepared to confront any new and unfamiliar force. I was ready to take on the reconciliation that had long eluded us, the reconciliation that Matace had neither bothered to conceal nor attempted to forge a treaty between the parallel worlds to strengthen and improve our standing.

Luke's absence weighed heavily on me today. His strong leadership and capable handling of affairs would have been invaluable as I set out to establish my reign over this realm. I yearned for his guidance to help me harness my power and leadership potential and lay the foundations for what I hope will be a new era of greatness. Instead, I am surrounded by a motley crew of hopeless wonders - those who eagerly fight amongst themselves, jockeying for position in the hierarchy. They are a hindrance, a distraction from my grand vision. I must cast them aside and pave the way for a truly powerful realm to emerge that will leave an indelible mark on history.

Each witch who now bowed down to welcome and accept me would have their own petty squabbles - small catfights that I was more than happy to resolve. I would bring peace and harmony amongst all these witches for the greater good of our cause. After all, many centuries ago, this realm had been established for the peace, harmony, and prosperity of the demons and strange creatures that appeared at the witches' doors almost daily. They were drawn to the magic and power like a powerful magnetic force, a force that no witch could truly comprehend.

I would not tolerate any discord or disunity amongst the coven. My role was maintaining order and ensuring that our collective power remained focused and unwavering. The witches may have had their differences, but ultimately, they would all submit to my authority and leadership. For the good of our cause, I would demand nothing less than absolute unity and cooperation.

Now, the time had come for me to make my mark, to etch my name in the annals of history - the destiny that had always been mine. Matace had crafted me for this moment to confront Lilly and be a formidable force against the renegades who futilely resisted the realm and all it stood for. In his foresight, Matace had secured this victory before his passing, leaving me as his sole heir to carry on our legacy and restore hope to the world.

Don't miss out!

Visit the website below and you can sign up to receive emails whenever Laurie Bowler publishes a new book. There's no charge and no obligation.

https://books2read.com/r/B-A-LVUW-SZOUE

BOOKS 2 READ

Connecting independent readers to independent writers.

Did you love *The Sequence of Immortality*? Then you should read *The Shadow of Light*[1] by Laurie Bowler!

"The Shadow of Light" is a thrilling tale of magic, mystery, and danger that follows the story of Ruby Blacksmith, a young woman with light and dark powers.

Ruby Blacksmith was raised orphanage, but her life took an unexpected turn when she discovered that she has been bestowed with both light and dark magic powers. However, her newfound abilities come with a price, as she becomes a target for magical enforcers who are tasked with eliminating all black magic from society. In fear for her life, Ruby decides to flee from her pursuers and embark on a journey to find a safe haven where she can harness and control her powers without being persecuted.

---

1. https://books2read.com/u/m2qw5O

2. https://books2read.com/u/m2qw5O

Ruby, a skilled survivor who uses her dark powers only when necessary, meets Harry Brimstone, a legendary enforcer with the unique ability to sense dark magic. Rather than taking her life, Harry chooses to investigate her past. Together, they must outsmart their enemies and prevent the darkness from consuming their world.

Read more at https://lauriebowler.com/.

Also by Laurie Bowler

The Chronicles of the Valenko Empire
An Empire at War

The Magical Intervention Agency
The Tyrants Rule
The Chaos Power
The Trial of Chaos
The Ghosts of Chaos
The Betrayals of Chaos
The Home of Chaos
The Chaos Entry

Standalone
Mythical
The Battle for Evov
Auras
The Darkside of Venus
Hidden Power
The Awakening
The Firaty Altar

Watch for more at https://lauriebowler.com/.

About the Author

Laurie Bowler is a bestselling author based in Hampshire, UK. She writes captivating fantasy, young adult, and sci-fi stories that have entertained readers worldwide.

Inspired by all the remarkable fantasy stories around her, Laurie regularly reads and writes to explore her creative side. When it comes to her writing, she likes to craft each story in a manner that will draw her audience in. Her writing is built upon intricate, interwoven stories with captivating characters.

Aside from writing, Laurie enjoys exploring new areas, divulging into fascinating and mysterious landscapes, and discovering new cultural experiences. She continues writing her heart out, incorporating her experiences and knowledge into captivating stories that carry through each page.

Read more at https://lauriebowler.com/.

www.ingramcontent.com/pod-product-compliance
Lightning Source LLC
Chambersburg PA
CBHW060750030726
47503CB00002B/229